T0372966

Alex Gray is the *Sunday Times*-bestselling author of the Detective William Lorimer series. Born and raised in Glasgow, she has been awarded the Scottish Association of Writers' Constable and Pitlochry trophies for her crime writing and is the co-founder of the international Bloody Scotland Crime Writing Festival.

www.alexgrayauthor.co.uk

Alex Gray

ACTS OF MALICE

SPHERE

SPHERE

First published in Great Britain in 2025 by Sphere

3 5 7 9 10 8 6 4 2

Copyright © Alex Gray 2025

The moral right of the author has been asserted.

A CIP catalogue record for this book
is available from the British Library.

ISBN 978-1-4087-3266-3

Typeset in Caslon by M Rules
Printed and bound in Great Britain by
Clays Ltd, Elcograf S.p.A.

Papers used by Sphere are from well-managed forests
and other responsible sources.

Sphere
An imprint of
Little, Brown Book Group
Carmelite House
50 Victoria Embankment
London EC4Y 0DZ

The authorised representative
in the EEA is
Hachette Ireland
8 Castlecourt Centre
Dublin 15, D15 XTP3, Ireland
(email: info@hbgi.ie)

An Hachette UK Company
www.hachette.co.uk

www.littlebrown.co.uk

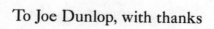

To Joe Dunlop, with thanks

PROLOGUE

*T*he moon emerged from a bank of cloud, casting silvery beams onto ripples crossing the dark water. Nothing else moved, only these arcs shimmering on the lochan's surface.

No bird cried, no grasses murmured on that windless night, a solitary figure watching as all movement ceased across the water.

There was nothing to tell that death had cast its shadow here, no portent of doom or even a sigh from the wind. And, as another ink-black cloud slowly covered the face of the moon, the silent figure slipped away into the night.

CHAPTER ONE

Abigail Brightman hated Mondays. The school gym hall was always cold after the weekend and the floor still smelled of years of sweaty feet despite the best intentions of the cleaners. Assembly was boring, the head droning on and on until the first piano chord signalled them all to stand up and sing whatever dirge had been chosen for that day. Very occasionally a pupil would be singled out for praise, having gained the Duke of Edinburgh Award or performed some feat or other of athletics. The head was big on sport, another reason that Abby usually switched off during his interminable talks. She loathed the school gym hall when all that cumbersome equipment was in place, especially the dreaded vaulting horse. She would wipe sweaty hands on her gym shorts, waiting in turn behind the other girls, hoping that this time she would not find herself scrabbling crab-like over the horrid thing or, worse, feeling the gym teacher's cold bony fingers grasp her thighs to heave her over.

Abby was stifling a yawn behind her hand that morning,

when she became aware of a bristling of attention from those pupils around her.

What had she missed?

'And if any of you have a parent or relative who might be of particular interest, do ask them to volunteer,' a female voice said.

Abby looked up to see the careers teacher standing behind the lectern, smiling down at them.

'What did she say?' Abby whispered to her neighbour.

'Shh!' The girl frowned back at her.

'Remember it is in your own interest to hear from as many professionals as possible before you make your subject choices,' the teacher continued, glancing around at her audience until her gaze came to rest on Abby.

Her smile and slight nod made a few heads turn Abby's way and she felt the heat in her neck travel all the way to her cheeks till she was certain they must be scarlet.

Whispers and nudges, a few turning to stare made it all so much worse.

Of *course* the careers teacher would single out Abigail Brightman, the daughter of a famous psychologist who had been on television and helped the police solve major murder cases, and of the mother who was the head of the Department of Forensic Medicine at the University of Glasgow.

I won't ask them. I won't! Abby thought furiously to herself.

As the assembled pupils trooped out, Abigail was unsurprised to see the careers teacher approach her, finger crooked to beckon her away from her classmates. Here it was, the inevitable question: would Abigail be kind enough to ask

4

her parents to consider giving a talk about their professions at the careers seminar?

It is perhaps not often that a young person of thirteen finds inspiration in the midst of their mental turmoil, but that day Abigail Brightman was struck by an idea that she hoped might save her from years of embarrassment.

'Oh, they are both awfully busy, miss,' she replied earnestly. 'But I could ask my uncle Bill. He's my godfather,' she continued, 'and a really well-known detective superintendent.'

'Phone for you,' Maggie Lorimer called to her husband. 'A young lady,' she added with a scarcely suppressed smirk as she handed him the house phone.

Lorimer's brows came together in a frown as he put the phone to his ear.

'Hello?'

'Hi, Uncle Bill. It's me, Abby,' came the reply, instantly banishing the lines around her godfather's eyes.

'Hello, you. To what do I owe this unexpected call?' he teased.

'Weeeell,' the word was drawn out as if the young girl needed a moment to gather her thoughts. 'I wanted to ask you a favour,' she said.

'Ask away,' he replied. 'Anything for my favourite girl.'

There was a pause and he listened, wondering if he had detected the faintest hint of a sigh. Relief? He hoped so.

'Would you give a wee talk at our careers fair at St Genesius? They're looking for parents or friends who have an interesting sort of job and can tell us about it. How you'd join up and everything . . . '

'Of course I will, if I'm free.'

'Oh great!' she exclaimed and this time he was certain of the relief in her voice. 'I really didn't want to ask Mum or Dad.'

'Is it an evening event or during the day?'

'It's an all-day thing,' Abby told him. 'Thursday the four-teenth of this month. We have to make our subject choices before the Easter holidays,' she explained.

'That should be fine,' he assured her. 'There isn't anything major at work right now and if something comes up one of our DCIs can deal with it.'

'Oh, thank you!' she squealed. 'I know it isn't that long since you and Aunt Maggie came back from your holiday. Mum said you might have a lot of catching up to do, and not to mind if you said no.'

Lorimer smiled. The trip to Zimbabwe had been eventful but neither of their godchildren had been told the full story of all that had taken place. Three weeks had elapsed since they had returned, along with Janette Kohi, the mother of their Zimbabwean friend, Daniel, who was now a serving officer in Police Scotland.

'Consider it in the diary, my dear.'

'I'll get Miss Webb the careers teacher to call you, if that's okay?'

'Fine,' Lorimer replied. 'Use this number, will you, Abby?' he added, reciting the main switchboard number at the Major Incident Team's headquarters in Govan.

'Bye, and thanks again,' she said breathlessly.

Maggie was looking at him quizzically.

'Abby's school is having a careers fair and she's asked if I'll go along,' he explained.

'Ah, we've had those in the past.' Maggie nodded. 'I think it does help kids to make up their minds what subjects to take. Of course, they must take English, so I'll always have bigger classes.'

'Any advice?'

Maggie chuckled. 'They're bound to ask how much you earn,' she told him. 'Especially the boys. It's not the first time a nosy wee rascal has wanted to know if I'm dead rich now that I write books!'

'Well, so long as they don't expect me to give any gory details about murder cases,' he laughed. 'Outlining the job should be fun. After all, I've given lectures at the police training college plenty of times. Maybe I just need to water it down a bit for young teenagers.'

He picked up the Sunday papers and resumed reading the sports pages, the object of Abigail Brightman's phone call put aside for the moment.

It would be a straightforward matter, speaking to kids, especially if they were bright like Abby, he decided. St Genesius had specialist departments related to the performing arts though pupils were also renowned for their academic prowess. Perhaps one of them might even be inspired to join the force in later years. Yes, this was a good opportunity to tell youngsters about the job he loved. He smiled as he thought of his goddaughter, now a gangly teenager, who blushed at the slightest provocation and who had probably worked herself up to ask this favour.

It was only much later that William Lorimer would look back at his ready agreement to visit her school and ponder at the things which followed.

CHAPTER TWO

She could not help shivering as they made their way
along Allison Street. Despite the nights becoming
lighter, March was still in thrall to winter winds and the
threat of snow. No wonder so many conversations began
remarking about the weather. Netta Gordon paused to
let her new friend catch up. There was so much for the
Zimbabwean woman to see in the city, Netta mused,
watching as Janette Kohi stood before the greengrocer's
shop, examining the different vegetables on offer. The
smell of citrus mingled with something earthier, probably that sack of Cyprus potatoes just inside the doorway.
Netta hopped from one foot to the other, willing Janette
to hurry up.

'D'you want tae go in and have a look?' she asked, turning
to stand beside the small woman whose head was swathed in
a brightly coloured shawl, an attempt to defeat the icy blasts.
'It's jist as cold in there as it is out here, mind.'

'There is so much . . . ' Janette raised a hand and let it fall with a sigh. 'I have never seen so much food. And put out like this?'

'Oh, naebody pinches stuff fae Mr Singh,' Netta laughed. 'He's goat thon CCTV and his laddie wid catch onybody that tried tae nick as much as a tattie. Fast? My, he'd gie Usain Bolt a run fur his money!'

Her companion stared at her for a moment and shrugged, a slight frown between her treacle-brown eyes. 'Tattie?'

Netta chuckled. 'It's short fur po-ta-to,' she explained. 'Mind we gave ye tattie scones fur yer breakfast at the week-end? Wi' black pudding an' all?'

Janette's face cleared as she nodded, though whether the Zimbabwean woman had genuinely understood every bit of Netta's Glasgow dialect was uncertain.

'C'mon alang here tae ma favourite wee café. They do brilliant flies' cemeteries, so they do,' she added, taking the smaller woman's arm and encouraging her to quicken her footsteps.

Janette was glad of the thick coat her son, Daniel, had bought for her and the warm boots lined with fake fur. This climate was so different from anything she was accustomed to, though Maggie Lorimer had warned her what to expect when they had landed in Glasgow airport the previous month. Nobody had mentioned the hard pavements outside every house, so unlike the dusty paths back home, or those towering tenement buildings that cast their shadows across each busy street. The noise of traffic was unrelenting, even worse than the centre of Harare, and the flat where Daniel and Netta lived was right on a road, cars and vans being driven past their front window all the time.

And yet everybody had been so kind, she thought, as she trotted by her penfriend's side, and the people in this city were friendly, complete strangers sitting beside them on the buses often striking up a conversation. Janette was used to these double-decker buses now although when she had first arrived Daniel had taken some leave from his work as a police officer to drive them to different parts of Scotland. Janette had gasped appreciatively at the view over Loch Lomond and the snow-capped mountain beyond just as much as she had enjoyed the delights of the city's Princes Square, its shops filled with luxury goods like some Aladdin's cave of riches. The food she had been given was all warm and wholesome and Janette had already begun to jot down a few of Netta Gordon's favourite recipes.

Everything would have been perfect apart from her lingering misgivings over the tall blonde woman who seemed to have such a hold over her beloved son.

'Here we are, best wee place in Govanhill!' Netta exclaimed, pulling Janette into the warmth of a bright café.

Inside, the air smelled of coffee beans and something sweet and syrupy, making Janette's mouth water as Netta bustled her towards a corner table well away from the draughty entrance. The hiss from the coffee machine created a small cloud of steam that rose to the ceiling, making Janette look upwards at a pair of silent fans, their blades motionless. Did this mean that there would be days hot and sunny enough for patrons to need them? Maggie Lorimer had promised that as the months went on, the weather would be so much warmer, and Janette could wear the cotton frocks that she had packed so hurriedly. She glanced across as the door opened to admit a mother with a small child, the chill wind blowing in a scattering of crumpled leaves. Janette shivered, tucking her coat around her knees.

'Feeling the cauld, hen?' Netta asked. 'How about a nice hot chocolate? Ma treat. An' ye must try wan o' the flies' cemeteries, eh?' She chuckled. 'They're better than these wans we had out of the supermarket.'

Janette smiled. She had been living here with Netta in the Southside of Glasgow just long enough to have discovered that these were actually fruit tarts made from well-soaked currants between layers of delicious sugary pastry, nothing at all to do with dead flies. In fact, it was the recipe for that particular cake that Janette Kohi wanted to seek out to add to her growing notebook.

As Netta strode over to the counter to place their order, Janette's thoughts returned once more to Detective Inspector Molly Newton. There was no doubt in her mind that her son was smitten by this lady but ... she sighed. Did she have the right to feel this way? Molly had no belief in God, she had stated with a small laugh when Janette had asked which church the white woman attended. And ... well ... she was so different from dear Chipo, Daniel's wife who had perished with their baby son in the horrific arson attack that had driven him out of Zimbabwe for ever. Janette pursed her lips. No, Molly wasn't a bit like her poor daughter-in-law. She had no compunction about sleeping with her son, Daniel sometimes staying over at her flat overnight. Loose morals, Janette had told herself in dismay when Molly had suggested slyly that Daniel would be more comfortable in her own bed.

11

Daniel had readily given his mother the smaller of the two bedrooms in the flat he shared with Netta, happy to sleep on the bed settee in the large living room. But his mother had noticed that he'd also taken some of his clothes and toiletries away to the West End of the city where Molly lived. She had still to be invited there, Janette thought, wondering if the police officer was a career-minded woman who preferred ready meals to the sort of home cooking a man deserved.

'Penny for them,' Netta said, sitting down heavily opposite her friend. 'You look fair lost in yer thoughts, lass.'

'I was thinking about Chipo,' Janette began, glancing down at her hands, afraid that this half-truth would somehow condemn her.

'Och, lass.' Netta took her hand and rubbed it gently. 'It's a terrible thing tae carry around with ye. Bad memories. But see now? He's goat Molly and the pair of them are that happy thegether.' She smiled then drew her hand back as a waiter arrived at their table bearing a tray with their order.

Janette attempted a smile. Netta was firmly on the side of this relationship and evidently saw nothing wrong with it. Was this a British thing? Were Christian morals so lacking here? She stifled another sigh as her hands clasped the warm mug of chocolate, its sweet smell wafting into her nostrils. Zimbabwe was a place of so much corruption, some of their leaders setting no good example to its citizens with immoral ways of living, and yet Janette had expected so much more of this cold northern country. After all, it had been Pastor John, Father Peter and the others who helped refugees escape from Zimbabwe, their mission trips good cover for these persecuted people.

'Wid ye look at that!' Netta exclaimed.

Janette followed her friend's gaze to see two large horses passing by the plate glass window of the coffee shop, their riders clad in black, helmets sporting the chequered emblem of Police Scotland. The clip-clop of hooves as they passed could be clearly heard, the hum of chattering voices stilled for a moment as folk gazed out at the sight.

'That's oor polis,' Netta whispered, a proud smile on her face. 'Ye see them at fitba' matches fur crowd control. They're that well trained, these horses, so they are.'

Janette gave a sigh. Her Daniel was undergoing a special training right now, she recalled, so that he might become a detective constable and even rise higher up the ranks sooner than he had expected. He had apologised for not taking off more annual leave, but the course out in a place called Jackton began today, and he was obliged to attend. No matter, her visa was valid until October. There was plenty of time to see more of Scotland. Janette Kohi bit her lip. What then? Maggie Lorimer and her husband had talked about seeking asylum, settling here in Scotland. But Janette was not so sure. She gave a sudden shiver, thinking of the immense skies of her beloved Zimbabwe, the sound of little children laughing, running barefoot on the dusty ground. She blinked back tears and swallowed hard. Was she destined to remain here, a small African lady of no importance, growing older, never to return to the place she once called home?

CHAPTER THREE

Abby could see each car arriving in the teachers' car park from where she sat at the very back of the school theatre, the windows to one side flooding the space with light. There was no way of telling when her uncle Bill would arrive, the order of guest speakers known only to the staff members who were sitting to one side of the lectern. As each adult arrived, their careers teacher would introduce them, giving a short explanation of what their job was and thanking them for taking the time to come to the school. Right now, Abby was supposed to be listening to a local GP who was speaking about the sorts of qualifications necessary to be admitted to medical school, but she had switched off, having long ago decided that profession was not one to which she aspired. There had been sufficient talk at home about bodies, blood and all sorts of disgusting stuff that her mother seemed to deal with on a daily basis to put her off anything gory for life. No, she was much more like Dad, who could not stand even the sight of a cut finger oozing a few red drops.

All morning Abby had been glancing out of that window, waiting for the sight of her godfather's car, and now it was after lunchtime and he still hadn't made an appearance.

Perhaps something had happened to hold him up, she wondered, gnawing the hard flesh at the side of her finger-nail. Maybe he wouldn't come at all. The thought made her sigh.

Then, just as she was beginning to despair, Abby caught sight of a large silver vehicle cresting the rise of the hill and turning towards the rows of parked cars. There was no mistaking the Lexus, an older model, long and sleek, that stood out from the four by fours that so many of the teachers seemed to favour nowadays.

He was here and hadn't let her down after all!

Lorimer strode away from the car park and headed down towards the main entrance of the school, glancing at his watch. No, he was still on time, thank goodness. The doors opened with a faint swishing sound, and he took a step towards a second set of glass doors, reading the notice instructing visitors to St Genesius High School to press the green button with their elbow, a safeguard against spreading any sort of virus. Schools were notorious for harbouring germs, Maggie had said on several occasions, bemoaning those parents who allowed their kids to arrive with streaming colds or fevers.

He gave the receptionist behind a glass window his name and she pushed a lanyard through a small space, instructing him to follow the signs to the theatre.

'You can't miss it,' the woman told him with a bright smile. 'There are red arrows pointing the way.'

Lorimer thanked her and headed along a corridor marked with the sign THEATRE, hearing a faint sound of laughter ahead. Whoever the current speaker was, they had at least elicited some response from the youngsters. Straightening the knot on his tie, Lorimer pushed on towards the sound, keeping one eye on the red arrows that had been taped onto the walls.

As he approached a set of double doors, a middle-aged woman emerged, heading towards him.

'Superintendent Lorimer? I'm Alexandra McIvor, deputy head teacher. Welcome to our careers fair and thank you so much for taking time to help us.'

Lorimer shook the woman's hand, feeling her strong clasp and warming to the smile crinkling her hazel eyes.

'Abigail is quite excited that you agreed to join us,' she confided. 'I think she's been on the lookout for your arrival all day,' she added with a grin.

Lorimer allowed himself to be taken backstage to a darkened area where a man sat behind a bank of serious-looking equipment.

'Ronnie will get you miked up,' Ms McIvor whispered, looking up into his eyes. 'I'm sure you are used to doing this sort of thing.'

Lorimer smiled and simply nodded, unwilling to disturb the speaker onstage as she finished her talk. The applause that followed was accompanied by a few whistles and whoops, no doubt heartening for the guest speaker as she came off the platform and joined them.

'Well done,' Ms McIvor said, 'and thank you.'

'Not a problem but I must rush now. I have a surgery in ten minutes,' the GP replied.

Lorimer followed the deputy head teacher onto the stage for her to introduce him to the assembled pupils. He let his glance rove over them, searching in vain for his goddaughter. They were so young, he thought with a pang. And having to choose the subjects that might lead to a career at this tender age! Still, he'd make being a police officer as interesting as possible. Who knows, there might be a budding cop or two amongst these rows and rows of youngsters.

They'd kept the best till last, Abby decided, beaming with pleasure as she listened to her uncle Bill tell stories about his career, some of the tales provoking laughter when he spoke about the silly sorts of things some criminals did. Like the would-be bank robbers who became stuck in a revolving door, or the burglar who broke into what he thought was an empty house, drinking so much of the owner's whisky that he fell asleep under a table, coming to only when a pair of handcuffs were put around his wrists. There was more serious stuff of course, like DNA and forensics, and he was happy for her fellow pupils to ask as many questions as they wanted.

When William Lorimer asked for a show of hands to see how many of them might be interested in such a career, there were so many that several heads turned in surprise, checking out who wanted to become a police officer, and she could see the grin of pleasure on his face. Promising to leave some information about the practicalities of joining Police Scotland with their careers teachers, he ended his talk by saying, 'Finally, I'd like to thank my goddaughter for inviting me to her school. I've enjoyed meeting you all.'

Abby sat silently, face reddening more with pleasure than embarrassment, since few of her year group were aware of who that was.

Then he was gone, a final wave of his hand, just as the school bell rang out signalling going home time.

The grin on his face lasted all the way to the car park, Lorimer feeling huge satisfaction that the time he had spent was worthwhile. He would probably be retired by the time any of those putative cadets joined up, but it was nice to know he had planted some seeds of interest, at any rate.

He was turning the car, following a one-way system clearly marked and headed for the exit, when a figure rushed towards him, making him slam hard on the brake.

Lorimer saw a young woman with bright pink hair, dressed in a long crimson coat, a green and red scarf flying behind her. What on earth ... ?

She raised gloved hands as though to signal stop, then drew close to his door, allowing Lorimer to see her in more detail. A tall, attractive woman, in her late twenties, he guessed, a slash of bright lipstick and violet-coloured eyeshadow in keeping with her retro look.

Lorimer pressed a button, allowing the window to open as she bent down, fingers clutching at the car.

'Please,' she breathed heavily, her eyes wide as she stared at him.

Lorimer frowned, wondering if he had forgotten something, but then she leaned forward, a sob catching her voice.

'Superintendent Lorimer! You must help me. You're my only hope!'

CHAPTER FOUR

'My name is Meredith St Claire,' she told him once he had invited her to sit beside him in the passenger seat and driven a short way from the car park to an area where polytunnels and painted boxes of yellow daffodils showed signs of a flourishing horticulture department. 'I'm sorry if I gave you a start.' She turned to stare at Lorimer.

He noticed how she had clasped her hands, an unconscious imploring gesture? Or a deliberate attempt to appear desperate?

'Why do you think I can help, Miss St Claire? Or is it Mrs?'

'Ms,' she replied with the faintest trace of a smile that disappeared as suddenly as it had come. 'Though I really hoped to be Mrs ... ' She turned away from him, covering her eyes for a moment as if to hide a moment of emotion.

Then she turned back and looked at him, biting her lip as if unsure how to continue.

'It's my fiancé, Guy,' she explained. 'He's ... ' He saw her swallow before continuing in a husky voice. 'Well, the fact is, he's disappeared, and I don't know what to do.'

'How long—'

'Days!' she jumped in before he could finish his question. 'I dropped him off in town last Sunday.' She hesitated, avoiding Lorimer's eyes. 'He was a bit vague about what he was doing. Sometimes he'd go off and buy me something nice, surprise me. He ... he is like that.' She pulled a crumpled tissue from her pocket, furiously wiping her eyes.

'Then, when he didn't come home, I rang around every Accident and Emergency in Glasgow. And *of course* I reported him missing to the police. But they're just not interested!' she exclaimed. 'Told me he had every right to disappear. How could they say that?' she demanded fiercely.

Lorimer suppressed a sigh. 'I'm really sorry that you are having this problem, but people go missing every day, many of their own volition. If your fiancé is an adult and there is no reason to be concerned about his welfare, then there is not much the police can do,' he told her. '*Is* there any medical problem? Physical or otherwise?'

She turned away slightly, dropping her head. 'They already asked me that,' she muttered. 'And, no, there is nothing to worry about on that score. Guy is a normal healthy individual with every reason to be happy.' She pulled off the emerald-green glove from her left hand and splayed out her fingers to show off a magnificent solitaire diamond ring.

'We were engaged recently and were planning our wedding,' she said quietly. 'Guy has no money worries, no worries of any kind ... at least ...'

She had stopped, making Lorimer wonder if Meredith St Claire expected him to do more than sympathise with her predicament.

'I feel ...' She turned her face towards Lorimer, her eyes full of anguished appeal. 'I know this sounds mad ... but ... I have this horrible feeling that something awful has happened to him.'

Lorimer tried not to show any reaction, though the woman's desperate tone had given him pause for thought. Yes, any partner would have grave concerns for a missing loved one, but it was best to be truthful and to reiterate what she had been told by those police officers who had already spoken to her.

'I am sorry, really sorry. And I can see how anxious you are, but this is just not the sort of thing I do, Ms St Claire. If there is any expectation that your fiancé is in trouble, then you must follow the proper guidelines that I am sure you were given by the officers who advised you.'

She was out of the Lexus as suddenly as she had arrived, slamming the door and marching away, scarf tails flying in her wake.

What a strange encounter, Lorimer thought. He might give Abby a call this evening, make discreet enquiries about this person, a teacher, perhaps?

She was certainly a woman he would find difficult to forget, with a rather beautiful but haunted face and wearing such striking colours that demanded attention.

'Abby! That's your uncle Bill on the phone!' Rosie called.

'Can I speak to him first? Can I?' Ben pleaded.

Rosie shook her head, laying a hand on her son's shoulder. 'Let Abby talk first then I'll get her to hand over to you, okay?'

'O-kay,' Ben heaved an exaggerated sigh and stomped off.

Abby grasped the handset and gave her mum a smile.

'Hi, Uncle Bill. You were great. In fact, you were the best speaker of the entire day!' she exclaimed.

Rosie folded her arms and listened as Abby continued to gush about the afternoon and how everyone had talked about her godfather on the bus on their way home.

'Miss St Claire?' she heard Abby ask. 'She's my drama teacher. We all think she's dead glamorous, some of the boys say she should have been a movie star. Anyway, she does give us some really fun stuff to do in class. Everybody likes her.'

The girl's chatter continued as Rosie made her way to the kitchen. Ben was sitting at the table and looked up hopefully.

'Are they done yet?' he asked.

'Abby will give you a call, don't worry. Uncle Bill will probably want to know all you've been doing at school and how your football practice is going,' she said. 'Didn't he promise to take you to a game next weekend?'

Ben nodded, mollified by the prospect of a whole Saturday afternoon with one of his favourite grown-ups. Dad and Mum were okay but neither of them had the slightest interest in what Uncle Bill called *the beautiful game*.

Lorimer put down the phone with a sigh. For a childless couple, he and Maggie were blessed with a couple of great kids who seemed to enjoy their company. Ben had reminded him of the forthcoming match next weekend, and he was looking forward to having the wee lad at the derby between his team, Kelvin FC, and Partick Thistle.

The mystery woman was in fact a teacher at St Genesius and one Abby seemed to know. A drama teacher, he thought. Interesting. Her flamboyant outfit was more in keeping with that subject than, say, physics or chemistry, though perhaps he was unfairly stereotyping those teachers. Her arrival in the car park had certainly been dramatic. A deliberate ploy? he wondered. Hopefully the errant fiancé would turn up safe and well, and he would hear no more about him, whoever he was.

And yet, there had been something else that Meredith St Claire had left unsaid that had aroused his curiosity. She had said that they *had* hoped to be married. Did that imply she had a reason to doubt his fidelity, perhaps?

Lorimer shrugged. Forget it, he told himself, ignoring the little voice that suggested otherwise.

CHAPTER FIVE

It might not be the warmest day for a fishing trip, but the morning was dry after the night's heavy downpour, the air now still. Brian Peters parked his Mazda in the usual place by the small loch and opened the boot. The hills around shimmered with the last vestiges of mist, a faint lemon light above them fading into sullen grey. He drew out his fishing gear and the lunch he had packed for himself, a corned beef sandwich and a bottle of fizzy juice. When Anne was alive, she would have added an apple or a couple of tangerines ... a slice of home-made fruit cake.

Brian gave a sigh.

Don't go there, he told himself. Who was it who had said, 'That way madness lies'? Shakespeare, probably. Anne had been fond of quoting the Bard, as she'd called him, as though he'd been a personal friend. And in some ways he had been just that, Anne's career as an actress flourishing before the onset of that ghastly illness that had changed their lives.

He slung a small haversack over one shoulder, grabbed

the waterproof case holding his fishing rod and slammed the boot shut with a finality that indicated a sense of resolve.

He'd already changed his trainers for walking boots, prepared for the path to the loch being a muddy track after last night's rain, though he would put on his waders once he reached the water's edge. Taking a deep breath of the fresh air, Brian headed along the path, his eyes scanning the loch for any waterfowl. He looked up suddenly, the mewing cry of a buzzard catching his attention. It was an isolated spot and yet he never felt lonely with so many creatures around. This was their habitat, he'd often thought; himself the interloper. He watched for a moment as the buzzard soared overhead, then disappeared beyond the nearby pine forest. In a few weeks there might be a second then a third bird, a mating pair raising their lone chick and teaching it to hunt. Such observations had been a solace to the man standing by the shore, a half-smile on his face.

There was a particular spot where he liked to sit on the mossy bank and fish, watching the ripples as ducks of every type swam towards him. He'd maybe throw them a few crumbs later. After a few minutes they departed, arrowing through the still waters. Once, someone had told Brian that fishing was the UK's most popular sport, but he found that hard to believe, given the masses seen at football matches everywhere. And yet, it was easy to believe in some ways, the peace that this provided, the sudden excitement when a fish rose to the bait and the satisfaction of bringing home a decent catch of trout.

The fisherman let his mind wander as he sat, rod in hand, casting from time to time and watching the surface of the loch for any movement.

He had been there for the best part of an hour before the familiar tug on the line made him stand up and pay closer attention to his catch.

His expression of eager anticipation became a scowl as Brian realised that he'd snagged something bigger than a trout, something that threatened to snap his line and perhaps even his precious rod. He waded into the water, mouth in a grim line as he felt the weight pulling his arms. This was a private fishing loch and yet he wouldn't put it past some yobs out for mischief having flung rubbish into its depths. Clenching his teeth, he pulled as carefully as he could, praying that the line would not suddenly snap.

Some bubbles broke the surface and then the tension on his line eased, the mysterious object floating closer to shore.

At first, he thought it was simply a black polythene bag stuffed with refuse.

Then the rounded shape became clearer, a pale hand floating upwards.

The sight of several white-clad figures by the shores of the loch had apparently been enough to scare off the ducks, the waters now a grey-blue mirror under the brightening skies.

'A hot drink, sir,' the female police officer said, handing the cup to Brian Peters, guiding it carefully into his shaking hands as they sat in the squad car. 'We have a senior officer on her way, a detective inspector who will want to ask you all about this.' She threw a glance across at the activity beyond them. 'Are you warm enough?' she asked sympathetically, tugging the blanket she'd wrapped around the man's shoulders. 'Shock can make you feel very cold.'

Brian nodded. Since he had dropped his fishing rod and scrambled to the bank to make that 999 call, he had felt as though every bone in his body was aching.

He could see the lights on the other police Land Rovers flashing, each of them having driven as close to the loch as the muddy path allowed. It had seemed hours since he had made that awful discovery and yet, checking his watch, Brian saw that it was not yet eleven o'clock.

Waiting for the first sign of help had been the worst part, he would tell people afterwards, hanging onto his rod, keeping the body close to the shore. At least whoever had fallen in was floating face down so that Brian did not have to see their features. That was some relief. Or so he had believed until the dreams that haunted his sleep began.

Detective Inspector Molly Newton parked her car beside a blue Mazda then grabbed the bag containing her white suit and bootees. Any discovery of a body was grim, but she loathed the ones that had been submerged in water, the depredations of small aquatic creatures often making the victim look like something from a horror movie. The scene of crime officers were already there, the forensic pathologist on her way. Thank goodness it was Dr Fergusson on call this morning, Molly thought as she zipped up the suit. Rosie and she had become quite good friends, through the pathologist's long association with Lorimer and his wife, Maggie.

On approaching the scene, she saw a uniformed female officer in a squad car sitting beside a man, his shoulders wrapped in a blanket. The poor sod who'd made the discovery, she decided. She'd head across to him first before looking at the body.

'Hello, I'm Detective Inspector Newton,' she told the man, crouching down to meet his eyes. 'So sorry you've had to be the one to find this victim.' She looked intently at the man's pale face. He was in his early sixties, she reckoned, the tweed cap showing some grey hair and a neatly trimmed beard.

'This is Mr Peters,' the constable said, and Molly nodded briefly.

'Brian Peters,' he told her. 'I was just fishing and then I caught something heavy . . . ' He sniffed and wiped his nose with the back of his hand. 'Didn't expect to see . . . '

Molly listened to the man; his voice strained as he tried to describe what he had found.

'I think it might be a good idea if you stay in the car a while longer, Mr Peters,' Molly told him at last. 'I'll be over there.' She stood up and gestured towards the edge of the loch before turning and making her way towards the other white-suited figures.

One of the SOCOs came and nodded to Molly as she approached the water's edge.

'We've put down plates, ma'am, and our photographer has taken the first few shots of footprints in the mud. Looks like the fisherman's waders are the main ones at the scene, though,' he said.

Molly stepped carefully towards the shoreline and a patch of flat ground where they had laid the body on a tarpaulin sheet.

'He was face down when your man over there found him,'

the SOCO told her. 'Don't think he touched him apart from pulling on his rod and line. Fellow was so shocked I doubt he'd have wanted to put a finger on him.'

'We'll ask but Mr Peters will still have to provide prints for elimination purposes. Bring me up to speed on this one, will you? Obviously not a simple matter of someone falling in and drowning.'

The scene of crime officer shook his head. 'You need to take a look, ma'am,' he said. 'Hard to tell exactly what might have happened till Doc Fergusson gets here. Oh, that looks like her wagon now.' He smiled, nodding towards a pale blue Audi. Sure enough, a slight figure emerged from the driver's side, her short blonde curls a halo against the brightening sky. Rosie would soon tell them what they needed to know, though an exact time of death was never something at which she would hazard a guess and Molly knew better than to ask.

The victim was not a pretty sight, bloated with the waters of the loch, his face damaged by whatever had been feasting upon it beneath the surface.

But as she lifted the man's coat collar with gloved hands, Molly's mouth tightened in a grim line.

That gash across his throat was not the work of pond life. A blade of some sort had done that. Molly swallowed down the bitter taste in her mouth. She let her eyes take in every detail that she could see. The victim was wearing a dark raincoat, jeans, trainers that had once been white and his right hand sported a heavy gold signet ring. Molly blinked as she gazed down at his face once more. Not old, maybe thirty? Possibly younger, stubble on chin and upper lip. Eyes closed, mercifully, for Molly hated looking into dead men's eyes, always feeling as though they might sit up and speak to her as if in some horror movie. She gave a slight shudder. No matter how often she had attended a scene of crime, there was always a sense of distaste mingling with the sorrow, particularly when a corpse had lain for any length of time, the smell of decomposition lingering long after she'd left the scene.

This was most certainly a crime scene. There was no chance that this poor chap had stumbled and fallen, inebriated, perhaps. Something she'd seen before.

'Morning, what do you have for me today?' a cheerful voice asked, and Molly turned to see the pathologist, now clad in her regulation white suit, every curl hidden beneath her hood.

'Fisherman found this fellow on the end of his line and hauled him to shore. Can't have been too far out,' Molly added, looking over the loch. 'A few yards perhaps on one cast? I'm not an expert, so we may have to ask him.'

Molly stood up to make room for the pathologist. 'Throat slashed. Was he dead when he entered the water, I wonder?' she asked, eyebrows raised as she looked at Rosie.

'All in good time, Detective Inspector,' Rosie replied, crouching down beside the body. 'Poor boy, what was your story, eh?' she asked softly, placing her bag to one side.

'Mr Peters, feeling any better?' Molly asked, slipping into the back of the Land Rover to sit beside him.

The fisherman turned to Molly and nodded. He did look less peaky, some colour now in his cheeks.

'I wanted to ask you how far out you think you had cast the fishing line when it hooked the body,' Molly began.

Brian Peters turned automatically to gaze out of the window to the figures milling about by the water's edge. Scene of crime officers were now painstakingly searching the area for a weapon, one of them wielding a metal detector. 'Hard to say, really. I didn't measure the amount of line that came in with . . . ' He bit his lip, evidently finding it hard to say the words 'the dead body with a dark slash across its throat'.

'Fifty feet? More? Less? See, I'd like to know where in that wee loch the victim came to grief.'

'You think he'd been swimming?' Peters frowned. 'Surely not. Far too cold . . . '

The poor man was still suffering from the initial shock, his response making no sense whatsoever.

'Perhaps he had been in a boat?' Molly suggested gently. 'I don't see one here today, however.'

Peters shook his head but remained silent, head hung low. Was he imagining a scene in his head? A fight that had ended in violence.

'Do you come here regularly?' Molly asked, turning the conversation to more basic questioning.

'Aye. It's been too wet and stormy for fishing lately, but I was here ten days ago. And nobody else was there that day either,' he sighed. 'Sometimes one of the club members rows out to the other side and casts from the boat. But it's been in for some sort of overhaul recently.'

Molly followed his gaze. There was no sign of a boat, not even a buoy to mark a mooring point, though she could see a flat grey slab of stone on the far bank which may have been a landing stage.

'Did you haul your line in further than the centre of the loch?' she asked.

Peters shook his head. 'No. Not that far. Maybe twenty feet? I couldn't see what I was pulling in,' he explained. 'There are lots of water weeds in there. Makes it hard to see anything below the surface. I think whoever it was had fallen in near the edge.' He turned to look at Molly again. 'It didn't take much time to bring it into shore.'

Molly nodded. The victim may well have simply fallen in after an assault and drowned. But this was no simple case of misadventure, no easy explanation. Once he was identified, she would have the unpleasant task of informing his nearest and dearest.

How do you tell someone their son, brother, husband has been murdered? She had done this before, but it never became any easier.

CHAPTER SIX

The last light in the auditorium was extinguished, reducing the chatter of anticipation to a muted murmur. Then the curtain moved silently, revealing an empty stage save for one hunched figure, the silence almost tangible. Behind the bank of equipment to the rear of the theatre one man looked out over rays of coloured lights filtering above the audience. All was as it should be, he decided, eyes on the stage and the actor now wakening from his slumber. No missing properties, all the flats just as they should appear. And yet, until the cast took their final bow on this, the last night of the play, he would not rest easy. Down at the front were certain people who might make or break this company, their reviews so critical to its future.

As the play progressed and other actors joined that figure onstage, the man felt himself relax. It was going to be all right. Their next production, if it was up to the standard of this one, would send their reputation rocketing. And, if he played his cards right, could make stars of several of his players. He smiled at the thought, absently stroking his beard. His leading man for the next production hadn't showed up tonight, though he might find him lounging about when the journalists gathered round the cast for the after party. It's what they did. Made an appearance when there might be press around, hoping to have their photographs taken. Guy would have his share of lionising once the new production reached the West End. Tonight, though, he would talk up the players in this performance, a few of them still fresh from drama college, their own big breaks still to come.

Before the curtain descended to mark the interval, he had slipped away, lights once more brightening the auditorium, picking out the gold-painted carvings between cream-coloured pillars, members of the audience already shuffling their way towards the bar.

CHAPTER SEVEN

'We've got an ID for him,' Rosie Fergusson told Molly later that afternoon. 'His wallet was zipped inside the coat pocket. Thank goodness most driver's licences are laminated nowadays, though I doubt if the issuing authorities had a scene like this in mind when they updated them.'

Molly waited patiently, resisting the impulse to butt in.

'Mr Guy Richmond, aged twenty-eight according to his birth date. A Gemini, if that helps. Here's his address,' she added, putting the licence card close to her computer screen.

Molly had a brief glimpse of a young man, his hair longer in this photograph than the man she had seen at the loch side, she noticed, as she scribbled down the address on the driving licence.

'Can you give me any idea when he may have entered the water?'

'Oh, this fellow had been in the water for at least a week, I'd say. As for time of death, no chance of being accurate with that.'

'No, of course.'

'PM's at eleven o'clock tomorrow,' Rosie said. 'We'll maybe know a bit more by then.'

The ground-floor apartment at 177 Glenlora Drive was on the outskirts of the Southside of the city, part of a new housing development that linked the districts of Thornliebank and Darnley. The housing scheme consisted of rows of pebble-dashed terrace houses and blocks of flats, the landscaping consisting of a few spindly trees planted in patches of green. Molly parked the car in a spare bay marked for residents and glanced across at her companion. Alisha was new to this sort of thing, just out of uniform and being fast-tracked into CID. It was her first time visiting the home of a murder victim and she heard the younger woman take a deep breath as they both left the car.

'Observe everything you can,' Molly told her. 'Details matter, remember.'

It was now approaching seven o'clock in the evening, skies darkening over the hills beyond the city.

'Hopefully someone is at home after work,' she added, knocking the door of the flat loudly.

After a minute they heard the rattle of a chain and the door opened sufficiently for them to see a young woman clad in purple fleece pyjamas, peering at them.

'DI Newton and DC Mohammed,' she said, showing her warrant card. 'Is this the home of Guy Richmond?'

The woman shook her head. 'He moved out,' she told them. 'I'm the tenant now. Why? Has he done something wrong?'

Molly smiled reassuringly. 'Do you have a forwarding address for Mr Richmond?'

'Yes. Wait a minute.' She unfastened the chain and opened the door wider. 'Better come in. Sorry, the place is a tip,' she murmured, casting a regretful look over her shoulder. 'Not quite recovered from the party. Last night of the play, you know. There's always a bit of a do afterwards and I got a bit ...' She grinned sheepishly and shrugged then looked around. 'Not long moved in here and, yes, there's still a lot to do.'

It was no exaggeration. Boxes lined the hallway, some of their contents spilling out onto the laminate flooring, and as she led them into the kitchen, they could see pots and crockery piled into the sink and a bin overflowing with rubbish, the smell of last night's takeaway curry a prevalent note. The only tidy element was a neat row of empty wine bottles lined up along the window sill.

'Here you are,' the woman said, pulling a postcard from an old cork pinboard hanging slightly askew on the wall.

Molly took it. There was a picture of a Rodin sculpture she recognised from Glasgow's Burrell Collection, *The Call to Arms*, a work that reminded her of a scene from *Les Misérables*. On the other side someone had written an address in fine flowing handwriting, ink not biro pen, Molly noticed.

'Can I keep this, Miss ...?'

'Sarra Milroy,' the woman answered with a shrug. 'Guy won't mind. He has loads of these fancy postcards.'

Molly glanced at Alisha before she continued. 'Good friend of yours?' she asked.

Sarra Milroy frowned. 'Well, not really a friend but we kind of work together. We met last year at St James's Theatre. I had a small part in the last play we did.' She made a face. 'Guy usually gets the lead male roles, of course, but he wasn't in this one. Didn't show up for the party, though,' she added with a frown. 'Not like him to miss a chance to schmooze.'

Molly's expression softened. This young woman would know soon enough to use the past tense when referring to Guy Richmond, but for now it was imperative to find his next of kin.

'Does he live alone or with his parents?'

Sarra gave a laugh. 'Guy, live alone? Not flippin' likely. Gets his gorgeous girlfriend to do everything for him.' Her face became more serious. 'Ach, his folks died not that long ago. Car accident. Poor Guy.'

'Thanks, Miss Milroy. That's been most helpful,' Molly told her, turning to leave.

'He is all right, isn't he? Only the director is about to tell us what parts we're having in the next production tomorrow night,' Sarra Milroy said, a note of anxiety creeping into her voice.

'Sorry, I can't say anything at the moment,' Molly told her. Then she walked out of the flat, the DC scurrying behind her.

'What now?' Alisha asked as they fastened their seat belts.

'Now we go and break the news to his girlfriend,' Molly replied with a sigh.

CHAPTER EIGHT

The lawyer gave a frown. She was a busy woman and had client meetings back-to-back in her diary all this month. What was it that this American fellow had wanted to discuss? He had insisted on a face-to-face meeting and would not give a single hint about why he needed to see her today. Her secretary had called his mobile several times, but it appeared to be switched off.

She drummed her fingers on the wood of the desk, thinking back to the previous visits the young actor had made here. She had shown him complete sympathy, of course. Such a dreadful thing to have happened but also good for her own client list to have a wealthy young man who had inherited such a fortune and who wanted her help, it seemed, with his financial and legal affairs. Still, he had a loving partner by his side, and it looked as if he meant to marry the girl. Perhaps he had wanted to put money in trust for her? There was certainly some reason why Guy Richmond had not wanted to explain the need for a meeting with his lawyer over the telephone.

The lawyer glanced at her wristwatch, realising that she ought to have been home hours ago. No, he wasn't going to be arriving this late. No doubt he'd send an expensive bouquet of flowers to apologise. He struck her as a man who made big extravagant gestures like that. She sighed. Young folk . . .

CHAPTER NINE

The address on the Rodin postcard led Molly and Alisha to a pretty cottage up a country lane, not far from the village of Milngavie. Molly parked the car then leaned over and gave the younger woman a pat on the arm.

'Always worse the first time. Got the paper hankies?'

Her DC nodded, gazing towards the red door and the ornate lantern lighting up the path. 'Terrible thing for them to hear,' she whispered. 'I can't imagine how she'll react. The girlfriend, I mean.'

'Just be ready to do practical things like making a pot of tea,' Molly advised. 'I'll do the hard bit.'

The cottage was hedged off on either side, enclosing a small garden. It was too dark now to make out very much, though as they drew nearer Molly noticed a large pot next to the front step with green spikes that might grow into tulips.

There was a bell on the side of the door and below it, a new brass nameplate with RICHMOND in flowing writing, reminding Molly oddly of the dead man's signature on his driver's licence. The shrill sound set Molly's teeth on edge, but her finger remained on the doorbell just long enough to hear footsteps thudding towards them.

'Hello?' A tall slim woman stood there barefoot, clutching a black and yellow silk kimono decorated with Chinese dragons around her, hair wrapped in a towel as though she had just emerged from the bathroom.

'DI Newton, DC Mohammed. May we come in?'

The woman stared at them both for a moment, her mouth opening as if to cry out.

Then, before Molly could move, she slumped to the floor in a dead faint.

Molly could hear the rattle of teacups from the kitchen as she sat beside Guy Richmond's girlfriend. She and the DC had lifted her between them and helped her to the nearby lounge and onto a sofa upholstered in bright turquoise velvet. The woman moaned a little, then looked at Molly through fluttering eyelashes.

'Come on, miss, lean forward a little, head between your knees, that's right. Good lass,' Molly soothed, her arm around the woman's shoulders. Soon she was sitting slumped back against the cushions, kimono gathered tightly around her body. The towel had fallen off in the hallway, revealing a straggle of dark pink hair.

'It's Guy, isn't it?' she whispered at last, casting a fearful look in the DI's direction.

Molly nodded, noting the ring sparkling on the woman's left hand. Not just a girlfriend, then.

'I'm afraid we have bad news. Mr Richmond was found dead this morning,' she told her. 'And you are Miss . . . ?'

'Ms St Claire. Meredith St Claire,' she whispered. Then, putting her face into her hands, she began to sob.

Molly patted the woman's back gently, feeling the bones of her spine through the silk dressing gown. She was pencil thin.

At last Meredith St Claire sat up and wriggled free of Molly's hand. Alisha arrived at that very moment, bearing a tray of hot drinks.

'I put sugar and milk out,' she faltered. 'What do you take?' she asked the distraught woman.

'Just milk,' she said, her voice husky. It was a lovely voice, thought Molly, cultured and with the sort of musicality that suggested an island heritage.

She took the cup from Alisha and clutched it as though warming her hands. 'I reported him missing,' she said, turning to Molly. 'I even spoke to a senior officer when he was at my school. But of course, you're police. You'll know that,' she added sorrowfully. 'I was so worried . . . ' She broke off with a shuddering sob.

Molly frowned. Lorimer had said something about a recent visit to his goddaughter Abby's school.

'Who was it you spoke to?' she asked quietly.

She shook her head. 'Can't remember his name . . . ' She turned and looked at Molly. 'Tall fellow . . . He was part of the careers seminar at St Genesius . . . that's where I work.'

'Was it Detective Superintendent Lorimer?'

'That's right. Do you know him?'

Molly nodded. The detective super was away for a couple

of days at Jackton but she'd check up on that later, she decided.

'Is there anyone you would like me to call? Someone who might come and stay here?'

Meredith St Claire looked at Molly and frowned. 'No. Nobody. It was just Guy and me. Always just Guy and me. I have nobody else ...'

Then, to the officers' dismay, she threw her head back, howling in anguish.

It was much later when they left the cottage with the promise of a return visit next day, a family liaison officer having arrived with an overnight bag.

'Is it always like that?' Molly's latest recruit asked, tucking a strand of glossy black hair behind her ear.

'Sometimes,' Molly admitted. 'More often it's stunned disbelief, the bereaved family insisting it is all a mistake, not *their* loved one that's come to harm.'

'It's a horrible job, though,' Alisha replied.

'I can't tell you that it's something you'll get used to because you won't,' Molly said. 'It's worst of all when it's a child,' she added, glancing across at the young woman. The lass would have to harden up pretty quickly in order to cope with the day-to-day elements of a murder case, though having a compassionate reaction was also a good sign if she really cared about the job. They had a duty to protect the public, though emotional involvement was not to be encouraged lest it blinded an officer to the necessary factors with which they had to deal.

'Dr Fergusson's got the PM scheduled for tomorrow morning,' Molly said. 'Do you want to ...?'

'I'll come,' Alisha said at once. 'It's not the dead that frighten me,' she added with a weak smile.

They drove along in silence, Molly thinking over the scene at that cottage, the woman eventually calming down sufficiently to give them her own details. So, Meredith St Claire was a part-time drama teacher at Abby Brightman's school, as Molly had guessed. Rosie and Solly's daughter attended St Genesius, which was situated in the West End of the city, handy for the Brightmans who lived close to Kelvingrove Park, and perhaps just a twenty-minute drive from the cottage. Molly gave a sigh, thinking about the bereaved woman's breakdown. She and Richmond had been engaged for a very short time though they'd lived together for almost a year. They'd met at the Conservatoire, Meredith had told them in that breathy voice of hers, and they had known immediately that they were destined for one another.

Molly had listened, piecing together the bits of background as she spoke, watching as Meredith's slender fingers twisted the huge solitaire as though it were all she had left to remind her of her dead fiancé. They would call in the next day, she assured her after the FLO arrived to relieve them for the night. Meantime, they would ask that she did not reveal the news of his death on social media, not until his body had been identified, a task to which Meredith had agreed, nodding sadly as though it were what she had expected to be asked.

CHAPTER TEN

'B ad day?' Daniel asked, pulling Molly closer. 'You look tired.'

Molly nodded, feeling Daniel's jersey soft against her skin, glad of the warmth of his body. Outside, rain was falling, the sound drumming against the windows of her flat in Lilybank Gardens. Daniel had arrived first after his shift and Molly had been glad of the curry he'd prepared for them both. It was a while since she had given him a key to the flat and he was an even more regular visitor now that his mother had taken over Daniel's room on the south of the city. They could not have the privacy that they'd enjoyed before Janette Kohi's arrival, Netta perfectly happy to have 'the two love birds' as she called them sharing Daniel's bed.

Molly had made an effort with the Zimbabwean woman but so far there had been no spark of recognition about her relationship with Daniel. That they were becoming serious about one another was not in any doubt, at least as far as Molly was concerned. Yet she must make allowances for the older woman's point of view. What was it Lorimer was fond of saying: imagine yourself in another person's skin. See how they might see the world.

'Hungry?'

'Starving,' Molly replied. 'That smell of curry is making my tummy rumble.'

All thoughts of Daniel's mother were brushed aside as Molly related her day's work.

'And you think that Lorimer had seen the victim's partner?' Daniel asked, after listening to Molly's tale.

She nodded. 'I think so. Rosie and Solly's daughter, Abby, she had Lorimer to her school a few days ago to speak at a careers thing. He was joking that he'd been recruiting for Police Scotland. I think the kids at Abby's school gave him a pretty good welcome, by all accounts.'

'Well, he'll want to know about the outcome,' Daniel said. 'Poor woman. Waiting and wondering till you turn up and confirm her worst nightmare.'

'She was in a state,' Molly told him. 'Took one look at us ...' She shivered suddenly. 'I guess our serious expressions must've given it away.'

'Well, don't be hard on yourself,' Daniel said, cuddling Molly closer to his side. 'You could hardly roll up with grins all over your faces, now, could you?'

Lorimer's face lit up when he saw DI Newton at his door next morning.

'Come in, Molly,' he said, rising from his seat behind the desk. 'I was just talking about you to the officers in Jackton Training Centre yesterday. They were extolling young

Alisha's progress. How is she doing under your guiding hand?'

Molly came forward as Lorimer beckoned her to sit in one of the comfortable chairs in his room, wondering how to begin.

'DC Mohammed is doing well, I'd say,' she began. 'We will be at a post-mortem examination later this morning. In fact,' she sat down and gave him a keen look, 'that's what I wanted to talk to you about.'

Lorimer nodded, but said nothing, folding his hands and waiting for Molly to continue.

'Do you remember a Meredith St Claire, sir?'

'Yes, indeed I do. Why?' His brow furrowed.

'The body of her fiancé, Guy Richmond, was found out in Whitemoss Loch yesterday morning.'

Lorimer looked up and gave a long sigh. 'Oh, dear lord, the poor woman. She asked me to get involved in finding him. Said she'd reported him as a missing person,' he explained. 'But when I tried to reason with her about the way the police respond, well ... she just ran off. As if she was in a real temper.'

'She did strike me as very emotional,' Molly admitted. 'When we broke the news, she fainted clean away then later gave the most unearthly shriek. Took both of us to calm her down and we had to get an FLO to stay the night with her.'

'And it's her partner's PM today?'

'Well, after she identifies his body,' Molly said. 'The FLO will bring her to the mortuary where she'll meet Dr Fergusson. She was on duty yesterday, too.'

'All the good ones gathering around,' Lorimer murmured.

'That will be of no consolation to her, of course, but I'm glad you are SIO in this case, Molly. And I know you will do a good job.'

'I thought you might want to see her, sir?'

'Me? Oh, no, I think I'd be the last person that Ms St Claire would want to see. However, if anything should escalate from this case, I'll be only too happy to become involved. What happened?'

'We don't know for sure, but he was probably assaulted at the loch or brought there already dead. Throat slit. PM will tell us a lot more.'

Lorimer frowned and shook his head. 'Bad business. They were just engaged, as I recall her telling me. Two young people with their lives all before them . . . ach, it's not right, is it?'

'It never is,' Molly agreed. 'Still, we'll be checking her story about dropping her fiancé off in town. CCTV ought to confirm that.'

Well, keep me posted, will you? I certainly want to know of any progress as it happens.'

'Of course, sir,' Molly said, rising from the armchair. 'I'd better get over to the mortuary and be there before Ms St Claire arrives.'

Glasgow City Mortuary was situated in an old Victorian building directly in front of the High Court of Justiciary, very handy for any of the pathologists that might be called as expert witnesses in a case. Rosie Fergusson had resisted the lure of one of the big city hospitals that wanted their department to relocate, her fondness for the old place as much a reason as the benefits of being close to the courts. Today she was awaiting the arrival of the woman who had agreed to identify the victim, though it was all but certain that Meredith St Claire would recognise Guy Richmond, her fiancé. The laboratory assistants had made a decent attempt to clean him up though only his face would be on view, a white sheet covering that injury to his neck.

This was the horrid part of the pathologist's job, meeting the nearest and dearest relations of the deceased. Molly Newton had informed her that the victim's parents were also deceased and that his fiancée was his official next of kin.

When the bell rang, Rosie left her office and stood in the corridor, waiting till the DI arrived. One of the lab boys was there to open the door and Rosie saw four people: a tall skinny woman with shocking pink hair, Molly Newton, an older woman she recognised as Heather Crawford, one of the family liaison officers, and a smaller young woman with dark hair. This must be the latest recruit to the Major Incident Team, the Asian lass who had been fast-tracked into CID and was said to have a bright future before her.

'This is Dr Fergusson. Meredith St Claire,' Molly said, introducing the visitor.

'Hello. So sorry for your loss,' Rosie murmured, offering the woman her hand.

'Thank you,' she replied, in a husky, tremulous voice.

'It's good of you to come in,' Rosie told her, leading them down towards the viewing room where the body lay. 'You only need to look through this window here, when the curtain is drawn back,' she explained, stopping at a large window set into the corridor wall.

'Tell me when you are ready,' she heard DI Newton say quietly as she took the victim's fiancée by the elbow.

'I'm all right,' Meredith replied, shaking the detective off and giving the pathologist a nod.

As the dusky pink curtain was drawn aside, Meredith leaned nearer the glass, her fingers clutching the window frame for support. Rosie watched intently, her heart filled with pity as the woman's mouth fell open then her hand was pressed against her lips as if attempting to stifle a cry.

'Is this Guy Richmond?' Rosie asked gently.

Meredith gave a brief nod, eyes still fixed intently on the body lying beneath their gaze.

It was important to wait in silence, making no move to disturb what might be the last sight a person would have of their loved one. Sometimes the bereaved wanted to scurry away as fast as possible, the process of identification too hard to bear, but more often it was like this, momentary calm when a silent goodbye might be made.

At last, the woman turned away. Rosie saw Heather, the FLO, take her arm and help her along the corridor to a room that was specially designated for the bereaved. Meredith St Claire was helped into a chair next to a low table furnished with a glass of water and a box of tissues. The room was painted in pastel shades of peach and green, a print of Monet's *The Artist's Garden at Giverny* hanging on one wall. Outside there was a faint hum of traffic but here, in this room, there was a sense of calm.

'Well done,' Rosie heard Molly tell the pink-haired woman and she had the chance to take a closer look now that the formal identification was over. She had a long, heart-shaped face with prominent cheekbones that suggested either a meagre diet or a recent illness. Grief? Or drugs? The question came unbidden into the pathologist's mind. She'd seen enough addicts in her post-mortem room. Could be. She watched as the slender fingers reached for a tissue and drew it to her eyes. Skinny or not, Meredith St Claire was a strikingly lovely woman. Abby's favourite drama teacher, she now knew, though Rosie had never met her at the school. Her eye fell on the woman's left hand as a shaft of sunlight made her blink. That was some size of solitaire on her engagement ring, Rosie thought, her pity for the victim's fiancée swelling.

'He was so happy,' Meredith said at last, wiping her nose and crushing the tissue in her fist. 'What happened?' she asked, turning a bewildered face towards Rosie.

'We will know more after the post-mortem,' she assured the woman.

'And I will make sure we find out the answer to your question as soon as possible, Meredith,' Molly said.

'You're in charge . . . ?'

'I am,' Molly assured her. 'But I must pass on condolences from my boss, Detective Superintendent Lorimer.'

The woman's eyes widened for a moment and then she looked at each of them in turn.

'You know him too?'

'He's the best,' Rosie said.

'But I . . . '

'Detective Superintendent Lorimer mentioned that you had met. And seriously, there was nothing else he could have told you at that point, Meredith,' Molly explained gently. 'Now matters have changed and we will make every effort not just to find out what happened to Guy but also to catch the perpetrator.'

'What about a funeral? I'm the only person he's got left, so ... it's up to me to arrange things.' She looked at each of them in turn, bewilderment on her face. 'And I have no idea how to go about that.'

Molly gave her a sympathetic look. 'Heather can help you when the time comes. Did Guy have a solicitor? That might be useful to know.'

She nodded then heaved a sigh.

'Can you spare us some time, Ms St Claire?' Molly asked.

'Yes, if you think that is necessary,' Meredith answered, sighing heavily.

'It would be good to ask you more about Mr Richmond, if you feel up to it.'

'You're being very nice.' Meredith gave them a tremulous smile. 'It's not like TV drama where the detective grills the poor wife of a victim,' she added, with a small laugh.

'You can either come with us to HQ where we'll find a space to talk, or Heather can take you back home, if you'd prefer?'

'I'm not ready to go home yet,' Meredith admitted. 'So many memories ... just seeing him there like that ...' She sniffed and swallowed.

'Okay, let's drive across town. We're situated beside Bellahouston Park,' Molly told her.

'We can get you a decent cup of coffee there,' Alisha added with an encouraging smile. 'Or herbal tea if you prefer.'

Rosie lifted her eyes from the task in hand. The main parts

of the autopsy had been performed and now the familiar Y shape had been stitched from just beneath the wound. That incision across the victim's neck had been made with a sharp blade, possibly a cut-throat razor, something she'd come across on several occasions after a gang fight where a lad had been slashed. But this chap was a different sort of victim, surely? An actor, Molly Newton had told her. Who had been happily engaged to be married, by all accounts. Her own part in his story was fairly straightforward, as she would tell the investigating officer and the Fiscal in due course. A single slash to the throat, administered from behind, his head raised slightly as the cut was inflicted, and slight bruising on his left shoulder where a hand had held him steady. One person or two? She would not find that so easy to determine, but from what she had seen, her impression was that it had been committed by someone at least as tall as the victim.

Other than that, she could tell them that his final meal had been salad and tuna steak, washed down with wine. Toxicology would determine if he had harboured any opiates in his bloodstream, though he looked fit and healthy with good muscle tone. He'd been a handsome-looking fellow, dark wavy hair over a broad forehead and a strong jawline that made her wonder about his character. Guy Richmond. She wasn't aware of his name but then neither she nor her husband Solly were regular patrons of the theatre. Perhaps he had still to make his fortune in the uncertain world of acting, a future now forever denied him.

The drive through Glasgow was quiet, none of them prepared to make conversation. For, what could you talk about after an experience like that? As Alisha drove across the Kingston Bridge and along the motorway, Molly glanced in the mirror at Guy Richmond's fiancée. She sat motionless, gazing out of the window. What did she see? Was it the Glasgow skyline passing them by? Or was Meredith St Claire revisiting those moments outside the viewing room at the mortuary? Impossible to tell from that still, impassive face.

The room was warm, sun streaming through the windows as though making a promise that winter was finally past. Molly pulled out a chair for the bereaved woman so that she had her back to the glare of light, seating herself at an angle to avoid the impression that this was an interrogation.

'It may help our investigation to know more about Guy, your fiancé,' Molly began, her hands over a notepad on her knees. 'Just tell us everything you know, in your own time.'

Meredith looked at each of them in turn, her brow furrowing.

'Where do I begin?' she asked but neither replied, expecting this to be a rhetorical question.

She heaved a big sigh then gave a little nod.

'We met at drama school. The Conservatoire here in Glasgow,' she told them. 'Guy was instantly popular, his good looks and American accent marking him out as someone special. Well,' she gave a faint smile and looked down at her hands, 'he was to me anyhow. We spent that first year together ... in groups and in rehearsals ... it seemed we were always chosen to perform roles with one another.' She paused, eyes looking over their heads into a distant past only she could see.

'It was in our final year that we really got together,' she explained. 'By then we were all auditioning for parts, Guy luckier than most of us to find work right away. TV ads, mostly, at first, then smaller parts in dramas. I . . . ' She broke off and made a face. 'I didn't cut it, I'm afraid. No sign of any work.' She shrugged. 'So, I retrained as a drama teacher and got a well-paid job. That helped. We had been pretty broke up till then, living hand-to-mouth in a small flat near Darnley.'

She bent forward to pick up her coffee and took a sip. Molly waited for her to continue.

'Everything changed for us last year when his parents died,' she said softly, shaking her head in sorrow. 'It was awful for Guy, but in other ways it helped.' She stopped then and looked directly at Molly.

'Can you explain what you mean?'

'Guy was an only child and he inherited . . . well . . . a small fortune, I suppose. I'm not very good at finance and stuff like that but he was going to be well provided for . . . not have to worry about work . . . and we, we bought our first home.'

Meredith's voice broke then, and she covered her eyes with both hands, her shoulders shaking as the sobs began.

That explained the huge rock on her finger, Molly thought. Poor lass! What hopes they may have had for their future, snatched away.

CHAPTER ELEVEN

Background checks were already under way even as Meredith St Claire was given a lift back home. The girl that Molly had spoken to at Richmond's previous address had mentioned that he was about to be cast in a new production. That might be worth following up.

Molly sat staring at her computer screen, reading the notes from one of the detective constables. Auditions were arranged for that very evening, in St James's Theatre, Paisley. Molly had been to pantomimes there every Christmas as a child and she remembered the old building tucked away behind the busy main streets, not too far from the University of the West of Scotland. It might be wise simply to turn up, relay the news of his death to Richmond's friends and colleagues and see their reactions. One thing was certain, they had lost their star performer, if all that Meredith St Claire had told them about Guy Richmond's acting prowess was true.

*

Molly drove around St James's roundabout then took the slip road and turned past the grounds of St Mirren Football Club. There were lots of cars in the car park, indicating an evening fixture at the stadium which had relocated to its modern home several years before. Molly nodded a silent approval as she drove on; the more facilities there were in communities like this the better, especially for bored teenagers who might be tempted into committing petty crimes. Or worse. There had been a spate of knife crimes in Renfrewshire over the previous winter and the chief constable had made a special appeal to officers everywhere to talk to groups in places like this as a way of preventing further crimes.

Molly stepped up to the main entrance of the theatre where double glass doors opened noiselessly. A bright, well-lit foyer had an old-fashioned box office to one side and corridors leading off to left and right, signs to the stairs and upper levels clearly marked. The patterned red and blue carpet was worn in places and Molly struggled to remember if it was the same one that had been there when she was a child.

There was no one about though she could hear voices dimly in the distance along the right-hand corridor and so Molly followed the sound, emerging at the back of the stalls. She gave the place a cursory look around, noting that there was a real lack of security here if anyone could simply walk in off the street as she had done. As she walked silently down one side towards the stage, she could see several people seated in a semicircle, including Sarra Milroy, the young woman who had given her Richmond's new address. Opposite them sat a long-haired man with a grey pointed beard, a scarlet cravat tucked into his dark tweed waistcoat. The director, she assumed, as she walked silently towards the darkened theatre pit.

The man looked down at Molly as she approached, an expression of fury on his narrow, pockmarked face.

'Get out! We're busy rehearsing!'

Molly continued her walk right up to the edge of the stage, even as the director glared at her from his seat, the rest of them turning to stare at the newcomer to their midst.

'Detective Inspector Newton,' she told them in a crisp tone, holding up her warrant card.

The effect on the man was immediate. He sprang to his feet and hastened over, bending a little to examine Molly's warrant card suspiciously.

'What do you want? Are you sure you've got the right place, young lady?'

'Am I correct in assuming that you were all expecting Guy Richmond to attend this evening?' she asked in a firm voice.

Several of the men and women began to murmur, shooting anxious glances at the detective.

'Well, yes, I mean ... ' The man who had shouted at Molly took a step back. Then his tone changed to something of a stage whisper as he asked, 'What's happened? Do you have some bad news about Guy?'

The murmuring grew louder, Molly able to glance from face to face to see their reactions. These were actors, after all, and might be practised in simulating an emotion. But the overall impression she had was one of surprise.

'I'm very sorry to inform you, but Mr Richmond is dead,' Molly said, her eyes still roving around the circle of faces.

'Good God!' The director slumped into his seat, his mouth falling open as if in shock.

'You came to see me,' Sarra Milroy cried out, coming forward and looking down at Molly. 'Did you know then ...? Why didn't you say?'

'What happened?' a slim, dark-haired young man stood up and asked. 'Was he in some sort of accident?'

'I'm sorry, due to our ongoing investigation I am not at liberty to divulge any details.' Molly noticed that they were all out of their seats now and beginning to crowd the edge of the stage, some kneeling down.

'Is Merry okay?' the Milroy girl asked, clutching the edge of the stage.

'Oh God! What a stupid question, of course she won't be!' An older woman dressed in a baggy denim dress and black cowboy boots glared at Sarra. Then she stared at Molly. 'Have you seen her? Meredith, I mean?'

'Ms St Claire has been informed,' Molly said. 'And a family liaison officer has been attending to her since we broke the news.' It was the least she could truthfully tell them at this stage of the investigation.

'Why have you come?' The dark-haired fellow frowned at her. 'Just to tell us?'

'I was hoping that you might give me some background information about Mr Richmond,' Molly told them.

'Is there something suspicious about his death, then?' the older woman asked, turning in her seat to stare at the detective. Molly declined to answer but noted the woman's eyes lighting up with excitement. Not so much concern as blatant curiosity, she thought.

'Madam, please join us,' the director said grandly, standing up and indicating his now vacant seat. 'Sarra, dear, go and fetch another chair,' he added, in an avuncular tone that Molly found less than convincing. 'Nigel, kindly show the inspector the way.'

The dark-haired man had now jumped off the stage to land by Molly's side.

'Come with me,' he said, nodding for Molly to follow him. She let him guide her through an exit into a shadowy area then to a door that led to a flight of stairs.

'Just go on,' he said and soon Molly found herself seated onstage next to the director, close enough to discern the scent of Hugo Boss cologne liberally applied to his person.

'Perhaps we ought to introduce ourselves, Detective Inspector. I'm Jeffrey Standish, director of this motley crew,' he said, giving a little bow and offering his hand to be shaken.

It was dry, Molly noted, and cold, though the stage itself was warm enough under the lights.

One by one the group introduced themselves. Sarra Milroy she had met already and the dark-haired chap who had led her to the stage was Nigel Fairbairn; the older woman who seemed to be relishing this visit from a police officer was Ada Galloway. Ahmed Patel, the only Asian member of their group, had mumbled his name and she caught the distinctive trace of a Glasgow accent. The others, including the director, were all holding what she assumed to be scripts, but Patel was the only member of the semicircle who was balancing a clipboard on his knee, pen in hand. Molly jotted down each name in turn, noting their expressions. Almost all seemed shocked, their voices husky with genuine emotion, Sarra

Milroy shaking her head, murmuring 'I don't believe it', over and over, her face drained of colour.

'Perhaps you might be kind enough to tell me what you know about Guy Richmond,' Molly said at last. 'To fill in any gaps Ms St Claire may have left. I take it you all knew him well?'

'It's not St Claire,' Ada Galloway, the woman in the denim dress, said drily. 'Poor Meredith has notions above her station, I'm afraid.'

Molly caught Sarra Milroy's outraged glare towards the older woman, but before she could speak, the director spoke up.

'That's true,' Standish agreed with a theatrical sigh. 'She was never going to be good enough for the stage. Changing her name was rather grasping at straws. Might have looked nicer on a programme than Sinclair,' he added waspishly.

Molly filed that particular comment for later examination. Meredith hadn't been universally well liked, it seemed, for all their protestations.

'Guy Richmond,' she continued, giving them all a determined stare.

One by one the actors told their own tale about Richmond, variations of how he was such a nice fellow, bright future ahead of him, terrible loss to the theatre (from Standish). Patel had just shrugged, mumbling *too bad*. Was he really a part of this group, Molly wondered, or a newcomer, listening in and making notes? It didn't seem, from his response, as if he had really known Richmond. Only Sarra Milroy looked genuinely upset, head down, a handkerchief balled in her fist. A few of them were either new to the group or had been brought in for this production, Standish explained, following their murmurs of *too bad, didn't know the chap* and *what a shame.*

Molly listened to so many platitudes, realising quickly how little in the way of real insight they gave into the victim's life. She would be better to interview those who'd known him well individually, though that would be time-consuming and these first few precious hours since the discovery of Richmond's body were ebbing away fast.

'What are you rehearsing just now?' she asked.

'Oh, not rehearsing, my dear, just a read-through of the script to see who can play which part. This is just a preliminary meeting. And Ahmed is making notes about props. That's his domain.'

'And the play?'

It was Nigel Fairbairn who answered in a tight voice, his reply sending an icy cold shiver down Molly's back.

'*Sweeney Todd,*' he told her. 'And we all expected poor Guy to be the demon barber.'

There was a pause, the actors glancing around at one another, as Molly took in the full significance of the man's statement.

'That'll be you now, Nigel, won't it?' Sarra stated at last, throwing a dark look at the man. 'You won't need to read for Judge Turpin after all.'

Molly was aware of the sudden silence that followed this and the way each member of the group avoided looking at Fairbairn. Something was going on here, she told herself. And she wanted to know just what undercurrents might have to be explored within this group of people who had known Guy Richmond.

CHAPTER TWELVE

'Would I like to ...?' Daniel Kohi stopped mid-sentence as DI Diana Miller smiled at him. Her presence at the training school in Jackton had been as much of a surprise as what she was now asking him to do.

'You won't be paid for it,' she told him, 'but it might bring some much-needed kudos to the force.'

Daniel said nothing, his mind whirling. His superior officers had been asked if PC Daniel Kohi might be willing to attend an interview with someone called Lynsey Ross and do a photo shoot for the Sunday supplement of a national newspaper.

'You did a marvellous job with the advertising poster,' Miller continued. 'You were the talk of the station all last week.'

It had been a surprise to the Zimbabwean constable to be selected as the face to help focus the public's perception of Police Scotland as an inclusive and diverse force but he had agreed, knowing that the top brass had laboured hard and long to stamp out the ugliness of racism.

'I know,' Daniel replied ruefully, not adding that it had not been universally welcomed by his colleagues at Cathcart. There was at least one officer who had thrown him a baleful look and another who had raised their eyes to heaven, making sure that Daniel saw their microaggression without any other witnesses.

'They think someone like you, a refugee who's turned his life around, would make a great story, of course. But think about it, Kohi, it might make a difference to the readers to see that we're doing all we can to "diversify and be inclusive",' she said, making inverted commas with her fingers.

'Okay, I'll do it,' Daniel agreed.

'Good man. That'll get the top brass off my back,' she said, laughing. 'Here's the number for the press office. They'll give you all the details. Oh,' she added with a sly grin, 'you do need to wear your uniform, but I think they'll be providing some posh civvies as well.'

'Thank you, ma'am,' Daniel said as Miller handed him a slip of paper.

'Ach, maybe you won't thank me when you become a star,' she joked. 'Just don't let it all go to your head.'

'The Sunday papers! Jings! Daniel, ye're gonnae be right famous, so you are.' Netta beamed after Daniel had explained why he was home from the training course earlier than expected.

'They want me to turn up this evening for a chat,' he explained. 'I'm to meet their reporter at the Blythswood Hotel.'

'My, very fancy,' said Netta. 'That's thon posh place beside Blythswood Square.' She leaned across the kitchen table towards Janette. 'Mind we walked up tae the gardens and looked back down at the city?'

Janette nodded, though she did not glance at her friend, unable to take her eyes off her handsome son, pride filling her heart.

'Oh, Daniel,' she sighed at last, clasping his arm. 'This is such good news. Now more people will understand what it was like for you working under that corrupt man and the dreadful things that brought you here.'

Daniel's eyes widened. 'You think they want to know all of that . . . ?'

'Of course!' Netta exclaimed. 'Your story is a' aboot good overcoming evil, isn't that whit ye were saying this morning, Janette?'

'In a way,' Janette conceded. 'A great deal of evil was done,' she added softly. 'You lost your wife and son, I lost you all . . . At least I thought I had until I came here.' Her eyes filled with tears.

'Now, Amai, if this is going to upset you, I won't do it,' Daniel insisted.

'No, no, this is a story that ought to be told,' Janette said, smiling up at him. 'You overcame such terrible things, and it is right that people should see how your courage and determination have led to your success.'

'Well, if you're sure,' Daniel said.

'Sure, we're sure,' Netta replied for them both. 'An' ah bet the Lorimers an' your Molly wid say the same.'

CHAPTER THIRTEEN

'Sweeney Todd, the demon barber,' Lorimer mused. 'Gruesome sort of film, wasn't it? Maggie and I went to see it. Too much blood, she thought. Well, maybe this lot will concentrate more on the love stories.'

DI Molly Newton shook her head. 'I don't like the fact that they are doing this production, sir. Too ... too much of a coincidence, if you know what I mean. Dr Fergusson's report says that it was a blade, most likely a cut-throat razor, that was used to inflict that fatal injury.'

'What did you make of the theatre people?'

She paused before answering, gazing over Lorimer's head at the window where white clouds were scudding past, traces of forget-me-not blue peeping through.

'I felt that some of them were putting on a show for my benefit, especially that director, Standish. He's a bit over-bearing, especially towards the younger women in the group. Or do we call it a troupe?' she asked, making a face. 'Sarra Milroy was the only one of them that really seemed upset about Richmond. I'd like to find out a bit more about those who were closest to him. And there was a bit of an unpleasantness when Meredith St Claire was mentioned.'

'Oh?'

'She wasn't good enough for the acting life so decided to teach instead. Well, she told us that herself, but there was a sort of sneering amongst a few of the actors as if that was somehow a lesser career. I felt like saying something to them about the importance of education but that wasn't the time or the place,' Molly admitted.

'They may be a bit envious, seeing that Meredith St Claire had fallen on her feet,' Lorimer reasoned. 'Whereas actors are normally living hand-to-mouth unless they hit the big time, Meredith has a steady income, shared a nice home with her fiancé. That was some size of diamond on her engagement ring,' he added. 'He'd inherited a great deal of money after his parents' death.' He looked at her thoughtfully. 'I wonder if Richmond had made a will?'

Molly nodded slowly. 'We've an appointment with his solicitor today, as it happens,' she told him. 'Meredith wanted to know when she might have his body for a funeral. And, of course, we had to tell her that was up to the Fiscal.'

'Well, let me know how that goes. Motive, means and opportunity,' he said softly. 'Money might even be a factor in the man's death if he had recently inherited a great deal.'

'We've checked her statement about when she last saw Richmond,' Molly said. 'CCTV can't verify their car's whereabouts on national highways, given the time that's elapsed, but their house phone records a whole series of calls to

Richmond's mobile that same evening as though she was concerned about him.'

Lorimer nodded, evidently satisfied that the woman's story had been followed up.

The solicitor's office was near the River Clyde in a modern building off Argyle Street, not far from Glasgow City Mission. Molly and Alisha entered the lift, and the DC pressed the button that would take them to the sixth floor.

The first thing they saw was the view from the top of the building, its frontage designed in a circular shape to give a panorama over the city and beyond. Today the view encompassed not just the immediate built-up area around the River Clyde but the distant Kilpatrick Hills in the west and the Cathkin Braes to the south where it was clear enough to discern the movement of windmills against the skyline.

'May I help you?' A voice to her right broke into Molly's reverie and she swung round to see a curved reception desk across the marble floor, a smartly dressed young woman regarding her with a faint smile of welcome.

'DI Newton, DC Mohammed,' Molly said, warrant card at the ready as she crossed the vast hallway. 'I have arranged to see Mrs McKay,' she continued, giving the girl the name of Richmond's solicitor.

'Ah, yes. Let me show you to one of our meeting rooms,' the receptionist said, rising from behind the desk and tap-tapping her way towards Molly on vertiginous high heels. 'This way.' She led them around the curving glass windows and along a nearby corridor. Molly could not help but take another look at the vista that presented itself, the city skyline south and west, stretching right towards a haze of grey-blue hills. The receptionist stopped when they reached a white wooden door and opened it with a keycard attached to her lanyard. 'Do come in, Inspector, have a seat. May I offer you both some tea or coffee?' she added.

'Coffee, thanks,' Molly replied.

'Nothing for me, thank you,' Alisha added.

'Mrs McKay won't be long,' the girl assured them and disappeared, leaving the door open.

Molly seated herself on a wine-red two-seater settee, one of a pair that were angled around a spotless glass-topped coffee table that gleamed in the sunlight. Had Guy Richmond sat in this very place, gazing out above the railway lines snaking out of Central Station? Meredith here too, perhaps?

She looked up as a middle-aged woman with short dark hair cut in a smooth bob entered the room.

'Janet McKay,' she said. 'You must be Inspector Newton,' she added as Molly rose to shake her outstretched hand.

'This is Detective Constable Mohammed,' Molly said, introducing her younger officer.

'I spoke to one of your detectives yesterday,' the solicitor remarked, her voice dropping as she acknowledged the reason for their visit. 'That poor young man. How dreadful! He'd made an appointment to see me and I thought it was odd that he didn't turn up.' She shook her head sadly. 'Now, of course, we know why.'

She sat opposite Molly but close enough for the DI to make out the familiar scent of Chanel No 5, the perfume that had been her mother's favourite. Dressed in a well-cut, dark navy suit, the pencil skirt accentuating her neat waist-line and shapely legs, Janet McKay looked every inch what she was, a successful partner in one of Glasgow's busiest law firms.

'Guy was a lovely fellow,' she began, then broke off as the receptionist returned bearing a tray with a cafetière of coffee, milk and sugar plus porcelain mugs and a plate of chocolate biscuits that Molly recognised from M&S.

'Thanks, Catriona.' Mrs McKay smiled at the girl as she laid the tray on the table. She waited till the receptionist had gone and closed the door behind her before turning back to Molly.

'Allow me,' she said, pouring coffee for them both. She took hers in both hands as though she needed to warm them and, crossing her legs, sat back, regarding Molly and Alisha with a detached sort of interest.

This was a woman who dealt in deaths all the time, Molly told herself. Wills and estates were all in a day's work, she supposed. Yet the tone of her sympathetic remark had sounded genuine.

'He was well spoken of by his theatre colleagues,' Molly agreed. 'Sadly, our own association with the man is some-what different.'

'Indeed.' Janet McKay nodded, uncrossing her legs and shifting forward a little. 'You will want to know his dealings with our firm, I take it?'

'Ms St Claire told us that he had made a will following his parents' deaths,' Molly said.

'Yes, we handled the transfer of the Richmonds' estate. We're an international firm, as you may be aware, so we had dealings with Mr Guy Richmond a few months ago. It was me who advised him to make a will,' she said with a slight shake of her head. 'Such a lot of money brings great responsibilities, and it is always advice we give to our clients in similar situations.'

'I see,' Molly murmured, sipping her coffee. It was good coffee with the distinctive aroma that came from freshly ground beans. 'I am interested in the terms of Mr Richmond's will.'

'Of course.' Janet McKay nodded. 'I was expecting that. There isn't much to tell you, frankly. He made a couple of bequests to charities but the bulk of his estate, including his new home, goes to his partner, Meredith St Claire.'

'He had no other relatives?'

'Apparently not. He was an only child. There had been a younger brother who died in infancy. Cot death syndrome. But nobody else. No surviving grandparents or cousins.' The solicitor paused for a moment to take a sip of coffee. 'I got the impression that Guy was glad to come over to the UK. His parents were high up in banking and had wanted Guy to pursue a similar career path. But he had rebelled a bit.' She smiled. 'Like most young people do. I have three of my own and none of them want to follow me into law.'

'Mr Richmond came to study at the Royal Conservatoire, here in Glasgow,' Molly said.

'I think his parents decided that acting was something he needed to get out of his system but from all accounts he had genuine talent. He wouldn't have been admitted to the Conservatoire otherwise.'

Molly nodded. This chimed with what had been said by

the St James's Theatre folk. He was expected to take the lead role in their forthcoming production.

'She is going to be a very wealthy young woman,' Janet McKay told her, then mentioned the figure that Meredith St Claire was to inherit. 'Thirteen million pounds, including some real estate in California. Though she won't see any of it until there has been confirmation of Mr Richmond's estate and probate has been granted. The house is in both their names so no problem there. If Ms St Claire requires funds we will, of course, be happy to advise her.'

Molly blinked for a moment as she considered the eye-watering sum.

'Of course, money won't bring back her partner. But it might help to ease some of the pain,' the solicitor continued. 'Help with the funeral.'

Molly cast her mind back to the distraught young woman who had collapsed at her feet in shock. She thought about how she might have reacted if news had been brought to her of Daniel's sudden death. No amount of money could compensate for that sort of loss.

CHAPTER FOURTEEN

T he police press officer stood at the close mouth of the tenement building, eyes searching for the name Kohi on the entry system.

'Ground floor left,' he murmured under his breath and pressed the appropriate buzzer.

'Gerry Cairns for PC Kohi,' he said clearly once the intercom crackled to life.

The main door to the flats opened with a noiseless jerk and he went in to see a dark figure standing in the doorway. Gerry's first impression was of an intelligent man, large dark eyes regarding him thoughtfully. The smile Kohi gave him lit up his face, in contrast to the poster now featuring in the foyers of every police office in the country, the Zimbabwean looking solemn and serious. It would be all right, Gerry told himself as he shook the man's warm hand and was ushered into the flat. The Sunday magazine editor had been quite specific about their brief and Gerry had given them the usual formal warnings about protecting the interests of officers.

And Kohi looked as though he was nobody's fool, he thought as he followed the man along the hallway and into a bright warm kitchen where two elderly ladies sat together round the table. He could smell home baking, bread or something else, his nose twitching in appreciation.

'This is Gerry, our police press officer,' Daniel explained. 'Mrs Gordon and my mother, Mrs Kohi,' he added with a wave of his hand.

'How do you do,' the small black woman replied, giving him a nod.

'See an' bring this wan back in guid time,' the white-haired lady insisted. 'He's oan an important training course. Gonnae be a detective, so he is.'

'Certainly.' Gerry smiled. 'Nice to meet you, ladies.'

'See you later,' Kohi said, stooping to kiss his mother's cheek.

'I've got my car outside,' Gerry told him.

Soon they were heading across the Kingston Bridge, the city lights twinkling on the dark waters of the River Clyde, then turning up the steep incline that would take them to Blythswood Square.

'What was your reaction to being asked to be the subject of the recent poster campaign?' the woman asked Daniel as they walked through the lobby of the hotel.

'I was surprised,' he admitted. 'There are several officers of colour in the force, here in Police Scotland and down south, so it wasn't just a matter of selecting me as an African but more to do with my experience as a refugee.'

'Here, this room's been reserved for us,' she said, stopping

75

at a dark wooden door and turning the handle. Daniel stepped back a pace, admiring her slim figure. Lynsey Ross was a well-groomed lady, her navy suit nipped in at the waist, a silk scarf of pinks and blues reflecting her rosy cheeks. She was not a beauty by any means, not like his Molly, Daniel thought, but with a low, calm voice that might be her most attractive feature.

'After you,' he said and then he and Gerry followed her in. She was older than Daniel, early forties, perhaps, and wore two rings on her wedding finger. When Lynsey Ross had been introduced to him, Daniel felt that it was a name with which he ought to be familiar, except that he didn't buy newspapers as a rule and so was dependent on others to fill in the gaps. Molly had told him that Ross was reckoned to be a good investigative journalist but that she currently wrote a satirical column for the *Gazette*. Netta had seen her on TV, she'd said, during one of the reports into some political scandal. *Afore your time, son*, Netta had said, wagging her head at him, meaning before Daniel had arrived in Glasgow on a cold wet November day that was to mark a turning point in his life.

'Right, let's get started. You don't mind if I record this?' Ross asked, turning to Gerry.

'So long as we can see the transcript afterwards,' he told her.

'Fine,' she said, settling herself on the edge of a chair and fiddling with the small recorder on the table.

'Can we test for sound first, please? What is your name?' she asked, looking at Daniel. 'Tell me what you had for breakfast.'

*

An hour and a half later Daniel and Gerry were laughing as Lynsey Ross regaled them with stories from her time as a young reporter. The interview had been far easier than he had expected, the woman a consummate professional, rapidly putting him at his ease.

The door to the room opened and a young man and woman entered, the latter carrying photographic equipment, the man a heavy suitcase.

'Ah, we'll leave you with Josie and Max,' Ross said, rising from her seat. 'Gerry and I will be in the bar. See you later, Daniel.'

Daniel turned to watch them go and then felt his sleeve being tugged. The young man stood before him smiling. 'Darling, you are just the most gorgeous man I've seen in months. This is going to be such fun.' He clapped his hands and gave a small squeal. 'Just wait till you see what I've got for you.'

Daniel frowned. What did he mean?

Seeing his face, Max gave a whoop of laughter. 'I'm your dresser, darling. Josie here is your photographer.' He came closer to Daniel and cupped his mouth with his hand. 'She's a dragon, you know. Best just do all she tells you.'

What followed was one of the strangest evenings of Daniel Kohi's life. He had never been one for dressing up much, finances always tight back in Zimbabwe, and since his arrival in Scotland he had been careful to spend only what was needed on essentials. Max, who was so exaggeratedly camp and light-hearted that he quickly endeared himself to the police officer, pulled out several suits and accessories from the bulging suitcase, making Daniel change several times till Josie was satisfied that they had caught *the look* that she wanted. So, the handsome Zimbabwean was photographed variously in a red velvet suit, white shirt with the buttons half undone and sparkling white trainers then jeans, a yellow long-sleeved T-shirt and patent leather lace-ups until finally he was instructed to put on his uniform.

At last Daniel felt more comfortable, though he'd been surprised at how that red suit had changed his appearance, Max teasing his hair into different shapes and the photographer capturing an expression on his face that was both thoughtful and intense.

Then it was over, the young woman nodding after scrutinising all the digital images she had captured.

'I'll send you the ones we think are best,' Josie told him. 'You might want a copy or two.' She smiled up at him suddenly. 'You've been a great subject. It'll be a fantastic piece with Lynsey Ross writing it. Well done.'

Max pulled the suitcase full of clothes behind him as they left the room where the photo shoot had taken place. 'Now, darlings. Time for a little refreshment before beddy-byes, yes?'

Daniel smiled. Max and Josie were both so young and, he had to admit, so talented at what they did. Max's constant chatter had ceased as soon as Josie had begun taking photographs, but he was in full flow again as they headed for the bar.

'I can't stay, sorry,' Daniel said as they reached the table where Ross was sitting beside the press officer. 'Have to get home and have some sleep before my early start tomorrow.'

'Oh, darling, what a shame. Not even one teensy-weensy drink?' Max said, putting on a huge pout of disappointment.

Daniel shook his head. 'Thanks for all of this. It was ... different,' he said at last. 'A once in a lifetime experience.'

Daniel tossed and turned, sleep eluding him, the flashes from the camera still making spots in front of his eyes. On arriving back at the flat, his mother was in bed, but Netta had waited up for him, not content till she'd given Daniel a mug of hot chocolate and a slice of home-made fruit cake, eager to hear as much about the evening as he was willing to tell her.

Now, however, in the darkness of the room, Daniel began to wonder if he had been right to accept that invitation. Yes, it had been a lot of fun and Lynsey Ross had been very good at making him open up to tell his story. But ... he bit his lip there, lying on the sofa bed, watching the shadow patterns on the ceiling as cars sped past outside ... what if it all went wrong and there was an unpleasant backlash? And, if he was asked to do anything else, would putting himself into the spotlight have any negative repercussions?

CHAPTER FIFTEEN

Daniel drew up to the kerb and parked, with a sigh. He had promised to be home in time for dinner after his training session out in Jackton and was eager to share his day with Molly. But she was involved in a new case and Netta had chided him for spending so much time with his girlfriend instead of seeing his flatmate and mother. *We might be two old biddies but she's your family*, Netta had reminded Daniel tartly when he had left that morning after folding up the bed settee in their lounge.

'Daniel!' Janette Kohi's face lit up as he walked into the kitchen where she and Netta were sitting at the table.

He went across and bent to kiss his mother's cheek, the fresh scent of something familiar and sweet lingering in her hair. A sudden memory came back to him, sitting on the stoep in the sunshine watching as she braided the hair of a little girl, their neighbour's daughter. These folk had left the township one night without any explanation, their home still half-full of furniture. Daniel had asked questions about Deborah, his young neighbour, of course he had, but Janette had fobbed him off without a satisfactory answer. Later, rumours circulated about Deborah's father, varying from fear of the authorities to outright calumnies against the man's character. He'd shot a man, one said, stolen food from the warehouse where he worked, robbed a bank, even; nasty pieces of gossip that were surely lies, Janette Kohi had insisted.

Still, the image remained of a sweet little girl who would let Janette braid her hair then sit and listen as she told her stories, a twelve-year-old Daniel sitting in the shade, pretending not to listen.

'Tea'll be ready soon,' Netta told them, breaking into Daniel's reverie. 'Toad-in-the hole tonight. And lemon pudding for afters.' She threw a grin at Daniel. 'Told yer ma it's not real toads, but sausages in batter. You want baked beans with it, Daniel?'

'Aye, lovely, thanks,' he said and turned back to his mother. 'How's your day been today?'

Janette reached across and clasped his hand. 'Netta took me into town,' she told him. 'We visited that marvellous place we'd been to before. So many expensive things in the shops, but very beautiful. Some were like Aladdin's cave from the fairy story.'

'Princes Square,' Netta said. 'Wait till you see it at Christmas time, Janette. My but it's bonny then with all the lights and a huge tree the height of the whole place!'

'Oh, my!' Janette exclaimed. 'It sounds wonderful.'

'What else did you do?' Daniel enquired.

'We had lunch in a very unusual place,' Janette told him.

'The chairs were tall at the back and there were strange carvings and so many choices of tea you would not believe it!'

'The Willow Tearooms?' Daniel guessed.

'Yes! That was the place. Netta showed me the menu that had some of the history of the artists who designed it all. Charles ... oh, I forget his name ... a famous man from Scotland.'

'Charles Rennie Mackintosh,' Daniel supplied. 'He was a famous architect and designer. Molly's taken me to some of the buildings he designed. Would you like to visit them? We could start with the House for an Art Lover, that's close by where Molly works.'

'That would be very nice, thank you,' Janette replied, though her smile was a little forced, Daniel thought. Was it the mention of Molly? He hoped not. So far, his mother had made little effort to engage his girlfriend in any meaningful conversation and he wondered if that indicated her disapproval of their relationship.

'That lassie's got a real head on her shoulders,' Netta remarked, handing Daniel a fistful of cutlery to lay the table. 'See she's involved in another murder case now.'

'Is that a good thing for a woman to be doing?' Daniel's mother asked.

'She's excellent at her job,' Daniel insisted. 'Being made a detective inspector shows how far she's come and how respected she is within the force.'

This was followed by a silence, Janette opting to turn her face away and look out of the window.

'Right, that's the tea ready,' Netta said as a ping came from the oven timer.

Soon they were tucking into Netta's delicious dinner, Daniel regaling them with snippets from his day at Jackton and the officers who were training him on fast track. If Janette Kohi noticed how many of these senior officers were women, she did not comment. However, the slight awkwardness of the previous conversation was lost as they enjoyed their food.

There was so much to learn living here in Glasgow, Janette thought, as she prepared for bed. Referring to the evening meal as tea instead of dinner, her son now saying 'aye' when he once replied 'yes'. The parlance was strange at times, but Janette supposed some of it came from Netta's own upbringing, the woman admitting to having had little formal education and not much time for reading books. And had that been a little dig at her for casting aspersions on Molly's chosen career? Making sure she knew that so many women were in senior positions within the police here? Back in Zimbabwe such things were rare although Janette approved of women making careers for themselves in suitable jobs like teaching or in medicine. Chipo had trained as a nurse before having little Johannes, a job she might have taken up again in time, but that was not to be.

Janette gave a sigh as she settled onto her knees to begin her nightly prayers, supplications for all her loved ones as well as good health and safety for Molly, though she did not truly know what the tall blonde woman might wish for herself, other than a lasting relationship with her own dear Daniel, something for which she simply could not begin to pray.

*

It was imperative that she took each of them in turn, beginning with Standish, the director, and Molly had arranged to visit the man in his home in the West End of the city. It was not far from Lilybank Gardens and the night was clear and dry, so she decided to walk there and back, knowing the exercise would do her good. Having time to go to the gym was impossible while the case was in its early stages.

There was a buzz of noise from Ashton Lane, the lights from the cul-de-sac flickering, swayed by a gust of wind. Molly looked up to the night sky to see scudding clouds. A couple passed her by, youngsters, probably students on their way back from the library, perhaps, their faces glowing under the lamplight. Molly smiled, remembering. Glasgow University had been her alma mater, psychology her subject of choice. Janette Kohi had raised surprised eyebrows when Molly had told her this. *Helps to understand a bit about human behaviour when you're in a job like ours*, she'd told the older woman.

Standish lived in one of the elegant, curved terraces that circled private gardens not far off Byres Road. The upper windows were of coloured stained glass, a pattern that might have been Arts and Crafts period. That was something Bill Lorimer would know, she thought, climbing the steps to the frosted glass front door and looking for a bell. There was an old-fashioned pull which when tugged responded with the chime of bells.

It was not long before a shadow beyond the glass transformed into the figure of a man and then the door was swung open, the theatre director taking a step back and making a sweeping gesture with one arm to invite Molly in.

'An inspector calls! Do enter my humble domain,' he said grandly, closing the night out and leading Molly along a reception hall that ended in two staircases, one to a lower apartment, the other a few carpeted steps upwards.

Humble it was not, thought Molly, noting the tall blue and white porcelain jar in a corner containing large stems of pampas grass, and several gilt-framed paintings that looked like original oils. Again, Lorimer might have an idea of their provenance, his career change from studying art history to joining the police as a young man had not diminished his interest in art. Standish led her into a lounge overlooking the terrace and adjoining gardens, though it was too dark now to see them very well. This was the sort of room her late mother would have loved, Molly thought, glancing at the white leather settees and matching footstool, the fireplace tiled with a design of red poppies, its carved mantel possibly original to the house. There was a blue pottery bowl of pot-pourri on the hearth, its dusty scent of old roses conjuring up images of a walled garden somewhere she had been with Daniel the previous summer.

'Do take a seat,' Standish murmured. 'May I offer you tea? Coffee?'

'Coffee, thank you,' Molly replied and watched as the director left the room and headed towards a door leading to what she guessed was the kitchen.

This place would have cost the man a great deal of money if he had bought it in recent years but perhaps it was a family home, inherited from wealthy parents? Weren't theatre people always hard up? Unless he had become a celebrated figure in his career, Standish surely could not command very much of an income. Weren't the arts in Scotland being perennially squeezed? Theatres losing revenue and literary festivals in danger of folding? The investigating team had given no indications that Standish had ever been more than a jobbing actor before moving into directing, his CV largely encompassing Scottish productions. She would love to know more about his background, but Molly Newton was here to talk about the relationship between the director and his deceased leading man.

'Here we are, best arabica.' Standish reappeared, handing Molly a cup of coffee, handle turned towards her. It was presented with a flourish, a bow and a sardonic grin as if the man was playing a part of some sort and Molly suspected that he was relishing his moment with a detective in a murder investigation.

As if reading her thoughts, he sat beside her and raised his own mug. 'A toast to our dear departed, bless him. Oh my, this is exciting, isn't it!' he exclaimed gleefully.

'I'm afraid this is rather routine, Mr Standish, I just need answers to a few more questions,' Molly told him sternly, clicking record on her phone. 'How long have you known Guy Richmond?'

'Oh, ever since he graduated, I suppose. I attend the students' performances at the Conservatoire, looking for promising actors, and I do recall seeing him in a performance of *As You Like It*. I thought then that he'd go far, you know. We'll have a couple of their students included in our next production. Always good to test the talent.'

'You sound as if you are more a scout than a director,' Molly said.

'Bit of both, my dear,' Standish replied. 'I tried my hand as an agent for a time, but I'm much better suited to directing. Not many people can say that, to be frank.' He smirked, examining his perfectly manicured fingernails.

'Did Guy have an agent, then?'

Standish gave a short laugh. 'If you could call him that!' he scoffed. 'Old Morgan had a whole load on his books at one time. I told Guy to find someone in London. That was where the money was, not in the provinces up here.'

Something was stirring in Molly's memory. 'Morgan? You mean D.D. Morgan, the chap at St George's Cross?'

Standish raised his eyebrows in surprise. 'You've actually heard of him! Old Desmond Dylan Morgan, my goodness, I didn't realise his fame had spread. Or has he been a naughty boy, up to no good?' He chuckled nastily.

Molly did not reply to these aspersions. Her memory came from an old murder case. The victim's fiancé was an actor and Molly and Davie Giles had visited the agent at his premises in St George's Cross. He'd been a colourful character, but kind, Molly seemed to remember, unlike Standish who was displaying not a jot of sympathy either for the deceased or for Meredith St Claire.

'And did he? Change agents?'

Standish gave an exaggerated sigh. 'No, but I'm sure he would have if . . . ' he ended with a shrug.

She made a mental note to pay a visit to the elderly Morgan who might help cast some more light on Richmond's life.

'Was he really good enough to play the West End?' Molly asked.

'Yes, I would say so,' Standish replied, a serious cast to his countenance now. 'I think he had a great future. And our next production may have sealed it for him.'

'Oh? How's that?'

There was another sigh, genuine this time, before the director spoke again. 'We have one of the top impresarios coming to watch our version of *Sweeney Todd*, shadow it from casting to production. We're playing it as a stage show, not a musical. There's TV interest in making a documentary but also a chance for the leading actors to be selected to perform in a London production. It would have been his big breakthrough.'

'And, what happens now?'

'Oh, my dear, the show will go on, as the saying goes. And young Nigel will have his moment in the sun and a chance to see his own name in lights.'

CHAPTER SIXTEEN

Money was no object, Meredith told herself. She'd give Guy the biggest and best send-off that everyone would remember. If only ... She gritted her teeth, casting her mind back to the cold corridor in the mortuary and the way that detective had looked at her, sympathy in her eyes as if she had a genuine understanding of what it was to lose the person closest to you in all the world. Perhaps she had? Or maybe her job entailed putting on that sorrowful expression, rather like actors she'd seen so often, leaning towards their mirrors, greasepaint ready to transform their faces.

She let the pamphlet from the funeral parlour fall onto the table. Not yet, the detective had told her, murmuring something about the Procurator Fiscal being in legal ownership of her fiancé's body. How could that be? How long was she to wait in limbo for closure of any sort? Meredith heaved a sigh. The school had been very understanding, not pressing her into giving them a date for her return, allowing as much compassionate leave as she required.

But she needed to move on, and until Guy was decently buried, that just could not happen.

Meredith looked out of the window at the field across the road. New lambs were frolicking there, close enough to their mothers for safety. There was no mother figure in Meredith St Claire's life, she thought with a pang. Nobody to advise her what to do.

She stood quite still as the idea began to form in her mind. Once, she had rushed away, snarling and angry, from his car. But perhaps Detective Superintendent Lorimer was the one person who might help to push the investigation forward, rather than the tall blonde woman who was currently in charge. After all, a senior detective, who was as good as they said he was, would surely make an arrest far more quickly than a mere DI, and let his goddaughter's teacher get on with the rest of her life?

Lorimer put down the phone, a small frown accentuating the lines between his eyebrows. She'd sounded contrite, apologising for her outburst that day in the school car park, but really, with hindsight, who could blame her? Strange that she wanted his help now that Guy Richmond had been found and Molly Newton was doing a sterling job as SIO.

I have faith in you, she'd told him, her tone so earnest. Flattery was not something that Lorimer succumbed to, however, and he'd endeavoured to reassure Meredith St Claire that DI Newton was a fine officer who was doing everything properly. And yet, there was more. Her sudden silence then the sound of quiet weeping had loosened his resolve.

Guy Richmond had been murdered and here was a woman

whose entire future was now changed for ever, Lorimer reminded himself.

He gave a sigh, wondering if his promise to help, to at least come and talk to her, would cross a professional line. Molly would understand, he'd told himself, even as he'd cast an eye on the diary, finding a free slot that very afternoon due to a cancelled meeting.

The house that Richmond and St Claire had bought together was situated on the outskirts of Milngavie, and Lorimer saw it from a distance as he drove slowly behind a farm tractor. It sat snugly in the fold of a hill and would enjoy a fine view across to the Campsie Hills. Not much of a consolation when there was nobody with whom to share it, he reminded himself.

He closed the car door and took a quick look over the landscape. Fields dotted with white sheep, a fresh smell in the air and the first haze of green on the hedgerows that heralded the beginning of spring. It should be a time of new beginnings for this bereaved woman, he thought as he turned to knock on the front door.

His first thought was how different she appeared from their first meeting. Then, she had been a colourful figure but today, with her hair tied back in an untidy ponytail, a drab grey tunic over black skinny jeans, she looked washed out.

'Come in,' she said dully, stepping back and waiting till Lorimer entered before closing the door behind them. 'Thanks for coming.' There was no token smile, no semblance of effort to welcome him to their home. *Her* home now, he reminded himself.

'We can sit in the front room if you like,' she continued, rubbing her arms. 'It's warmer in there.'

Lorimer followed her through a door to the left and into a pleasant room that overlooked the meadows and the hills beyond. Here was more evidence of the woman's natural preference for colour. Not for her the fashionable greys and beiges he saw so often in people's homes, but a turquoise settee with green and purple embroidered scatter cushions and two comfortable-looking armchairs with pink fleecy throws. The flooring was uncarpeted and looked as if someone had restored the original wood, the sun through the window burnishing it to a shade of copper.

'I was just going to have some tea ...?'

'Tea would be fine, thanks,' Lorimer said. 'Milk and no sugar.'

Meredith disappeared from the room, and he heard the faint sounds of a kettle being filled then cupboard doors opening and closing.

He looked around the lounge, processing his thoughts about the grieving woman and the man who had lived here for such a short time. There were pictures on every wall, black and white images of Guy Richmond. He stood up and walked around, realising that these must have been taken as press shots during performances, the man dressed for several different roles as well as for a television advert that Lorimer remembered. Richmond had been smiling out from their own television set, repeatedly offering a better way to clean a kitchen. The photo showed the actor grinning at the camera, product in hand, his perfect white teeth gleaming as brightly as the Belfast sink in the background. Americans always had beautiful teeth, Lorimer thought, looking at the photograph and running his tongue over teeth that required regular scaling and polishing due to all the black coffee he drank.

'Here you are.' Meredith was back in the room and putting two mugs of tea onto a small side table next to the chaise. She perched on its edge and handed Lorimer his tea.

'Thanks,' Lorimer replied, taking the mug from her. 'He took a great shot, your Guy.' He nodded towards the walls.

Meredith sniffed hard and he saw her swallow. 'Yes, he was very photogenic,' she said. 'And I have all of these to remind me of him. Lucky old me.'

Her sour tone was not lost on Lorimer. There was a hint of the bitterness she'd displayed on their first meeting, her fury at the police for not immediately hunting a missing person.

Lorimer looked at her. 'It is a dreadful thing to lose someone you love,' he said softly. 'But you are young and talented. In time you'll find the joys you think are lost for ever.'

Meredith looked down at her mug of tea. 'Right now, I feel as if life stopped the minute your detective came and told me ... ' She broke off, tears in her eyes.

'What do you think I can do to help?' Lorimer asked gently.

'Find out who killed Guy!' she exclaimed, leaning towards him. 'Isn't that what this is all about? Someone must have hated him enough to do that.'

'That is a good place to begin,' Lorimer agreed. 'Now, tell me, who do you think would have had a reason to kill Guy Richmond?'

Meredith shot him a startled look. 'Well, nobody,' she began. 'Guy was well liked by everyone. Most popular student at drama school, always laughing and joking around. You know?' She shook her head, seemingly unaware that she had contradicted her earlier statement. 'I simply cannot think of anyone who knew him bearing the sort of malice required to ... ' she stopped and swallowed, 'to kill.'

'Was there anyone who bore him a grudge? A good-looking fellow like that, perhaps he attracted some form of envy?'

Meredith gave a wan smile. 'Oh, loads of people envied Guy,' she agreed. 'Rich, successful, though I doubt if choosing me for a life partner would have incurred anyone's jealousy.'

Lorimer gave her a quizzical look.

'Well, I'm not a leading lady, am I? Just a teacher, nothing very special, really.' She looked a little downcast and Lorimer began to wonder why, as he looked around the walls of this room, there were no photographs of Meredith St Claire, or even one or two of the couple together. Had Guy Richmond's ego prevented anything other than total adoration from his fiancée? Or had she been so utterly obsessed by him as to decorate every wall with his image? Something didn't feel right, though at that moment Lorimer could not have said what it was.

'He obviously thought you were special,' he said at last, resisting the bait to flatter her. 'I've not seen many engagement rings that make a statement like that one.' He smiled, pointing at her left hand.

'Oh, that,' she said, twisting the ring and letting it slide around her finger to hide the stone. 'Well, maybe ... I mean we were so in love with one another ... ' She broke off and turned her face away. 'We had such plans ... ' she whispered.

'Tell me, if it isn't too hard for you,' Lorimer asked gently.

He watched her sighing then she turned back and looked him in the eyes.

'He lost his parents, you know,' she began. 'It was his dearest wish that we would honeymoon in The Hamptons, take time out to see the places where he grew up.' She gave a sad smile. 'He wanted to create some sort of a memorial garden back in his hometown, you know. A small place near Boston.' She shrugged. 'I was happy to go along with all of that, if it made Guy happy. Guess I'll never go there now.'

Lorimer did not pursue that line of thought, yet surely carrying out her dead fiancé's wish would have been something this poor woman would have wanted to do, in his memory?

'Guy had inherited money,' Lorimer began. 'So can we assume he had no debts at the time of his death?'

'What are you suggesting?'

'It is not completely unheard of for unscrupulous persons to threaten their debtors,' he told her. 'And if Guy had unpaid debts, perhaps it might be wise to investigate them.'

'Oh.' Meredith looked lost for a moment. 'I never thought of that. I mean ... I wouldn't know ... ' She began to fidget with the tassels on the scatter cushion, clearly ill at ease.

'What are you not telling me, Meredith?' Lorimer asked.

A faint pink began to blossom on the woman's neck then she began to cry.

'I couldn't tell that other detective, I just couldn't,' she gasped between sobs.

'Tell her ... ?'

She turned and stared unflinchingly into his blue gaze. 'Guy had a regular dealer,' she told him. 'Coke, mostly. I think ...' She turned away again, shaking her head. 'I'm not certain but it might have been someone in the theatre.'

'But, if he was so well off after his inheritance, surely they would know he'd pay up?'

There was a moment's silence before she looked at him again.

'I don't know, honestly. I never had anything to do with that. Drugs, I mean. Well, not since my student days, and after I got my job.'

'And are you sure you can't name this person?'

This time Meredith St Claire's eyes did not meet his gaze as she merely shook her head.

'You can't name them? Or you don't know their identity?'

'I really don't know, and I'd rather not guess,' she whispered, picking up her mug of tea and clasping it in both hands.

'What do you want me to do, Meredith?' Lorimer asked once more.

'Find who killed Guy. Lock him up and throw away the key!' she exclaimed, tears now streaming down her cheeks.

Meredith wrapped the picture in several layers of white tissue paper before putting it into a bubble-wrap envelope. It was the image he'd loved most and the one she would use for the order of service when the investigation was at an end, and she could bury him in peace.

Now that Detective Superintendent Lorimer had agreed to investigate, surely things would lead to a satisfactory conclusion?

CHAPTER SEVENTEEN

Her meeting with Lorimer had left Molly feeling wounded. That he'd gone to visit the St Claire woman without even telling her had rankled. He'd explained it all, of course, how she had called him and asked for his personal assistance. And, to be fair, he'd written a full report of their meeting and handed a copy to her. But it felt as though he were pulling rank and that was just not like Lorimer. Not like him at all. Was he allowing himself to become personally involved just because the woman had accosted him in that school car park? She gritted her teeth as she entered the room to face her team, forcing herself to put it behind her and carry on as normal.

'Right, let's see where we're at.'

Molly turned to the officers assembled in the muster room. 'Scene of crime report first, please,' she said crisply, nodding towards DS Christopher Pearson, her scene of crime manager, a tall slim man with reddish-blond hair and the fine complexion that was typical of some Scots.

'There were footprints, but the fisherman who found the body had trampled over them too badly for any decent prints to be obtained,' Pearson began. He made a face. 'Poor fellow wasn't to know that was probably the deposition site.'

'No other signs of activity along that shoreline?'

'No, ma'am, none at all. There had been heavy rain in the preceding days so it would have been easy to see if anybody had left prints in the mud. However,' Pearson cleared his throat, 'SOCOs did find tracks on the same path that the fisherman and our own officers used. They've been sent for analysis but so far, they've not got back to us with an identification for the tyres.'

'What about the body itself? Any joy there?'

'Dr Fergusson said that his clothes were far too water-logged to have retained any significant traces,' Pearson said, a note of regret in his voice. 'But she estimates that the body must have lain in the water for at least a week.'

'Making the date of his death approximately Sunday the tenth of March,' Molly said, tapping the whiteboard behind her. 'He was last seen earlier that day by his fiancée when she dropped him off in town. Got worried when he never returned home. Then his body lies undiscovered till Monday the eighteenth when our angler caught the body on his line.' She stopped for a moment, considering. 'We need to know if anyone else had a sighting of him after they left their cottage in Milngavie.'

'We've got traffic onto that, ma'am, to see if there is anything on CCTV.'

'Meredith St Claire, his fiancée, reported Richmond missing on Monday the eleventh. Evidently it was out of character for Richmond to go AWOL, so she was well within her rights to start panicking.' Lorimer had seen the woman at Abigail Brightman's school several days before the discovery of the body and had told Molly how frantic she had been. Having spent time with her, Molly could understand that. Meredith was brittle, like thin glass, easily broken, she thought, easy for a nice man like William Lorimer to pity, her earlier rancour thawing a little.

'We know the MO, a slash to the throat, probably done from behind, the victim caught unawares. Let's go through that scenario,' Molly said, turning to look at her officers.

'They grab him from behind, pull back his hair, one swift stroke of that open razor then ... either they let him topple into the water or gave him a shove to make sure he would sink.'

'Could it have been done from a boat?' Alisha asked. 'There was mention of a boat at the loch, wasn't there?'

Molly shook her head. 'Unlikely unless they'd brought one with them and taken it away again. The usual boat belonging to the angling club is away for repair at present. And to be frank, I can't see the perpetrator going to so much trouble. Now, let's get back to the moments before his death, shall we? What do we think? Premeditated?

'Whoever it was came prepared with a cut-throat razor,' DS Davie Giles chipped in. 'That surely indicates a level of foresight?'

'And that suggests that Richmond may have been at ease with his killer. It was someone he knew.'

'But why go all the way out to a wee loch?' another officer asked.

'That is an excellent question, and I was going to come to that. As far as we know Richmond had no interest in angling or even birdwatching. The super tells me it is a good place to see a variety of waterfowl. So, what was Richmond doing there in the first place that Sunday night and who was with him?'

Molly picked up her scarf and wound it around her neck ready to venture out once more. The officers had been given their different actions and now she was going to visit one of the other members of the theatre company. A knock came on her door, and she looked up to see the tall figure of Lorimer smiling at her.

'Got a minute, DI Newton?' he asked, walking into the room.

'Would you mind if I tagged along?' Lorimer asked a few minutes later.

He was sitting on the edge of Molly's desk, repeating some of his thoughts from his afternoon's visit to the cottage Meredith had shared with Guy Richmond.

'I think she'd like me involved a little bit, but over to you, Molly. I don't want to tread on your toes.'

'Not at all, sir,' Molly replied. 'If that's what she wants?'

He heard his DI's voice, somewhat stiff and possibly annoyed but trying hard not to show it.

'You've seen it before, Molly, a grief-stricken person demanding that only the top cop will suffice to solve a case. Now, we both know that's not true, but I would like to spend at least a little time with you when you make the rest of your visits to that theatre group.' He held his hands up submissively. 'You're still SIO in this case, don't worry. It would have to escalate into something far bigger for me to oversee.'

The smile of relief that she gave him was gratifying as he slid off her desk. 'Right then, let me know what you propose to follow up next.'

Lorimer followed his DI into the block of flats that towered above the city. It was clean enough as they stepped into the lift though there were scrawls on the metal doors and walls, mostly the sort of teenage angst that found its outlet with a thick-nibbed felt pen and a dirty mind. Nigel Fairbairn would have to stand here surrounded by that graffiti day in and day out unless he was the athletic type who enjoyed running up and down nine flights of stairs. The lift stopped with a creak and a shudder, and they came out onto a concrete floor and an enclosed passage to the four flats that were situated at this level. Fairbairn lived at number 901 and Lorimer reflected that it was the sort of numbering that hotels normally used. The pale blue door was scuffed at the base as if muddy boots had given it a kicking at one time. There was a spyhole beneath Lorimer's eye level, and he wondered if they would be peered at by the occupant before Fairbairn opened the door.

Several sharp knocks did bring the sound of feet approaching and yes, there was a pause before the door swung open, confirming Lorimer's thoughts.

'It's Nigel, isn't it?' Molly asked. 'You remember me? I spoke to you at the theatre.'

Lorimer saw a young man of below average height, slim,

with dark hair that flopped over his forehead, his face reminding him for a moment of a young David Tennant, the Scottish actor who had been Maggie's favourite in the TV series *Doctor Who*.

'This is my boss, Superintendent Lorimer,' Molly said, making the introduction.

'Oh, you'd better come in, then,' Fairbairn said, looking Lorimer up and down with more suspicion than interest.

His voice was almost bereft of any trace of a Glasgow accent and Lorimer wondered if he had been educated at one of Scotland's public schools. Either that or he had ironed out any familiar accent in his quest to achieve stardom. That was an interesting thought, and he'd keep it in reserve for now.

'Better come in, though the place is a tip,' Fairbairn told them. 'My flatmate isn't the tidiest of people.' He sighed, raising his eyes to heaven. 'I suppose this is about poor Guy?' He led them through a dark hallway and into a square room that served as lounge-cum-dining room. A table pushed against one wall was littered with sheets of foolscap and what Lorimer guessed was a script, folded open at a particular scene, a round grey stone laid on its edge as a paperweight.

'Here, take a seat,' Fairbairn said, sweeping up a pile of newspapers from a three-seater settee and dumping them in a corner of the room.

Lorimer wondered about the amount of newsprint. Didn't young folk eschew printed papers for the freedom of the internet, only interested in soundbites rather than reading their way through entire features? Maggie had expressed as much the other night as she despaired of encouraging some of her third-year boys to read. He'd caught a glimpse of copies of *The Times*. There would be theatre reviews in such papers, of course, the sorts of things an actor would like to read.

Fairbairn pulled a chair from the side of the table and placed it in front of them then sat down. It gave him a little advantage in height, Lorimer thought. Was he self-conscious about his own height or was he simply trying to offset the superintendent's six foot four? Neither, perhaps, the chair he'd pulled to face them probably the very one on which he'd been sitting before they'd arrived.

'Now, how can I help you?' Fairbairn began, evidently eager to take charge of the meeting.

Molly shot Lorimer an enquiring glance, but he gave the merest shake of his head, enough to let her know he was still a bystander.

'We'd like to know a little more about Guy Richmond,' Molly began. 'What was he like? How did he relate to other people? Was he popular?'

Fairbairn gave a snort of mock laughter. 'Popular? You could say that. Especially when he came into all that money.'

'Go on.'

'Look, you people know about human nature, right? Of *course* everyone was fawning over him, sympathetic at first, naturally, but that kind of thing can make a difference in relationships.'

'Care to elaborate?'

Fairbairn scratched the back of his head for a moment. 'His folks sponsored a couple of his plays, got him on the right side of old Standish. He knew which side his bread was buttered!' he exclaimed, with a cynical curl of his lip. 'But our Guy was always the golden boy, even at drama school.'

'You were at the Conservatoire too?'

'Same year as Guy and Merry. God, I must stop calling her that,' he sighed with a shake of his head. 'She'll be anything but merry now that he's gone.'

There was a genuine note of regret in his voice now, Lorimer noticed, and he wondered if Fairbairn had ever had a crush on the tall, pink-haired woman.

'You're a friend of Ms St Claire?'

The young man gave Lorimer a curious look then nodded.

'We were at school together.' He shrugged. 'Did things like school plays. Mackay Brown's *Witch* ... you probably never heard of it.'

Lorimer did not reply to that. Yet it rankled to think that being a police officer was, in this fellow's eyes, tantamount to having no interest in the arts.

'Was Guy Richmond popular with all the students?'

'Oh yes, and the tutors. See, he was outwardly a nice chap, friendly, talkative ... When you hear folk saying that everyone liked a person after they're dead, you think that's an exaggeration. But Guy really was different. Charismatic. Girls fell at his feet,' he finished with a hollow laugh.

And perhaps not at yours? There was a thought to store away for later, thought Lorimer.

'How did Ms St Claire feel about that? She was his girl-friend even back then, wasn't she?'

'Oh, Meredith was like a little puppy, following Guy around with her big wide eyes. It could be quite nauseating at times if it hadn't been so sweet.'

'Can you think of any reason why someone would want to harm him?'

Fairbairn pursed his lips, no trace of mirth on his face now. 'No. Absolutely not. He had everything going for him.'

'Did you like him?'

Molly's question hung in the air for a moment as the two detectives looked at Fairbairn.

The man gave a twisted sort of smile then shook his head.

'Not really. Guy could be quite cruel to those he considered beneath him.'

'Care to elaborate?'

They watched as Fairbairn chewed his lower lip, pondering the question.

'There was one time . . . ' He broke off and glanced at each of them in turn. 'I overheard him having a bit of a run-in with one of our tutors. She was primarily our voice coach and had been castigating Guy for his reluctance to do his exercises. Wanted him to iron out his American accent.'

'Go on.'

'It turned nasty,' he continued. 'This lady was in a wheelchair. Had been a good actress in her day, by all accounts, and Guy mocked her. I remember his very words. Called her a washed-up cripple. I was pretty shocked, but to my shame I slunk away and didn't intervene or anything. Guy had that sort of effect on people. You didn't want to get on his wrong side, I suppose.'

'Who was this tutor?' Molly asked.

'Anne Peters. Have you heard of her? Bit before my time, I'm afraid,' he replied.

Molly blinked but Lorimer was relieved to see that she

105

resisted the urge to make eye contact with him. This new bit of information suddenly gave more insight into Richmond's character as well as Brian Peters' discovery of the man's body giving them more food for thought.

'Was he a good actor?' Lorimer broke in suddenly, making Molly turn towards him.

Fairbairn thought for a bit before answering. 'Not as good as he thought he was,' he murmured. 'Like I said, he could have done with ironing out his American accent more, at times. And,' he sat up a little straighter, tilting his chin up, 'his final results were pretty mediocre. Wasn't mentioned in the prize list. He certainly wasn't a contender for the gold medal.'

'Oh? Who got it that year?' Lorimer asked, though he was pretty sure he knew the answer already.

'I did,' Fairbairn said, giving them both a small smile of satisfaction.

'Weren't you a bit bothered then, that Guy was given all the lead parts?' Molly asked. 'Especially Sweeney Todd. I understand from Mr Standish that there's a lot riding on that production?'

Fairbairn gave a shrug, but they could see his gesture of indifference was all pretence.

'My turn would come,' he said at last. 'And, before you come to any silly conclusions, stepping into Guy's role is hardly grounds for murder.'

Lorimer said nothing. If Nigel Fairbairn had worked hard at the Conservatoire and gained that prestigious gold medal, then, yes, he might in time have captured the attention of the big producers. On the other hand, had years of being in the less talented but undoubtedly charismatic Richmond's shadow caused his pain of playing second fiddle to fester into something manic?

'Getting back to what you mentioned earlier,' Molly said. 'Was there anyone in particular who changed towards Guy Richmond after he received his inheritance?'

Fairbairn stroked his chin thoughtfully. 'Mm, not really sure. Ahmed was a bit funny about things, but he was never a great fan of Guy's in any case.'

'Ahmed?'

'Yeah, the props person at St James's Theatre. We'd both been cast in productions there recently. He didn't like Guy messing about with girls. He's quite a religious type, comes from a strict Muslim family.'

'When you say messing about, what exactly are you implying?' Molly asked sharply.

Fairbairn shifted in his seat, looking uncomfortable for the first time. 'Guy wasn't exactly a paragon of virtue when it came to women,' he said. 'Merry put up with it. Or pretended not to see it, but he had a few flings with other girls. At the Conservatoire ... and later on, I think.' He crossed his arms now, an automatic sign of defence, Lorimer noticed. What was he hiding?

'If that's all, officers, I really have to get back to my script,' he said, a wave of his hand indicating the papers on the table behind him. 'We're having a new read-through at the theatre this evening.'

'What do you make of him?' Molly asked after the lift doors closed.

'I don't think he fits the bill for your killer,' Lorimer said. 'For a start he's a bit too small to have grabbed Richmond from behind and slashed his throat. Unless, perhaps, Richmond had fallen to his knees ... ?'

Molly nodded. 'I suppose so. He doesn't seem big and strong enough to have overcome the American, though, does he? But height's never been a barrier for a successful actor, has it? I mean, look at Tom Cruise! And he does all his own stunts.'

'He was quite insistent that playing second fiddle to Richmond was hardly motive for murder. That's obviously what he wants us to believe, though I do wonder if he resented Richmond a lot more than he was letting on.'

'Yes. I don't think there was any love lost between them.'

'And that incident when he insulted Anne Peters.' Lorimer gave a frown. 'Could it be a coincidence that her husband found Guy's body? Did he know of the actor's cruel remark?'

'A wife would confide something like that to her husband, don't you think?'

Lorimer nodded. 'And had that rankled all these years? Enough to drive a man to commit murder? Nursing his wrath to keep it warm,' he murmured, paraphrasing one of Maggie's favourite poems.

'Mm, not so sure about that. I saw Brian Peters at the locus. I believe he was genuinely shocked. But, getting back to Fairbairn, he was quick to let us know who'd won the gold medal, wasn't he?'

'Yes,' Lorimer replied as the lift shuddered to a halt and they made their way out into the cold air.

They walked in silence back to their cars then Lorimer

stopped and laid a friendly hand on Molly's as he aimed his car keys towards the Lexus. 'Where now?'

'I think we ought to pay a visit to Ahmed before tonight's rehearsal – sorry, read-through,' she said. 'I was curious about what Fairbairn said about the fellow's distaste of Richmond's playing around. Not a normal reaction amongst boys, surely?'

'Agreed,' Lorimer said. 'There is definitely more to this than meets the eye.'

CHAPTER EIGHTEEN

*T*he sense of euphoria had melted away now to be replaced by something quite different. Certainly not guilt since Guy Richmond had deserved that quick dispatch. One swift slash across his throat followed by a guttural sound then a splash as his body hit those dark waters. Nor was it a feeling of relief, although the aftermath of careful planning might have merited such a moment. And the only regret was that he had not been made to suffer for longer.

Was it fear? Perhaps. Fear of discovery, fear of the consequences that might follow should their identity be known.

But that was not going to happen. There were so many of them who had held grudges against the American actor that the police would find themselves running around in circles. Any one of them might suffice as a suspect and be no loss to the world of the theatre once behind bars. So, what was this hesitation to move forward? Caution, perhaps, born of many years of honing one's skills and seeing their effects on others.

The feeling of regret was, of course, the sense of a job that was only half done.

CHAPTER NINETEEN

Ahmed lived at home with his family in a grand red sandstone house in St Andrews Drive, not far from the site of Craigholme, once an exclusive private school for girls that had closed several years before. Now many of the locals sent their children to nearby Hutchesons' Grammar, a modern co-ed private school founded centuries ago by two brothers who had been intent on giving orphan boys a good education. Maggie had mentioned all this to Lorimer when a new deputy head working previously at Hutchesons' had been appointed at her school.

'Nice place,' Molly murmured. 'Must have a gardener to keep these hedges so neat.' She nodded towards a line of golden privet surrounded by a low wall of the same red sandstone as the large Victorian villa that occupied a corner site of the street. It was a very desirable area indeed, and yet Lorimer had memories of another house, not so very far away, that had belonged to one of Glasgow's foremost drug barons, his current home for the foreseeable future at the hospitality of His Majesty's Prison Service. Nice houses were not always inhabited by nice people, and it remained to be seen if the Patels' home was tainted with any criminality.

'Ahmed is . . . how old did you say?' Lorimer asked as they opened the gate to the property.

'Young-ish, maybe early twenties?' Molly replied.

Lorimer nodded to himself as they walked up the path towards the main entrance. Few youngsters could afford to have a place of their own in these straitened times and being the properties manager in the theatre company was unlikely to command a high salary. It made sense for the young man to live at home. Had that excluded him from the social life of the stage folk? And did he resent that in any way?

'Ahmed,' Molly began as the door opened to reveal a slight figure wearing black jeans and a cream polo neck sweater standing in the hallway. 'This is Detective Superintendent Lorimer. May we come in?'

Ahmed Patel looked up at Lorimer, a tiny frown of disquiet between his brows.

'Of course, do come in.' He looked at Molly and held the door open until they had entered.

Inside, Lorimer saw a large reception hall where a half-moon table was placed against a pillar separating two doors, a huge vase of lilies on its well-polished surface. Lorimer wrinkled his nose as their pungent scent wafted past, Ahmed leading them along a corridor to a room that looked out over the rear gardens. He was pleased to see the sitting room furnished in keeping with the age of the house, some Arts and Crafts pieces like a sideboard with lozenges of coloured glass set into rosewood panels and a pewter mirror, its scrollwork so reminiscent of the contemporaries of Rennie Mackintosh. Thick carpeting masked any sound as they were ushered to take a seat on one of the high-backed primrose-yellow settees that looked out towards French windows and the gardens beyond. There were several trees, still bare branched at this time of year, and Lorimer guessed there would be a froth of pink cherry blossom in the weeks to come, a swathe of yellow daffodils planted on the lawn beside them.

'How do you do, sir.' Ahmed put out his hand to Lorimer. 'I did not expect a senior officer to accompany you,' he said, glancing at Molly. 'But please, be seated. And may I offer some refreshments?'

'Not for me, thank you, Mr Patel,' Lorimer answered.

'Thanks, I'm fine,' Molly murmured. 'Sorry to trouble you, but we really did need to talk to all of Mr Richmond's closer associates as soon as we could.'

'Please, no apologies,' Patel said, seating himself on a large pouffe so that he was looking up at them both. 'How can I help?'

He sat quite still, Lorimer noticed, no fidgeting, his hands clasped neatly in front of him, those large dark eyes turned towards the police officers.

'How well did you know Mr Richmond?' Molly began.

'Not well at all,' Patel told them. 'I have only been with St James's Theatre since last September. And I was mostly busy with props, not with the actors themselves.'

'How did you get the job?' Lorimer asked.

For a moment Patel seemed lost for words. He opened his mouth as if to speak then closed it firmly, his jaw tightening.

113

'Usual way. Answered an advert.' He shrugged, glancing away as if he could not meet their eyes. Lorimer noted the deflection, putting it away for now. There was something he didn't want them to know. Interesting.

'Did you like him? Guy Richmond?' Molly asked.

Again, Patel avoided their eyes. 'Not my type of person.' He shrugged again. 'Bit full of himself, I'd say. We had nothing in common except for the plays.'

'Did you get along?'

'Well enough, I suppose. I didn't socialise with any of them, really.'

'Oh?'

'They'd all go to the pub after rehearsals, but I don't drink,' Patel explained.

There was nothing to stop him having a soft drink to keep them company, Lorimer reasoned, but left that thought unspoken. If he was still living at home, perhaps money was tight, or maybe his upbringing had been fairly strict, prohibiting the sorts of things most young men his age enjoyed.

'I'd like to ask you about the props,' Molly went on. 'Have you sourced all that you need for the next play?'

Patel nodded, a small sigh of relief escaping his mouth as Molly moved onto less personal ground.

'Yes,' he replied, sitting up a little straighter. 'Everything that is on Mr Standish's list.' A smile tugged the corners of his mouth. 'An awful lot of fake blood for their next show. It is all there.'

'Where are these properties kept?'

'Oh, in the theatre, always in the theatre unless we are touring, then I have other people to help box or crate them.

If we're moving around, they're kept in the van, under lock and key after each performance.'

'And they are kept somewhere backstage?'

Patel smiled properly now. 'Actually, I store everything *under* the stage. There's a big basement area for furniture, flats, etc, and cupboards for the smaller stuff.'

'You're doing *Sweeney Todd: The Demon Barber of Fleet Street*, right?' Lorimer asked.

'Yes.'

'Did you source a genuine cut-throat razor or a fake one?'

There was a moment's silence as Ahmed Patel looked from one officer to the other, his eyes widening. 'Well, a real one as it happens, why? It has a safety guard that the audience can't see ...'

Lorimer exchanged a meaningful glance with his detective inspector.

'Ahmed,' Molly leaned forward a little, 'would you take us to the theatre? To show us where all the props are kept?'

St James's Theatre sat in a block between tenement buildings, just a stone's throw from the bustling streets of Paisley, next to St James's Church, its steeple almost dwarfed by the grey stone flats and the lofty theatre. Ahmed pushed open a gate to the side of the theatre and stood aside politely to let the two detectives in.

'Don't we go in this way?' Molly asked, pointing to the sign for the stage door.

Ahmed shook his head. 'Round the back. Come with me.'

They followed him along a side path bordered by an untidy strip of grass, where a few half-hearted daffodils struggled for light. Lorimer looked up at the mullioned windows of the old church next door, long since closed to worshippers, noticing some stained glass though it was too dark now to make out any sort of design. At least some features of the original church appeared to have been preserved, he thought with approval. So many buildings like these had been deserted due to falling numbers of worshippers, some of them being given residential status or even becoming bingo halls or nightclubs. Nothing seemed to be happening with this building, however, and he wondered if perhaps the theatre had plans to take it over.

Ahmed unlocked the back door and stepped inside, his hands reaching up for the light switch. Soon they were inside, following him along a corridor and around a corner till they came to two doors that faced each other, one marked **KITCHEN**.

'Basement's down here,' Patel explained, pushing open the other door. 'Just watch your step, it's very steep.'

Lorimer nodded to Molly to follow the props manager, and watched as she slid one hand along the wall to steady herself. Patel was already down in the area below the stage, a dimly lit place that had a dry, dusty smell. It was a huge space, Lorimer realised when he reached the foot of the narrow staircase, encompassing far more than the area beneath the stage. Stage flats were propped up against two walls, rails and rails of costumes swathed under heavy-duty plastic covers taking up about a third of the room. Pale shapes of furniture could be seen under their dust covers, some stacked almost to the ceiling. Patel had headed across to a set of cupboards and so they followed him, Lorimer glancing around, taking in the enormity of storage that this basement afforded.

'Do you keep it locked?' Lorimer heard Molly ask.

'No need. It's only me and the wardrobe folk and tech lads who come down here as a rule,' Patel explained. 'Nothing much of value. All the jewellery is paste.' He smiled at them for the first time, a man more confident in his own familiar realm, Lorimer guessed. 'Close up you can see that, but from an audience's viewpoint it all looks pretty real.'

'But you have a genuine cut-throat razor for the next production, right?'

Patel's smile disappeared. 'Guy wanted me to have it,' he said. 'It was among his parents' effects after their deaths, said it had belonged to his grandfather. Anyway, I thought it would be okay with the safety guard on. Mr Standish okayed it as well.' He looked from one of the detectives to the other, a small frown troubling his expression. 'Why? What's wrong?'

'Can we see it, Mr Patel?' Molly asked, slipping on a pair of blue nitrile gloves.

'Sure. It's in a box in this drawer.' He turned to tug a pair of handles in an old-fashioned chest of drawers. Lorimer moved to look over the young man's shoulder and was impressed by the neat arrangement of carefully labelled boxes. This chap evidently took some pride in storing his various properties, be they large or small.

'Here it is,' he said, pulling out an old leather box and handing it to the detective inspector.

Molly opened the box. Inside was a layer of white satin, the shape quite discernible of where a razor should have been. Lorimer looked at Patel whose mouth was now hanging open, his eyes staring at the empty box in horror.

'It's gone!' he whispered, lifting his head to stare into Lorimer's eyes.

'When did you see it last?'

Patel shook his head. 'Sorry, I don't remember. Guy showed it to everyone when he brought it here one night. Maybe a couple of weeks ago? He thought it was a good laugh, but Standish told me to put it away till the proper rehearsals began.'

'And, did you?'

'Of course!' Patel's voice rose into a squeak, his stress evident. 'I put it in there', he turned and pointed to the space in the open drawer, 'and there was no reason to take it out again.'

Lorimer and Molly exchanged a grim look.

'Oh!' Patel gasped suddenly. 'Was that . . . was that how he was killed? Oh, my God!' he cried, wrapping his arms around his thin body, shuddering uncontrollably.

Molly had her phone out now and was calling up for a team of SOCOs.

'This area will need to be dusted for fingerprints,' Lorimer explained to the shivering boy. 'We'll have to take yours for elimination purposes, do you understand?'

Patel nodded, his narrow face bleak, the full realisation of what he had found dawning on him.

CHAPTER TWENTY

'They say he'd been murdered,' the girl whispered behind her hand as the class trooped into the gym hall at St Genesius High School.

'Who says?' Abby asked, drawing her brows down. 'Is that why she's off?'

'Jenny heard Miss Taylor talking about it to Mr Williamson. You know what a loud voice she's got. All that yelling across the hockey pitch. Bet you that's why we've been called for a special assembly.'

Abby's mouth tightened. Her mother had said nothing about this but that was not unusual, Rosie tending to keep her working life as distant as possible from her family. She knew enough about the Department of Forensic Medicine and the sort of things that her mother did, like performing post-mortems on dead people and teaching students how to do them. Still, she'd ask once she came home. Her mum was always open and truthful and, if she did know anything more, she'd tell her. Poor, poor Miss St Claire! Abby felt her eyes stinging as she thought of how her favourite teacher must be feeling.

'Maybe your godfather is running the murder enquiry,' her friend, Isabel, whispered. 'He was pretty good that day, wasn't he?'

The girls fell silent as they entered the hall, lining up in their classes. Assembly was about to begin, and all eyes were on the figure who appeared on the platform, his academic gown billowing out behind him.

The head teacher faced his pupils, a grave expression on his face.

Abby sat in the classroom, unable to concentrate on what her maths teacher was telling them. Miss St Claire's husband-to-be (as their head had expressed it) had been brutally murdered and the pupils were to expect interest from the press. *Don't talk to strangers, whether they seem like real newspaper reporters or not,* he'd instructed them. But the ripple of adolescent excitement that had followed their dismissal from the hall gave Abby the uneasy feeling that some pupils would be only too eager to tell what they knew about their drama teacher.

She thought about the tall, slender woman with the bright pink hair and colourful clothes who had enthused them all about her subject. *How awful to lose the man you loved like that!* Isabel had gushed. Now everyone would make up stories about Miss St Claire being *their* favourite teacher, even if they'd only had her standing in for an absent member of staff. Abby didn't want to join in with the gossipy girls, her own heart too full to express the sadness she was feeling. She had secretly nourished a teenage admiration for her teacher ever since she had arrived at St Genesius and now all she wanted was to know what was really happening to her.

Uncle Bill would know, she realised. He was used to solving murder cases. Perhaps she'd call him tonight, tell him about the assembly and what had been said.

At going home time Abby saw a small crowd at the school gates and guessed, correctly, that this was a posse of reporters bent on catching one of the pupils and quizzing them about their drama teacher. As she approached the gates, she saw several members of staff standing either side, waiting as the pupils came out, stern frowns on every face.

The bus journey home from school was noisy with speculation, but Abby stared out of the window at the tenements passing by, wondering about the lives of all the anonymous people who lived in these flats and whether any of them concealed a killer. *An overactive imagination*, her English teacher had scrawled in the margin after reading one of Abby's more lurid stories. But her psychologist father had encouraged her to express all her thoughts and now Abby lost herself in musing about the lives of strangers, anything to keep images of a pink-haired teacher at bay.

'I did do his post-mortem,' Rosie told her daughter. 'Sad case. Your poor teacher was distraught, as you might imagine.' She gently pulled Abby into a hug. 'I'm sorry it's affected your school like this. But d'you know what your uncle Bill often says when a person has been the victim of a killing?'

'No. What?'

'Well, he says it is like a stone being thrown into a deep pool of water. The ripples keep coming and so there is always more than the one victim. So many others are affected by the killer's act.'

Abby nodded. 'It's so sad,' she sighed. 'I can't stop imagining how she is feeling.'

Rosie bent and kissed her daughter's head. 'You have more than normal empathy for people,' she said. 'That's not a bad thing, of course. But don't brood about it. That's not helpful to you or anyone else, darling.'

'Is Uncle Bill going to find who killed him?'

Rosie shook her head. 'It's Molly Newton who's in charge of this one, dear. And she'll do a fine job, I'm sure,' she added, unconsciously echoing Lorimer's own thoughts.

Molly took a deep breath then knocked on Lorimer's door.

'Come in. Ah, Molly, sit down.'

'Sir, that's the results from the basement of the theatre,' she told him. 'Lots of fingerprints, as we'd expect, but one rather worrying anomaly.'

'Oh?' Lorimer looked up thoughtfully, fingers clasped beneath his chin.

'No fingerprints on the razor box apart from the fresh ones from last night when Ahmed Patel handled it.'

'So, you think whoever took that razor out of its box wiped it clean?'

Molly nodded. 'All the other props had several sets of prints. And we would have expected to see Guy Richmond's prints on a box that he'd clearly held to show it off a couple of weeks ago, like Patel said.'

'And the basement isn't kept locked, so anyone might have sneaked in and taken the razor,' Lorimer mused.

'Anyone who had a right to be there,' Molly added. 'Patel said that all members of staff had keys to the back door so that they could access costumes and the like. There's a back-stage crew that changes from time to time, mostly students looking to earn a bit of cash in hand when the stage manager needs more bodies, but the lighting engineer and the sound technicians are employed full time by the company. All of the orchestral musicians are freelance, some from Scottish Opera, others from the Royal Scottish National Orchestra. But they are only required for certain productions.'

'And I guess you have your team looking into a list of all these personnel?'

'They've been hard at work all day,' Molly agreed. 'Unfortunately, that area of Paisley isn't covered by CCTV – the nearest camera is in Causeyside Street – but even that isn't much help as any vehicle parked at the theatre wouldn't access it from there.'

'You'd have thought a big theatre like that would have had access to better security,' Lorimer mused. 'So many people coming and going, especially for performances. Ah well, no other information from Traffic, I suppose?'

'Not so far, though they wouldn't be much help since we don't know what date the razor was taken from that props drawer. And Patel says there's been a lot of coming and going since the new show was announced early in the new year.'

'Is there a wardrobe mistress?'

'A lady from Renfrew who works from home. I believe she's some sort of relation of Jeffrey Standish. She has a couple of assistants, but they are rarely at the theatre as costume fittings take place in the woman's house.'

Lorimer gave a sigh. 'You've got your work cut out, DI Newton. Thanks for keeping me up to date.'

Sir.' Molly gave him a nod and rose to leave.

Lorimer frowned, recalling the size of the theatre basement and the musty smell. Fingerprints would have been easy enough to secure in that dusty area, he thought. And somebody had figured that out. Somebody who might have taken the cut-throat razor with the explicit intention of slitting Guy Richmond's throat. The weapon of choice had given a high probability of a premeditated murder. And now the box had been found to be so clean that theory was growing ever stronger.

CHAPTER TWENTY-ONE

SWEENEY TODD ACTOR MURDERED WITH HIS OWN RAZOR

Up and coming actor Guy Richmond has been found murdered, his throat slashed with what is thought to be his own cut-throat razor, a prop he had supplied to the St James's Theatre Company for their forthcoming show. Richmond, 29, trained in Glasgow's Conservatoire after graduating from the University of Massachusetts. He was an only child whose parents perished tragically in a car accident in Boston last year.

Police have not yet released more information about the man's death though it is thought to have taken place near Whitemoss Loch in Renfrewshire, a few miles from Paisley. The senior investigating officer, DI Newton, has asked for anyone who had been in that area around the tenth or eleventh of March to come forward to assist with enquiries.

Sarra Milroy put down the newspaper and sat staring into space. The printed words made it all so real, she realised with a shudder. Since the detective had broken the news, the young actress had been wondering about another place to stay, the memory of Guy in this flat all too poignant. Sometimes she imagined she heard his laugh or that a shadow across the hallway was him stepping out of the bathroom. Nights were the worst, taking hours to fall asleep only to have her dreams haunted by visions of Sweeney Todd.

The sound of her mobile shook Sarra out of her thoughts.

'Hello? Oh, it's you. I've just been reading about Guy in today's paper ...'

There was silence for a fraction of a second before her caller responded.

'Oh, you got it, then?' Sarra said, a faint smile playing about her mouth. 'I did wonder if you really meant what you'd said.'

She listened to the familiar voice on the line, words spilling out, the tone both querulous and demanding.

Sarra pulled her feet off the couch, a frown crossing her pale face. 'Now? But ... oh, I see ... Yes, of course I'll be there. I mean, it's to my own advantage, after all, isn't it?' She laughed.

Then, as the call ended, she sat for a moment staring at her phone, the crease between her eyebrows deepening. Could she put her trust in her caller? It would be foolish to refuse the offer that had just been made, she told herself, swinging her legs down at last and getting to her feet. If all went well, then she'd be out of this crappy flat and on the next plane to LAX airport. Hollywood practically guaranteed.

Minutes later the young woman was out of the door, a warm scarf under her parka, the fur-trimmed hood pulled up against a blast of icy wind.

It would take a good twenty minutes to reach the place and goodness knows when she'd be home again. A taxi for the return journey instead of a bus. Still, it was important to be there tonight. Heart thudding, Sarra Milroy crossed the road and waited at the bus stop.

There was no other person to see her shivering on the pavement, the flickering light from a streetlamp casting a circle around the slight figure as though she were, for once, in the spotlight.

CHAPTER TWENTY-TWO

'Smile! That's it!'

Daniel Kohi felt his cheeks begin to ache from the effort of grinning at the camera. The unexpected arrival of the photographer to Jackton had been a welcome break for his tutors, he supposed, but it had come as a surprise to the police constable.

'You're a perfect example of everything we stand for!' his divisional commander had exclaimed, slapping Daniel on the back. The senior officer had waited until the photographer had taken some shots of Daniel standing beside him before shaking hands all round and leaving them to carry on with the afternoon's photo shoot. The Sunday supplement might only be the first, Daniel had been warned by Gerry, the police press officer. There might be even more requests to interview PC Daniel Kohi, perhaps even an appearance on Scottish television.

Being picked as a poster boy for Police Scotland had seemed just a nice gesture to Daniel but his divisional commander had insisted on putting out a press release to accompany whatever photo would be selected. *It is in keeping with the force's determination to stamp out racism and show the public that Daniel Kohi, a black refugee, has not only been made welcome in our country, but is making a positive contribution in his role as a police officer*, he had written, enthusing about the training north of the border and Daniel being selected for the fast-track scheme that would take him back to his previous job as a detective.

Daniel had been sent a copy of the statement and now, as he stood glancing over his shoulder, as instructed by the photographer, the words came back to him. Yes, he was proud to have been chosen for that role, but he was also wise enough to know that there might well be a less than positive reaction to the publicity – now that the media were clamouring for his attention – not just from the public at large but from within Police Scotland itself too. Racism had reared its ugly head more than once since his first days at Tulliallan Police Training College and Daniel was not so stupid as to imagine his presence in Glasgow would be hailed by all his fellow officers as a good thing. Especially now that he was on the training scheme that would soon transfer him from uniform to plain clothes.

'That's nice, head up a little, look straight at me, good,' the photographer said.

He had been told to come downstairs into a room at the back of the college where there was less direct sunlight streaming in the windows, apparently a feature that was anathema to professional photographers.

Daniel was in uniform for this photo shoot, his hat either

held in both hands or tucked under one arm, whichever suited the young man taking the pictures. It was for another newspaper and this picture would be in black and white.

'Think that's us done,' the photographer said at last, standing up and grinning at Daniel. 'You're a great subject, you know. One or two of my shots could be worth submitting for a portrait competition, if your boss and you would allow that?'

'I don't mind, but you'd better clear it with him,' Daniel advised, rolling his shoulders to ease the stiffness.

'I can send you a few of the better ones, but it isn't going to be up to me which one they choose for the paper,' he replied. 'Anyway, thanks for your time. I enjoyed that.' He stepped forward and gripped Daniel's hand warmly.

Back home the two older ladies were eager to know all about Daniel's training day.

'Had my photo taken for another newspaper,' he told them, over a dinner of shepherd's pie.

'Good-looker like you, that'll do well,' Netta laughed, nudging Daniel's elbow. 'Wonder what Molly will think, eh?' She winked.

'You didn't mind being asked to do that?' Janette asked, looking uncertainly at her son.

Daniel smiled at them both. 'It's no big deal.' He shrugged. 'I'm not exactly a rock star, am I? Any publicity in the local papers will be used for tomorrow's fish suppers. I don't expect to be hassled by the general public, Mum, don't worry about that!' His words were intended to reassure his mother, despite his own inner misgivings.

*

'Didn't manage to speak to Daniel today,' Lorimer told his wife, Maggie, as they settled down that evening. 'Seems he was busy being photographed. Something to do with the new poster campaign, I think. Or was it a newspaper feature?'

'Because he is black? Or because he's an example of how a refugee can make a new life here in Scotland?' Maggie asked, a frown on her face. 'Hope he wasn't railroaded into this.'

'I think he was fine with it,' Lorimer told her. 'And in answer to your question, it will be a bit of both. Our chief constable has a soft spot for our Daniel, and she wouldn't want to exploit him unfairly. I can only see this campaign doing some good for the force. Perfect example of inclusiveness and diversity,' he said, grinning. 'See, even I know all the buzz words.'

'Well, I just hope he isn't targeted by the wrong sort of people,' Maggie sighed. 'There's still a nasty racist element in our country that should shame us.'

'Don't worry,' Lorimer said. 'Daniel's come through a lot worse than that and I think he's well able to take care of himself.'

Molly Newton was far less interested than his flatmates in her boyfriend's moment in the limelight, her attention focused on the investigation into the death of the actor, Guy Richmond, and the publicity surrounding that. So far, she had dodged the individual members of the press, only putting out a very brief statement on the early evening news.

Right now, she was poring over the results of the man's

post-mortem examination, trying to figure out just what had happened out at the side of that lonely loch.

Toxicology results showed a higher than normal level of a sedative that the man was prescribed to help him sleep. Molly frowned as she read on. Might he have taken this by mistake? Unlikely, since the prescribed drug was meant to be swallowed at bedtime. Had someone slipped it into a drink, led him to Whitemoss Loch in order to overpower him more easily? She lifted the phone and dialled the number that the FLO had given her for Meredith St Claire.

'Hello?' The husky tone of the bereaved woman made Molly bite her lip. Her voice sounded as if she might have been weeping.

'DI Newton here, sorry to bother you this evening, but I wanted to ask you about Mr Richmond's medication.'

'Medi ... medication? You mean his sleeping pills?' The woman's voice rose anxiously.

'Yes. Did he keep them at home?'

'Well yes, he did. In the drawer of his bedside table. Why?'

'Would you mind very much taking a look to see if they are there?'

There was a pause and then she heard a heavy sigh. 'Oh, all right, but they are always there, you know. Guy just takes ... I mean took ... one a night. It was after the crash, you see. He kept having the most awful nightmares. Hold on and I'll look.'

Molly nodded, though there was nobody there to see her response. She could barely imagine the shock of losing both parents like that and the grief the young man had experienced. Thank goodness he'd had Meredith by his side to comfort him. She waited a few minutes but there was no instant reply. What was keeping the woman?

Then she heard the phone being picked up.

'They've gone!' Meredith exclaimed. 'I looked under the bed, all through the drawer and the cupboard underneath. Not in the kitchen cupboard either. I'm really sorry.' There was a catch in her throat as though she were trying to hold back tears.

'That's all right, Ms St Claire. I just needed to check. His pharmacist gave us the information about dosage, so we don't need to see the pill box itself,' she reassured the woman. 'I'm so sorry to have troubled you. Good night.'

How the poor woman was feeling right now was anyone's guess, Molly thought as she cut the call. It was a horrible part of the job, probing for answers when someone was so emotionally raw. But answers she must have, Molly told herself, tapping a pencil against her lips. There were several possibilities. Someone had accessed their home and taken the pills to deliberately sedate the victim; Guy Richmond had taken too many himself for some unknown reason; or he'd carried them on his person after disappearing that Sunday.

It was a mystery that she must solve, Molly thought. One more strand in a case that was becoming increasingly strange.

CHAPTER TWENTY-THREE

The back door to the theatre creaked as a vagabond wind blew it wide, letting a flurry of dried leaves sweep into the building. A worried blackbird cried out its alarm call and flapped away into the night as the door slammed shut again.

Nobody saw the hooded figure in black make their way along the side of the building or disappear into the night.

Somewhere deep in the heart of the town a bell tolled midnight and a car revved its engine as the traffic lights changed to green. Then, all was silence.

There was not usually much mail for the theatre, but today the postman on his early round was delivering a large package with the address of St James's Theatre Company on a pre-printed label, no name attached. He walked smartly around the old church, noting that the few daffodils on the verge had been trampled into the mud.

'Bloody vandals,' he muttered to himself, turning the

corner only to see the back door lying open, a puddle of rainwater on the worn linoleum inside.

'Hello!' he called into the dim interior.

But there was no answer.

Had there been a break-in? The trampled daffies seemed to be telling that story.

For a moment he dithered, calculating how soon he had to be back at the sorting office. Then, reaching into his jacket pocket, he drew out his mobile and dialled 111.

It did not take long for the first patrol car to sidle up to the main gate, two uniformed police officers emerging.

'I didn't like to go in,' the red-jacketed postman told them as they walked up the side path towards him. 'Think there might be a mess, if that's anything to go by.' He jerked his thumb towards the remnants of yellow flowers fading against the muddied verge. 'And you always see the polis telling folk not to contaminate a crime scene, right?'

'Yes, sir, that's correct.' The older police officer's mouth twitched as he cast a sly glance at his younger neighbour. 'Watch a lot of crime drama on TV, do you?'

'Oh, aye. Never miss an episode of *Vera*.' The postman nodded.

'Let's have a wee shuftie inside, then, shall we?' the older cop suggested.

The postman remained outside, watching them walk into the building, not even stopping to don a pair of blue nitrile gloves. Not what Vera Stanhope would do, he thought, shaking his head as the officers disappeared out of sight.

He'd be asked for a statement, though, surely? Wasn't

that what they all did? He blew onto his ungloved hands, listening as the officers' booted feet made their way along the corridor. There was silence then the sound of thudding feet returning, the crackle of a radio springing into life, then the younger officer stumbled out of the open doorway, eyes wide as if in shock.

'Bad, is it? Make a right old mess, did they?' the postman asked, wondering why the officer's face was so pale and drawn.

'There's a body down in the basement,' the officer gasped. 'Need to call this in. Stay right where you are, okay?'

Rosie Fergusson crouched over the body of the woman at the bottom of the stairs, her torch illuminating the scene. Down here in the basement the light was poor, only a couple of bulbs suspended from the ceiling, certainly not enough for the pathologist to see the victim in any great detail.

From the way she was lying, Rosie estimated that the woman, whoever she was, had fallen down the steep flight of stairs and broken her neck. There was enough initial evidence to state that, at least. Though how she had come to be in the empty theatre was anybody's guess. It had all the hallmarks of a simple accident, but further examination might help to show what had really happened.

'Did she fall or was she pushed?' Rosie murmured to herself. Strange that this should be the second death associated with the St James's Theatre, but perhaps the postman outside was right and this person had broken into the place intent on an act of vandalism and simply stumbled down the steps.

Too much of a coincidence? she wondered, with a cynical twist to her mouth. Lorimer would be the first to make that remark. She looked up as white-suited figures at the top of the stairs appeared, cavalry in the form of the SOCOs.

'There's no ID on the victim,' she told them. 'No handbag, no wallet in her jacket pocket. Think this is one for Detective Inspector Newton over at the MIT. First responders were from Mill Street HQ but DI Newton's in charge of the other death out at Whitemoss Loch, and that victim is associated with this place.' She waved a gloved finger around at the shadowy basement. 'I think she should be here as soon as, don't you?'

Molly drew up behind the police car and the SOCOs' familiar white van. A woman's body found at the foot of the basement stairs, she'd been advised. She donned her white suit and pulled on the regulation gloves, then, slamming the car door shut, Molly strode along the pathway. She remembered that staircase, steep and poorly lit. Hadn't she let her hand slide along the wall as she made her way down into the basement on her first visit, no handrail on either side? Could this have been an accident?

There was barely enough room to manoeuvre past the body, but Molly found her feet meeting the metal treads that had been laid out. It was a woman, her head twisted to one side, hair obscuring her features. Molly hunched her way around until she had a clear view of the victim, then nodded at Rosie who pushed the woman's hair back from her face.

'No ID, I'm afraid,' Rosie sighed.

Molly stared at the dead eyes, still wide open on a world that continued without her. Then she caught Rosie's glance.

'I know who she is,' Molly said. 'I've met her before.'

Rosie's eyebrows rose expectantly.

'This is one of the women from the theatre company,' Molly said quietly. 'Sarra Milroy.'

It was every police officer's least favourite job, breaking the news of a loved one's death to their nearest and dearest. In the case of Sarra Milroy, it was her mother, Angela, who answered the door to DI Molly Newton's knock, DC Alisha Mohammed by her side.

Angela Milroy lived on a housing estate in Craigbank, not too far from where her daughter had lived in her rented flat. It was now mid-morning and Molly was in a hurry to catch the victim's mother before her working day began. The caretaker at the theatre had informed them that Sarra's mother worked part-time in a city centre department store and so it was imperative that they broke the dreadful news to her before she set off for her journey into town.

'Yes?' A pleasant-looking woman stood on her doorstep, dressed in the regulation black suit that most sales assistants chose for their working outfit. A string of pearls and a pink scarf knotted loosely around her neck were the only adornments.

'Mrs Milroy, I am Detective Inspector Newton. May we come in, please? I'm afraid I have some bad news,' Molly asked, her expression sombre as she watched the woman's mouth open.

*

'I can't believe it,' Angela Milroy repeated, shaking her head. 'Not Sarra.' She looked up at the two officers, a bewildered look on her pale face. 'She was so young, just starting out ... a good girl, Inspector ... never in trouble, never ...' She broke off, tears streaming down her powdered cheeks.

Molly gave her DC a silent nod and Alisha rose from her chair and left the living room to find the kitchen. She'd return with hot tea, milk and sugar, the panacea for all ills. It was the second time the younger detective had come to the door of a grieving woman, but somehow this felt much, much worse.

'Tell me about Sarra,' Molly asked gently.

Angela Milroy gave a tremulous smile. 'She is our youngest,' she began. 'Three big brothers who spoiled her, but she had the sweetest nature, never took advantage of ... of anyone ...'

'She seemed a nice lass,' Molly murmured. 'I really am so very, very sorry for your loss.'

'I did warn her, you know,' Angela said, looking up suddenly as Alisha came back into the room with the tray of drinks.

Molly waited till her DC had made sure that the mother had a mug of tea clasped in her shaking hands before she commented on that statement.

'You warned her?'

'Oh, maybe I was being silly. Overprotective, but I honestly couldn't see a future for Sarra in the theatre. She had very little experience, you know. Just what she'd done at school, Higher in drama. An A,' she added, a trace of pride in her voice. 'But not enough to take her into drama school.'

'But she was in a rehearsal for a professional production,' Molly pointed out.

'Mr Standish was giving her a trial, said he'd help her prepare for another audition. He knew her drama teacher from school, you see.'

Molly waited, wondering what was coming.

'Sarra was a scholarship pupil, Inspector. Clever lass, too bright for the local school here. So, we let her apply for St Genesius.'

'Her drama teacher ... was that ... ?'

'Ms St Claire, yes. Sarra adored her. We were all very cut up about that dreadful thing ... her poor boyfriend. Sarra got the lease of his flat out in Darnley after they'd bought their cottage, you know,' she added, not meeting Molly's eyes as she set down her mug onto the coffee table.

'It was an accident, what happened to Sarra, wasn't it?' she asked suddenly, looking from one officer to the other.

Then she saw the young Asian officer look across at her boss, her dark eyes full of questions.

Angela Milroy gave a gasp, her hands flying to cover her mouth.

'You said she was dead, fallen down some stairs ... are you saying ... oh, no ... '

'I'm sorry, Angela,' Molly said softly, sitting next to the woman and putting an arm around her shoulders. 'We can't be sure just yet whether or not it was an accident.'

'Did she fall or was she pushed?' Lorimer asked, unconsciously repeating the forensic pathologist's very own thoughts.

'Dr Fergusson said she'd have a better idea once the PM is done, sir,' Molly replied.

They were back at the MIT, leaving the scene of crime officers to continue working in that cavernous basement. Molly had already accompanied Sarra's tearful mother to the city mortuary where she had formally identified her daughter.

'There's something else you should know,' Molly said. 'Sarra had been a pupil at St Genesius, same school that Abby Brightman attends. Meredith St Claire had been her drama teacher just a couple of years ago.'

Lorimer raised his eyebrows. 'Well, that's interesting. Nobody told us they had been teacher and pupil. Meredith can't be that much older than the girl?'

'Sarra left school at eighteen, almost two years ago. It explains why she may have been closer to Meredith than the others. And why she shed some tears when she heard Guy had died.'

'I wonder why nobody ever told us,' Lorimer mused.

'Do you think this is some sort of escalation, sir?'

'We can't be sure of anything, yet, Molly,' Lorimer told her. 'Strange that she should be down there at that time of night, though.'

'The caretaker told us he locked up at nine p.m. after the stagehands had cleared everything away following a rehearsal by a kids' theatre group.'

'Who was last to leave?'

'Caretaker said he was. And he insisted that he'd locked the back door properly.'

'No sign of a break-in?'

Molly frowned. 'Funny you should ask that, but the postman who found the door swinging open thought that was exactly what had happened. Flowerbed all trampled underfoot. SOCOs will have made impressions from any footprints.'

'Perhaps it was meant to look like a break-in. Staged,' he said with an ironic half-smile.

'I wonder why she was there,' she murmured. 'No wallet, no phone or handbag. How did she arrive from her flat in Darnley?'

'If that was where she travelled from,' Lorimer added. 'Check CCTV around the nearest bus stops.'

'Looks odd, though, doesn't it? Someone must have taken her things.'

Lorimer nodded. 'If this does turn out to be a suspicious death, you know I'm at your disposal, DI Newton.'

Molly nodded. The mystery surrounding Guy Richmond's death was proving difficult enough to solve. If Sarra Milroy had been a second victim, then Molly would need all the expertise that the Major Incident Team could provide, starting with the man at her side.

CHAPTER TWENTY-FOUR

It was unusual for so little evidence to be found at the scene of crime. For, after Rosie had examined the body in situ and the photographer had submitted so many shots of Sarra Milroy, that was the pathologist's conclusion. The bruising on the woman's shoulder suggested that someone had grabbed her viciously before flinging the young woman headlong down the stairs. On reaching the bottom, her neck had snapped and death would have been instant. The woman's jacket had been unzipped, either by Sarra herself or by whoever had pushed her. Rosie was inclined to believe in the latter scenario since whoever had committed this deed had removed any identification from the body. Had it been a simple act of aggravated theft? But if so, what was the young actress doing there in the first place? Matters for DI Newton to ponder, Rosie told herself.

'No mobile phone, so no way of tracing where she had been in the hours before her death till we find her phone provider

143

and get some idea of locations,' Molly sighed. 'Whoever did this was intelligent enough to leave very little trace. However, there was a CCTV camera near the Darnley bus stop that lets us see Sarra Milroy getting on a bus to Paisley at ten-fifty-five. Forensics are hoping to find some DNA but so far it looks as if Sarra's assailant came prepared.

'A premeditated act, then?' she said to Lorimer, the question purely rhetorical. 'Who would want to lure her there to her death? What advantage could anybody possibly have in wanting her dead?'

'She lived in the flat that Guy Richmond used to rent. Start there,' Lorimer suggested. 'And let's keep this from the public eye as long as we possibly can, okay?'

Molly nodded. She remembered the untidy flat, and that pinboard in the kitchen. Might there be something there that could give a clue not just to this latest murder but to Guy Richmond's death too? She'd get members of the team to turn the place inside out.

'Sweeney Todd,' Maggie Lorimer said slowly, as they finished dinner. 'The Demon Barber. He threw his victims into the basement after slitting their throats, as I recall from that Johnny Depp film. Odd that this young woman should have been found in the basement of the theatre, don't you think?'

Lorimer stared at his wife. Trust Maggie to know the details. And she was correct, of course. 'Just don't want any pies turning up filled with human remains,' he said grimly.

'Maybe whoever killed Richmond had a thing about the play?'

'You mean, could it point to someone in the theatre? Could

144

certainly be one of them if there's motive and opportunity. Molly has interviewed a few of them and I'm accompanying her to talk to the others this evening,' he said, glancing at his watch. 'Actually, I need to go now,' he said, dropping a kiss on Maggie's cheek.

As he turned to leave, he looked at his wife. 'There was a casting session the other night. It may be interesting to see which parts have been allocated to each player.'

Ada Galloway lived in a ground-floor flat off Byres Road. No news had been given to any of the actors about the death of Sarra Milroy, but it was only a matter of time before questions would be asked about her non-appearance when rehearsals were due to begin. The casting had given the girl the role of Sweeney Todd's young wife, Lucy, in the forthcoming production, the main female part of Mrs Lovett having been scooped up by the more mature Ada Galloway. Now there were two characters' parts to fill.

'Rehearsals don't begin till Monday,' Molly said as they walked stride for stride up Great George Street then turned to Kersland Street where Galloway lived, a stone's throw from Molly's own flat.

'Have you time for a coffee afterwards? Might let us brainstorm a bit once we've interviewed the latest member of the group,' Lorimer suggested.

'Of course.' Molly smiled warmly at her boss. 'Netta gave me a batch of her home baking so I can offer you something nice to eat as well.'

Lorimer stopped for a moment and caught her arm. 'It might be an idea to let this woman know about Sarra Milroy,'

145

he said. 'See her reaction. I'll give you a nod if I think the timing is right.'

The building was in shadow as they rounded the corner and headed for Ada Galloway's address. It was not unusual for flats in this area to be rented out, the proximity to the University of Glasgow enabling landlords to command decent rents, properties here at a premium since there was always a high demand. Ada Galloway had done just that, letting out two rooms in her home to postgraduate students, the team at the MIT had discovered.

There was a tinny sound as Lorimer pressed the ground-floor buzzer.

'Yes? Who is it?' a woman's voice asked.

'DI Newton and Detective Superintendent Lorimer to see Mrs Galloway,' Molly said, leaning down next to the line of names posted on the entry system.

There was a harsh buzz and then a click as the main door opened and they stepped into a cold hallway, a defective stair light flickering above them.

The door to their left opened and Ada Galloway beckoned them into her flat.

'Come on in, straight down the hall. Nice to see you again, Inspector.' She beamed at Molly, raising her eyebrows appreciatively as she looked Lorimer up and down.

'Ah, policing's gain was the theatre's loss,' she sighed. 'You'd have made a lovely leading man, Superintendent,' she told him, with a wink. 'Come on through to my salon, won't you.'

Lorimer entered a dark sitting room lit by a pair of Tiffany lamps in jewel colours that complemented the rich burgundy velvet curtains draped across the windows and the Persian rugs on the floor. Another light drew his eyes to the fireplace where a huge Jo Malone candle was placed, its mandarin and basil scent filling the room.

Ada Galloway was dressed in a low-cut black frock that showed off her ample bosom, a ruby-coloured pendant around her neck that glinted in the candlelight as she sank into a chair by the fireplace, gold and silver bangles jangling on her wrists, hair piled up in a messy bun, tendrils escaping to soften her face.

'Do take a seat, officers,' she said, waving a beringed hand towards a settee that had seen better days, the red fringes at its base in tatters, peeking beneath a couple of scarlet fleecy throws.

It had been an opulent room at one time, Lorimer decided, but its former glory was past, faded creases on the curtains and stains on the rugs showing some neglect.

The actress had chosen to sit where the light did not illumine the lines on her face or neckline, he noticed. A deliberate ploy to hide her age, perhaps? He smiled at her, politely, wondering about the woman's background. There was no wedding ring on her ring finger though several others glinted in the light as she clasped her hands, still gazing at him with a coquettish smile. Widowed? Divorced? Their background checks would turn up these facts soon enough. For a moment he felt a certain sympathy for a woman no longer in the first flush of youth, her face heavily made-up as though trying hard to stem the advancing years.

'I hear you will be the next Mrs Lovett. Congratulations,' he said with a nod.

'Oh, yes, not that I expected any less, of course. Standish knows what he's about when he's casting,' she cooed.

'We wanted to ask you about Guy Richmond, the man who would have played Sweeney Todd,' Molly began.

Ada Galloway's face changed immediately as she turned to the detective inspector. 'It was horrible,' she said in a whisper. 'That poor young man. It would have been his big chance, you know.' She sighed. 'Nigel will do all right, of course. He'd have made an excellent Turpin, but I bet he's secretly delighted to have the better role now.' She glanced slyly at the detectives as though to gauge the effect of her words. 'Consummate professional, but the poor little dear doesn't have the same stage presence as Guy did. Still, it's wonderful what they can do with shoe raisers these days. He'll have heels of course,' she sniffed, 'costumes are to be true to the period.'

'How well did you know Guy Richmond?' Molly asked.

Ada shrugged for a moment, letting her sleeve slip off one shoulder to reveal a crimson bra strap. 'Who really knows anyone, darling? I mean, we play parts on the stage, go for drinks after rehearsals, gossip about anyone who isn't there, you know? The theatre can be a place where one confides in one's opposite partner, if he's the right sort,' she said. 'But I'm afraid the poor boy never thought to confide in me.'

'What was your impression of him?' Molly asked, changing her question ever so slightly.

'Oh, he wasn't so bright, you know. Settled for that drama teacher. Far too early to make a commitment like that when the whole world is waiting for you to become a star. Honestly, he could have waited for better than Meredith Sinclair, if you ask me.'

'You didn't like her?'

'Oh, darling, *liking* wasn't the point. She'd have tied him down, stopped him going for the really juicy parts. Might even have whisked him back to that island of hers. I hate to see all that sort of potential wasted,' she said irritably.

'Island?'

'I heard she was born on one of those little places in the Orkney Islands. Not Kirkwall. That's where Nigel Fairbairn came from, incidentally. Some other smaller place.'

Lorimer listened, intrigued by how much Ada Galloway appeared to know about Meredith's background. Yes, he mused, Sinclair was an Orcadian name, wasn't it?

'She gave herself airs and graces, you know.' The woman leaned forward, in a confiding way. 'Said she was descended from the earls of Orkney. Stuff and nonsense.' She grinned. 'Just wanted to make a name for herself. That's why she changed her surname to St Claire. Sounded grander, you see.'

'She would have been Meredith Richmond,' Lorimer reminded her quietly. 'They were newly engaged and had plans to be married.'

'Really?' Ada Galloway looked confused for a moment, then shook her head and sighed. 'Well, there's no accounting for . . .' She tailed off, biting her lip. 'Oh dear, I'm being bitchy, aren't I? Sorry, we seem to have strayed away from poor Guy. Terrible thing to have happened. And with the grandfather's razor he'd brought for his own role!' She gave a shudder that would have looked good on stage, Lorimer thought. 'Are you anywhere further on in finding the culprit?'

149

'The investigation is ongoing,' Molly told her firmly. Then, throwing a glance towards Lorimer, he saw her waiting for him to nod. First, though, he wanted her to ask her other questions.

'Do you know of any reason why someone would kill Guy Richmond?'

Ada Galloway's face changed at that moment, her previous coquettishness gone.

'Yes, I'm afraid so,' she began. 'Jealousy, of course, the green-eyed monster, and ... how can I describe it ... a sense of entitlement?'

'Can you be more explicit?' Lorimer asked.

She shook her head with a sigh. 'I had hoped not to be asked that question. However, you have asked, and I suppose it's my duty to tell the truth. No matter whom it might hurt?'

Lorimer looked at her intently and nodded.

'Oh well, I suppose you'd have found out eventually,' she said. 'Young Ahmed might have killed him. Or Fairbairn. Both of them had motive enough, you see.'

'Go on.'

'Nigel was crazy about Meredith. He'd had a thing for her when they were younger. At school, probably, you know how these things happen. Pair of lovesick teenagers, both accepted for drama school. One makes the grade with distinction, the other has to settle for teaching.' She leaned forward towards the two police officers, wagging a finger at them.

'But as soon as Guy came on the scene it was all over for Nigel. Meredith ditched him and cosied up with Guy. Is that

150

not reason enough? Added to which the blue-eyed boy from the States takes all the plum parts, leaving Nigel seething with fury.'

Lorimer nodded. 'And the props manager?'

Ada Galloway sat back again with a sniff. 'Well, maybe he had more reason than most to dislike Guy. Very traditional fellow, religious, you know?'

When there was no response from either officer, she continued. 'Guy was popular with the ladies, played around, you know? Well, when you're young that's what you do,' she added airily, with a wave of her hand. 'Only, when it came too close to home, Ahmed turned nasty.'

Lorimer frowned. The actress was enjoying telling her tales, despite her earlier claims.

'Guy went after Ahmed's sister. Not a very bright move, though the girl is exceptionally good-looking. Let me tell you about it.' She leaned forward a little and lifted a finger as if to ask for silence before she began her tale.

'One night Ahmed tore into Guy as we were rehearsing for the pantomime. Walloped him across the jaw till Standish flung him out. We thought Ahmed might lose his job, but he was still there the next day, though he and Guy never really spoke after that.'

'And Meredith? How did she react?' Molly asked.

'Oh, who knows? I suppose the poor girl was used to it. But it looks as if she'd clipped his wings right enough.'

Lorimer turned to Molly and gave her the signal she'd been expecting.

'Mrs Galloway, something very bad happened last night,' Molly began, staring into the woman's eyes, knowing that

Lorimer was watching the actress's body language and listening intently for her reaction.

'Yes, dear?' Ada turned away from Lorimer to face the detective inspector.

'Sarra Milroy died,' Molly stated.

'Sarra?' Ada frowned. 'What happened? Has there been an accident? I didn't see anything on the news . . . ' She clutched suddenly at her heavy necklace.

'Sarra was killed. At St James's Theatre,' Molly told her. 'Where were you last night, Mrs Galloway?'

The woman's mouth fell open, in genuine shock this time, nothing theatrical about her response to Molly's words.

'Sarra? Wee Sarra? Dead?' She shook her head. 'I can't believe it. And you're asking where *I* was? Goodness . . . ' She tailed off and turned to Lorimer as if he might be of some help.

'You don't think *I* had anything to do with this . . . surely.'

'Just answer DI Newton's question, please.'

'Well, I was here all night. After the casting I needed time to read my script, memorise the lines . . . ' She turned and flapped a hand towards a table by the curtained window. Sure enough, a black folder lay there.

Ada rose to her feet, snatched it from the table then brandished it under Molly's nose.

'See. My alibi!'

'And can anyone vouch for that?'

The woman sank back into her chair. 'Well, yes, of course, the girls who live here. They were all in last night. Exams coming up soon. You can ask them, if you like. We were all in the kitchen at one point, making coffee. I was here in the flat all evening and so were they.'

152

'I'm sorry if I was rather blunt,' Molly demurred. 'It is a question we will be asking of several people who might have had reason to be at the theatre last night.'

'Oh, I see. Well, rehearsals don't begin properly till Monday ... Oh my God, we can't continue now, can we? Scene of crime, and all that?' She shuddered visibly.

'I'm afraid we will be keeping everyone away from the theatre meantime,' Molly replied.

'We do not want you to speak to anybody about this latest fatality,' Lorimer told the actress. 'Please keep it to yourself until it is made public. Can you assure us you will do that?'

Ada Galloway nodded. 'I can,' she said stiffly. 'But I do resent being treated as if I might have done something like that! I had no reason to harm a single hair on that young girl's head!' she exclaimed indignantly.

Lorimer smiled at her. 'And I'm glad to hear it, Mrs Galloway. Thank you so much for giving us your time. What you have told us has certainly given DI Newton and me more insight into Guy Richmond,' he said with a nod as he stood up, ready to leave.

They walked down the hall, leaving the actress in her salon. Then, as they reached the front door, they heard her call out.

'Wait!'

Lorimer and Molly turned around to see her marching hurriedly towards them.

'She might have been one of his conquests,' Ada said, breathlessly. 'Guy Richmond's, I mean. I'm sure he had a fling with Sarra. Poor kid thought the world of him, and of Meredith. Star-struck, so she was. Delighted when she moved into that place in Darnley.'

'More tea?'

'Thanks, you make it nice and strong, just the way I like it,' Lorimer grinned.

They were sitting in Molly's flat, close by the window that overlooked the treelined street.

'What did you make of her?' Molly asked.

'A proper flirt.' He smiled. 'Bet she tried it on with Richmond despite the age gap. She must be well into her fifties, or even older, don't you think? And she's a gossip, too. It may take all her willpower not to lift the phone and tell her friends about this latest murder.'

'She seemed to know a lot about the other actors' backgrounds,' Molly remarked.

'Aye, and gave us information about Fairbairn and Patel that might have taken a while to find.' He frowned. 'Could Richmond have been continuing some sort of dalliance with Patel's sister? He wouldn't be the first Asian to have committed a murder out of so-called honour.'

'We need to follow that line of enquiry,' Molly said firmly. 'Ahmed Patel did not express the same sympathy for Richmond's death as the others did, when I first met them.'

'And now we know why.'

CHAPTER TWENTY-FIVE

Dundee was a different city from Glasgow, DS Giles thought, as they drove along the road, his driver's window down for a few moments. He breathed in, smelling the salty tang from the nearby River Tay, a wider stretch of water than the Clyde that ran through his home city, its blue surface a reflection of this March sky. So many changes had rendered the city a magnet for tourism, with the old sailing ship, *Discovery*, by the quayside and the very modern V&A art museum close by. A swathe of bright yellow caught his eye, making Giles blink. Daffodils, thousands of them across an embankment by the road, planted by supporters of Marie Curie, the charity. Then the sight was gone as the city approached.

Eventually they reached their destination at the student residency where Jasmine Patel, Ahmed's sister, had a room. It was a typical modern building, purely functional, no real soul to its design.

'C'mon, we know which room she's in,' Davie said, leading the way.

155

They were soon upstairs, knocking on Jasmine Patel's door, but there was no answer. Davie scribbled a note on the back of his business card and shoved it under the door.

'Should we try the refectory? Ask around to see if anyone knows where she is?' Alisha suggested.

'She could be in a class,' Davie said. 'We need to try the office, see what her timetable is like.'

After waiting patiently for the secretary to find a timetable for Jasmine Patel, Davie and Alisha headed for the refectory after all, Jasmine's classes apparently over for the day. It was just after twelve o'clock and her previous lecture had finished.

Davie eyed the swarm of young people in the large dining hall, a long queue snaking around the place, students lifting plastic trays as they inched towards the serving hatches.

They had split up, Alisha asking the students already at tables if they knew where Jasmine was likely to be, Davie walking the length of the queue.

It was at the table nearest the large swing doors that Alisha struck lucky.

'Jazz? She doesn't usually eat lunch here. Anyway, you're more likely to find her in the library,' a girl with bright red curls and wearing a baggy green cardigan told her, eyeing Alisha's warrant card with concern. 'She's not in any trouble? She's a really quiet lassie. Nice girl.'

Alisha smiled. 'Not at all, we just want her to help with one of our enquiries, that's all,' she replied with a reassuring smile.

As the DC turned away to join Davie Giles, she did not

156

see the girl flicking open her mobile, fingers rapidly tapping out a message, the activity hidden from sight by the oversize cardigan.

'Any luck?' Davie asked.

'A friend said she could be in the library,' Alisha explained.

'Okay, let's grab a sandwich and a coffee to take away while we're here then head over to the library.'

Two hours had passed since their arrival and Davie and Alisha found themselves back at the same student residence as before. They had knocked on several doors, but nobody had seen Jasmine Patel that afternoon, though one of them claimed she had been at a class earlier in the day.

'This is hopeless, sir,' Alisha grumbled. 'Where is she?'

'Ach, it's something you have to get used to, DC Mohammed,' Davie told her. 'Lots of investigations are grunt work like this. Easier for plain clothes to find a student. Uniforms can put some of them off. I remember being called plenty of names before I joined CID.

'We just need to call it a day, knowing we've done our best. If she gets our note, she'll call. If not, we try her home address if DI Newton wishes us to pay the family a visit. Come on, if we go now, we can be back in Glasgow before the rush hour begins.'

Of course, Patel's DNA would be all over that basement, Lorimer thought, putting down the latest forensic report with an exasperated sigh. *Motive, means and opportunity*, he reminded himself, the mantra drummed into detectives from the moment they began their training. Any of the principal actors and staff who held a key for the building had the opportunity, of course, and Sarra Milroy may well have let herself into the building, albeit no key had been found on her person. Every member of the theatre group had now been questioned by his team of officers, yet their focus remained on those closest to Richmond. One hard shove down those treacherous stairs was the means, something that even a slight figure like Fairbairn could have achieved. But what sort of motive would any of them have had? What on earth was the reason for that young woman's death? And did it have anything to do with her crush on Guy Richmond?

Perhaps it was time to talk to Meredith St Claire again. The bereaved woman had been Sarra's drama teacher and perhaps the person who knew her best. Even if young Sarra had been a love rival, the object of her affections was dead and so there was nothing to be gained from eliminating her now. Besides, Molly had assured her that Sarra had voiced concern for Meredith (Merry, as she'd called her) and Ada Galloway had asserted that the girl was fond of both Guy and Meredith.

Who would have gained from these deaths? Meredith had been expecting to become Mrs Guy Richmond, the cottage purchased in both their names and, though she was chief beneficiary in Richmond's will, what would her life be like now without him? The way she had stormed into Lorimer's life that day at the school car park had shown a woman half-mad with worry, something that had tragically come to be justified. From others' viewpoints, Meredith had been devoted to Richmond; *his little puppy* as Fairbairn had described her. And Ms St Claire had apparently turned a blind eye to

Richmond's flings with other women, bagging the man for herself, that huge diamond ring testifying to her success.

Being an outsider, a teacher of drama rather than one of the players, might give Meredith St Claire a fresh perspective on them all, Lorimer decided.

There were several others in the theatre world who might have gained from Richmond's death. Fairbairn's envy may well have escalated into something manic and who knew what other grudges he may have held against the popular American? He'd spoken of his rival's unkindness towards the crippled Anne Peters but had that been only one of many things Richmond had shown to raise Fairbairn's ire?

Then there was the sullen props manager whose sister had been linked with Richmond. An honour killing? It was not something Lorimer had come across in his caseload before but there had been plenty about such things in the press. That was certainly worth deeper investigation.

Standish, now, only seemed to have been a beneficiary of the victim when he was alive and, so far, Lorimer could not attribute any motive for murder to the director. Ada Galloway, too, had no apparent motive but she had struck Lorimer as a practised flirt. Had she tried it on with Richmond? Would a rebuff from the American have enraged her sufficiently to have him killed? Hell hath no fury like a woman scorned, he thought, shaking his head doubtfully. Had any one of them stood to gain from Richmond's death?

Then, there was the man who had fished Richmond's body out of the water. Could Richmond's nastiness to the late actress have resulted in some form of retribution by her husband?

Envy, spite, revenge, lust and greed were all elements in Shakespeare's canon, the Elizabethan dramatist a keen observer of the human condition, as Maggie was wont to remind him whenever they discussed a play they were about to attend.

Perhaps the drama teacher might indeed reveal more about these people, he mused.

CHAPTER TWENTY-SIX

It was one of those March days that presage springtime and make one believe that the fearful cold of winter is finally past. A light breeze was blowing cirrus clouds across a sky of heavenly blue as Lorimer drove out of Glasgow and towards the hinterland of Milngavie and Bearsden. As he turned onto the Stockiemuir Road, he kept glancing to his right, aware of a grassy slope where he sometimes caught a glimpse of roe deer. Sure enough, he saw three familiar shapes in the distance, heads down grazing as he swept past then focused on the road ahead once more. Soon he was turning up the farm road that led to the couple's pretty cottage, sheep grazing in the sloping fields on either side.

As he parked the car, he heard a faint sound coming from behind the cottage. Was that a female voice singing? Or a radio turned up loudly? Lorimer stepped quietly along the grassy path at the side of the cottage and was surprised to see Meredith hanging out washing on a line behind the house, an apron tied around her waist, her pink hair blowing in the wind.

He stopped for a moment, listening as she sang. The tune was a familiar one, but he could not make out the words, as she had her back turned to where he stood. It had a plaintive, yearning sound, the notes carried towards him on the westerly breeze. Then it came to him, the old legend of Sulskerry where a seal king had shed his skin and appeared on dry land as a handsome man. A shape-shifter who had left a mortal woman heartbroken.

The singing stopped abruptly as the woman turned around.

'Oh, Superintendent Lorimer! I didn't hear your car!' she gasped, dropping the last of her laundry into a plastic basket.

'Sorry if I gave you a start,' he apologised, walking towards her. 'These hybrids are notoriously quiet vehicles.'

'I was just . . .' She paused, gesturing towards the washing now blowing merrily on the line.

'Don't let me stop you. I have an old friend who would tell me that it's a grand day for a washing. It'll all come in smelling fresh, I'm sure,' he laughed, thinking about Netta Gordon.

Meredith's cheeks reddened a little as she nodded and continued to peg out the remaining towels on the clothes line.

'You're happy to keep up the old traditions, then?' Lorimer asked as they walked back to the cottage.

'Oh yes. Far better to use wind and solar power than a machine, though I have used the tumble dryer on occasions, too,' Meredith admitted.

'You have a lovely singing voice,' Lorimer remarked as Meredith opened the back door and they entered the kitchen.

'Thank you,' she said quietly. 'I didn't think I'd ever want to sing again after . . . ' She bit her lip and shook her head, letting her hair fall over her face.

'Sometimes it takes a day like this to lift one's spirits,' Lorimer said gently.

She nodded briefly then turned tear-filled eyes to his. 'Sorry, can I offer you coffee? I was just going to have a cup.'

'Thanks,' Lorimer replied, leaning his tall frame against the door, watching as Meredith busied herself with a bag of coffee beans. The buzz of the grinder prevented any conversation and so it was not until she had poured hot water into the cafetière and set out two porcelain mugs that he felt ready to talk.

'May I?' he asked, reaching out to take the tray the woman had prepared. He carried it through to the same room he had been in before and set it down on the low table.

'Have you got news?' Meredith looked at Lorimer expectantly, a flicker of hope in her eyes.

He nodded briefly. 'Take a seat, Ms St Claire, please. There is something I need to tell you.' He paused, regarding her with a serious expression. 'Sarra Milroy has been found dead.'

Meredith sat stock-still, hands clutching her apron, staring at him in disbelief.

'We are treating her death as murder,' he added. 'She was found in the basement of the theatre, after having been pushed down the stairs.'

'*Pushed?*' Meredith gasped, both hands covering her mouth, eyes wide with shock.

'I'm afraid there is no doubt in the pathologist's mind about that.'

'No ... ' she whispered, shaking her head in disbelief.

'I believe she was one of your pupils at St Genesius.'

The woman nodded silently, her face drawn.

'You were friends with Sarra?'

Meredith nodded again, swallowing down sudden tears. 'She was my star pupil,' she said huskily. 'Oh, the poor, poor girl ... ' She looked up at Lorimer. 'Who on earth would want to harm Sarra? She's ... she was ... lovely ... ' Meredith gasped.

'Who indeed,' Lorimer said. 'Where were you the night before last, Ms St Claire?'

'*Me?*' Her word came out in a squeak.

'We have to ask the same question of everybody close to Ms Milroy. Standard procedure,' Lorimer explained gently. Leaning forward and lifting the coffee pot, he poured some into each mug then took his own cup and sat back, waiting.

'Night before last ... I've been here every evening,' Meredith said, reaching into her apron pocket for a handkerchief. 'Watching television. Let me think ... night before last ... yes, that was when I watched *Vera*. Eight till ten. Then I watched the news till eleven and went to bed. Couldn't sleep till the sedative the doctor gave me had kicked in.' She gave an apologetic grimace. 'That was me till after eight. Same last night. Only it was a different programme ... ' She broke off. 'It's living on my own here. So quiet. Nobody to talk to. I need the television or radio on in the evenings after it's dark,' she explained.

Lorimer did understand. This was a very lonesome spot, only the bleating of sheep and the distant sound of farm traffic, an occasional plane heading for Glasgow airport, background noises that must have become a familiar tapestry of sound.

'Sarra Milroy. Can you think of any reason someone would want to harm her?' he asked.

'*Sarra?* Are you kidding me?' Meredith looked at him in horror. 'She was the sweetest kid. Her whole life ahead of her. All these dreams she had of making it in films one day ... Oh, I can't bear to think about this ... ' She lifted the skirt of her apron and covered her eyes, sobbing quietly. 'It's too, too horrible. Sarra was ... ' She gulped back further tears and gave a huge sigh. 'I'm sorry, coming so soon after Guy ... '

Then she looked straight at Lorimer, her mouth falling open as though she had seen something terrifying. 'Are we all in danger, Superintendent? Is there someone out there killing all Guy's friends off? Some madman ... ?'

'Have you any idea who might have had access to the theatre, other than the professional staff and the actors in the company?'

'Well, there is still Guy's key somewhere,' she said. 'I suppose I could have used it, but I have no idea where it is.'

'It was on his person,' Lorimer told her gently. 'Once this whole thing is over, we'll return all of Guy's possessions that were with him when he died.'

Meredith gave him a sharp look. 'You knew this and yet you asked where I was? As if I might have harmed that poor child!' she scolded.

'Routine, as I told you. I have no intention of upsetting you, Ms St Claire. I know you must still be raw with grief.'

And yet he'd found her on this lovely spring morning singing, something that had surprised the detective.

As if she had guessed his thoughts, Meredith gave a watery smile. 'Some days like this I try to blot it all out. Pretend I'm back home again in Kirkwall.'

'You lived there?' Lorimer asked. 'I'd thought you were from a different part of the islands.'

She gave a small laugh. 'Oh, I was born on Hoy, but my parents moved to Kirkwall before I started school. I don't remember much about my early years. Except the Old Man, of course.'

Lorimer nodded. The Old Man of Hoy was a famous challenge for intrepid rock climbers, the narrow stack of red sandstone emerging from the swirling seas, often depicted in travel brochures advertising the islands.

'And you knew Nigel Fairbairn?'

She nodded. 'We've been friends since primary school,' she admitted. 'Such a talented lad. He was always the star of our school shows.'

'And you studied together at the Conservatoire.'

'Yes. We were both thrilled to get away to "the big city".' She smiled, making inverted comma shapes with her fingers. Her smile faded as quickly as it had flitted across her face. 'Times like this, I feel I could go back there and never return.'

'Islands are special places,' Lorimer said. 'My wife and I often take a holiday on Mull.'

Meredith nodded. 'But it's home to me. Where my folks are. Maybe I should just go back? Make a new start? Try to forget I ever knew Guy.'

Lorimer did not reply at once. Was she asking his advice? Or permission?

And she'd mentioned her folks, yet hadn't she claimed to have nobody in her life? 'Perhaps not the best idea until after you've laid him to rest,' he said gently.

He regarded Meredith thoughtfully. 'You never mentioned your parents,' he said.

The woman dropped her head. 'No. We ... we didn't really get on, you see. They were furious when I left to go to drama college. Wouldn't speak to me. It was only because of a legacy I had from my grandmother that allowed me to go away. I'm afraid we haven't been in touch since then.'

Lorimer said nothing. Estrangement like that was sad when it was clear this young woman could do with family support right now. But her relationship with her family was none of his business. Finding the killer of those two people close to Meredith was, however. 'I know that DI Newton has been here and that we have Guy's laptop to try to help us with our investigation, but would it be an intrusion for me to see the other parts of the cottage?'

When the woman looked doubtful, he continued, 'I find that when I can see where a person has lived it helps me to get a sense of them. Do you know what I mean?'

Meredith nodded. 'Let me show you around,' she said quietly.

The house was more spacious than it appeared from the front, with three sizable rooms upstairs, one of which was used as a study by the drama teacher. Lorimer looked around slowly. A side window looking west gave plenty of light as well as a view across to distant hills and he reckoned this was a place in which Meredith enjoyed working. There were colourful posters including one from a performance of *King Lear* in Stratford-upon-Avon dated a few years back, its corners now curling in the sunshine. Above her desk was a pinboard with her current school timetable and various post-it notes relating to work. One entire side of the room was shelved with books, including, he noticed, several by the late Orcadian, George Mackay Brown, one of Maggie's favourite authors. He ran his eye across their spines.

'You like Mackay Brown?' he asked.

She nodded. 'We did a lot of his stuff at school.'

Lorimer hunkered down to take a closer look at the books then picked out one that had clearly been well used.

'May I borrow this?' he asked. 'It's not one I've come across before.'

Meredith gave a shrug. 'Of course. It's an old copy.'

He stood up and, casting his eye around walls that were painted in buttercup yellow, he did not see any other pictures of Guy Richmond. Nor was there one on her desk. Perhaps living with all his images downstairs was enough.

There was a guest bedroom that had the look of a 'tart's boudoir', as Maggie might have said, her pet phrase for some of the more outrageous interiors she had spotted in the colour supplements. Curtains in rust and gold satin were pulled back in ornate brass fittings, heavily fringed tie-backs securing them in place. The counterpane on the double bed was made of some silken fabric in similar dark colours, the pattern of a golden dragon dominating the design and repeated on pillow shams and scatter cushions. The blood-red walls had some pictures of bright yellow or ochre flowers behind unframed glass, which on closer inspection proved to be botanical prints, adding to the exotic look. Opposite the bed was a black and white Aubrey Beardsley print of *The Climax*, the first thing a guest would see on awakening. The wooden floor had been sanded and varnished in bright oak which creaked a little as Lorimer stepped around. Once more, there was no sign of Richmond.

'Striking room,' he murmured. 'Did you design it?'

Meredith smiled. 'Thank you. I did. It's my sort of taste but Guy wasn't as keen. I created it with my girlfriends in mind.'

'Have any of them come to stay?'

She shook her head. 'But maybe once we have the funeral arranged . . . ' She turned away and Lorimer wondered if she was hiding tears.

'Just our room to see,' she said in a gruff voice. It's pretty ordinary. Guy liked pale colours. Wanted something that reminded him of home, I suppose.'

The master bedroom was to the back of the house, and Lorimer guessed from its size that it had been extended from the original plans of the cottage as it reached over the kitchen which had probably been added since the old house had been built.

It was, as Meredith had said, different from the guest room. Wallpaper in narrow blue stripes instantly reminded Lorimer of the US flag and the bedding was also in shades of white and blue, a red fitted sheet peeping from the duvet that had been dragged over on one side. Was she having trouble sleeping? What must it be like to accustom oneself to being in bed without your partner? As he turned to take in the room, one huge image dominated the wall opposite

169

the king-sized bed. It was a blown-up colour photograph of a younger Guy Richmond, dressed in baseball gear, a club clutched in one hand, the man grinning into the camera, his teeth white against a glowing suntan.

'That was a gift from his folks,' Meredith mumbled. 'They wanted him to have it as a reminder of everything he loved about his youth.'

Lorimer moved closer to the huge picture and saw the inscription, *Love from Mom and Dad*. Behind him, Meredith said nothing.

'They were close,' Lorimer remarked.

'Very,' she replied. 'He adored them, you know. Took it so hard after the accident. For a while I thought I'd lost him.'

'Oh?'

She heaved a sigh and sat down on the side of the bed. 'If he'd been over there he'd probably have gone to a shrink. Therapy. They all seem to have a therapist like we have a hairdresser,' she said, a note of disapproval in her voice. 'Instead he ... '

Lorimer saw her bite her lip and look down.

'Took some relief in drugs?'

Meredith nodded. 'He wasn't an addict, you know,' she said, looking up at Lorimer. 'Please don't think that. Guy would have worked through it all with my help, you know. Once we were married ... ' She trailed off again and Lorimer saw her shoulders heave as the tears came once more.

'I get the sense that he was a much-loved young man,' Lorimer said gently. 'And a talent that might have gone far.' Meredith rose from where she had been sitting and walked back into the upper hallway.

It was time to go, and Lorimer had the feeling that he may have outstayed his welcome.

Lorimer looked in the rear-view mirror as he turned onto the main road. A black four-by-four was slowing down, then it was driven up towards the cottage he had just left. He pulled into the side, making a note of the vehicle's registration. Someone was paying Meredith St Claire a visit, and he was curious to know who that was. He'd run it through the system when he returned to the office, see who had come to see the grieving woman so soon after his own visit. He hoped it wasn't a nosy reporter from the press. Their intention would be to dig for any salacious bit of information about Richmond, not caring whose feelings they damaged in the process.

The black car was registered to a man named Joshua Pettifer, living at an address in the village of Killearn. Certainly, the car had come from the Stirlingshire direction to Meredith's cottage, a twenty-minute drive away. Who was he and what business did he have with the drama teacher? Lorimer wondered.

It was a matter of minutes to check the man's name on the police database and, sure enough, up it came, the man flagged for crimes related to drug dealing. Aged thirty-eight, he'd served a few short sentences in the past, but nothing in recent years. A reformed character? Or just far more careful not to be caught? he thought cynically. Could this be Guy Richmond's supplier? And, if so, why was he visiting Meredith now that her fiancé was dead?

171

He thought about the tall, slim woman with those high cheekbones. Did Meredith St Claire also have a drug habit? There had been no behaviour to indicate that, no nervous tics or a rapidly tapping foot so familiar to the detective used to interviewing drug users. Had Guy owed money to his dealer? He frowned, a sudden qualm of anxiety for the woman living alone in that lonely spot. Perhaps he'd ask the family liaison officer to drop by later, just to check that all was in order. After all, theirs was a duty of care to the public and Meredith St Claire might be more vulnerable than most right now.

He didn't normally sit up this late reading, each day's early start demanding a decent amount of shut-eye, but once Lorimer had begun to read the play by Mackay Brown, he found it hard to put the book down. *Witch* was the story of an innocent girl accused of witchcraft and her ensuing torture was told in prose that was at once simple and beautiful, conjuring up a time long past. Meredith's pencil marks were all over the margins and some sections had been underlined, probably back in her school days.

And it made William Lorimer ponder the cruelty of those who were sure of their own power and just how they might kill to get what they wanted.

CHAPTER TWENTY-SEVEN

'I haven't seen your Molly for ages,' Netta remarked as Daniel sat down opposite her in the kitchen.

'No, she's very much occupied with this double murder case,' Daniel murmured, glancing up at his mother who was sitting next to Netta. 'Lorimer's pretty much in charge now that it's moved up a gear.'

'He's in charge? Doesn't that let Molly off the hook?' Netta continued.

Daniel shook his head. 'She's part of the team, still officially SIO in the Richmond case, but now they'll have more manpower to tackle the ongoing investigations.'

'SIO?' Janette Kohi looked puzzled.

'Senior investigating officer. Sorry, Mum, police talk uses so many acronyms. Keep asking if you don't understand.'

'Took me a while to make sense of it all,' Netta chipped in.

'Not as bad as it was for me interpreting Glaswegian,' Daniel nudged his friend with a grin.

'Ach, ye're almost a native speaker now, son,' Netta

laughed. 'An' you need to jist ask away when I say something that sounds strange, Janette. Dinna haud back, mind?'

Daniel noticed his mother staring at her friend. She blinked, then smiled. But had she even caught the gist of what Netta had said? Perhaps. He remembered how long it had taken him to understand the Glasgow parlance a few years ago after he'd arrived in Glasgow on a cold, wet November afternoon. But Netta's warm welcome had never been in doubt, something that transcended the language barrier, just as it seemed to be doing for his mother.

'That's me finished my first week of detective training at Jackton,' Daniel told them. 'I'll be back in uniform on my usual shifts at Cathcart in two days' time.'

'I thought you were going to be a detective right away,' Janette said.

Daniel shook his head. 'I have to wait until there is an opening in one of the CID teams,' he told her. What he did not say was that there was a possibility that he might find himself sent to anywhere in Scotland, should the need arise. 'So, how about I take you two ladies on a trip once Molly can join us? You haven't been to Stirling yet, Mum. It is a lovely drive, and the castle is well worth seeing, for the view alone.'

'Stirling?'

'It's right bang in the middle o' Scotland. A wee thing short o' Perth,' Netta said. 'Isn't it the place where thon Highland fault line is, Daniel?'

'Not that far away, Netta. Aberfoyle and Crieff are on the geological fault line, but Stirling is considered as the place where Highlands and Lowlands meet. We'll maybe visit the Bannockburn Centre. I can show you where

174

the famous battle of Bannockburn took place,' he added enthusiastically.

'My, ye're turnin' intae a real Scot, so you are, son,' Netta said proudly.

'Well, I'll soon have my British citizenship,' Daniel smiled, 'and I'm an officer of Police Scotland. Lorimer has even persuaded me to support his beloved Kelvin FC.'

If he'd glanced across at his mother just then, Daniel might have noticed the shadow crossing the older woman's face.

Janette Kohi stared out at the dark sky full of clouds, not a star to be seen. The lump in her throat had been growing all evening as they'd sat in the lounge, making plans for the trip to Stirling. She had tried to sound a note of enthusiasm but knew deep down that all she really wanted was to stand under the wide, open skies of Africa, listening as night sounds began their velvety chorus. It was too quiet here, despite the occasional car swishing past on the wet street outside, and Janette knew in her heart that she would never settle in this busy city.

She bowed her head, feeling ashamed of the wave of homesickness that had engulfed her. Didn't she have so much for which to be thankful? She began to say her nightly prayers, listing all her blessings and asking God for protection on her loved ones, even including the tall blonde lady whom her son loved so much. Then, after a moment's consideration, she prayed for those poor souls who had been affected by the deaths of those actors Daniel had told her about, Guy and Sarra, and asking God to bring justice for them all.

*

Meredith switched off the light and rolled over in bed. Guy's side was cold, and she immediately turned back with a shiver. Outside, everything was quiet. No sheep bleating, no tractor rumbling past the cottage. Even the rain had stopped its earlier pattering on the windows. How long . . . ? She turned restlessly, wondering if the police had come to any conclusion about the murders. If they had made an arrest . . . ? Once that happened, she might find some peace. Bury her fiancé and begin a new life somewhere else. But for now, she must remain here, in the place they had shared with hopes and dreams for a future that was never going to happen.

The woman closed her eyes and gave a huge sigh, bidding sleep to come; a dreamless sleep, rather than one where her nightmares contained images of a drowned man, his pale face breaking the surface of ink-black waters.

CHAPTER TWENTY-EIGHT

'That doesn't look good,' Molly agreed as they sat in the DI's office. 'A dealer turning up like that. Still, she's an adult and it is her own affair, I suppose.'

'You don't seem too worried about her,' Lorimer said.

'Should I be?' Molly retorted. 'She's been given all the support we can offer. And until we find out who is behind these deaths, we'll continue to do just that. But she's turned down any further visits from our FLO. Wanted to be on her own, she said. And fair enough, we have to respect that.'

Lorimer frowned. 'What was a known drug dealer doing up there, today? I think we should bring him in for questioning. If he was Richmond's dealer, I'd like to know where he was when the man went missing.'

'Josh Pettifer?' The grizzle-haired desk sergeant laughed. 'Oh, we've known him since he was a nipper. Came from a bad family of drug dealers down the road in Wine Alley,' he added, naming a notorious part of Govan that had long gone after the area had been subject to urban revitalisation. 'In and out the nick as a juvenile but haven't heard of him for a good few years now.'

Lorimer nodded. There wasn't much about the local Glasgow drug scene that Billy McRae didn't know, which was why they were sitting in Lorimer's office having coffee on the man's lunch break.

'What is he like, Pettifer?'

'Chip off the old block,' McRae replied. 'Caught dealing at primary school. Ach, the lad had nae chance. Young Pettifer was brought up used to police raids at their house. Never indulged in the stuff, unlike his poor big brother, Michael. That one OD'd when he was still in his teens.'

'I was wondering if he was Guy Richmond's dealer,' Lorimer explained.

'Actor fellow found out at Whitemoss Loch?'

'Yes. Seems he had a coke habit, nothing too serious to hamper his acting career, but worth looking into all the same.'

'Well, Josh is a slippery customer. He's got this huge house up in Killearn. Profits from dealing, of course, though nothing to prove it. Has a genuine cash and carry business over in Govanhill. It's been turned over a couple of times, but nothing ever found. Good luck with pinning anything on that wee squirt, sir,' McRae grunted, laying down his coffee cup.

'Thanks, Billy. Good to have first-hand background,' Lorimer said.

*

If Josh Pettifer was surprised to be stopped by a police vehicle as he drove along the narrow road past the Devil's Pulpit, a favourite spot for tourists, he certainly did not show it, the officers reported to their superiors at the MIT. His presence requested at Helen Street had brought no refusal to attend, not even a dark look at the officers who had brought his black Range Rover to a halt, Lorimer was informed.

Now he was sitting in an interview room, having been left to stew for twenty minutes, a uniformed officer at the door, while Lorimer and Molly discussed the best way to question the man.

'Joshua Pettifer?' Lorimer asked the slight figure sitting at a table as he entered the room followed by Molly. 'Thanks for coming in.'

The man stood up, glancing at each detective in turn, his eyes lingering longer on Molly.

He made no attempt to hold out a hand to greet the officers, merely sitting back down and grumbling, 'Hope this won't take long. I'm a busy man, you know.'

Pettifer was dressed in jeans, a smart leather jacket, his open-necked shirt with double cuffs fastened by heavy monogrammed gold cufflinks. His immediate impression was of a man appearing cool and casual but with the smell of money about him.

Once Lorimer had turned on the tape and established the date, time and Pettifer's identity, he made the introductions.

'I'm Detective Superintendent Lorimer and this is my colleague, Detective Inspector Newton,' Lorimer said, sitting down opposite Pettifer.

The man looked older than his years, bald-headed with

deep wrinkles around his eyes and mouth, designer stubble that was already grey.

'Big guns, to greet me, eh?' Pettifer's smile did not deepen the lines around his eyes. 'Do I need a lawyer?' He gave a dry, mirthless laugh.

'We want to ask you about your relationship with the late Mr Guy Richmond,' Lorimer told him. 'Do you feel the need to have a lawyer representing you?'

'Only if you lot think I killed him.' Pettifer smirked. Then, when both Lorimer and Molly stared gravely at him, his smile disappeared.

'Hey, you don't think *I* had anything to do with that?' Pettifer protested, leaning across the desk, arms outstretched.

'We'd like to know about your relationship to Mr Richmond, as Superintendent Lorimer has told you,' Molly said quietly. 'In a murder investigation it helps to talk to any of the deceased's associates.'

Pettifer remained silent, eyes flicking from Molly to Lorimer, whose blue gaze seemed to draw him back like a moth to a candle.

Lorimer saw him swallow hard. If Pettifer had nothing to do with Guy Richmond's death, then he might well prefer to incriminate himself with the truth about his supplying the man with cocaine rather than risk a murder charge. Lorimer guessed that was the man's dilemma as the ensuing silence continued.

At last, Pettifer gave a sniff and nodded. 'What do youse want to know?' he asked gruffly.

'Were you supplying drugs to Mr Richmond?' Lorimer asked.

'Maybe.' Pettifer dodged the question. 'Why d'you ask?'

Lorimer smiled. 'Just answer yes or no,' he told Pettifer, gesturing towards the recording device.

Pettifer ran a hand across his bald pate. 'Aye, on occasions. For recreational use only. No big deal,' he added with a half-smile. 'In both senses of the word.'

'What was he like? Richmond?' Molly asked, startling Pettifer with the change of topic.

'Guy? Oh, he was a decent enough bloke, I suppose. Had the airs and graces you'd expect from a theatrical type.' He leaned forward again, addressing Lorimer. 'See his coke habit, I reckon most of it was for show. Actors sometimes need a wee bit of a high after they've been onstage. All that adrenalin pulled out of them. No energy left to party.' He shrugged. 'Seen it time and again.'

'He wasn't the only actor you supplied to, then?'

Pettifer tapped the side of his nose. 'Cannae rightly say, now, can I?'

'Do I take that as a yes?'

'S'pose so. But ah'm no' in a hurry tae name names.'

'If it's relevant for us to ask you about other customers you were supplying with a class A drug, then we will. Is that understood?' Lorimer insisted, never letting his eyes off the man across the table.

Pettifer nodded.

'Speak for the tape, sir,' Molly told him.

'Aye,' Pettifer grunted, slumping back in his seat with a defeated air.

'Did you ever visit him at his former home in Darnley?'

'Mibbe, once or twice,' Pettifer admitted reluctantly.

181

'And did you know the person who took over his tenancy? Sarra Milroy?'

Pettifer shook his head. 'Never heard of her.'

'When did you last see Guy Richmond?' Lorimer asked.

Pettifer raised a hand to his face, turning away for a moment as if thinking hard. A delaying tactic, or was he genuinely trying to remember? Lorimer wondered.

'I seen him at the theatre week afore he was found out in that loch,' he said at last, turning back to the detectives. 'We had a wee chat outside the back door.'

Lorimer tried not to smile, the man's phrase a euphemism for doing the business of a drug deal.

'And how much did he buy?'

'Och, his usual wis a couple of wraps, but ... ' Pettifer stopped and licked his lips, his eyes darting worriedly from one officer to the other.

'And ... ?' Lorimer encouraged.

'Well, he wanted a lot more that night.'

'So, there was a big deal?'

'Not anything remarkable. Just more than his usual,' Pettifer insisted. 'I gave him what I had, but he said he couldn't pay me there and then. Wanted me to come to the cottage and get the money later.'

'What did he mean by later?'

Pettifer shrugged. 'Said he'd square up with me the following Tuesday ... but ... '

'But by then he had been found dead,' Lorimer finished for him.

'Is that why you were visiting Meredith St Claire this morning?' Molly asked.

Pettifer shook his head. 'Offering my condolences, wasn't I? Poor lassie's got enough tae deal with. A wee debt like that could wait. I'm no' exactly desperate tae be paid back,' he said, shooting out an arm to glance at his Rolex watch. 'Am I tae be detained here much longer?' he asked. 'Ah've a business tae run, you know.'

Lorimer resisted the urge to wipe the smirk off the drug dealer's face. What he had told them was probably true. Pettifer was a wealthy man and Richmond's delayed payment for the drugs was unlikely to cost the dealer a sleepless night. They might step up their inspections of his cash-and-carry business, see if they found any large quantities of drugs, but right now it was Pettifer's cooperation that they needed. Still, it would do no harm to rattle the man's cage a bit.

'What were you doing on Sunday the tenth of March?' he asked.

Pettifer blinked but said nothing.

'Sunday, March the tenth,' Lorimer repeated, as if re-phrasing the question might help.

'Sundays I'm usually at home,' Pettifer said slowly, his foot beginning to drum an anxious tattoo on the floor.

'And that particular Sunday? You might remember it? Guy Richmond died that night.'

'Cannae mind,' he said breathlessly. 'Wan Sunday kinda drifts intae the next, know whit I mean?'

'It would be useful to know your whereabouts, sir,' Molly said lightly. 'An alibi to verify it would also be nice.' She smiled, as if they were discussing what Pettifer had had for breakfast rather than how he might be in the frame for murder.

183

'I wis at hame. The wife can verify that,' he said at last, sitting back and folding his arms.

'Thank you,' Molly said sweetly. 'And your wife's name and mobile number?'

Pettifer reeled off his wife's name and number, a sullen look on his face.

'Interview terminated at fourteen-twenty-three,' Lorimer said aloud, then switched off the tape.

'Not that we've finished by any means, Josh,' he said, rising from his seat and towering over the man. 'Got a wee call to make right now,' he chuckled.

They left him there, sweating in the interview room while they walked back to Molly's office nearby.

'Here. Might be better coming from you,' Lorimer told her, handing the slip of paper with Mrs Pettifer's number.

Molly put her phone on speaker, tapped out the number and waited. It rang out for a few seconds before a young woman's voice answered, breathlessly.

'Hello?'

'Mrs Mary Pettifer? DI Molly Newton here from the Major Incident Team. Your husband gave us this number to call.'

'Josh? Is he all right? What happened?' Her girlish tone sounded genuinely anxious.

'Oh, he's fine, Mrs Pettifer, just helping us with enquiries into a case. He asked us to call you,' Molly said sweetly. 'It's about March the tenth, a Sunday. Can you help your husband by telling us where you were that evening?'

'Me?' Mary Pettifer squeaked. 'Sunday's my dance night. I go to ceroc with my mates, we go for a drink, and we take turns to sleep over at each other's places. Killearn's that far out and I don't drink and drive,' she said, a tone of righteous satisfaction entering her voice.

'And Josh? He doesn't go with you?'

'No, he stays at home on Sundays,' she said. 'Leastways, that what he tells me,' she added with a giggle.

'Home alone?'

There was a pause then Josh Pettifer's young wife began again, as though the penny had finally dropped as to why these questions were being asked of her. 'Erm, Sunday the tenth? Oh, maybe, um, maybe I was at home that night as ... as well,' she stuttered. 'That's right. I had a bad cold and didn't go out.'

'So, you were both there at home in Killearn all night.'

'Aye, ask Josh. He'll say the same,' the woman replied, her voice suddenly harder.

'And you can make a signed statement to the police about that?'

Again, there was a pause before Mary Pettifer said, 'Aye,' and cut the call.

'Believe her?'

'Not a chance. She sounded really young,' Molly said. 'Inexperienced too. An older woman would have twigged right away. Looks like Josh has got himself a child bride. Bet she's bonny but not very bright,' she mused.

'Well, whatever, he's got himself an alibi. Meantime, it might help if you got some of the team to talk to Mary Pettifer's friends. Find out if she was at a dance class and stayed out in Glasgow that night.'

*

Josh Pettifer slouched out of the building and turned to the car park where his car was parked, bristling with hurt pride. Thank God Mary had told them that they'd been home that night. Admitting to supplying Richmond had been inevitable and he might yet be dragged up to court, although that could just be a waste of police time. This was a murder case, after all.

As he drove down towards the motorway, Josh Pettifer drummed his fingers on the leather steering wheel.

Whatever happened now, they must not find out where he had really been on that cold Sunday evening, so far from the city centre.

CHAPTER TWENTY-NINE

'Sarra's phone provider shows that a call was made to her at 10.27 p.m. on the night she died,' Alisha told Molly. 'It was made from a landline.' She looked at the DI excitedly. 'A telephone in the theatre building itself!'

'Can we pinpoint exactly where it came from?'

'Yes. There's an office on the ground floor near the rear of the building.' Alisha pushed a sheet of paper across to the DI that had a diagram of the theatre's layout.

Molly examined it carefully, noting that the DC had already drawn a red line from the back door to the basement, indicating the direction where Sarra had probably gone before being pushed to her death.

Alisha came around Molly's desk now, leaning over her shoulder and tracing a route with her finger.

'Anyone coming in from the rear of the building could access kitchen, toilets and the office from where we believe that call was made. According to the caretaker it was Mr Standish who used it most of all,' the young DC told her.

'Good work,' murmured Molly. She gave a sigh. Alisha had been disappointed by the fruitless trip to Dundee, so this was a boost to the young woman's confidence. 'That helps, but doesn't pinpoint anyone in particular,' she said. 'Any of them who had a key had access to the theatre. So now we need to establish where they all were the night Sarra was killed.'

Murder enquiries used as many resources as possible in the early stages of an investigation and now there would be house-to-house visits in the area around the theatre, a trawl of CCTV cameras in the nearest streets and another round of questioning. Surely this time they'd find one of the people who had wanted both Guy Richmond and Sarra Milroy dead? And yet, Molly chewed her lower lip thoughtfully, were the two deaths necessarily connected? Lorimer was going to address them all in the incident room shortly and she'd bet he'd make the very same observation.

'Abby Brightman?'

Abby turned to see a lady in a red coat, her silk scarf tucked round her neck, smiling at her. She frowned. Did she know her? Was she one of Mum or Dad's friends?

'I hoped it was you,' the lady said. 'Have you got a minute before you go in?'

Abby followed her glance at the school gates. It was early, the bus dropping them off a good half hour before the bell summoning them to registration.

'So glad to have caught you before the bell goes,' the woman said, still smiling at Abby as if the girl ought to recognise her. 'Can we talk?'

'What about?' Abby asked, suddenly suspicious of this woman who might be a perfect stranger, despite the well-dressed look and confident manner.

'Oh, it's so sad.' The woman's smile faded in a sigh. 'Poor Meredith. I just wondered if you knew how she was getting on? Especially now her little friend has been found dead. Wasn't she a pupil here, too?'

Abby stared at the woman through narrowing eyes.

'You're from the newspapers, aren't you?' she accused.

'That's right, dear. The *Gazette*. We wanted to find out about your drama teacher. From a pupil's perspective,' she added in a low voice.

Abby had a sudden urge to swear at the woman, tell her to f— off, but could not bring herself to let such a word fall from her lips.

'Go away,' she said instead. 'You aren't meant to talk to pupils. It's not right.'

Then, turning away, she marched through the school gates.

'I can make it worth your while, dear,' the woman called out. But Abby kept on walking, her face pink with fury. She vowed to tell her godfather about this, see if he knew who this auburn-haired woman was.

Once in the seclusion of the girls' bathrooms, Abby took out her phone. Uncle Bill had told her that WhatsApp was the safest way to leave a message. She sat on the lid of the lavatory, wondering just what to tell him. How had that reporter known who she was? And why did she think a mere schoolgirl would know anything about her absentee drama teacher?

*

189

Lorimer frowned at the message. He'd have the press officer make an immediate complaint. The woman from the *Gazette* must know who Abby was and her relationship with the detective superintendent. Did she imagine he'd discuss a case with a thirteen-year-old girl? Or that her pathologist mother might chat about it around the dinner table?

What if some of the kids had been spreading rumours? He sighed. The imagination of teenagers could do more damage than they realised. Perhaps he ought to have a word with one of the senior staff.

A few minutes later, Lorimer was assured by the head teacher that every effort was being made on the school's part to stop the pupils talking to the press. However, what they did out of school hours was beyond their control. It was a fair comment, but worth having made the call to alert them to the reporter trying to hassle Abby, offering her money as well. Had any of the pupils spoken to the reporters since Guy Richmond's death, tempted by a fee? It was possible. Meantime, he had asked his goddaughter to keep her ears open for any silly gossip about Meredith St Claire. After all, the poor woman was grieving badly, without the added pressure of reporters swarming around her door.

It had not taken the reporter long to find out the address. One of the kids she'd spoken to after the Brightman girl had shaken her off had been only too keen to give her the information she'd sought. The girl had promised to find it as soon as she could, two ten-pound notes folded into her blazer pocket. The reporter's suggestion that the pupils might want to send a condolence card had been taken up by the girl and their unwitting registration teacher had supplied the address. She smiled as she drove around Baljaffray roundabout and headed for the open countryside. Devious ways were all part of her stock-in-trade and she'd bet that none of her rivals had yet found the cottage where Meredith lived.

Meredith jumped as the doorbell rang. Walking on slippered feet, she peered through the curtains to see a woman in a red coat standing on her doorstep. She blinked, wondering. Surely this wasn't someone else from the police? Hadn't they given her enough hassle lately?

She drew back and hid along the wall as she saw the woman step onto the grass, evidently deciding to look through the front window. If she stayed still long enough, whoever it was might just go away. Meredith's car was in the garage so there was no obvious sign that she was at home. She waited, listening as she heard footsteps on the path and the doorbell ring out again, one long single shrill note as if the stranger had her finger on it, determined to be heard.

At last, the noise stopped, and Meredith heard a clatter as something was dropped through her letter box.

Not until she'd heard the sound of a car engine starting up did Meredith dare move away from her hiding place and slip into the hall. There, on the floor, was a note folded in half.

She gave it a quick read then tore it into shreds. Asking for an interview, offering to pay good money. Her lip curled. No money in the world would make her speak to the press. Grubby little newshounds! Surely they must realise that she was grieving the loss of her fiancé?

But, if one of them had discovered the cottage, then

others would surely follow? The thought made Meredith sigh. Hadn't the family liaison officer warned her this might happen? Maybe it was time to do some packing, leave this place with all its memories?

But where could she go?

And how would she avoid being found?

CHAPTER THIRTY

'Detective Inspector Newton, do come in.' Desmond Dylan Morgan waved a hand towards Molly and her companion, inviting them in with an elaborate bow.

The theatrical agent had changed little since she had last met him, the intervening years evidently kind to him. He was just as corpulent as she remembered, his wispy white hair and pink cheeks more like those of a kindly cleric than the man whose professional life revolved around the theatre. Today he was wearing a red paisley-patterned waistcoat over a pale grey silk shirt and a pair of raspberry-coloured cord trousers. A faint whiff of something spicy drifted from a room opposite his office as he ushered the two officers in.

Molly noticed Alisha casting her eyes around the room, the walls filled with images of some famous actors and stage advertisements for shows from yesteryear.

'Now, ladies, to what do I owe this visit?' Morgan asked, clasping his chubby fingers together and smiling at them like a benevolent uncle.

'We are investigating the death of one of your actors,' Molly told him.

The smile immediately disappeared from the elderly man's face.

'Ah, of course. Guy Richmond. I should have realised,' he said, drawing a long sigh. 'Please, take a seat. May I offer you a refreshment?' Morgan waved his hand in the air once more.

'No thank you,' Molly answered for them both. 'And we'll try not to keep you long.'

Once seated on an old chaise longue, Molly introduced Alisha to the theatrical agent, who had taken the chair from behind his desk to sit closer to his visitors. A considerate move, Molly observed, making the arrangement far less formal.

'What can you tell us about Guy Richmond?' Molly asked.

'Ah, what indeed,' Morgan said slowly, his eyes flitting from Molly to Alisha with interest. 'He was a likeable boy, well, young man by the time of his death, poor fellow. I first met him when he asked me to represent him. That was in his second year at the Conservatoire. He'd been getting quite a few parts by then,' he explained, nodding towards Alisha. 'I'm fairly well known in the city and many students come to me and remain on my books long after they've left Glasgow to go on to greater things.' He lifted his chin with a little smile of pride. 'I was expecting Guy to leave me for a bigger London agency, once *Sweeney Todd* reached the West End. I'm not the biggest or the best and I believe that Guy would have gone on to find real stardom.'

'He was that good?' Molly asked.

Morgan paused for a moment. 'I think he would have

become very good in time,' he said slowly. 'An actor needs experience to hone his or her craft, but there is one quality that cannot be taught, and Guy had it in spades.'

'Oh? And what is that?'

'Charisma, my dear. Something that one is born with. A gift, if you like. Guy Richmond could sweet-talk his way into lots of things ... and into the beds of many a young lady, if the rumours were true,' he said with a chuckle. 'He turned their heads, you know.'

'What about his fiancée, Meredith? Wasn't she aware of this?'

Morgan raised his eyebrows. 'His fiancée? You mean Meredith St Claire? Who knows? I didn't meet her very often, I'm told she wasn't a gifted actress, I'm afraid, despite her training. You know that saying: "those who can, do; those who can't, teach".' He shrugged.

'Who told you that?' Molly asked.

Morgan's eyebrows rose, 'Oh, Guy, of course. He wasn't unkind about it, merely realistic.'

'But you had met her?'

'Oh, yes, hanging onto Guy's arm at social occasions. She's a striking-looking young woman. Pity she never made the grade, she'd have been sensational with that angular look of hers, those cheekbones ... almost Cate Blanchett, don't you know?'

'But she didn't mind her fiancé having affairs with other women?' Alisha burst out in a tone of indignation.

Morgan laughed gently. 'He was young, he was an actor ... it is what they all seem to do.'

'What did you think of their relationship?' Molly asked,

remembering what Ada Galloway had commented about the pair.

'Oh, if he'd asked my advice, which he didn't, I'd have told him to steer clear of becoming involved in a serious relationship so early on. It gets in the way, you know. Much better to stay single if you have a fan base. Just look at all these top pop stars.'

'What was he like, as a person?'

'A nicely brought up American boy,' Morgan began. 'Sowing his wild oats but quite determined to follow his dreams. I don't think he would have hurt Meredith. He was, as I said, a nice chap but I do believe he might have changed his mind about her later, if she'd tried to tie him down, but she wasn't that type. She was a follower, you know. Would have gone along with all of Guy's plans. Well, who wouldn't, especially if she hoped to be married to a man with that sort of fortune and the expectation of fame?' he added cynically.

'Here's another question, Mr Morgan,' Molly said slowly. 'Have you any idea who would have wanted to harm Guy Richmond?'

Morgan pursed his lips together thoughtfully before replying.

'You know, I have been thinking a lot about this ever since the news and manner of his death,' he said. 'I wonder ...' He broke off with a frown.

'Go on,' Molly said.

He looked up at her, the customary twinkle now lost from his eyes. 'I wondered if it was some sort of stunt. A publicity stunt gone wrong.'

'Really?'

'Someone pretends to cut his throat, someone else is on hand to take a picture then ... did Guy slip, was the blade only meant to rest against his neck? Was it, in fact, a tragic accident?'

Molly stared at him for a moment. Morgan was a nice man who probably wanted the world to be a less cruel sort of place. But, with the death of Sarra Milroy, surely there could be no possibility that Richmond's had been accidental?

She kept those thoughts to herself as she rose from her seat.

'Well, thanks for your time, sir.' She nodded towards Morgan.

'My pleasure,' he replied with a courteous bow.

As the agent walked them towards the door, Molly stopped to look at one of the many posters on the wall, the image of a young woman dressed in flowing robes, her chin resting on one hand. Her name, in black capitals beneath, **ANNE PETERS**.

'That picture,' Molly said, turning to the theatrical agent. 'Was she one of your actresses?'

'Ah, yes,' Morgan replied, stopping beside Molly to look at the poster. 'Poor Anne. Such talent, such a dreadful pity.' He turned to both women. 'She developed multiple sclerosis, you know. Ended her acting career for good, though she did teach for a bit in the Conservatoire. In a wheelchair by then.' He sighed and shook his head. 'Anne Peters could have been a household name by now. Poor thing died a few years ago. No family, sadly. Husband must be retired by now.'

Molly felt a cold sensation running down her spine. Was

the incident between the dead man and Anne Peters something they ought to be considering? Perhaps.

'Do you think that is a possibility, ma'am?' Alisha asked as they left the building near St George's Cross. 'Could Guy Richmond's death have happened the way he described?'

'An accident? Two people there at that loch on a dark Sunday night?' Molly drew her brows down and shook her head. 'I don't think so. Perhaps Mr Morgan was being a little bit fanciful. Or maybe he simply could not fathom why anybody would want to kill Guy Richmond.'

Molly was silent for a few moments as they walked back to where they'd parked the car.

Alisha slipped into the driver's seat. 'He seemed a nice old fellow, Mr Morgan.'

'He is,' Molly said. 'And I suspect he was good at doling out advice to his clients. I think his notion of a publicity stunt gone wrong is a bit far-fetched, though I'll certainly be interested to know what the rest of the team make of it.'

However, as her DC drove back to Helen Street, Molly's thoughts turned to the widower who had found the body in that out-of-the-way loch, and his late wife, Anne Peters. Glasgow was a village, some said, and paths crossed more often than one might imagine. Still, it might be something to bear in mind, especially after Fairbairn's revelation about how Guy Richmond had treated the actress. Could this possibly show a significant link with the murder victims?

CHAPTER THIRTY-ONE

William Lorimer did not normally take an instant dislike to anyone he'd met for the first time, but the man sitting opposite was an exception. What was that old rhyme Maggie's mum used to recite?

I do not like thee, Doctor Fell.
The reason why, I cannot tell.

'Superintendent Lorimer.' Jeremy Standish gave the tall detective a long, lingering look as if assessing him for a part in a play. Then he smiled and shook his head. 'Terrible business, just terrible,' he repeated, giving an exaggerated sigh.

They were standing at the front of the theatre where Lorimer had asked to meet the director. Scene of crime tape was still barring the way in, but Lorimer lifted it with one gloved hand and nodded to Standish. The man raised his eyebrows as if it was somehow beneath his dignity to stoop, but nevertheless he skipped under with surprising agility.

'Here, you'd be better to put these on, sir,' Lorimer said, handing Standish a pair of bootees and matching blue gloves.

Standish took his time to lean against the wall and made a bit of a stramash putting on the protective overshoes, sighing now and then as if it were all a bit of an unnecessary palaver. At last, they were both kitted out to enter the building safely and Lorimer led the way, nodding to the uniformed officer on duty at the back door.

'I think we'll start in the office,' Lorimer said, placing his feet carefully on the metal treads that led along the corridor.

'Fine by me,' Standish murmured, looking around as if seeing the place for the first time. And in a way he was, Lorimer decided, looking back at the man. He was seeing these familiar surroundings as a scene of crime, something that was entirely new to the director.

'Let's have a chat here,' Lorimer said, pulling out a chair and offering it to Standish while he seated himself behind the office desk, the telephone close to hand. It was an old-fashioned Bakelite model, updated by British Telecom and plugged into a socket in the wall, the sort of appliance more usually seen in old films or in TV adaptations of Agatha Christie novels. More interestingly, it was on a different line from the main switchboard, something Sarra Milroy's killer may have known.

'Were you in the habit of using this, sir?' Lorimer asked, gesturing towards the telephone.

'That old thing?' Standish gave a snort of laughter. 'No, can't recall that I was. I used the mobile, don't you know,' he said brightly, flicking a blue-gloved finger through his moustache with the air of a gentleman from a bygone era. 'Much more convenient, m'boy.'

Lorimer found the man's attitude interesting, as if he had a need to act out a character, a way of distancing himself from the reality of these two murders. For a moment he wondered what his friend and sometime colleague, Solomon Brightman, would make of this odd scenario. Still, he'd pretend to ignore it for now.

'It had incoming calls, though?'

'Oh yes, sounded like being in a wind tunnel, mind you. Distorted one's speech. Not a good way to be articulate. Can't stand sloppy speech, people can be so damned lazy when they talk, don't you think?' he added, deliberately emphasising the T and K sounds as if demonstrating a point to this policeman and inferring that the detective superintendent probably knew no better.

'Had you ever heard any of your actors' voices on that telephone?'

Standish stared over Lorimer's shoulder, stroking his bearded chin thoughtfully, again his gesture all part of whatever act he was playing out.

Then, turning his gaze back to the detective superintendent he shook his head and smiled. 'Nope,' he said, making a popping noise with his lips as he uttered the word. It was almost as if he was trying to make a farce of this interview, and that was beginning to annoy Lorimer.

'A call was made from this phone on the night that Sarra Milroy fell to her death,' he said quietly but clearly, staring at the man for a long moment until Standish dropped his gaze.

'It was late. A good while after the caretaker had locked up for the night.'

Standish frowned under his bristly eyebrows. 'So? What do you expect me to say about that?'

'Where were you between ten p.m. and midnight on the night in question?' Lorimer asked, unwittingly falling into the old-fashioned parlance that Standish had initiated.

'Where I always am, Lorimer,' he said stiffly. 'Having a nice glass of malt. Last orders at the Curlers then home.'

Lorimer nodded. The Curlers, or the Curlers Rest to give it its full name, was a popular pub in Byres Road, a ten-minute walk from where Standish lived. Last orders might well have been called at a quarter to midnight, enough time for someone to have driven from the theatre in Paisley and sauntered up to the bar.

'Can anyone verify that, sir?' Lorimer asked, his tone quite bland.

Standish drew himself up, back rigid, bristling with an indignation that was wholly theatrical. 'Now look here, Detective, I have several witnesses at the Curlers who can tell you of my whereabouts. Do I have to search them out for you?'

'Possibly, sir. We will want to know the whereabouts of several people who were close to Miss Milroy.'

'Close? What do you mean by close! Good heavens, man! She was a mere child! You don't think I had any interest in her? Preposterous!' Standish exclaimed, thumping a blue-clad fist onto the table between them.

Was this man protesting too much? Or was his act designed to throw Lorimer off? He could not be quite certain

202

and again he thought of Solly and how he might interpret the director's behaviour.

'Were you intending to allocate a part to Sarra?' he asked, changing the subject.

'Well, yes, quite a good part, in fact. Lucy, Sweeney Todd's young wife. There isn't much for her to say except at the start and a few lines in the last act. She's still ... I mean she *was* ... just an aspiring actress. Might have had real star potential ... ' he mused.

'But we will never know now, will we?' Lorimer reminded him, quietly, still staring into the man's eyes.

'No,' Standish said and gave a quick sigh that seemed the most genuine reaction he had made since they had encountered one another at the theatre.

'Have you any idea who might have wanted to harm her?' Lorimer asked.

Standish pursed his lips. 'No, nobody. She didn't have an enemy in the world, not that I knew of at any rate. She wasn't long out of school, doted on all of the cast. Especially Guy. So eager to be helpful,' he added, as if remembering something. 'Nothing was too much trouble for her.'

'So, it would not come as a surprise if someone asked her to arrive at the theatre late at night?'

Standish frowned. 'It would certainly be a surprise but ... well, she was a bit gullible, if you want to know the truth. Took everyone at face value. Yes,' he broke off with a slow nod, 'so, yes. That would be like her to drop everything to do a favour for ... '

'For ... ?"

Standish moved uneasily in his seat. 'One of us,' he said at last, giving Lorimer a mournful look.

Having just seen the basement and the director's office so far, Lorimer asked Standish for a tour. The theatre was much bigger than it appeared from outside. The main auditorium was a traditional shape, curved around the central stage, the Corinthian-styled capitals atop the columns painted in gold. There were rows of seating in the stalls, the familiar red plush seats that he associated with his infrequent visits to the theatre, and balconies above, including a box at either side of the dress circle. The stage itself was as big as any he had seen in Glasgow theatres, the pit now a darkened empty space.

Standish led him backstage, pointing out the technical equipment then taking him down a few steps and along a narrow passageway.

'Dressing rooms in here,' Standish said, opening one door after another to allow Lorimer to look inside.

There was a smell of linseed oil, Lorimer thought, then, catching sight of a bank of mirrors with bare downlights, he realised that it was probably greasepaint. This was where these strange transformations took place to change a mere mortal into a playwright's character. He followed the director, listening to his comments about plays he had produced in the past and well-known actors he'd directed. Behind the stage area was a large hall.

'Was this always here?' Lorimer asked, wondering if it was an annexe from the original building.

'Yes. Even back in the day there was the need for

corporate sponsorship. We use it as an entertainment suite.' Standish nodded towards a bar area that had a steel shutter locking it shut. 'We open it before and during performances. Got a proper licence, of course,' he said, tossing his head as if Lorimer were about to challenge him on that. 'We have part-time bar staff who freelance if we are hosting a big group, students mainly, as well as our full-time staff in the theatre bars.'

Lorimer nodded. He would ask for their details before he left.

'By the way, I have to warn you that there may be a visit from Health and Safety in the near future. Not only is there a distinct lack of security inside and outside the theatre but the lack of a handrail to the basement is something that will have to be sorted. Once the press get hold of that snippet of information, they'll point the finger at the theatre's management.'

Standish did not reply, merely nodded, a worried expression on his face.

Later, after Standish had given him his tour of the theatre, pointing out all the different areas that Sarra and the rest of the group used regularly, Lorimer bade him goodbye, waiting at the front of the theatre till Standish had walked away, turned a corner, then disappeared from sight. He retraced his steps and re-entered the building.

It was a veritable rabbit warren of a place and now that he was alone, the lights extinguished, he saw that there were many dark corners in which Sarra Milroy's killer may have hidden. The auditorium itself, with its balconies and curving staircase where a person might linger unseen in its shadows; the dressing rooms with their smell of greasepaint; even some hidden angles in the technical area backstage. He trod carefully now in the dim light, lest he disturb any wires trailing from monitors to equipment on a table. There were several that would have been perfect places for someone waiting for Sarra's arrival. A few swift steps to encounter the girl at the top of the basement steps, the door already open ... then one fatal shove.

It would have to be a person familiar with this place, as Lorimer had already told the team. Someone who had lured the girl to the theatre late at night. Someone whom she had trusted.

A quick call was all it took for the action to begin on finding out whether Jeremy Standish's alibi could be verified. He was not in a hurry to eliminate the man, despite his protestations about his vast seniority to the dead girl. Motive was a puzzle, of course, but means and opportunity had also to be established. And Lorimer knew the very person who enjoyed a thoughtful conversation about all three.

CHAPTER THIRTY-TWO

'Hello, this is a pleasant surprise,' the dark-haired man said, his brown eyes smiling behind tortoiseshell-rimmed spectacles. 'Come for a cup of tea? Or to pick my ageing brains?'

Lorimer sat down with a thud into one of the chairs by the window that overlooked University Avenue. 'Tea first, if you don't mind, Solly.' He grinned. 'And yes, there is something I'd love to discuss with you, though it might be a wee bit close to home.'

Solly smiled but said no more as he filled the kettle jug and plugged it back in. The evidence of recent tutorials lay all around, small piles of books, printouts of essays and a wastepaper bin full of crumpled biscuit wrappers. Several unwashed mugs littered the floor beneath Solly's ancient wooden table where the kettle began to hum quietly.

'Busy day?' Lorimer asked, eyeing the detritus of Solly's office post-seminar, an empty biscuit tin with only a few crumbs lurking in its corner.

'Here you are. I've left the bag in as you like it so strong,' Solly said, handing Lorimer a chipped white mug with a green shamrock on one side. 'Biscuit?' he offered, looking around hopefully as if a new packet might somehow materialise from nowhere.

'I'm all right, thanks,' Lorimer told him, suspecting (correctly) that Solly's students had gobbled up the last of his stash.

'Really good to see you,' Solly said once more. 'Rosie has kept me up to date with this case. I take it that is why you're here?'

Lorimer poured a little milk into his mug, stirred it a few times then squeezed the bag against the side of the mug before reaching over and dropping it into the bin. 'Aye,' he replied. It was always good to have a talk with the professor of psychology who had supplied the police with criminal profiles in past cases. Solly was more than a colleague who assisted in murder cases, though – he was a good friend. Bouncing ideas off this man sometimes helped to clarify Lorimer's own mind since Solly had a way of looking at things that often made him see them in a different light.

'It is a difficult one for us all. Not much progress yet, and these theatrical types are making it even harder. Putting on an act, some of them; well, most of them probably. It's what they do, isn't it? Assume a part.'

Solly nodded, his dark eyes full of sympathy. 'Abby was stopped by a reporter from the *Gazette*,' he murmured, changing the subject for a moment.

'Yes, you've got a sensible lass there, Solly. She messaged me right away. The school is doing all it can to protect the kids and to stop them from talking to reporters, but outside their gates, there isn't much the staff can do.'

'But that's not why you've come to visit, is it?'

'No. It's more complicated than that. You see I am not convinced that these actors are telling us the truth. I had Standish, the director, in the theatre today, and he put on this absurd, almost comical persona. Like an actor from the 1930s.'

'The Golden Age of Crime Fiction,' Solly murmured.

'Yes, that struck me, too. But why? What was his need to adopt that sort of act?'

'He was hiding behind it?'

Lorimer nodded his agreement. 'Yes, but why? What is his motive? Standish has everything to lose with Guy Richmond out of the picture.' He went on, explaining to the professor how the role of Sweeney Todd might have catapulted its star to a West End show and brought kudos to the provincial theatre company.

'Now with this other death, St James's will only attract adverse publicity. Plus, it is doubtful whether the show can proceed now that their theatre is a crime scene.'

'And who would want to do that?' Solly suggested, thoughtfully stroking his beard.

Lorimer stared at him for a moment. 'You think Sarra Milroy's death was a deliberate attempt to stop the play going on?'

'It is certainly one motive, though I'm sure you have others in mind,' Solly said, eyeing Lorimer with a smile that invited further confidences.

'At this point there are several people who might have had a motive to kill Guy Richmond, but this latest death simply baffles me. Until we can find out more about the young woman, I'm stymied for a reason behind her death.'

'Money?'

'She had nothing on her person when she was found, but I think we can rule out a mugging. The last known phone call to her mobile, which is still missing by the way, was made from the theatre office. Forensics have examined it thoroughly of course but not a single trace of a fingerprint was on that old Bakelite phone.'

'An old Bakelite model? Interesting.'

'It was modernised to plug into the wall like any other handset, but to be honest it looked like something from their props cupboard.'

'Someone liked the old-fashioned style,' Solly mused. 'And your director chappy put on this sort of persona. I wonder if he was instrumental in choosing that particular phone for the office?'

I could find out,' Lorimer sighed. 'Looks more like something left over from the war years. But I can't see how that will get us any further forward.'

'Probably not,' Solly agreed. 'So, let's look at your *dramatis personae.*'

Lorimer smiled. 'Well, the fellow who has replaced Richmond as Sweeney Todd will get any plaudits going if it eventually reaches an audience,' he began. 'Then there's the props manager, Ahmed Patel. Richmond had some sort of fling with Patel's sister, and the props manager had a go at him. Could it be a killing to avenge his sister's honour?'

'Have you spoken to Miss Patel?'

'Not yet. She's currently at the University of Dundee,'

Lorimer said. 'One of our team tried to track her down but couldn't find her in halls. Or anywhere else, for that matter.'

'She should be back home soon,' Solly reminded him. 'Easter break has already begun for some of our students, though you might not think it.' He looked ruefully at the messy floor. 'I'd guess she'll be back in the family home fairly soon. Unless you think that Patel is worried about her?'

Lorimer nodded. 'We've no evidence that Ahmed is worried but since we've had information about how he assaulted Richmond, it's important we speak to his sister as soon as possible.'

'Who else might be under suspicion?'

'There's a drug dealer we have our eye on,' Lorimer told him. 'Visited the fiancé just after I'd been there. Richmond owed him money apparently, but I honestly can't see that as a valid reason for slitting the man's throat and dumping him into the water.'

'A sign to others, perhaps?' Solly mused. 'See what you get if you don't pay up on time? But, no, I agree that is unlikely, given that Richmond was a wealthy young man.'

'It was the deliberate use of that cut-throat razor that seems to point to one of the actors,' Lorimer said. 'We've still to establish a motive but the means was just too handy for them all. The razor was in the props cupboard till someone removed it. And cleaned its box completely,' he added with a wry look at Solly.

'All carefully planned and worked out then,' Solly agreed. 'What about his fiancée, Abby's drama teacher?'

Lorimer gave a sigh. 'She inherits his vast wealth, right enough, but if they had married there would have been no need to worry about money. From what we've seen of her I think Meredith St Claire would have been happier with him still alive and having a future together.'

'How does she seem to you?'

'Every time we've spoken she appears to be devastated,' Lorimer answered with a frown.

Solly stroked his beard thoughtfully as he listened to his friend.

'And Molly? How does she feel about the heartbroken fiancée?'

'I think she's been very supportive of her,' Lorimer assured him. 'Think how she'd feel if it was Daniel.'

'So, let's set aside money, for the moment. What about the old "green-eyed monster that doth mock the meat it feeds on"?' Solly asked, quoting from *Othello*.

'Well, there is an interesting strand there. Not only did the actor replacing Richmond have an envy of him getting the plum parts, but he used to be the boyfriend of his fiancée.'

'And now? What is their relationship?'

Lorimer thought about that for a minute. Nigel Fairbairn had seemed more absorbed with his career, but then ... he was an actor ... had he too been playing a part during his interview with the detectives? Lorimer liked to think he was adept at sussing out people after all this time, but had they skills that might outwit even the most experienced officer?'

'That might be worth keeping an eye on,' he admitted. 'Though the fiancée does not seem to be in touch with any of Richmond's colleagues from what we've seen. Besides, Fairbairn's career would only have suffered if the play was cancelled after Sarra's death.'

'Your breakthrough will come when you find a proper link between the two deaths,' Solly told him. 'A different modus operandi does not mean that the killer hadn't planned each of their deaths carefully.'

As he drove across the city, Lorimer pondered the psychologist's words. Was there one of these players capable of both killings? Anybody could have pushed Sarra to her death, though how could they be sure that the fall would kill her? That suggested a risk taker, surely? And to lead Richmond to that lonely loch, slit his throat from behind ... a tall man who had gripped him firmly, had enough guts to do the deed and push him into the loch afterwards? Desmond Dylan Morgan's idea of a publicity stunt had been mere fantasy, the team had agreed.

He imagined the scenario, the dark water before them, Richmond groggy from the drugs he'd been given, easily overpowered. But it must have taken some nerve to draw that blade across his throat.

Was it done by someone playing a part right there and then? His thoughts flitted to Fairbairn, the smaller than average fellow who was now in the lead role. Taking his place in a play, no matter how profitable the consequences for his future fame, seemed an unlikely motive. But if he added the availability of the woman he had once loved – perhaps still did – then that might create sufficient reason to do away with his rival, in turn giving him access to Meredith's inheritance.

The only problem was, why then kill Sarra Milroy? Solly was right. Tie those two together and perhaps he might then find their suspect.

CHAPTER THIRTY-THREE

The woman in the orange and tan sari stood looking at them speculatively. 'You want to see our Jasmine? Why? What is this all about? She is just home from the university, and she has to study for her final exams,' she scolded, her small frame barring the way of the two detectives. 'You've already upset my Ahmed. Now you want to bother Jasmine?'

'I am sorry, ma'am,' DS Giles apologised. 'But this is a murder enquiry and we really do need to speak to your daughter.'

Mrs Patel looked from the detective sergeant to his female companion, her eyes lingering on Alisha for a long moment.

'You seem like a nice young woman,' she said softly. 'You understand these things—'

At that moment a squally wind swept a shower of rain and wet leaves into the porch, making Mrs Patel step back.

'You had better come in,' she said stiffly, pursing her lips in a disapproving line.

They followed the woman through a pleasant reception hallway and into a small sitting room where a dark-haired girl in skinny jeans and a roll-necked sweater sat surrounded by books and papers, a laptop on her knee.

'Jasmine, these police officers are here to see you,' Mrs Patel announced.

The girl looked up, her large dark eyes reminding Davie of a startled deer.

'Hello.' He smiled, offering a hand for her to shake. 'I'm Detective Sergeant Giles and this is my colleague, Detective Constable Mohammed.'

Jasmine Patel sat awkwardly, trying to balance the laptop at the same time as shaking hands with each of the police officers. Like her mother, she was more inclined to stare at Alisha.

'We tried to find you up in Dundee, but I think you must have returned home by the time we arrived.' Alisha smiled warmly.

Jasmine was sitting up very straight, long black hair cascading down her back, hands clasping each side of the laptop.

'We're part of the Major Incident Team investigating the deaths of Guy Richmond and Sarra Milroy,' Alisha explained.

Jasmine's mouth dropped open as she transferred her gaze to Davie, an expression of panic on her pretty face.

'Mum, you don't need to be here,' she said, staring at Mrs Patel until the woman muttered something inaudible and scurried out of the room, leaving her daughter alone with the two detectives.

'Miss Patel—' Davie began.

'I've not done anything wrong,' she interrupted, her voice high and shrill.

'We aren't here to accuse you of anything, Miss Patel. We are hoping you might help us with some background enquiries,' Davie told her gently. 'Nothing to be scared of.' He smiled as he noticed the girl flick her hair from behind her ears, letting it fall either side of her face, an unconscious gesture signalling a desire to protect herself.

'We're investigating the death of the actor Guy Richmond,' Davie continued. 'Can you tell us how you knew him?'

Jasmine kept her head down and said nothing for a moment then mumbled, 'Ahmed took me to the theatre, showed me the backstage area. He thought I'd like to see what goes on behind the scenes.'

'And . . . ?'

She shrugged. 'That's all. I met him there . . . ' She looked up at them, tears filling her eyes. 'I thought he was nice . . . friendly . . . ' She shook her head and sighed. 'He was a good-looking man, I thought . . . I thought . . . ' She stopped then, swallowing hard.

'What did you think, Jasmine?' Alisha asked.

'I imagined it would be fun when he asked me to go out for a drink. That was all.' She raised her head and looked at them, a spark of defiance in her expression. 'I wasn't doing anything wrong. I didn't lead him on, you have to believe me!'

'It came to our notice that your brother was angry with Guy Richmond after he had . . . tried it on with you . . . shall we say?'

Jasmine's face darkened. 'Don't!' she said firmly. 'Just don't try to belittle what he did to me!'

'Did Guy Richmond assault you?' Alisha asked quietly, her expression softening as she saw the tears begin.

Jasmine looked down at her hands, her long hair hiding her face as though she were ashamed to look at the two detectives.

'We need to know what happened, Jasmine,' Alisha told her.

'It wasn't my fault,' the girl whispered. 'I thought he was just being nice, asking me out for a drink ... ' She looked up suddenly in alarm. 'You won't tell my parents, please? We're not supposed to take any alcohol, but it was just a couple of cocktails.'

'Did he spike your drink?' Davie asked.

Jasmine shook her head. 'No, I wasn't woozy or anything, just a bit giggly. Then he asked me to go and visit the theatre again. Said he wanted to show me around while it was empty.'

'When was this?'

She paused for a moment before answering. Then she took a deep breath.

'November the second. Before last Christmas. They'd been rehearsing for the pantomime earlier that day. Guy was Aladdin.' She sniffed. 'He said ... he said ... I'd make a lovely leading lady because I was his Jasmine ... and then ... '

She burst into sudden tears, rocking to and fro so that Davie had to swoop forward, and catch the laptop as it began to fall.

Alisha immediately came to sit beside the distressed girl, an arm about her shoulders, offering her a clean, folded handkerchief. 'Hey, it's all right, it's all right.'

After a few hiccups, Jasmine dried her tears, gulping, 'I'm sorry, I'm sorry ... '

'Right, now, take your time and tell us exactly what happened,' Alisha soothed.

Jasmine wriggled free from the other girl's arm, shifting slightly as though any human touch was unwanted.

Then she gave a long sigh and looked straight at Davie Giles.

'You want to know what happened,' she said. 'Well, I'll tell you. Guy Richmond raped me.'

The shame attached to the event had been too much for the girl to go to the police, she told them, but her brother, Ahmed, had found her in a terrible state after Jasmine had taken a cab back home. When DS Giles asked if Ahmed was at home, Jasmine's brother was summoned from his room upstairs to verify Jasmine's account. Yes, he insisted, she had told him the truth of what had happened, resulting in his assault on Richmond. They'd left them there together, Mrs Patel still none the wiser why two detectives had needed to call on her daughter.

'And neither incident was reported,' Davie told Molly when he and Alisha were back in the office. 'Richmond never admitted to what he'd done, told Ahmed that Jasmine had been a willing partner. And the poor girl could never bring herself to go to the police.'

'It would have been her word against his,' Molly said grimly. 'It makes a sort of sense, but it is far too late now to establish whether Richmond did rape the girl or if she had let things go too far and had been too scared to tell him to stop. We may never really know.'

'She was in a real state when the brother saw her,' Davie went on. 'The parents and other siblings were never told a thing and she has begged us to keep it that way.'

'Richmond is dead now, so, unless we find that this was a motive for Patel to kill him, then it could remain their secret.'

'Why wait all those months?' Davie asked.

'Why indeed? Patel had the motive and the means. Was he simply waiting for the opportunity?'

CHAPTER THIRTY-FOUR

.

'My next rest day is Sunday,' Daniel said. 'A good opportunity to have lunch out somewhere nice. If Molly could join us that would be even better.'

'Oh, are we going to Stirling Castle, then?' Netta asked. 'You'd like that, Janette. You have tae see the view frae the esplanade. An' then mibbe we can have lunch?'

Janette Kohi smiled. 'I would like that very much,' she said. 'But you must let me pay. It should be my treat. After all, I am staying here as your guest, and you have not let me buy a thing!'

'No need, Mum—' Daniel began, but his mother raised her hand to stop him.

'I have plenty of money, Daniel. The sale of your plot . . .' She let her hand fall. 'Oh, my dear, I don't mean to upset you,' she said, seeing Daniel turn away for a moment.

'You did the right thing,' he said. 'Richard and Campbell Mlambo now have space to build a bigger home for themselves next to my old neighbour Joseph and look after him.

And legally, that was yours to sell. After all', he gave them a rueful grin, 'I was supposed to be dead and buried. It was your inheritance.'

Netta watched them, gnarled hands wringing her apron as she listened. It had been a terrible thing, those wicked people burning Daniel's home to the ground, killing his wife and child and thinking that Daniel had also perished in the fire. But his good neighbour, Joseph Mlambo, and his pastor had spirited him away, leaving Janette and just a handful of close friends to know the truth. Happily, Lorimer and his wife had helped to bring Janette to Scotland, her airfare paid for after the sale of Daniel's property.

'Well, perhaps we should all jist pay for wurselves,' Netta suggested, before Daniel could argue any further. 'An' see if your Molly can manage a day aff. She's been workin' that hard oan these murder cases, so she has. Lassie deserves a wee break.'

Molly glanced at her mobile as the text came through. Daniel. Her face softened as she thought of him, his kind smile and the way he held her close. *Never let me go*, she had told him recently, murmuring into his pillow. She read the message, a smile lighting up her eyes. *Yes. Count me in*, she replied, pressing the X button several times. There was no reason to be here on Sunday, Molly persuaded herself. She hadn't had a break for days and besides, she'd been busy handing out so many actions and doing all the work of an SIO that she deserved a day off. Lorimer would approve, too, she reasoned. He'd always told his team that their relentless hours on the job made for fatigue. And he'd dinned into them that detective work required them to keep up their energy levels and sustain a clear mind. She smiled at the memory. Lorimer didn't always practise what he preached, working all hours whenever a difficult case demanded his attention, endless mugs of black coffee sustaining him.

There was no answer. Again. He had tried the cottage landline, but it simply rang out until the answering service kicked in, plus Meredith's mobile appeared to have been switched off. Lorimer frowned. It was odd. He had been given the impression that the grieving woman wanted to be at home. Hadn't she seemed to be finding a little peace and comfort in domesticity on his previous visit? He remembered that tranquil scene watching Meredith hanging out her laundry, singing some folk song, not realising that Lorimer had been her audience.

The haunting music came back to him now, the Selkie of Sulskerry. It was an old legend about a seal, or selkie, that transformed into a man once it was on land, leaving its sealskin behind. There was something in that song that reminded him of shapeshifting legends. Didn't actors do much the same, donning a mask to appear other than themselves? He brushed the fleeting memory away to concentrate on where he might find the drama teacher.

He wanted to ask Meredith about Jasmine Patel's claim, and only a face-to-face meeting would be appropriate, given the delicate nature of the incident. Had she known about Ahmed's attack on Guy? And, if so, had she been given any idea what had prompted it?

He looked up at the clock and sighed. There really

wasn't time for him to drive over and pay a visit until later this evening. Perhaps he and the family liaison officer might go together? Another woman, one whom she already knew, might help her to discuss the matter. It was a horrible situation, not just for Ahmed's sister, but for the drama teacher, too.

A ping on his computer alerted Lorimer to an incoming message. Could it be Meredith St Claire returning his calls? He read the email and scrolled down to open the attachment, his eyes crinkling into a grin as he saw the dark face of PC Daniel Kohi staring intently from the new Police Scotland poster. Soon the Zimbabwean's image would adorn the noticeboards of every division in the country, as well as billboards, railway stations and the subway walls here in Glasgow. The poster campaign with its image of the handsome black Zimbabwean was intended to add strength to their anti-racist message; *anyone can make a difference by becoming a police officer here in Scotland, ours is a police force that welcomes every race and colour to its fold.* How proud he had been to watch as Daniel Kohi marched in his passing-out parade, wearing the uniform of Police Scotland, and how pleased he would continue to be watching the younger man as he aspired to his role as a detective.

Was this the feeling a father might have for his son? Lorimer suddenly wondered. Solly would probably have nodded that wise head of his had he asked him. He was getting old, he thought to himself. Fifty now, with his goddaughter a teenager already. His thoughts turned to the way he had met Meredith St Claire at Abby's school. He would keep trying the woman's number, then, if there was still no reply, maybe the FLO would agree to accompany him this evening.

Heather chattered brightly at his side as they left the city behind and climbed the road that led to their destination. It was a clear March evening, the nights lighter now, the sun setting by seven o'clock, the western skies bright with the promise of stars to be seen. His companion was enjoying their journey through the countryside, commenting on the new lambs that were big enough now to run and leap, their antics a source of delight.

'Poor woman, such a lovely wee spot to live, but all alone now,' Heather remarked with a sigh. 'I'd love a place like this. See how that side window catches the setting sun.'

Lorimer pulled into the narrow farm road that led to Meredith St Claire's cottage and parked. 'Right, let's hope she doesn't mind another visit so soon,' he said.

'Well, here's a wee cheery-up flower,' Heather replied, clutching a bouquet of red and yellow tulips, chosen for the drama teacher's penchant for vivid colours.

Lorimer rang the bell and heard it echo through the house but there was no answer.

'Maybe she's around the back,' he suggested, starting to walk in that direction, the FLO close on his heels. But when they came to the back door, it was firmly locked. 'No washing out on the line.'

'And no car in the drive,' Heather added. 'You're tall enough to see in the side window of the garage to look for it, aren't you, sir?'

Lorimer strolled further along the driveway and squeezed

in between a hedge and the side of the garage to peer into the back window.

'Nope. Nothing here. She's gone out,' he sighed.

'Oh, what a pity. I had hoped to talk to the poor woman again,' Heather said. She wandered back to the front of the house, crossed the grass and looked in the lounge window.

Lorimer heard his colleague gasp.

'Sir! Come and see! I think there's been a break-in!'

In three strides he was by Heather's side, peering over her shoulder to see inside the room.

It looked as if a fight had taken place, the coffee table lay on its side, broken glass littered the floor and a table lamp had been wrenched from its socket.

Lorimer pulled out his phone and tapped out the number then looked at Heather, his expression grim. 'I don't like this. She's gone missing and this place has been turned over. We need to have a look inside.'

The family liaison officer nodded, knowing that a police presence would soon be there, and that any crime scene should not be contaminated. However, she was wearing leather gloves and approaching the front door, she turned the handle.

It opened noiselessly.

'Sir! Look!' Heather took a step back and pointed to the floor where thin slivers of wood lay to one side. It was not hard to see that the door had been forced, long scars on the paintwork near the lock.

'Should we go in, sir?'

Lorimer nodded, his face worried. 'She could be lying unconscious somewhere. But be careful. Scene of crime officers will not want any contamination.' He pulled out a pair of nitrile gloves and put them on before entering the cottage.

'Meredith! Meredith! Are you in there?' he called. But there was no answer, just the hollow sound of his own voice falling in the stale air as if they were alone in this house.

There was a scattering of mail on the floor directly beneath the letter box and he stooped to pick it up.

'Looks like this has been lying here for at least a day,' Lorimer murmured. 'Go through to the kitchen, Heather. Check if she's there.' Then he raced up the stairs, looking into each room. All was as he had seen it before except for the couple's bedroom where he paused for a moment, shocked to see the picture of Richmond lying ruined on the floor.

There was no sign of the missing woman.

'No one here,' Heather's voice came from below, confirming his suspicion that they were alone in the cottage.

He hurried back down and looked more closely into the room where he had recently talked with Meredith St Claire.

'Good grief!' he said quietly, blinking as he saw the mess. Every picture of Guy Richmond had been wrenched from the walls, now peppered with dark holes, and smashed as if in a frenzy. Some of the photographs had even been yanked from their frames, torn fragments of the late actor's face scattered in a mad collage.

Lorimer sensed Heather come and stand beside him. Then, as she followed his gaze, an expression of horror came across her face.

'This was done by someone who must have hated him a lot,' she said.

Lorimer nodded. 'It doesn't take a detective to come to that conclusion, does it,' he agreed. 'I found another portrait of him vandalised upstairs.'

But what Lorimer did not add were the names of those people who had harboured a grudge against Guy Richmond, enough to wreak havoc on his home. And whoever had done this with such passion might well have been the very person who had murdered Meredith St Claire's fiancé.

Now, more than ever, it was imperative to find Abby's teacher in case she too was in danger.

CHAPTER THIRTY-FIVE

'No fingerprints apart from Richmond's and Meredith's.' Molly sighed. 'They found some smears along the frames, so it looks like the person who pulled these pictures off the walls wore gloves,' she said, an exasperated twist to her mouth.

Lorimer nodded. The cottage had been gone over with meticulous care in the hope that they might find a trace of whoever had smashed up those rooms in the cottage.

'I saw upstairs is just the same,' Molly added, referring to the huge poster of Guy that had been ripped to shreds and strewn over the floor. 'Only the guest bedroom and Meredith's study were unharmed,' she said. 'And the garage, which was padlocked. No sign of an intruder trying to break in there.'

'It's as if some malicious spite has been deliberately taken out only on places with Richmond's image. Someone really hated him,' he murmured, echoing Heather Crawford's words. He paused for a moment, pondering an idea that had flickered through his mind several times before being dismissed. An idea that might cause him sleepless nights were he to follow it up.

'Any word from Meredith?' Molly asked.

Lorimer shook his head. 'Goodness knows where she is. Her phone is still switched off.'

'Let's see what this might show us,' Molly said, indicating the landline telephone that had been tipped off a small side table.

Soon Lorimer was listening to his own voice repeatedly asking Meredith St Claire to call him.

'Nothing else on the answering machine,' Molly said at last. 'Do we have any reason to be concerned about her?'

'Well, there's the small matter of her home having been broken into,' he replied with a slight tone of sarcasm.

'Of course,' Molly sighed. 'But surely this happened after she left? You saw the mail in the hallway.'

Lorimer did not reply at once, his eyes staring into space.

'Imagine if Meredith had returned to the cottage and found this mess, would that have been enough to have made her want to leave?' he reasoned.

'Surely she'd have called us,' Molly protested. 'I know she's terribly on edge, who wouldn't be? But a quick call to us would have been the sensible thing to do.'

'We should make every effort to locate her,' he decided. 'We have a killer on the loose ... perhaps the same person who trashed this place so violently ... ' He turned and looked straight at Molly. 'So, yes. She may well be in danger.'

*

Meredith stood at the window looking out over the back court below, then raised her eyes to the rows and rows of chimneys on the nearby rooftops. The sky was a mass of steel grey clouds blotting out a weak sun that had given up the struggle several hours ago.

She could not stay here much longer, she thought, turning back into the room where she had spent so many hours, its four walls now closing in on her.

With a sigh, she picked up the small haversack, fished out her mobile then switched it back on to read her missed calls.

Lorimer. A faint smile tugged at her mouth. He was persistent, she'd give him that, and probably deserved an explanation by now.

She tapped out a message and then paused for a moment. Would he come? Yes, she decided, firmly pressing *send*.

Lorimer looked around the hotel bar until he spotted the woman sitting in a corner, a purple scarf tied over her vivid pink hair.

'Hello,' he said, sitting down opposite her. 'Good to see you alive and well. We've been concerned about you.'

'Hi,' Meredith replied, casting her eyes down for a moment. 'Sorry if I've caused any bother.' She sighed, picking up her coffee cup and taking a sip. 'I just had to get away,' she explained quietly.

'You should have called me,' Lorimer told her. 'Don't forget that two people have been killed.'

'I know, and I'm sorry, but when I saw that reporter arriving . . . well,' she raised a hand and let it fall again, 'I just couldn't face talking to anyone about Guy.'

'When did you leave the cottage?'

'Two days ago,' Meredith replied. 'I just needed some space without these awful people hounding me.'

'And you locked up and drove into the city?'

Meredith nodded. 'I thought it might be good to have a little time to myself. But to be honest, I'm missing the peace and quiet of the cottage,' she said ruefully. 'I'll go back today, once I've seen the solicitor.'

Lorimer regarded the woman thoughtfully. She seemed to be more in control of herself since he had last seen her so perhaps the break in this city hotel had done her some good. Pity to have to spoil whatever solace she'd found here with his news.

'I'm very sorry, Ms St Claire, but the cottage was broken into in your absence and there's rather a lot of mess.'

Meredith looked at him, her eyes widening. '*My* cottage? Are you sure?'

He nodded slowly. 'I hate to have to tell you this. I was worried enough by your absence to make a visit the evening before last. The front door had been forced.'

'What?' She leaned towards him and gripped his hand suddenly. 'Tell me. What have they done?'

Lorimer explained about the smashed glass and the destruction of all the photos of her fiancé as well as the torn poster in their bedroom. As he spoke, he saw the woman's eyes widening in horror, her mouth opening in shock.

'No, no ... how could anybody be so cruel?'

Lorimer did not reply. During his career he had seen so many examples of human cruelty and malicious damage inflicted upon precious things belonging to another.

Sometimes a person's anger was vented in a mindless moment of passion, no thought for the consequences. How often had he seen a drunken brawl resulting in a body lying bleeding on the floor?

'Is ... is there much damage?'

'A lot of broken glass. The scene of crime officers are finished now, so you can go back and begin to clear it up. If you feel up to it,' he added, sliding his hand out of her grasp. 'And I think you might be advised to get a joiner out to repair the door. And maybe even a locksmith to change the locks. I'd also advise having CCTV fitted.'

Meredith gave a huge sigh and shook her head. 'I don't know ... well, I suppose I have to, don't I? I guess this is something you see a lot?' she asked, looking at Lorimer. 'Being a policeman must be a horrid job at times.'

Meredith's words still rang in his ears as Lorimer returned to the Helen Street office. Yes, there had been times when he wished he was anywhere else but a crime scene, the evil deeds that people had perpetrated causing him grief. Once, he had almost given up the job, the carnage at a murder scene too much to bear, taking him down into a dark place. But the rewards of this job outweighed those bad times, ensuring that people who had committed crimes were brought to justice.

Now, it was up to him and to his team to find out who had killed the two young actors. And if that same killer's rage had strewn those broken pictures across the floor of Meredith St Claire's cottage.

*

As Lorimer entered the main door in Helen Street, he stopped suddenly. There was a large noticeboard at reception and there, right in the centre, was the familiar face of Daniel Kohi looking out at him.

'Friend of yours, sir, isn't he?' the desk sergeant asked, nodding towards the poster. 'I mind when he came here that first time, looking for you. Spoke with that funny accent. Poor bloke looked half frozen to death.'

'And what a change in him now,' Lorimer replied proudly. 'An officer of Police Scotland.'

'Aye, it's a grand thing he's doing,' the sergeant remarked. 'Showing that anybody can join up. Make a difference.'

Lorimer smiled and nodded then headed for the stairs leading to the upper floor where the MIT had its offices. So much had changed for Daniel Kohi since that dark winter's day when he had come searching for a detective named Lorimer. Not only had their friendship grown but he had met Molly Newton, resumed his career as a police officer and now had a future here in Scotland.

As he walked along the corridor, Molly appeared at the door of the muster room.

'May I have a word, sir?' she asked.

Lorimer entered the room where officers were busy behind screens, all manner of investigative work being carried out, the minutiae of which might take hours of their patience.

'Something's not right,' Molly said. 'SOCOs have found very little in the way of trace evidence from that break-in. A few hairs, mostly Meredith's, and some DNA relating to Richmond and Pettifer. But it looks as if Ms St Claire was a good wee housewife who kept the place spotless. SOCOs remarked that there was hardly a corner of dust in the entire place.'

Lorimer raised his eyebrows. 'There was never a mention of a cleaner coming in, was there?'

'No, sir. But that's something we need to check with Meredith.'

'Well, we can now,' Lorimer told her. 'I've just left her at the Arthouse hotel in Bath Street.'

'You've seen her?' Molly's eyebrows rose in surprise. 'Is she okay?'

Lorimer nodded. 'She wanted to get away from the attention of reporters,' he said. 'Said they'd been harassing her. But she's going to drive back now that I've told her about the break-in.'

Molly looked at her boss and nodded, but, as he turned away to go into his own office, she looked at him for a few more moments, a frown of disquiet on her face.

CHAPTER THIRTY-SIX

'Okay,' Daniel said, rolling onto his side. 'Out with it. You've been gazing into space all evening. Something's troubling you, isn't it?'

Molly nodded sheepishly. 'What am I like? Thinking about another man while I'm here with you,' she laughed, rolling her eyes.

'Terrible woman!' Daniel teased, taking a strand of her blonde hair and tugging it gently. 'Come on, tell me all.'

Molly sighed and shifted closer to Daniel. 'It's Lorimer,' she said. 'I'm worried about him.'

Daniel propped himself up with an elbow and looked at her. 'Is he ill?'

'No, no, nothing like that. It's just ... ' She bit her lip as if afraid to continue.

'What is it, then?'

'I think he's paying an awful lot of attention to that woman I told you about, Meredith St Claire.'

'The one with pink hair,' Daniel laughed, as if he were finishing a rhyming couplet.

'Aye, her. And it's not funny, really. He seems a bit besotted with her. I mean, he even took the FLO with him to her cottage when she hadn't answered her mobile.'

'He's a careful man, Molly,' Daniel told her, his handsome face becoming serious. 'I don't know anybody quite like him. I don't think you need to worry about his relationship with Maggie either. If he's obsessed by this victim, it's just because he is so keen to see the killer brought to justice.'

'Oh, I don't worry about him and Maggie!' Molly replied quickly. 'It's just ... maybe he's having some sort of mid-life crisis. Sees the woman like the daughter they never had, or something. Solly would be able to put a name to it.'

'He's turned fifty,' Daniel said. 'Do you think that's made some sort of difference to the way he looks at people?'

'Maybe. He's always been a decent boss, very professional but sympathetic, looking beyond an officer's rank ... seeing the human side of everybody's situations.'

'Well, there you have it,' Daniel said. 'Like I said, he sees this woman as a victim of a dreadful crime and realises that she is having a terrible time coming to terms with it all. You did say she was a nervy type of person, right?'

'But that's what an FLO is for,' Molly protested. 'Lorimer doesn't have to go the extra mile. But for some reason he wants to.'

'I shouldn't lose sleep over this,' Daniel told her, curling an arm about her shoulders and drawing her close. 'In fact,

I have the very cure for a sleepless night.' He chuckled, leaning over to kiss her.

Janette stared straight ahead as the road wound its way to their destination. Till now the journey had given her some spectacular views of mountains and moorland, sheep grazing, their little lambs gambolling across the green pastures.

'There it is! Look!'

Netta's voice behind her made the African woman blink. There on a craggy hilltop was a cluster of buildings, one of them shining golden in the morning sun. That was a castle? Janette was not certain whether to be disappointed by the absence of pointed turrets and flags waving or be delighted at the sight. She thought of those days from centuries past when kings had to repel invaders. Yes, this high, craggy hill was a sensible place to have one's stronghold, she realised. And Molly had told her that it was more of a fortress than a Disney castle.

'Wait till ye see the view frae the esplanade,' Netta said. 'And it's a grand clear day the day.'

'Let's hope we can park close to the castle,' Molly reminded Daniel. 'I've got my Historic Scotland pass that entitles me to free entry, but I'll pay for the rest of you.' She tapped Janette on the shoulder. 'My treat.'

'Thank you, my dear,' Janette murmured, covering the younger woman's hand with her own for a moment. Molly was trying to be friendly, she realised, so she must do the same, even though there was a certain sadness in her heart every time that she watched the tall blonde woman walking hand in hand with her son. She must make more of an effort, Janette told herself. And today, she would seek for an opportunity to be nice to Molly.

The city of Stirling was a revelation to the older lady, many of its towering buildings so very old and yes, there were some turreted corners to be seen as the car climbed the steep hill that would lead them to the castle. The street itself was bumpy, full of cobbles and tiny corners that had to be navigated carefully. At last, they drove through a gateway onto a huge open space and Janette saw the imposing entrance to Stirling Castle.

'There! Told you it was magnificent, didn't I?'

Netta had slipped her arm through Janette's and now they were both staring at the panoramic view from the top of the esplanade. A breeze blew through Janette's grizzled curls making her shiver. These Scottish kings and queens must have been hardy creatures to endure life up here, she thought, although they would never have been lost for the spectacular sights below and all around them. Any enemy would have been easily spotted before he could ascend these black rocks, she saw, turning to look down.

'Come on, I bet you're dying for a coffee. Or a cup of tea,' Molly said. 'Let's get in out of this cold and find the café.' She laid an affectionate hand on Janette's shoulder and smiled. 'I'm so pleased you're here. Stirling's a wonderful place, so full of history.'

'Aye, yer heid'll be fair rattlin' wi' a' the information here by the time we're done,' Netta laughed. 'It wis the same fur me first time I came. I cannae mind half the stuff I read oan a' they wee notices.'

'I'm going to buy your mum a guidebook,' Molly said firmly, taking Daniel's hand. 'Then she can read it at her leisure and remember bits from today.'

Janette smiled shyly up at her and was rewarded by Molly's warm grin.

She really was a pretty lady, Janette thought, as the young couple strode ahead of them, despite being so different from dear Chipo. And there was no doubt that she and Daniel were fond of one another.

Leaving the warm cafeteria, Molly glanced at the two older women. Netta was chatting away nineteen to the dozen, pointing out things to the little African lady as if Janette did not understand the signs written in English and needed them translated, a shy smile on Janette's face as Netta explained every one of Historic Scotland's notices. Once she even intercepted a wry look between his mother and Daniel but not a word was spoken. She was bearing it all with patience and good humour, Molly realised, and the DI found herself hoping that Janette Kohi was enjoying the visit and not becoming bored.

'Oh, look!' Daniel stopped and signalled to the other three as they turned a corner. They were still a short distance away but there was no mistaking the grand figure of Mary, Queen of Scots and her entourage of fine ladies, surrounded by a group of tourists and their guide.

She was indeed a stately personage, her black costume and white ruff a stark contrast to the golden hair peeping out from under a white headdress and billowing gossamer veil. The woman's face was painted white, with the merest hint of pink on each cheek, possibly testament to the brisk wind swirling around the castle.

Daniel signalled for them to draw closer, as several other visitors were now doing, to hear what was being said.

Molly was on the edge of a small crowd by the time they reached the Queen and her courtiers but could hear every word as Mary spoke in an accent tinged with her French heritage. The DI looked at Daniel, his mother and Netta, glad to see that they were evidently enraptured by this unexpected show. A small ripple of applause rang out as the Queen ended her speech, gave a nod of acknowledgement to her audience and swept on past them and into the Great Hall, followed by those lucky enough to have a ticket to hear more.

Molly stared as she went past. That face ... She found herself frowning. Hadn't she seen her somewhere before? There wasn't a lot of time in her life for watching television, but perhaps that was where she'd seen her.

The moment passed as Janette tugged her sleeve. 'I would love to take a photograph of the view from the battlements. May we borrow your camera, please?'

'Of course! Here, let me take one of you, Daniel and Netta. Stand over there ...' Molly said, pointing to a gap between visitors who were gazing at the scenery.

It was much later, as Daniel drove them back along the motorway, Netta and Janette dozing in the back seat, that Molly thought once again about the figure of Mary, Queen of Scots.

She knew suddenly whose face was behind that mask of paint and whose voice had imitated the Queen. But, even as the name came to her, Molly began to doubt herself.

Surely, it couldn't be? No, she must have been imagining it.

Yet, the more she looked back on that moment when the tall woman had swept past them, the more Molly's thoughts centred on Meredith St Claire.

'We really do not recommend your return to school just yet, my dear,' the deputy head told her.

'I am only part-time,' Meredith reminded her.

'Even so, Meredith. There have been reporters pestering the pupils. They've had the audacity to huddle around the school gates!'

'I see,' Meredith replied. 'In that case ...' she sighed, 'please let me know when you consider it safe, won't you.'

'Perhaps you ought to wait until after the Easter break,' the deputy head advised. Then, lowering her voice, added, 'Or until the funeral is past, don't you think?'

Meredith put down the phone with a sigh. Would this never end? Was she to be kept in a sort of limbo until the police made an arrest? Surely by now they would have had some clues as to who might have wanted to harm Guy? She walked back and forth in the empty room, its walls now bereft of photographs, the furniture pushed to one side, marks where fingerprint dust could still be seen. If only ... She bit her lip and felt tears of frustration welling up.

Lorimer had reminded her over their coffee that she was a victim of crime, too. He was a nice chap. Kind, thoughtful. But was he really the whizz at solving crimes that the tall blonde DI had described?

CHAPTER THIRTY-SEVEN

W as she guilty of dogged determination to be proved right? Or had that last call been simply to satisfy her curiosity? Molly wondered as she laid down the telephone. Yes, that had been the drama teacher at Stirling Castle the day before, her trademark pink hair tucked out of sight beneath a wig. She was one of the actresses employed by Historic Scotland on an occasional basis, Molly had been told. The young man who had spoken to her had been enthusiastic about Ms St Claire's acting abilities, telling Molly how popular she was with groups visiting the castle.

It made sense for Meredith to be doing this sort of work, she supposed. The woman might be mourning the loss of her partner, but changing into a different role could be something she could easily slip into. Wasn't that what actors did? Inhabit the character that they portrayed? And perhaps it gave the grieving woman some sort of relief to dress up like the famous Queen of Scots rather than to be herself.

It was an idea that suddenly had Molly Newton thinking

hard. What if all these actors who had been interviewed by the police were playing roles all the time they were being questioned? The director, Standish, perhaps? And that older woman, Ada, had definitely been acting out a part. Hadn't Lorimer warned her about just this very thing?

Had all these interviews with the people closest to Guy Richmond been a waste of time?

Molly recalled her first impression of the theatre group; Standish's overbearing manner, Sarra's anxiety about her friend, Merry (her former teacher, as Molly now knew), and the surly-faced Ahmed who had every reason to dislike the dead star. What about Fairbairn? He had seemed a conscientious sort of fellow, keen to learn his script, quite open about the others in the group. Had that been an act? Were they all covering up their true feelings about the handsome American who had become heir to a vast fortune?

And what about Meredith, herself? No, Molly decided. Surely the shock on hearing about Guy Richmond had been genuine. She had seen that sort of reaction before, poor souls failing to grasp the reality of the death of a loved one and collapsing like that. It had been a horrible time for the drama teacher, and she ought to feel glad that Meredith was beginning to pick up the threads of her life again. And yet she surely didn't need the money that Historic Scotland were paying for her time. As the solicitor had told them, Meredith St Claire would soon be a very wealthy woman. There was no need for her to work, Molly reasoned, but perhaps the impulse to resume her role at Stirling Castle fulfilled a different need. Subsuming her own personality for a little while as a way of keeping the horrors of reality at bay. Would Solly

Brightman say something like that? she wondered, recalling her own years as an undergraduate at the university.

A knock at her office door was followed by Davie Giles entering, a grin on his face making Molly sit up expectantly.

'Mary Pettifer's story doesn't hold up,' he told her. 'One of her pals spilled the beans. Mrs Pettifer *was* with her girl-friends that Sunday night, not at home cuddled up with her drug-dealing husband.'

Molly thumped her desk and grinned back at him. 'Right, let's get that wee toerag back in. Find out why he had to lie about this. And give Mrs Pettifer a warning, too. Lying to the police in a murder case might turn out to be one of the stupidest things she's done. Apart from marrying that creep,' she added with a grimace.

'Could Pettifer have murdered his client?'

Molly drew her brows together. 'I can't think of a motive. And Lorimer agrees that the weapon of choice indicates one of the St James's group.' She sat back in her chair and sighed. 'Plus there's Sarra Milroy's death to consider. 'It's highly unlikely Pettifer knew her.'

'Unless she was also on his client list?'

Molly shook her head. 'We have no evidence of that at present, but stranger things have happened. Besides, how would Pettifer have got into the theatre that night? No, he's hiding something, but to be frank, I can't see him as Guy Richmond's killer. Can you?'

Davie Giles paused for a moment to consider the DI's question. 'What was he doing visiting Richmond's fiancée, then? Do we buy that guff about comforting the bereaved woman?'

'No, I don't. But there's something going on that's scared him enough to lie about being at home with his wife. Let's bring him in again. Take DC Mohammed with you.'

The house in Killearn was at the end of a sweeping drive of dark green rhododendrons, gravel crunching under the car's wheels as Davie and Alisha drove up. It was a large modern property, sunlight bouncing off huge glass windows and doors to the front, making the detectives shade their eyes as they approached. To one side was a triple garage but no cars were parked outside nor was there any sign of life after they had stood on the doorstep ringing the bell and hammering the solid metal door.

'Let's have a gander. See what we can see,' Davie told the younger detective.

There was a flagged path around the house leading to another entrance, double bifold doors above a long, decked veranda, protected by the overhanging roof.

'Looks like the kitchen,' Alisha said, as she stood on the decking, peering inside. 'Come and see, sir. It's like something out of a magazine!' she exclaimed.

Davie Giles joined her, shading his eyes so that he could see inside better.

It was indeed very modern, pale dove greys and dark brown, a huge island dominating the centre, dishes and pots piled up in the middle.

'Looks like they left in a hurry,' Davie murmured. 'See that counter?'

Alisha looked to where the DS was pointing. Two plates of half-eaten toast beside a couple of mugs, a glass dish of butter uncovered, its contents melting in the sunlight, and an open carton of milk, evidence of a hasty breakfast and possibly hastier departure.

Davie looked at Alisha. 'They knew we were coming. Bet that friend of Mary Pettifer's tipped them off,' he said.

'Should we try to get inside?'

'No. We'd need a warrant, Alisha. Everything we do as detectives is done strictly by the book. The only reason we'd have for a forced entry is if we were suspicious that someone in this house was in serious need of our help. There's absolutely no evidence of that so we just take as close a look around the grounds as we can, report back and see if DI Newton or Lorimer want to ask for a search warrant. There has to be a cogent reason for that request, too. Simply suspecting Pettifer's done a runner won't be enough to demand a search.'

'What about drugs?'

'If we have any reason to think he has a quantity of illegal substances in his home then we can ask the Fiscal for permission to search.' He made a face. 'But I'm not sure that's going to happen.'

'Pity,' Alisha said wistfully. 'I'd love to have a look in there. See the rest of the property.'

Davie patted her shoulder as they turned to walk around the house. 'Got the makings of a detective, so you have. Nosiness being a first requirement,' he teased her.

Despite a careful examination of the extensive grounds, including a summerhouse which was locked, and a croquet lawn marked with metal hoops, there was nothing to indicate any wrongdoing. By the garage Davie stooped down to see tyre marks deepening the pale grey gravel. He sniffed the air for a moment. 'Burning rubber,' he muttered. 'Looks like they left recently and in a real hurry,' he said, looking up at Alisha. 'And I wonder where they are now.'

CHAPTER THIRTY-EIGHT

I t was another good day for fishing, the clouds scudding across the sky, a warmth in the sun that made him stop and turn his face upwards.

The boat was back on the loch, bobbing on its mooring, several waterfowl dipping here and there on the far side of the water. Brian Peters raised a hand to the other two men who had taken up their stance, rods held at an angle from the bank. He would have to walk further around the shoreline than usual, he realised, his fellow anglers having chosen the place that he normally took. No matter, there were plenty of decent spots and the fish were as predictable from any part of the loch; either they were biting the flies dangled on the end of their lines or they weren't.

Brian walked carefully along the edge of the bank then stepped to one side as a slick of mud threatened to make him slip. It wouldn't do to injure himself, nobody at home to patch him up. The grass was cropped short further away from the water's edge, the local farmer's sheep having grazed there recently. It was lambing time now and the animals had been taken to a field on the opposite side of the farm, so the fishermen had no cause to be concerned about their presence. The smoother grass soon gave way to clumps of reeds, his boots swishing through them. The mewing of a buzzard made Brian falter for a moment and look up.

The sound of the bird's cry was abruptly drowned out by the approach of two vehicles. Brian turned to see the dark vans stopping right where the police cars had parked on that fateful morning. Nothing happened for several minutes then he watched as several figures emerged in wetsuits, fastening their diving apparatus before heading towards the spot where he had found the young actor's body. They spoke to the other fishermen, who were soon winding in their lines and moving away from the edge of the bank.

Police divers, Brian realised, probably searching for the murder weapon. Well, good luck to them, searching amongst the waving fronds of waterweeds. Surely they'd never find anything there?

He stopped to gather up his own gear and walked slowly back to his Mazda, nodding to the other fishermen as he passed them by.

He was about to unlock the car when a voice called out.

'A word, sir, if you don't mind.'

'Just as we thought,' Molly said. 'Whoever killed him did chuck it into the loch. We'll ask Patel to identify it.'

The discovery of the murder weapon ought to have been helpful, but it was raising even more questions for the team. Any traces on the razor were probably gone by now but nonetheless the weapon would undergo several tests to see if there was anything that could be used as evidence.

There were no fingerprints, partial or otherwise, on the cut-throat razor. Whoever had flung the razor into the water had probably ensured it had been thoroughly wiped. However, there was a trace of a type of solvent that had shown up, its oily substance still clinging to the blade. On closer examination it proved to be a pre-paint cleaner used for treating metal surfaces before applying paint.

'Could this have been used anywhere in the theatre?' Molly wondered out loud as she tapped her cheek with a pencil. The person whose name sprang to mind was Ahmed Patel, who was in charge of props. But perhaps one of the other backstage crew would have had more use for stuff like this. It was a readily available solvent, something anyone might have in their garage or under their sink at home, the forensic scientist had informed her.

Just then her phone rang.

'DI Newton. Oh, hello, sir.'

'There is something else we haven't considered,' Lorimer told her from his office. 'It might be nothing, but I wondered if it was just a coincidence that the man who discovered the victim was also at the scene when our divers found the razor.'

'Brian Peters?' Molly tried to keep the scepticism out of her voice but knew from the pause that followed that she had failed. If Lorimer wanted to gnaw that particular bone, she was happy to let him but the man she remembered at the edge of that cold loch had been genuinely shocked at hauling a body in on his fishing line.

'Worth a bit of investigation,' she heard her boss say. 'Especially in the light of what we know about the deceased's run-in with Peters' late wife.'

Stifling a sigh, Molly replied, 'Yes, sir.'

After she'd put down the phone, Molly closed her eyes and took a deep breath. Why wouldn't Peters be at that lochside, fishing? He'd been one of three anglers out to cast their lines into the water when the divers had turned up. This case was becoming more and more complex, and she really didn't need another possible suspect in the mix. She'd ruled out the fisherman in her own mind, concentrating on those within the theatre world.

So far there was no sign of the Pettifers and Molly could not afford to deploy any more officers to hunt them down. Still, this new development about Brian Peters would give young Alisha plenty more work to do.

DC Mohammed looked at her computer screen once again. Nothing about Brian Peters had shown that the man had had anything to do with Guy Richmond, apart from being the one to find his dead body. She decided to look a bit further. He was a widower, the report said, so maybe it would be worth looking at his deceased wife. She'd died some years ago of multiple sclerosis, a horrible wasting disease, that theatrical agent had told them. Alisha shuddered as she looked at the images on her screen of patients who had suffered this. How awful to have been fit and healthy then unable to walk or even talk.

It surprised the DC when the name Anne Peters came up in so many links. She read carefully through each one, her eyes widening as she learned about the woman who had once been a successful actress, appearing on television as well as in several theatres throughout the UK. Hers was not exactly a well-known name, her parts in television dramas tending to be that of supporting actress, though there was one older review that had praised her Juliet in Stratford. Anne Peters had been Anne Maillie before her marriage to Brian but she had no longer used her maiden name for the stage, unlike so many of her contemporaries. She had been a good actress, perhaps going on to be famous, as Desmond Dylan Morgan had insisted, before the onslaught of MS had cut her career short. Despite being confined to a wheelchair, Anne Peters had been a drama tutor at the Conservatoire.

Then, as she scrolled down the page, Alisha saw it. The name of a show in which Anne Peters had performed. *Sweeney Todd*.

Alisha felt a thrill run through her body at the discovery. There *was* another link between Brian Peters and the world of the theatre. And she had found it.

Molly listened as the younger woman told her about the result of her search. That was down to her, she thought. She should have found this out long since, not left Brian Peters out of the circle of interest. Had his discoveries been mere chance? Or was Peters involved in some way? Lorimer was right, she scolded herself.

'Well done, Alisha. Good work,' Molly said, heartened by the young DC's beaming smile. 'Right, let's get Mr Peters back in for a wee discussion,' she sighed.

CHAPTER THIRTY-NINE

That part of the plan was bearing fruit. After all, it was to be expected that a team of divers would locate the razor. Now that it had been located, there would be more questions directed towards the cast. The artistry of the scheme had been so appealing, made possible by Guy Richmond's acquisition of his grandfather's cut-throat razor and his glee at having it as a prop. Ah, well. To shadow the events of the drama was not an option now but perhaps the symbolism of both deaths might already have resonated sufficiently to make all of them afraid. Actors were a notoriously superstitious lot, after all. Yet to have the assurance that they were trembling in their shoes barely assuaged any disappointment.

The murder weapon had been found so there was a possibility that the police might rake over old ashes. A smile played about the killer's mouth. In doing so, might they not find out even more about Guy Richmond?

Now there was the next Act to figure out and decide which characters might grace each scene.

Or leave the stage for good.

CHAPTER FORTY

B rian Peters parked his car at the end of a row, glancing at all the different makes of vehicles. One car caught his eye, an older Lexus 450 model, the silver saloon standing out from the others due to its length. Someone had good taste in cars, he thought, stopping for a closer look before heading towards the entrance to the police station.

It was a mild spring day and he'd had no plans to spend it fishing, somewhat put off by his recent visit to Whitemoss Loch, so a visit to the police office filled the afternoon, although he was not quite sure why the officers had asked him to be there at all. Was it because they had found that razor? Or were they still doing work on the body he had found?

'Hello, I've an appointment to see Detective Inspector Newton,' Brian told the desk sergeant.

'Ah, just sit over there, sir. Someone will be down to meet you shortly,' the police officer replied.

Brian watched from his seat opposite the reception desk as the man lifted a phone, presumably putting things in motion for his visit. He could not really remember the detective inspector, that day at the loch a bit of a blur now, but when the tall blonde lady in a charcoal trouser suit approached him, Brian stood up, the memories suddenly flooding back.

'Mr Peters, thanks for coming in,' she said, extending a warm hand to shake.

'I'm a bit puzzled why I'm here at all,' Peters said with a half-hearted laugh. 'I already gave my statement on both occasions.'

'Oh, we just wanted another chat,' she told him as they ascended a staircase to the upper floor of the building. Brian did not reply but he could feel the bacon roll he'd had for breakfast suddenly churning in his stomach. What were they going to chat about?

'In here,' the DI told him, opening a door to a small office and ushering him inside. She gestured to Brian to take a seat then sat behind the desk, reminding him uncomfortably of the occasions when he had been summoned to his head teacher's office as a young boy.

'Thanks again, for giving up your time to come in,' the woman said.

Brian made a non-committal noise. After all, his days were empty now that he no longer had to go out to work, retirement not always the blessing he had expected.

'We wanted to ask you about your late wife,' she began.

'Anne?' Brian raised his eyebrows. 'She died five years ago,' he said. 'What has Anne got to do with your investigation?'

The DI clasped her hands and looked straight at him. 'We have found that your late wife was an actress,' she said.

'That's correct.' Brian nodded. 'But she had to give it all

up when she got MS. She was only thirty-eight when she was diagnosed. Far too young. And she suffered for years. Do you know what sort of progressive disease that is?' he asked, leaning forward a little.

'Yes, I do,' Molly replied. 'But it is something else I wanted to ask you about. We discovered that she did some drama coaching at the Conservatoire, is that correct?'

Brian nodded, feeling beads of sweat begin to trickle on his brow.

'Did you or your late wife know anybody from St James's Theatre?'

Brian frowned, thinking hard. The man whom he had found was one of that lot. Surely the police weren't thinking he had any connection with them?

'No.' He shook his head. 'Anne was mostly working for television before her illness. And yes, afterwards she did a little work with students at the Conservatoire. When she was younger, she did a season at the Royal Shakespeare. But that was before we met. She wanted to stay in Scotland after we were married, said she'd seen too many couples splitting up because of the long spells apart during the run of a play or on tour.'

'Did you know her agent?'

Brian smiled then. 'Ah, yes, dear Desmond Morgan. Lovely chap. He read a poem at her funeral, you know.'

'He also represented Guy Richmond.'

'Not a surprise, Detective Inspector,' Brian said stiffly. 'Mr Morgan's agency is well known, and he has had a lot of successful actors on his books over the years.'

'Did either of you know a man named Standish?'

Brian frowned again and shook his head. 'Doesn't ring any bells, sorry. And Anne never acted at St James's. She was more often at the Theatre Royal,' he said proudly. 'Stage was her first love, though television paid well.'

'Did you ever visit St James's Theatre, sir?' the woman asked, her stare sending a shiver down Brian's back.

'No. Never. Look, what is this all about?' he asked, his heart beating fast. Was it annoyance at these questions making him feel the heat suffuse his face? Or were these police officers actually thinking that he might be a suspect? 'I've had two horrible experiences when I was doing no more than taking myself off for a quiet day's fishing,' he told her, his voice beginning to sound shrill. 'I resent the thought that you see some sort of link between my late wife and these actors,' he went on, his hands clutching the edge of the desk. 'Anne gave up acting before that poor young man was even born!'

He saw the blonde officer sit back and tilt her head to one side as if she were considering his words.

'But she did know Guy Richmond,' the detective insisted, her stare beginning to unnerve him.

Brian licked his lips. 'Did she? I wouldn't know. Anne never talked much about her students. By the time I picked her up from the Conservatoire she was too tired to say very much.' He gritted his teeth before adding, 'In the end she lost her power of speech altogether. Can you imagine what that does to someone whose whole career depended on her voice?' The question ended in a high strained tone.

He saw something like pity flash across the detective's

257

face but then it was gone, replaced by her usual determined stare.

'We have been told that Guy Richmond was rather nasty towards your wife, called her a "washed-up cripple". Were you aware of that?'

Brian swallowed hard, the memory of his wife's tears coming back forcefully.

'Yes,' he said, his voice strangely gruff.

'And did that make you want to harm Guy Richmond?'

Brian sat very still. Was this the moment he should tell this woman exactly how that had made him feel?

'That was years ago,' he whispered. 'Besides, I never set eyes on the man till I fished his body out ... never made the connection until I read about him in the papers.'

His throat was dry now and all he wanted was for this to be over so he could go home.

'Your wife had a part in a production of *Sweeney Todd*,' she said slowly, never taking her eyes off the man opposite her.

'Did she? Well, I don't remember all of her plays, you know. I was working too at that time,' he said. 'What of it?'

He dabbed a handkerchief on his forehead, realising how such an action gave away just how stressed he must appear. Was she taking that small action as a sign of guilt?

'*Sweeney Todd* was the performance that the St James's Theatre was about to begin rehearsing,' she reminded him.

Brian Peters' mouth fell open then closed again. 'The cut-throat razor ...'

Molly watched as the man made the connection. Somehow, he was telling her the truth, she thought. This wasn't one of those actors who were expert at the art of dissimulation. But was he simply an ordinary chap who'd had the twin misfortunes of stumbling across a dead body and being at the loch when the murder weapon was found? She might not regard herself as adept at seeing through a person telling lies as Lorimer was, but DI Molly Newton reckoned she had the true measure of Brian Peters right now. And what he was telling her was the whole truth.

'I apologise for any distress I may have caused asking these questions, but in a murder investigation we must be very thorough. Don't you agree that it was a strange coincidence that the same man who discovered the victim was also on the scene when the murder weapon was found?'

She heard the man's sigh of relief, noted the tension in his shoulders easing a little.

'Yes, I do agree, Detective Inspector. It was a very strange coincidence but nothing more than that. And I wasn't on my own when the divers arrived, remember. Yes, there was a time when I could cheerfully have punched that young man on the nose but I'm not a man given to violence. Never have been. And I don't hold grudges.'

Molly looked at him, his face pink with emotion, and felt a sudden pity for the man.

'You know, it was simply my bad luck to have been there by the loch that day,' he told her, shaking his head wearily. 'Anybody might have fished that ... that poor man out of the water.'

She stood up then and came around the desk, resisting an impulse to pat his shoulder.

'Thanks for coming in, sir. I like to speak face to face with people rather than talk over the telephone,' she explained with a smile, beckoning him to follow her. 'Let me show you out.'

Molly watched as the man turned a corner and disappeared from sight. Had that been an unnecessary meeting? Had she simply raked up bad memories for that poor man? Or was he hiding something? She had noticed the sweat and redness appear in his face and the way he had gripped the desk.

Was her estimation of the man as accurate as she'd believed a few minutes ago? Was she beginning, even now, to doubt herself?

For a moment Molly Newton wished that it had been Lorimer who'd spoken to Brian Peters, for her boss was well known for seeing into the hearts of guilty men and women. She wanted to take Brian Peters at face value, though, and to believe all that he had told her. Any hurt caused to his late wife by Richmond surely did not amount to a motive for murder. After all, what would that retired man have been doing out by the loch late on a cold Sunday night? It just didn't make any sense.

CHAPTER FORTY-ONE

They will never find me. I have covered all my tracks and ensured that these investigating officers run around in circles. It is amusing seeing them hare off in so many different directions.

The snippets in the newspapers keep me informed about all that is going on and I have listened to the television as often as the subject is shown. Not even the cleverest of them is a match for me. For I am like a spirit who hovers over the scene, watching and waiting. If I feel the need to take another life, so be it. There is no stain upon my conscience.

I am like the person hidden behind a screen, pulling at the strings of marionettes, deciding which way they will dance to my direction. If I make one of them fall, who will shed a tear? For to me it is all make-believe. I am writing the script, choosing the cast and directing the show. But none of them can see me.

None of them can even feel my touch.

Until the moment I play my part.

CHAPTER FORTY-TWO

'Please let me come over and see you,' he pleaded.

'What's the point?' Meredith said dully. 'You never were very keen on Guy. So what sort of conversation do you expect us to have about him?'

There was a pause as she waited for him to speak again. She turned towards the window that looked down onto the country road, watching the cars in the distance slow down behind a farm tractor.

'I don't want to talk about Guy,' Nigel Fairbairn said at last. 'I want to see how *you* are, Merry.' She could hear the softening in his tone, the faint echo of an accent he thought he'd left behind in the Orkneys.

'All right,' she sighed. 'But this place is a right mess. Someone broke in, you know.'

'*What?* Are you all right?'

'Yeah, yeah. It happened when I was staying in town for a couple of nights. Avoiding nosy reporters, if you must know,' she sighed.

'Oh, you poor peedie lassie,' he said gently, his use of the Orcadian word making her smile. 'Let me come over, Merry. Please. I can help you tidy up.'

'When do you want to come?'

'Now would be as good a time as any,' Nigel told her. 'We don't have rehearsals till tonight.'

'See you later, then,' she said and clicked off the phone.

Was this a good idea, having her old friend come all the way over from the city? What if he were also being trailed by reporters? For a moment Meredith regretted her decision to let Nigel come to the cottage. But then, they were old friends, had been childhood sweethearts, she reasoned. Seeing him couldn't do her any harm. Could it?

Nigel Fairbairn felt the old familiar sense of envy creeping over him as he rounded the bend and drove his ancient Golf up the farm track. Meredith and Guy's cottage was set on a small plateau against the hillside, green fields full of sheep and new lambs on either side. A place like that would have cost a goodly sum, he reckoned, somewhere far and beyond his own dreams. Unless he could find a way to make his name in the theatre. Or by some other means.

She was standing at the door when he arrived, pink hair blowing in the wind. As he approached, he saw her smile and remembered with a pang the way they used to meet down at the harbour after school most afternoons, the constant breeze from the sea part of everyday life, something that visitors to the Orkney islands sometimes whinged about.

For a moment Nigel wondered what would happen if he

began to run towards her and held out his arms, the over-dramatic gesture of teenagers that had had them giggling as he'd spun her around and around till she was dizzy.

No, he decided. Closer now, that smile was a bit forced and he realised with a qualm what a strain his old friend was under. Nobody expects to lose their lover quite like that, he told himself as he stopped.

'Merry,' he began, then, without thinking harder, he wrapped her in a hug, dismayed to feel how terribly thin she had become.

'Nige.' She broke free and gave him a proper smile, tears brimming over and sliding down her pale cheeks. 'I'm glad you came,' she said. 'Come on in.'

Nigel followed her through the house till they reached a bright kitchen with windows overlooking a garden, washing out to dry in the sunshine.

'Let's sit here,' Meredith said, pulling out a bar stool from the table top that was part of the counter. Its metal legs and shiny white plastic seat were modern, probably some high-end brand that he'd never heard of. They could afford the best, he reminded himself, that nagging bitter voice still not quelled, despite Guy's death.

'Coffee? I have some good stuff. Caff or decaff?'

'Oh, definitely caffeine for me.' He grinned. 'I have a long night of rehearsals ahead.'

'Oh. So they've begun – I thought the theatre was out of bounds?'

Nigel shook his head as Meredith busied herself grinding coffee beans. When the noise of the grinder had ceased, he gave a laugh. 'Old Standish sweet-talked that blonde detective woman, apparently. We can't use the basement, of course, but the stage area and auditorium are available.'

As Meredith tipped the coffee into a glass cafetière and added hot water from a fancy kettle with a mirror shine, Nigel glanced around the kitchen. It was a far cry from his own digs.

'I'm surprised they let you back in so soon, I mean . . . ' As Meredith tailed off, he saw her bite her lip.

'Aye, poor wee Sarra. That was horrible. Still can't get my head around that, never mind what happened to Guy.'

Meredith sat down suddenly beside him, her head drooping in an attempt to hide the tremble on her mouth. Then she gave a sigh. 'Do you mind if we don't talk about any of that, Nige? I've hardly slept ever since it happened,' she said.

'Sorry,' he murmured. 'Here, let me do this.' He sprang up and plunged the cafetière slowly till he saw the edge of crema appear.

'Black with sugar?'

Meredith nodded, looking down at her hands clasped on her lap. She was wearing a gypsy skirt, its purple and patterned flounces covering legs that he remembered as slim and shapely. They'd run along the sand barefoot many a time in the old days, carefree and full of hope for a dazzling future together. They would both be West End stars, they'd told themselves, Meredith specialising in musical theatre while he trod the boards in all the modern plays they so eagerly read or watched on YouTube, on the occasions when the island's signal behaved.

'Do you remember singing in St Magnus?' Nigel began.

'You had all these solo parts. Old Fitzpatrick loved giving you the best bits. The other girls in the choir were dead jealous.'

Meredith looked up at him and for a moment he saw the eager teenager she had once been, her eyes still glistening but now bright with memories.

'Nobody had a voice quite like yours,' he said, giving her arm a small stroke then shifting forward to pick up his coffee cup.

'I loved that,' she said. 'The acoustics in the cathedral were wonderful. Remember when we heard Nicola Benedetti playing at the music festival? You couldn't take your eyes off her,' she teased.

'Do you blame me? What a woman. Aye, we were lucky to do so much even while we were living there.' He took a sip of the coffee. She was right, whatever posh brand this was, it was really good, not the cut-price stuff he bought in the supermarkets.

'It wasn't so bad back then, was it?' he whispered, drawing a little closer and catching her eyes. 'Remember our walks along the shore? I still have that stone you gave me. You said the Selkies had left it there. Pretended it had magical powers. We had some good times, didn't we?'

'We did,' she agreed. 'Maybe best to leave the past where it is, though, don't you think? Someone said to me recently to hang on to all the good memories. They meant Guy, of course. But it could mean anything from the past.'

'Merry, listen to me, they are right, whoever they were, but you need to think about your future. You're a young, talented woman. You have years ahead of you and now you can do anything you want. You don't have to stay in that job, for instance. Why not go back to performing? I wish everyone knew just how good you really were.'

Meredith gave him a strange look, her eyes narrowing.

'Don't you remember what Guy used to say? "Those who can, do; those who can't, teach."'

He heard the bitterness in her voice and inwardly cursed the dead man for his casual cruelty.

'I never understood why he said that,' he murmured. 'You did so well at school and in your audition for the Conservatoire. I always thought . . . '

'What? What did you think?' He heard her voice harden.

Nigel took her hand, running his fingers over the cold skin. 'I thought you were better than anyone,' he whispered.

Meredith pulled her hand away. 'Don't sweet-talk me, Nige. What we had in the past should stay there. You know that.'

'I'm not,' he protested, throwing his hands into the air. 'I truly believed you had the making of a great singer and actress. What happened to change all that? Was it when you met Guy?'

There was a sudden silence as Meredith looked away, confirming his words.

'I thought so. Guess being in love does funny things to a person,' he muttered.

'Well, I like teaching, as it happens,' Meredith said. 'Some of these kids are great. And Sarra . . . Oh, dear God, who brought that young life to its end!' she exclaimed.

'Shh, don't dwell on that. Poor kid, though. Her folks must be in bits.'

'Oh, don't. I can't bear to think of that.'

'Well, don't think about it. Or even of going back to teaching. I mean, you'll be able to do anything you want to now, won't you?'

Meredith shot him a sharp look. 'You mean because I'm going to be a millionairess?' She gave a hollow laugh. 'It's like one of our old Greek tragedies, Nige. Dream about the best thing you want and when you find it, it's snatched away from you. Do you really think a lot of money will make up for what I've lost?' she cried, dashing a hand across her eyes to wipe away fresh tears.

'Sorry,' he mumbled. 'I didn't mean to . . .'

Meredith put her hand on his shoulder. 'I know it's been hard for you being in Guy's shadow for so long. I mean we all had it hard as students and struggling actors, but you'll make it big one day, I'm sure.'

'Well, money won't be a problem for you now,' he said. 'And you don't need to do anything at all, do you? You could take a long break, travel the world, buy a house in the South of France . . .' He broke off with a hollow laugh.

Meredith smiled then. 'That was our dream, wasn't it, Nige? Become famous and have a second home in Cannes.'

'We could still do it, Merry,' he whispered, moving towards her and clasping her around her waist. 'You and me.'

At first, she seemed to resist his soft kisses then she was kissing him back with an urgency that surprised him.

It was working. The old magic was still there, he told himself, gazing intently into Meredith's eyes as she led him towards the stairs.

*

Afterwards, she watched from the doorway as his car drove down the track and turned into the main road, one hand raised in farewell. Had Nigel Fairbairn got what he'd come for? she wondered. He was good, she'd give him that. Nige had acted out his part as a friend and lover, but not quite well enough to hide the mendacity that had shone in his eyes when he'd listened to her offer.

And, as his car disappeared from view, Meredith St Claire suddenly wondered what Detective Superintendent Lorimer might make of it all.

CHAPTER FORTY-THREE

Nigel picked up the smooth grey stone and turned it over and over in his hands. Maybe it did possess a kind of magic, the sort of elemental force that the old poets had written about. He laid it down again and picked up his script. Perhaps his future would now be assured but right now it was time to head off, he told himself, get back to the real world of rehearsals for the play where, for once, he had the starring role.

'This is Tony,' Standish told them, looking at the thick-set man beside him. 'You all know him from his television career, of course. Detective Turner in the *Dead Men's Shoes* series.'

Nigel looked up and caught the man's eye. Judge Turpin, of course, the evil character who had deported Sweeney Todd, creating a madman who had gone on to his many crimes till he came upon his original tormentor. The part he'd have been playing if Guy Richmond had not been killed. Tony Fernandez was still a well-known face, though his star was now in the descendant since the TV series had been terminated, and viewers might struggle to remember the actor's name. Still, he'd better look out lest the more experienced man tried to upstage him in any way. He'd seen it before, a supporting actor playing to the gallery, infuriating the lead character onstage, contrary to whatever the director had intended.

'Tony, meet your Sweeney Todd.' Standish grinned, waving his hand in an exaggerated flourish.

Tony Fernandez stepped forward and nodded to Nigel, no attempt to shake his hand. The older man looked him up and down for a moment then gave the faintest of smiles. Was he already becoming Turpin, the judge who'd crossed him and evoked such malign hatred in Sweeney?

'Pleased to meet you, Nigel,' he said at last. 'Looks like we'll be seeing a lot of one another.'

'Good to see you, Tony. I'm sure you'll enjoy playing Turpin,' Nigel replied politely. He gave the man a courteous nod. There would be antagonism between their respective characters, of course, so no need to begin on anything but a civil footing.

Nigel sat back down as Standish went around the semicircle of actors, introducing them one by one. Ada Galloway had pulled at his sleeve and was making some gushing remark to Fernandez, evidently caught up by the excitement of having the once-famous TV actor join the cast. She'd probably coax him to one of her favourite haunts after the evening's work, he decided, seeing Ada licking her lips as Standish took Tony to one side, speaking so quietly to the man that he could not hear what was being said. However, as they turned back to regain their seats, Nigel was aware of both older men staring in his direction and he knew instantly that they'd been talking about him. Was Standish telling Fernandez that his new Sweeney Todd wasn't up to the part? Nigel ground his teeth silently, vowing to show them all that he was more than capable of carrying it off. This rehearsal would confirm to them that he had always been the better choice for the leading role, he decided, raising his head and staring around at each of the cast in turn.

It was dark now, the space between streetlamps barely sufficient to see the pavements. All the shops were shuttered against the night, even the chippy closed, the lingering smell of vinegar wafting up from crumpled papers discarded in the gutters.

Nigel Fairbairn hesitated as he walked back to the flat then turned around.

Had he heard someone following him?

But when he looked there was nobody there. And yet he'd been so sure that he had heard another set of footsteps some way behind him.

Nigel started as an animal howled, a dog fox calling for his mate. He shivered at the eerie sound then quickened his pace.

The smell in the entrance was worse than usual, a stink of urine filling his nostrils and a puddle in the corner near the lift where some idiot had relieved themselves.

Nigel pressed the button and waited for the lift to make its descent. Voices outside in the street made him turn, but whoever was there had walked on, their chatter becoming fainter.

When the lift arrived, Nigel stepped inside. As he pressed the button and turned to face the door, he was suddenly aware of a shadow by the foot of the stairs, a swishing sound, then the doors shut and he was left alone, a puzzled frown on his face. Had someone crept down the stairs and slipped out of the building?

That movement suggested something furtive, Nigel told himself. Or was it his imagination playing tricks after the rehearsal when he'd succeeded in putting every ounce of passion into his lines?

Once inside the flat, Nigel flicked on the light to the living room and gazed around, listening for any faint snores coming from the adjacent room. But all was silent. Of course, Graham was away home for the holidays, the flat his for a glorious two more weeks. He frowned, trying to see what it was that was different about the room, but nothing appeared to be out of place. The couch was still sagging, cushions heaped to one side, his cereal bowl was where Nigel had left it on the coffee table, a milky residue still to be wiped up. His computer was open on the table by the window where he usually worked. All things that he might expect to see when he returned from the theatre. He laid down his script and yawned. Too much excitement in one day, he reasoned, just his imagination playing tricks.

Still, Nigel Fairbairn could not shake off the uneasy feeling that some sort of malign presence had been here in his absence.

And it was a feeling that persisted into the night, robbing him of sleep.

CHAPTER FORTY-FOUR

The BBC studios were situated in Govan, looking across the water to Finnieston where its famous landmark dominated the skyline, the one hundred and seventy-five-foot giant cantilever crane. The words **BBC Scotland** dominated the top storey of the building that stood right on the edge of the river, its layers of glass windows reflected in the water. Today, blue skies and scudding white clouds seemed to float across the surface of the building as he approached the bridge that would take him across to Govan. Close up, the building looked much bigger than Daniel had expected, and he felt a momentary qualm. What business did he, a mere police constable, have being interviewed by some of Scotland's best-known personalities? He took a deep breath and remembered what Molly had told him that morning. 'You've done things that most people will never experience. Don't forget that, Daniel.'

There were steps leading to a glass door and, just as Daniel reached the top, a good-looking man in a navy quilted jacket stepped out, holding the door open for him.

'Thanks.' Daniel smiled, as he walked forward.

'You're welcome,' the man replied and nodded. Daniel saw him reach up and take off a lanyard that was around his neck, stuffing it into the pocket of his coat. He gave Daniel a brief smile and then suddenly his face was familiar. Of course, that was the weatherman who often appeared right at the end of the news programmes. Daniel smiled to himself as he approached the long reception desk, hoarding away the moment to relate it to Netta and his mum later.

Soon he was seated around the corner from reception, fingering his own visitor's lanyard and waiting *for someone to fetch him*, as the lady on the desk had explained.

It was not long until a young woman appeared on the far side of a security barrier and looked across at him as she let herself through and approached Daniel.

'Mr Kohi? I'm Laura,' she said, giving him her hand to shake. 'Please follow me, we're going up to the studios now.'

As Daniel was taken through the security barrier and onward to a bank of lifts, he gazed upwards at the four layers of what he presumed were offices surrounding an internal bank of staircases leading to different levels. Looking up at the glass ceiling and seeing clouds moving slowly across the sky made him feel dizzy, as if he might fall sideways, so he focused instead on the grey steel lift doors.

'No trouble finding us?' the girl asked as they waited.

'None at all, thanks,' Daniel said. It was funny how well he had come to know his adopted city. It might be Scotland's largest, but he had found his way around with little difficulty after those first months when he'd walked and walked its streets, the central grid system easy to navigate, the river running through it like a great artery.

Once out of the lift, Laura led him along a balcony and Daniel marvelled at the glass walls that allowed him to look out over the water. Then they were in a narrower corridor, and she waved him towards a row of bench seats.

'Morven, the lady who is going to talk to you, is in the studio with another guest right now,' she explained. 'There will be a short break after that, and I'll take you in to get miked up.'

The words were hardly out of her mouth when a door to the studio where they were sitting opened, and Daniel saw a small man emerge. He was dressed all in black, head shaved, one bright silver earring glinting from his ear.

'Thanks for coming in, Tommy. Your taxi will be waiting outside,' Laura told him.

Daniel watched Laura's eyes following the man and then she turned, eyes bright with excitement.

'Tommy McQuatt,' she said in a breathless voice. 'Bass player with the—' but Daniel never found out the band's name as Laura jumped up suddenly, a man with earphones around his neck beckoning her from the studio doorway.

The next few minutes saw Daniel being hooked up to the radio microphone, carefully attached to his lapel by the sound engineer, and led to the wings of the studio where he saw two huge cameras at different angles to what looked like a small sitting room, the glass wall behind it showing the sky. The stage set was much smaller than he had expected, the cameramen swivelling their focuses on a petite

276

woman wearing a purple dress and matching high heels, sitting beside a younger man who was talking to her. Daniel listened intently. He did not know what had gone on before, but the pair were now discussing the current Scottish policy towards immigrants.

'You'll go in and sit between them after a count of ten,' a voice in Daniel's ear told him.

He swallowed hard, remembering his mother's advice that morning not to mumble and to speak slowly and clearly. What if he became nervous and stuttered?

The count began and on ten, Daniel stepped forward as he'd been instructed and sat between the woman, Morven McDermott, and her co-presenter, Archie Anderson. He did not see the camera swivel and focus on him or the thumbs up sign that Laura silently gave from the wings.

'It was like being in somebody's home,' Daniel told the two ladies afterwards. 'I couldn't make myself think of anybody actually watching me on television at that point.'

'You were great, son.' Netta beamed, turning to Janette. 'Wasn't he?'

Janette nodded, smiling at Daniel.

'It was quite an experience for an old lady from Zimbabwe, seeing my fine son speaking so easily to these well-known television people,' she said. 'And telling the story of how you came to live in Glasgow.' She hugged him then, motherly pride radiating from her.

He'd keep the rest of his feelings to himself, Daniel decided, at least till he could confide in Molly. To say out loud how much he'd enjoyed it might make these two ladies feel he was too full of himself. But Molly would understand. The way the interviewers had made him out to be a person of some importance was a new experience for Daniel Kohi. And it had given him a few moments of pride.

'It must be how stars feel when they're being made a fuss of,' Daniel murmured as he lay in bed with Molly later that same night. 'Or an actor when the play is ended, and the audience clap and cheer.'

Molly raised herself up on one elbow. 'What do you mean?'

Daniel breathed out a contented sigh. 'Being made to feel that your life is worth something,' he said. 'All the hardship I went through to get to Glasgow pales in comparison to other refugees whose lives are torn apart in war zones. But still. Managing to make a new life and do what we do,' he pulled Molly closer to him, 'being a police officer means making a difference for other people. Remember the phrases that were trotted out at Tulliallan? They're not just to encourage cadets to get on with the real job. A duty of care is something that should be ingrained in us all. Right? And sitting there in that studio, telling the public how I had a second chance to live the life I was meant to ... well ... it made me feel a little bit special,' he admitted.

'You are special,' Molly told him, looking into his dark eyes. 'A very special person. And, oh dear Lord, am I glad you came into my life.'

As they settled down against the pillows, Molly knew that she meant every word. And yet, even as he nestled into her side, she could not help the small shiver of doubt that clouded her thoughts.

She had no worries that the interviews, especially the television show, would make her beloved swollen headed. No. That wasn't what was causing her disquiet. Molly Newton had seen enough in her time as a police officer to be aware of the vagaries of human nature and the possibility that not everybody might applaud the Zimbabwean refugee for his success here in Scotland.

Even as they fell asleep in one another's arms, were there dark forces at work to banish the good feelings PC Daniel Kohi had expressed to the three women who meant so much to him? No, it was just the job, she told herself with a yawn, this constant work to find the perpetrators of vicious crime shadowing her thoughts. *Be happy*, a small voice told her. *The best is still to come.*

CHAPTER FORTY-FIVE

Ada Galloway watched the younger actor as she sat near him, script in one hand for easy reference though she had memorised it now. There was something different about Nigel's demeanour this morning, Ada thought. He was perkier, more assured of himself, a brightness in his eyes that she recognised. Good for him, she chuckled inwardly. Someone's making him happy. Her eyes flitted around the cast who were sitting on the stage, reading their lines to an auditorium that was empty except for Standish who sat right at the very front, a clipboard on his lap. But Ada was reading more than the lines of the Demon Barber, concentrating on the facial expressions and body language of others in the cast, hoping to see one of them display that tell-tale smug look, but none of the women, or men for that matter (despite his previous relationship with Meredith, who knew what sexual proclivity Nigel favoured these days?), seemed to be gazing his way.

Ada was an old hand at this game, her flirtatious nature helping her to bed any keen male who might be available, and she recognised the signs of recent conquest. She was suddenly aware of Standish looking her way and she gave him a faint smile and nod to let him know she was following the script.

'Well done, Nige,' Ada cooed as they broke up for lunch. 'You were made for that part.' Easy flattery always worked on guys like this, she thought, clapping the man on his shoulder. 'Fancy a wee refreshment later? My treat.'

Nigel gave her a grin. 'It was a good morning, wasn't it? Tony's fitted right in, as well. Shall we ask him to join us?'

'Oh, not today, darling,' Ada gave him a coy look. 'I'll save Tony for another day.' She linked her arm through his. 'Just the two of us. We've hardly had a chance to get together as a twosome since the casting, have we? Sweeney and his pie maker,' she said, nudging his ribs. 'Let's have a good old gossip, shall we? Make mince of a few reputations.'

The afternoon passed with Standish shouting at a few of the younger actors, insisting that they thought more about their diction. 'The audience are paying to hear you, not to gawp at a silent screen!' he exclaimed to the young fellow playing Anthony, recently graduated from the Conservatoire, who blushed at being given a rollicking.

At last, the director called a halt and the cast gathered up their scripts and headed off the stage to their dressing rooms. Ada was first offstage, eager to gather up her coat and bag, glancing over her shoulder at Nigel.

'See you outside in five,' she said and dropped a wink as he passed her.

*

The pub was quite full with after-work office drinkers but Ada swept through those close to the bar, elbowing her way to the front. Several decades of asserting herself amongst men and a voice that penetrated any babble had made the older woman adept at being served as soon as she reached the bar.

'There you are, sweetheart.' She plonked the pint glass down on their table. 'G&T for me,' she said, taking her first sip as she sat close to Nigel. 'Right, now, tell Aunty Ada all the latest. I noticed you're in a particularly good mood today. Who's the lucky woman?'

Nigel grinned at her as he raised his glass of lager. It was a look Ada knew well, that sly expression in a man's eyes evidence of a secret he was bursting to share. Whose bed had he been in?

'Went to visit my old friend Merry, the other night,' Nigel said, smiling to himself then glancing up at his colleague.

'Ah, comforting the poor dear, were you?' Ada gave him a suggestive grin. That was news indeed, she thought with a frisson of excitement. Was Nige trying to pick up where he had left off, perhaps?

'Something like that,' he replied, a twinkle in his eyes that was enough of a boast to reveal what he really meant.

'Good for you.' Ada beamed, lifting her drink in a salute. 'So nice to cheer the girl up. I mean. You two are such old chums, aren't you?'

'Yes, we are,' Nigel said. 'We go back a long way.'

'Well, that is just lovely,' Ada gushed. 'Maybe she'll come to her senses now.'

'What do you mean?' Nigel began to frown.

Ada moved a little closer and leaned towards him. 'You two were meant for one another,' she whispered. 'Don't you think? And now that poor Guy has left the scene, God rest his soul,' she laid a fluttering hand on her chest looking earnestly into Nigel's eyes, 'Meredith can enjoy a proper future with you.'

'You don't think it's too soon?'

Ada shook her head and took another sip of her gin. 'Not in the least. Do you?'

'Well, it might look as if I'm after more than wanting my old girlfriend back,' Nigel said quietly, a tone of doubt creeping into his voice. 'She's a rich woman now.'

'Nonsense!' Ada exclaimed, patting the back of his hand. 'Life's for living, dear boy. And if Guy's demise has taught us anything it is to make the most of every day. Who knows what misfortune lies ahead of us, eh?'

Sitting in the bay window of her flat, Ada thought back to the day's rehearsals and that mask of hate young Fairbairn put on as he'd played the part of Sweeney Todd slicing a man's throat.

She gave a sudden shudder.

Had he looked that way as he'd dispatched another victim? Guy Richmond?

Ada had already flagged up her suspicions to those detectives, the blonde and the tall man with the wonderful blue eyes. But now, after that little session in the pub, Ada was certain that she must tell DI Newton and Superintendent Lorimer that she knew the identity of Richmond's killer.

*

That morning Molly had left Daniel sleeping, her need to arrive early at Helen Street, the double murder case, taking priority over spending time with the man she loved. As she drove, Daniel's words about his BBC appearance came back to her. He'd felt special, he'd told her. *Like an actor at the end of a play.* For a moment Molly recalled times when she had clapped loudly from the audience, watching as the cast of a play took their curtain calls, the loudest roar of approval for the stars of a show. Was that the moment under the spotlight that every actor aspired to have? Did it matter enough to kill for such fleeting applause?

She frowned, wondering if they had been wrong to dismiss the aspirations of the actor, Nigel Fairbairn, as insufficient motive to murder the man who'd stood in the way of his success.

'Letter for you, ma'am,' the desk sergeant said as Molly came through the main door of the police station.

Molly looked at the white envelope. A first-class stamp and her name and address typed out. But there was no post-mark to tell when it had been sent or from where. She turned it over, but it was blank. Walking up the stairs, she ripped it open, the self-adhesive strip coming apart easily.

Inside was a piece of A4 printer paper folded neatly to fit the long envelope.

Molly stopped outside the DI's room, pausing to read it.

```
Dear DI Newton,


It has come to my attention that Nigel
Fairbairn is sleeping with his old
girlfriend. Meredith is now a wealthy
```

woman. Don't you think you should ask
him where he was the night that Guy
Richmond disappeared?

From a concerned member of the public.

Molly read it again then a third time before raising the
paper to her nostrils and sniffing. Did she detect a whiff of
something fragrant? Was this written by a woman? And, if
so, by whom?

She frowned. Who could have sent this? Her immediate
suspicion fell on the middle-aged woman playing the part
of Mrs Lovett, the pie maker infatuated by Sweeney Todd.
Ada Galloway would be working in close association with
the Orcadian actor. Was this true or just a dirty bit of gossip?
Surely Meredith wouldn't have let another man into her bed
so soon ... and yet ... grief made people do the strangest
things, didn't it?

Ada jumped as her mobile phone rang. How weird to be on
the point of tapping out a number, only to see it appear on
her screen. She gave an involuntary shiver. *Goose ran over
your grave*, an inner voice whispered.

'DI Newton, what a coincidence! I was just about to phone
you,' Ada exclaimed.

'Really?' The detective inspector sounded sceptical. Why
was that?

'Yes, it's about—'

'Nigel Fairbairn and Meredith St Claire,' Newton finished
for her.

285

'You know about that!' Ada gasped.

There was a momentary silence and Ada wondered if they had been cut off.

'You already sent me a letter about that matter,' Newton said, pausing before adding, 'Didn't you?'

'No! What on earth makes you think that, Inspector?' Ada trilled nervously.

'Sure about that?'

'Of course I'm sure. I was on the point of calling to tell you all about it when you rang!' Ada protested.

Once again, there was no immediate response and Ada stood still, chewing her lip as she wondered if the tall blonde detective thought that she was lying. Nobody could see that phone in her hand, nor guess her intention to call the detective inspector's number, after all.

'I think perhaps we ought to have a little chat face to face, Mrs Galloway,' Newton said at last. 'Don't you?'

'You think it's true?' Lorimer frowned.

'Could be. But I don't like it. Smacks of a troublemaker rather than a concerned member of the public to me,' Molly Newton said, nodding towards the letter now safely encased in a plastic cover.

'And Ada Galloway categorically denies sending it,' he said.

'She's coming in shortly so we can see if she's telling the truth or not,' Molly replied.

'Maybe she is telling the truth as she sees it.'

'You don't like the idea of Ms St Claire hopping into bed with her old boyfriend?'

Lorimer shrugged. 'It's none of my business what she does in her own bedroom,' he said. 'But it does seriously impinge on the case, doesn't it?'

'Gives Fairbairn additional motives for killing Guy Richmond. Leaves the way clear for him to get back with Meredith. *And* her fortune.'

Lorimer chewed his lower lip for a moment, his blue eyes clouded with doubt.

'We need to see Fairbairn, then, as a person of interest,' he said at last.

Molly watched Lorimer walk back to his own office, wondering just what he was thinking at that very moment. He had seemed genuinely concerned about Meredith St Claire's welfare up until now. Did that mean he was disappointed by her behaviour, if the accusations in this letter were true? Backed up as they were by Ada Galloway's phone call, Molly was pretty certain that she had found the person who had wielded that cut-throat razor. If Fairbairn were to confess, then all that remained was to tie him to Sarra Milroy's death. Still, the detective inspector was uneasy about Lorimer's reaction.

Ada Galloway was dressed in a calf-length black coat, her shoulders swathed in a pashmina of varying shades of purple and blue, a magenta felt trilby perched on her head.

As they sat down in the interview room, Molly wondered how much the woman spent on cosmetics, a thick layer of foundation and powder covering her skin, smoky eyes ringed in black kohl, her front teeth showing a scarlet stain, a give-away of recently applied lipstick. The actress was certainly dressed to impress, she thought, but outward appearances cut no ice with the detective inspector or her colleague, DS Giles.

'Thank you for coming in,' Molly said, after introducing the detective sergeant. 'Now, it is important that we clear up the matter of this letter.'

Ada Galloway sat up straight, glaring at the two detectives, positively bristling with indignation. Watching her, Molly felt a bubble of laughter inside that she had to suppress as she wondered which of the actress's previous stage roles were being played out at that moment.

'I did not send any letter to you, Detective Inspector! And I want to make that *absolutely clear*!'

Molly nodded. She'd let that pass, for now. 'You did want to tell me about Nigel Fairbairn and Meredith St Claire,' she said.

'Yes!' Ada's eyes brightened as she leaned forward. 'Yes! I know what's going on there. Nigel was far too ready to spill the beans,' she declared. 'Saw right away that he'd been having fun with someone, and it didn't take a lot to guess whose bed he'd been in! Besides, he told me he'd been to see poor Meredith and it wasn't long till he was boasting about it.' She wagged a purple-gloved finger at the two detectives. 'Thinks he's in with a chance now that poor Guy's out of the way. So,' she stopped to take a deep breath, 'my thinking is that he's been planning it all along! Gets rid of Guy, takes over his starring role and fiancée all in one swoop.'

'That is a very serious allegation,' Molly said severely.

'Not an allegation, darling, just my own thoughts on the

matter,' Ada said sweetly. 'Besides, if you've had a letter stating just what I've told you, then it's obvious, isn't it?'

Molly swallowed hard. The woman was infuriating. But she was right. She'd take the actress's prints to match with the letter and envelope, see if there was any evidence that she was lying.

CCTV showed a figure clad in black, hoodie disguising the face. It must have happened in seconds, the envelope dropped onto the desk as the man on reception had turned away. Whoever he or she was, they had taken a huge risk to deliver that letter. The external cameras at the Helen Street police office showed the same figure mounting a bicycle then pedalling madly in the direction of Paisley Road till it entered Bellahouston Park then disappeared.

'It isn't Ada Galloway,' Molly said.

'Possibly some youngster bribed to take it into the office,' Lorimer suggested. 'Whoever delivered that letter took plenty of trouble to disguise himself.'

CHAPTER FORTY-SIX

Today, Daniel was heading back to the Cathcart office till such time as he was offered a detective's post. It could be anywhere, his friend, Lorimer had warned him. Police Scotland covered the entire country now. Daniel thought about what he might do if he was offered a job far from his adopted city. He would not just be leaving Netta and his mother in the flat here at Nithsdale Drive but his beloved Molly too. He sighed. Face that problem if it arises, he told himself. With a bit of luck, he would be posted to the Glasgow area. After all, it had the highest population of any part of Scotland. And there was never a shortage of crimes to solve. Whatever happened, he would make sure that a change in his working life would not affect his relationships with the women he loved.

'Good morning.' DS Knight grinned at Daniel. 'Looks like you've got a pile of fan mail,' he added, dropping him a wink. 'Loved the interview on BBC, by the way. You came across brilliantly. Well done.'

Daniel's eyes widened as he saw the stack of envelopes waiting for him. That all those viewers had taken time to write to this African refugee was humbling. He placed them into his locker, vowing to open them only after he'd finished his shift and arrived at Molly's duplex flat in Lilybank Gardens. He gave a grin as he thought of her reaction as he read them out. Would she tease him about it? Probably.

Molly gritted her teeth. If only they could find out what had taken Guy Richmond into the city centre that Sunday afternoon, some sort of a lead might be followed up. But there had been no further sighting of the man until his waterlogged body was fished out of that loch. Had he met with Pettifer? That might explain why the drug dealer and his wife had apparently scarpered. Traffic was on the lookout for his black four-by-four but so far without any luck. Guy Richmond had somehow managed to evade any more of the all-seeing eyes of the city's many cameras and now Pettifer was doing a similar disappearing act.

And yet, were either of these things relevant now that they had information about Nigel Fairbairn? She glanced at the clock on the wall of the DI's room. Fairbairn should be arriving any time soon, under a police escort. Would this be the day that they resolved those two murders? Would the man admit everything? Molly frowned, a niggle of doubt making her uneasy. It didn't fit, somehow. The slightly built actor did not seem a match for the much taller Richmond and yet . . . motive was there, and means. Had he taken the actor out to that lonesome place, pushed him to his knees and slit his throat, half a mind on the role of Sweeney Todd? Were they dealing with a man who had two opposing sides to his nature, one which so far had been hidden from the investigating team?

Nigel sighed as he heard the ringing. Someone had probably pressed the buttons on every floor. Och, let some other fool buzz them in, he thought, crossly. But when the ringing became more insistent, he flung down his pencil and stormed across the room. Was it one of his flatmate's friends? Had they forgotten he was away on holiday?

'Hello, who is it and what do you want?' he snapped.

Then, as the voice came across loud and clear, Nigel blinked, and pressed the entry button. What had brought the police here again? Was Meredith okay? After that break-in, surely she should have had some protection? His mouth twitched in a smile at the thought. It was perhaps just as well that there had been no nosy cops around the cottage, otherwise that would have spoiled what he had waited for . . .

The heavy thumps on the door made Nigel break into a trot and pull the handle.

Two uniformed officers stood there, staring down at him.

'Mr Nigel Fairbairn?'

Nigel nodded dumbly.

'Please come with us, sir. You are wanted for an interview by the Major Incident Team.'

Something within him turned cold at that moment and he felt as though a hand was clutching at his heart.

Lorimer sat quietly beside DI Newton as she began the interview. Fairbairn had already been offered a solicitor but had shaken his head, staring at each of the detectives in turn.

He was a young man still, Lorimer thought, regarding the actor as Molly stated for the record the date, time of interview and the persons present. Would this meeting be brought up in court at a later date? Talking to his DI before the actor arrived, Lorimer realised how certain Molly seemed to be that Fairbairn was her main suspect. Looking at the man's pale face and that expression of shocked disbelief, Lorimer wasn't so sure. He'd seen so many suspects grimly sticking to their stories or parroting out a 'no comment' when questioned, but he had also witnessed those who had committed their first crime and looked nervous or just plain bewildered, the enormity of their actions finally dawning on them. Those were the suspects most likely to crumble and confess, tears and sobs evidence of genuine sorrow and regret.

'Where were you on Sunday the tenth of March, Mr Fairbairn?' Molly began.

'At my home in Glasgow,' he replied, shifting a little in his seat. 'I already told you both that,' he added, a trace of annoyance in his voice.

'And where were you three days ago?' Lorimer saw Molly make eye contact with the man, her question piercing his defences. Fairbairn looked away first, head turned to one side.

'Don't remember,' he muttered.

'Oh come on, Nigel, you can do better than that,' Molly scoffed. 'At a rehearsal? Or, were you in bed with Meredith St Claire?'

The young man's head shot up, his mouth open to protest, but when he saw the two detectives staring at him, he closed it again and nodded silently.

'Please can you speak for the tape,' Molly said. 'Were you in bed with Meredith St Claire three days ago?'

'Yes,' came the reply, Fairbairn's pale cheeks reddening.

'Comforting an old friend?'

'Something like that,' he mumbled, looking down at his hands.

Lorimer saw the raised shoulders, the man's body language showing a severe attack of nerves.

'And Ms St Claire was quite happy for you to make advances of this nature?'

Fairbairn glared at Molly. 'That's not a crime. Anyway, we're old friends,' he insisted.

'And former lovers?'

'Aye.' The word came out softly as he fidgeted with his hands.

Hearing his change of tone, Lorimer wondered if Fairbairn was recalling his boyhood days with the pink-haired beauty. They'd been a couple for years, they'd been told, till Guy Richmond appeared on the scene. No secret there. And these may have been halcyon days on the Orkney islands, two talented youngsters with dreams of stardom, the big city still ahead of them. Something about a time of innocence ... the words of a song came back to Lorimer then. But was the man sitting opposite him today really so innocent now?

'What were you hoping to achieve?' Molly asked, her tone quite bland, almost bored. Lorimer listened approvingly. An accusatory voice might have made this fellow clam up.

'I ... nothing,' he said, looking from Molly to Lorimer as if seeking help. 'What do you mean?'

'Look at it from an outsider's perspective,' Molly reasoned.

'Your rival in the theatre as well as in love is banished from the scene and so this is your chance to step into both roles. Besides which, Ms St Claire has become heir to a fortune with her fiancé's death. Wouldn't you say that puts you in somewhat of a predicament?'

Nigel Fairbairn stared at her for a long moment, all the colour draining from his face.

'You think I killed Guy?' he whispered, shaking his head. 'Well, you're wrong, quite wrong. I'd never do anything so horrible to another human being! How can you even think that?'

Molly leaned forward. 'Perhaps you were not where you said you were on Sunday the tenth of March,' she countered. 'Perhaps you were playing the part of Sweeney Todd for real, dispatching the man who stood in your way?'

Fairbairn shook his head. 'You're mad,' he said. 'How can you think like that? What kind of suspicious minds have you people got?'

Lorimer saw his fists clench as Fairbairn sat up a little straighter in his chair. Molly had riled him, for sure, the actor now angry, rather than tearful.

'Not just us, Mr Fairbairn. We have others who evidently think the same.'

'Who?' Fairbairn's eyes snapped with sudden temper. Was he showing a different side to his personality? A hidden temper that could be stretched to breaking point?

It was at that moment that Lorimer made his decision. Whoever had killed Guy Richmond had planned it carefully, whereas he felt that this man was more likely to have acted on impulse. His was an emotional character. No. Fairbairn wasn't the person who had lured Richmond to that lonely loch and pulled a razor across his throat.

'We are not at liberty to disclose that,' Molly said stiffly.

'Do you have any evidence that I killed that man?' he snapped, beginning to rise from his seat. Then, when neither detective replied, Fairbairn nodded. 'Thought not. Right. I don't need a lawyer to tell me I'm done with this interview.'

Molly and Lorimer also stood up, acknowledging the truth of the man's words. They had no concrete evidence with which to charge him and he was within his rights to walk out.

'Thank you, Mr Fairbairn,' Molly said. 'You are certainly free to go but please stay in the area, should we need to ask you any further questions.'

'Well, that was a shame,' Molly said. 'I thought we had him just then.'

He's not our killer, Molly, Lorimer wanted to tell her.

'But there are too many things that don't fit, Molly,' he said quietly, instead. 'Inferior height and weight to overcome the victim, to start with. Fairbairn might have lashed out on impulse, but he doesn't strike me as a man who planned things out in advance.'

'Don't you think he planned that visit to Meredith? Surely that is evidence that he was trying to take Guy Richmond's place?'

'He'd want to see her, of course he would. Probably still holds a candle for the woman,' Lorimer said. 'But my bet is that he called her on impulse. Then things developed.'

'I can see your point, sir,' Molly replied. 'But he still has a motive.'

'And what motive would he have for pushing Sarra Milroy down those basement stairs?'

Lorimer regarded her carefully. She was still SIO in this case, and it didn't sit well with him to pull rank, no matter how much he felt that Fairbairn didn't fit.

'Do you think we ought to pull him out of our list of suspects?'

'Do you?'

He saw Molly's mouth tighten before she replied. 'He had all of it,' she said at last. 'Motive, means and . . . well, we don't know what happened by that lochside, but surely we can't rule out opportunity?'

Lorimer did not answer her for a moment or two. 'Good question,' he said at last. 'Perhaps that will be the most determining factor of all. Meantime, let Fairbairn think about this interview and see what he does. He'll be feeling pretty rattled at this invasion of his privacy, besides anything else. If he is guilty of anything, we might even see him dropping out of the play.'

'They were horrible,' Nigel told her, gasping back tears. It was so good to talk to Merry, tell her what he'd been through and hear her comforting words. 'See if they haul me back in again? I've a good mind to tell them just what a brute Guy could be— No, don't argue, you know he had a mean streak. Putting you down the way he did when I know you were a great performer.'

'Don't,' Meredith said. 'You mustn't speak about Guy like

that. You're just upset. Now, tell me everything they said. Is there any chance they're nearer to catching his killer?'

'Don't worry,' she said at last, once Nigel had poured out his experience at the police office. 'Nobody in their right minds could think of you taking a real weapon and killing someone.' She gave a slight laugh. 'Remember what our PE teacher told you when we tried out karate?'

Nigel frowned. 'No, I don't remember. That was ages ago. Why? What did he say?'

He heard the woman breathing a sigh before replying.

'He said,' Meredith paused before adding, 'that you couldn't hurt a fly.'

'I was so sure I had him,' Molly told Daniel as they sat by the window of her flat later. Outside was becoming dark, bare trees ink-blue against the crepuscular skies, the dying embers of sunset towards the west. 'Then, after Fairbairn marched out, Lorimer really stunned me. Didn't actually tell me we had the wrong man. But that was what I sensed.'

'Molly, you know him better than I do, but please, let me assure you that I have faith in Detective Superintendent Lorimer. He has such an insight into human nature ... you know that, don't you?'

Molly sighed and nodded, letting her head fall onto Daniel's shoulder.

'It all made such a lot of sense, though. That letter, Ada Galloway's statement. And now I feel we're back to square one again.'

'Cheer up.' Daniel gave her a hug. 'I've brought something

to show you.' He extricated himself from her arms and walked over to where he'd put his jacket on the back of a chair.

'Look at this lot!' He grinned, pulling the packets of letters from each deep pocket. 'I'm led to believe it's fan mail. Shall we read them together and you can have a laugh at me?'

Molly raised her eyebrows. 'Gosh, that's amazing. You're a real celeb now, Constable Kohi.'

Daniel sat beside her again and tore open the first envelope. Soon they were smiling together at the wealth of accolades that had been directed to the Zimbabwean officer.

'The media has celebrated something positive for a change,' Molly murmured. 'Nice to see that. And all this coverage about your life has given you more confidence, hasn't it?'

'Maybe. It's been very flattering to be in the spotlight for a time, but I shan't do any of this sort of thing again,' Daniel said. 'I'm a police officer first and foremost, not a media star.'

Lorimer gazed out as the last rays of sun finally gave way to darkness. He was sorry if Molly Newton had seen his opinion of Fairbairn as damaging her case. He sighed. There were things about this whole business that had troubled him from the start. Evidence was needed, or else the perpetrator had to come forward and make a confession, something that he highly doubted would ever happen. No, if his instincts were right, the person behind the murders was still a few steps ahead of them, confident that their careful planning had worked. It would take just one small slip, however, and they would be unmasked, like the villain at the end of a tragedy.

CHAPTER FORTY-SEVEN

'Whit's up, lass? Ye look like a week of wet Wednesdays, so ye do,' Netta declared as she put the bowl of porridge in front of Janette.

'Sorry,' the lady replied, attempting a smile. 'I am a little sad today,' she admitted. 'It is what we call a sickness of the heart.' She looked at Netta. 'A longing for home,' she added.

'Oh, well, I can understand that,' Netta said. 'Scotland is a bonny place but we've no goat the weather like youse have, and a' thon wildlife ye've telt me aboot. Like yon weaver birdies you said nest near your auld place.'

Janette nodded. 'You have all been very kind, but I think my heart is still in Africa.'

'You're surely no' thinkin' o' goin' back tae Zimbabwe?'

Janette shrugged. 'I am not sure,' she admitted. 'Things are still dangerous for me there, despite all that has taken place. But I have a brother who lives just over the border in Botswana.'

'You'd go back to Africa?' Netta looked at her penfriend.

'Perhaps. Daniel has settled here and Molly . . . '

'You've no' taken tae Molly, huv ye, hen?'

'She is a good person,' Janette said. 'And good for Daniel but . . . '

'She's no' an African wumman and doesnae go tae church, is that it?'

Janette bit her lip. 'I am guilty of comparing her against those I held dear. It is a sin for me, I know this.'

'But they two are so good thegether, lass. She makes your Daniel so happy. Somethin' lights up when I see them here. Give it time, Janette, get tae know the lassie better, eh?'

'You are right, dear Netta, as always,' Janette smiled tearfully.

'Now come oan an eat up yer porridge afore it gets cauld,' Netta told her, picking up her own spoon, taking some sugar and sprinkling it onto her bowl.

She had been in Glasgow for nearly two months now and still she felt so much like a stranger, Janette thought, despite her friend's kindness and generosity and as well as being with her beloved Daniel once more. Could she really bear to lose him again? Or, Janette thought sadly, had she already lost him to the tall policewoman?

As he changed into his uniform in the locker room, Daniel thought about Molly's disappointment concerning her person of interest, the young actor who had been given the victim's starring role. If the man was to go on to fame and fortune, he too would be at the mercy of the media, his life picked over for anyone to see. No, Daniel thought, I will not agree to any more interviews. Molly assured him that his head had not been turned by being chosen as a poster boy for Police Scotland, had even teased him about it. *It'll be tomorrow's fish and chip wrappings*, she'd said after they'd read his story in the newspaper. Well, it was too late now to turn back the clock and he would have to live with its consequences, some of his own colleagues here in Cathcart no doubt ready to mock him gently about his media success.

Across the city, William Lorimer stared out of his office window. The distant hills were shrouded in a veil of mist, a portent of rain to come. DI Newton had done well to interview Fairbairn and follow up on Ada Galloway's titbit of gossip and he had seen the dejection in her face when he had called time. However, there were other lines of enquiry being followed up even as he stared out of the window, officers all across Scotland on the alert for any sighting of the Pettifers, the drug dealer and his wife's sudden departure a possible sign of guilt. Had it been Pettifer who had handled that razor on the night when he'd claimed to be at home? If so, how had he obtained it? Only those in the theatre group had ready access to the props in the theatre basement. Besides, what link did he have, if any, to Sarra Milroy?

No, he told himself. The culprit had to be someone closer to the group of actors, even one of their own number.

Should he go and visit Meredith again? Hear her side of the story about her affair with Fairbairn? Or would that be seen as an invasion of the woman's privacy? On balance it was better to leave her alone, let things take their natural course.

He continued to gaze across at the hills, his mind turning over several possibilities, one of which caused him to sigh heavily.

CHAPTER FORTY-EIGHT

W hen he turned the key in the lock, Nigel found the
door opening under his hand.

Surely he hadn't forgotten to shut it properly when he'd
gone out? He frowned, standing still for a moment, listening
intently.

His hand reached up for the light switch and he heard the
faintest click, but the hallway remained in utter darkness.

A power cut?

Or had someone pulled a fuse?

His heart began to beat faster, ears straining for the
slightest noise of another person within the flat. He fumbled
for his phone, wondering what he might see if he switched
it on.

Had there been a break-in? Was he going to find the place
trashed?

There was no sound from within, nothing that should have
made the hairs stand on the back of his neck.

Nevertheless, he entered cautiously, the thin light from his phone sweeping the hallway, relieved to see that everything looked just as he had left it.

Stupid man! He scolded himself, pushing the door and closing it behind him till the lock clicked. Yet the feeling that someone was there persisted.

Or was that unlocked door a sign they'd been in the flat during his absence?

Once inside the lounge, he gazed around as he had the previous occasion that he'd felt like this, nerves on edge. Nothing appeared to be amiss, Nigel realised, until he felt a faint draught from the open window.

Had he opened it this morning? He frowned, trying to remember.

A faint rustle from one side made him start, fists clenched. But it was just the pages of his foolscap notes on the table by the other window, lifting slightly in the current of air.

Nigel frowned. That wasn't right, he thought. There should have been—

The blow to the back of his head stunned the slightly built actor, felling him to the ground.

Nigel groaned, putting out an arm in a weak effort to raise himself up.

Then something hard hit his head over and over again, blood spattering as an artery burst in a cascade of crimson spray.

Then there was silence once more, darkness covering Nigel Fairbairn's sight for the very last time.

CHAPTER FORTY-NINE

'Where the hell is he?' Standish demanded, pacing up and down the stage, his pockmarked face contorted with anger.

The actors began to murmur with one another, casting awkward glances towards the director whose temper was well known to them all. Fairbairn would be in for a rollicking once he appeared, was the general consensus, but one person amongst them remained silent, her eyes fixed on Standish. Ada Galloway watched as the man paced backwards and forwards, mobile phone to his ear.

It wasn't like Nigel to be this late for a rehearsal. In fact, the young man who had stepped into Guy Richmond's shoes had been so eager to play the part that he'd often been first to arrive at the theatre now that rehearsals were taking place on stage. Ada looked around to see if everyone else was there. Yes, even Ahmed was with them, fussing with something in the wings, his perpetual scowl marring an otherwise handsome face.

'Nothing,' Standish growled between clenched teeth, glaring at the assembled actors as if one of them might be responsible for the absence of his leading man. 'That's all we bloody need.' Then his gaze fell on Ada.

'You were with him the other day, had a drink together,' he began. 'Any idea what's on his mind?'

Ada shook her head. It wasn't her call to say anything about Nigel rekindling the romance with his old flame. The stern warning she'd had from that DI still resonated with the woman. Perhaps the silly boy was out at the cottage? Had he decided to chuck the stage for a future with Meredith and her millions? It was possible, but, no, on balance, Ada thought that Nigel Fairbairn was more likely to be swayed by the allure of West End stardom than throw in his lot with the drama teacher. What was it Guy used to say? *Those who can, do; those who can't, teach.*

She shivered for a second. He'd been a confident man, the American, perhaps too confident. And in the end ... well, she wouldn't dwell on that right now.

'Maurice, you take over for now,' Standish called out to the actor who had been asked to understudy the main role.

Ada stood up, ready for the scene they had been asked to rehearse for this morning's meeting, trying to put Nigel Fairbairn completely out of her mind.

'Hello?'

'Merry, it's me, Ada. Is Nigel there?'

There was no reply for a moment and Ada wondered where exactly the woman was as she strained to hear Fairbairn whispering in the background. Were they still in bed?

'Nigel? Why on earth did you think he might be with me, Ada?'

'I know all about you pair,' Ada scoffed, adding a chuckle to disarm the younger woman. 'Nigel was all too keen to tell me he'd been ... seeing you again.'

'I don't know what you're talking about,' Meredith replied stiffly.

'He visited you, though, didn't he?'

Again, that pause. Was she about to deny it? Ada smiled to herself.

'Nigel did come to see me recently. First time we had met since Guy's death,' she said, a sigh in her voice that gave Ada a frisson of guilt. Poor cow was still cut up over Guy's death and here she was casting aspersions ... She bit her lip, wishing she'd never called.

'He was very sweet,' Meredith said at last. 'Sometimes it's old friends you need at a time like this. And as you know, Nigel and I go back a long way. But ... shouldn't he be with you? Isn't it a rehearsal day?'

Ada took a deep breath. Was it any of her business what was going on with Meredith St Claire and her old boyfriend? What if Nigel was seeing someone else? Asleep in another girl's bed right now? Or, ill? But Standish had called his mobile ... Ada frowned.

'Sorry, honey, it's just that he hasn't turned up today and I thought ...'

'You thought he was with *me*? Goodness, Ada, you have got a fertile imagination. I finished with Nigel years ago. We're still pals, but that's all,' Meredith insisted.

'Okay, just checking. You know what Standish is like.'

'Yes. Light touchpaper then scarper,' Meredith laughed softly. 'Still, not like Nigel to miss a rehearsal, is it? If that's all, I'd better go. I've an appointment in town.'

Ada frowned as she sat alone backstage. Had she been wrong to call the woman? Meredith had sounded sincere, perhaps Nigel had just been showing off the day he'd hinted that he'd got back together with her. Still, his non-appearance was a mystery and the longer it went on, the more Jeffrey Standish would fly into one of his unreasonable rages.

'I've had a call from Jeffrey Standish,' Molly told Lorimer. 'He's concerned that his new leading man hasn't turned up all day. Asked if we could send an officer to his flat, just to check.'

'That is odd,' Lorimer replied. 'Fairbairn wasn't so worried by his interview that he would go off somewhere, surely?'

Molly shook her head. 'I don't like it, boss,' she frowned. 'And Standish was obviously worried.'

'Why doesn't he go to see Fairbairn himself, then?'

Molly exchanged a look with Lorimer that told him more than words. The director had some sort of reason to want an officer at the actor's flat. What did he expect them to find?

'Let's go,' he said, gathering up the jacket on the back of his chair. 'And I think we want to bring two uniformed officers with us.' He paused for a moment. 'And Alisha. Could be a wild goose chase . . . ' He shrugged, but his jaw was set in a way that belied his words.

The building glowed with light from the setting sun, turning its bland concrete into a wash of pale gold. Lorimer could hear a blackbird's warning cry from the depths of evergreen shrubbery to one side of the flats, an answering call taken up a distance away.

There was a smell of paint as they entered and the detective superintendent noted the badly finished edge of the surrounding walls, no masking tape used to cover its skirting. It wasn't the sort of place where tenants or residents made a fuss about that sort of thing, he thought, or even had a choice of the primrose yellow freshening up the entrance.

Soon the five officers were out of the lift and standing at the door of Fairbairn's flat.

'Does he live alone, sir?' one of the uniformed officers enquired, after knocking loudly on the door.

Lorimer shook his head. 'Shares with a student from Caledonian University but the fellow is off on holiday. Easter break.'

The officer tried the door handle, his hands already protected with nitrile gloves.

'Locked.'

'Usual, sir?' the other uniform asked, the red enforcer in his hands.

'Give it another knock first,' Lorimer suggested.

'Police, open up,' the man called, hammering again on the door till it shook visibly under his fist.

'Right. We have reason to suppose the occupant may have come to some harm,' Lorimer said seriously. 'Two of his acting colleagues have been murdered. And he didn't turn up at the theatre as expected. Go on.'

After several swings of the thick hammer, the door began to tremble then flew open with a sudden splintering crash.

Lorimer let the two uniformed officers go in first then beckoned to Molly and Alisha to follow him, all now wearing protective gloves.

'In here, sir!' Lorimer heard the man call.

Lorimer stood in the doorway to the lounge looking straight ahead. In death, Nigel Fairbairn looked even smaller than he had in life, arms spread out as he lay on the floor. Blood from a head wound had soiled the carpet beneath him, flecking red spots across the nearest wall.

'Need scene of crime team here immediately,' he said, turning to Molly, but the DI already had her phone to her ear.

Lorimer glanced at the DC, catching her wide-eyed gaze as she looked at the body. She was learning fast, he thought, seeing the young woman backing out of the room. The less contamination of a crime scene the better.

'Want me to wait for the SOCOs?' Molly asked.

Lorimer shook his head. 'I'll stay here, DI Newton. Three corpses ... all connected to the theatre ... Can you get over to St James's? Have the team question every one of them. When did they last see Fairbairn? Where were they last night? And get Ada Galloway on her own, will you? She's got a sharp pair of eyes, never misses a trick, that one.'

Lorimer was now dressed head to toe in a white suit, like all the other figures in Fairbairn's flat. Blue and white tape across the doorway indicated a scene of crime and already neighbours were being questioned by his officers from Helen Street. Had there been any noises from the neighbouring flats? The police presence soon attracted a small crowd outside, despite the chilly night air, among them the inevitable clutch of reporters hoping for something to make the front pages of tomorrow's edition.

Here on the ninth floor, it was more peaceful, scene of crime officers busily collecting what might be evidence; electricity soon restored, the thrown switch dusted for prints.

'Oh, aye, you working late too?' A familiar voice made Lorimer turn to see the diminutive figure of Rosie Fergusson, Abby's mum.

'You on call, then?'

'Yes. Daisy has gone back to Melbourne for a funeral and Dan is away in Belfast helping out there,' Rosie explained, naming two of her fellow pathologists. 'We've got a locum on hand for PMs, though,' she added, Scottish law demanding a double-doctor system for post-mortem examinations. 'Right, where's our body?'

As yet there was no distinctive odour of decomposition and Lorimer had decided that Fairbairn's death must have taken place late the previous night. He said as much to Rosie, who nodded and waved him away as she knelt to examine the body.

'Someone's bashed his poor head in right enough,' she said softly, her gloved finger turning the dead man's head slightly to show the damage to his skull. 'We'll know more at the PM but looks to me he was attacked from behind and whoever did this was in a foul temper. That's our weapon, right?' She indicated the smooth grey stone smeared with blood, now encased in a plastic evidence bag and laid to one side.

'Yes, we think so. No other object in the room unless the perpetrator took it with him.'

'DNA should show a match for him,' Rosie murmured. 'It

happened less than twenty-four hours ago but I'm not sticking my neck out yet to be more precise. Think it may have been during the hours of darkness, though.'

Lorimer nodded. Fairbairn's corpse had been both cold and stiff when he had first seen it around six-thirty that evening, so death may have occurred during the previous night.

'Someone had cut the electricity off,' he told her. 'So it was probably dark when Fairbairn arrived home.'

Rosie glanced up at him. 'That day you came to Abby's school. Never thought it was going to turn out like this, eh?'

Lorimer blinked. She was right. A nasty coincidence, doing his goddaughter a favour, had grown into a murder investigation that pointed to someone wanting to kill off several of the actors involved with St James's Theatre. But who had borne such a grudge against these people? And why?

'It's all finished,' Standish groaned, head in hands as he sat in front of the detective inspector. 'We may as well shut the whole production down.' He looked from Molly Newton to the window of his office. Sounds of clamouring reporters could be heard, officers trying to reason with them, admittance to the building prevented for now. 'Publicity like that will finish me,' he said bitterly.

Molly listened to the director, wondering just how truthful he was being. Known for his flashes of temper, Standish was quite capable of lashing out at someone, wasn't he? The death of Fairbairn appeared to have been frenzied, by what she'd seen in the flat. And Guy Richmond's slashed throat? Had that been premeditated or had the actor carried the razor with him for some reason and had it taken from him by his killer in a moment of rage? Had Sarra been pushed to her death, deliberately? Hastily? She tried to stifle a yawn as she faced the director. It had been a long night and was nearing the witching hour already. Thoughts of sharing her bed with Daniel Kohi had long been abandoned, a quick call to tell him she'd not be home for hours yet.

'Let's go over this again,' Molly said patiently. 'You last saw Nigel when?'

'After you lot had had a go at him,' Standish said, narrowing his eyes at her. 'We met up at the theatre, had a chat and then he went home.'

'And what time was that?'

'Eight, nine o'clock, I can't really remember. It was dark here when I locked up. None of the junior groups are rehearsing as it's the Easter school holidays. Nigel said he was going home for something to eat, and I went back via the Curlers in Byres Road. You can check that if you like,' he added with a sigh.

'Can anyone verify the time you left the theatre?'

Standish shook his head. 'Caretaker left earlier. I mean, we all have keys for this place and I've every right to come and go at whatever hour I see fit.' He sat up straighter and tried to look down his nose at Molly. 'I'm the director of this company. And all of this has been detrimental to my business!'

Molly regarded him for a moment. 'Are you insured against performances not being carried out for any reason?'

'Insured? What the hell are you suggesting? That I kill off three good members of my cast to get my hands on a paltry amount of cash?' His voice rose, trembling with emotion, and Molly noticed the fists clenched by his side.

'I was due to make a small fortune out of our run up here and the promise of a West End production,' Standish yelled at her, his face becoming an unhealthy shade of puce. 'And you try to accuse me of murdering them!'

'Nobody is accusing you of murder, Jeffrey. Calm yourself or those newshounds out there will hear you,' Molly cautioned. 'But you must see that we need to establish where Mr Fairbairn was last seen and by whom.'

As suddenly as he had built himself into a rage, the director subsided, slumping into his chair, no doubt chastened by the mention of the press who, despite the late hour, had formed a small crowd behind the police cordon.

'I said goodnight to him. Locked up then went for my car. I was parked on the strip of ground to the far side of the theatre. Used to be a hall there in the old days but it was demolished when the church closed down.'

'Where did he go then?'

Standish sighed. 'I wish I could remember. I just got into the car and switched on the lights. Don't remember seeing him as I did a three-point turn and drove towards High Street.'

'He hadn't parked beside you?' Molly was curious. Their own CCTV had shown Fairbairn driving away from Helen Street after his interview and she had presumed that the actor must have driven straight to the theatre.

'No, come to mention it, he didn't appear to have had his car there. But of course, he'd left before me. I had to lock up, remember?'

Molly looked at Standish. It was a small but significant point. Was Standish lying? Easy enough to do that as there was no camera covering the theatre area. Perhaps it was true, and Fairbairn had left in a hurry, eager to get home, probably hungry too. PM results would show when he'd had his last meal.

'Did you hear his car?'

Standish's eyes glittered with emotion. 'I told you. I. Can't. Remember! Okay? I'm sorry he's dead, sorry for myself as much as the rest of the people who knew him. All right?'

'I think you can go home now, Mr Standish,' Molly said quietly. 'But please don't go anywhere far as we may need to talk to you again.'

CHAPTER FIFTY

Abigail tapped the bedroom door then pushed it open. 'Mu-um, cup of tea,' she called out, stepping around the bed to the hump that lay to one side beneath the duvet.

'Mmm.' Rosie rolled over and began to sit up. 'What time is it, Abby?'

'Eight o'clock. Dad and Ben are already away for the train to Edinburgh. The zoo, remember?'

'Thanks, love, this is good of you.' Rosie yawned, taking the mug of hot tea from her daughter. 'Need to be in by nine-thirty this morning,' she said.

'Post-mortem?'

Rosie glanced over the rim of her mug at Abby's face. There was no sign of a shudder from the girl. Perhaps she was becoming accustomed to the gorier side of her mother's profession at last.

'Afraid so. Your godfather has a triple murder on his hands now,' she admitted. 'No doubt you'll see it on the news.

Another of the actors from the theatre group. Orcadian chap, Nigel Fairbairn.'

Abby nodded. Orcadian? Wasn't it the islands of Orkney where her drama teacher had lived? She stored the thought away meantime, a pang of pity for the lady who had suffered so much heartbreak already. A memory of her pink hair and colourful clothes reminded Abby of how much she and her classmates had enjoyed their teacher's lessons, how much fun they'd had. It seemed so long ago now but it was only a few weeks since Ms St Claire had demonstrated all these different accents and they'd fallen about laughing at each other's attempts. She should have been an actress herself, Abby thought, but their teacher seemed really dedicated to helping her pupils to success instead, her smile lighting up the room whenever they arrived in class.

As she set the table for breakfast, Abby's thoughts turned to the rest of her day. Aunt Maggie would be coming over to be with her soon, Mum still on call after the events of the previous evening. Her godmother was one of her favourite grown-ups and Abby was keen to know what surprises Maggie Lorimer might have for their day together. Besides, Maggie had promised Abby a belated present, something special.

'Hello-oh!'

'Aunt Maggie!'

Abby pressed the entry button and stood waiting at the top of the stairs. Before long she could see a dark-haired figure below in the reception hall.

Soon Maggie Lorimer had reached the Brightmans' flat, a beaming Abby arms open for a hug.

'Great that we're both off now for the Easter break,' Maggie said when she'd untangled herself from her god-daughter's grasp, 'and I have a surprise for you as well.'

Abby looked down at her hands but all she saw was Maggie's shoulder bag. Was there some small gift hidden inside?

'It's too big to bring all the way up the stairs by myself, though you'll no doubt find a place for it in your cellar.'

'What is it?' Abby bounced up and down, any teenage notion of being too cool to show her excitement disappearing in an instant.

'You'll see. It's in my car,' Maggie replied. 'We'll go down together in a few minutes, once I have a chat with your mum.'

Abby gave her another hug then raced through the house till she came to her father's study, his window the best one to look down at cars parked in their private bay.

But, despite standing on tiptoe, she could not see Maggie's white Toyota anywhere.

'Abby, go and get your rain jacket and a scarf. You and Maggie are going out,' Rosie told her, a smile on her face that showed she had been let in on a secret.

Abby needed no second bidding and rushed to her room. Soon she was wearing her waterproof jacket and a tartan scarf that Daniel's friend, Netta, had given her for Christmas.

'Okay, honey, I'm off to work. You and Maggie have a great day,' Rosie told her, planting a kiss on Abby's cheek.

'Ready?' Maggie smiled at her. It was only then that Abby noticed her godmother was also wearing a weatherproof jacket and scarf. Were they just going for a walk? A wave of disappointment hit the teenager, her initial excitement dampened.

'Okay,' she replied, forcing a smile. Whatever was going

on, it was an outdoor sort of thing, and she had no notion of taking a long walk on this chilly March day.

'You're going to love this,' Maggie told her as they made their way downstairs, and Abby nodded, curious to know what she was going to see on the other side of the large front door.

Outside, the rainclouds that had threatened all morning had disappeared and a hazy sun was struggling to appear.

They walked side by side in silence for a couple of minutes till they reached Maggie's car, parked a little way along the street.

Abby stopped at the sight of the white Toyota, a cycle rack fitted with two bicycles attached.

'Happy belated birthday, darling girl,' Maggie said suddenly, squeezing Abby's gloved hand. 'That red one is yours from Bill and me,' she added, pointing to a brand-new red cycle beside her own.

'Wow!' Abby was almost speechless as she watched her godmother lift the bike from the rack and wheel it towards her.

'Oh, thank you. How did you know . . . ' she said, grasping the handlebars and gazing at her present.

'Oh, wee chats with your mum and dad. We knew you'd outgrown your old one and the way you've shot up this past year, we reckoned you needed a full-sized bike now.' Maggie opened the rear door of her car and pulled out two cycling helmets, a new one for Abby.

'It's fabulous! Oh, thank you, thank you so much!' Abby exclaimed, fastening the helmet strap under her chin.

Soon Maggie had taken her own cycle off the rack and

the pair were wheeling their way into the park, Abby beaming, heedless of the chilly air reddening her cheeks as they picked up speed. Overhead the skies cleared, patches of blue emerging as they cycled further along familiar pathways and onto the roads nearby.

Abby followed her godmother carefully along the busy roads, taking care to signal whenever they had to turn into another street. Part of Kelvin Way was now traffic free, but cyclists could still use the treelined street that bordered the park and the art galleries. Abby glanced at the landscaped grounds as they passed, swathes of yellow and pink primroses covering the grasses. Everything looked so fresh and pretty, she thought. Maybe the cold winter days were finally over, and she could look forward to more bike rides with her family and friends, though Ben was still too young to go out on the roads by himself.

The thought came to her then, of a place she might like to go, her new cycle enabling her a greater freedom. Abby smiled to herself. She was old enough to ride on the roads and speeding along on this beauty would be a joy.

'Fancy stopping for tea and cake?' Maggie called over her shoulder, one arm out to indicate a right turn into the galleries.

'Yes please!' Abby called, delighted at the thought. Soon she was locking her new bike on the cycle stanchion and shaking her hair out of the helmet, her thought of a much longer trip shelved for the moment.

The magnificent red sandstone building of Glasgow Art Gallery and Museum had been one of the Brightman children's favourite haunts since early childhood. Lorimer had shown them the peregrine falcons nesting in one of the museum's towers and they had grown up familiar with all the exhibits inside, Ben especially fond of the natural history section.

Abby was soon seated at a table by the window from where she could see her new bike.

'That is so nice of you to give me that bicycle,' she said.

'It's from both of us,' Maggie told her with a grin. 'And Bill made sure you had a new helmet and that good strong padlock and key.'

Abby rolled her eyes. 'Typical policeman,' she laughed. 'Making sure to keep me safe.'

'Right, what shall we have? Coffee? Hot chocolate?'

'Oh, hot chocolate please, with all the toppings. And a bit of iced gingerbread if they have any.'

Abby looked at her godmother. She was probably as old as Mum, older even, she thought, but there was not a single strand of grey in Maggie Lorimer's long dark hair, and her complexion was smooth and unblemished. *Good genes*, Maggie had told her once with a laugh when Abby had commented on her appearance. She never took offence when Abby made personal comments or asked about stuff. None of her own teachers at St Genesius were as much fun as Aunt Maggie, Abby reckoned, and though she enjoyed English as a subject, her godmother's stories were far more intriguing than those she had to read at school.

'Dad told me that Uncle Bill had gone to visit my drama teacher, Miss St Claire,' Abby began. 'How is she?'

'Yes, he did. Oh, that poor young woman. Well, you know

what happened,' Maggie sighed. 'I don't need to go into details. Her home was broken into, and she'd been bothered by newspaper reporters. It'll take a long time for her to come to terms with all of this . . . ' She broke off, shaking her head.

'Where is the cottage?' Abby asked. 'Is it far from here? What does it look like?'

Maggie nodded. 'I must have passed it once or twice on my way to my friend in Drymen, so I was curious enough to check it out on the internet to have a look. It's a pretty cottage, white walls and a red front door. One could probably cycle to it from here, but it would take a good hour or more. Remember the concert your friend Lisa's mum took you to at Douglas Academy?'

Abby nodded. 'It was way out in the country, but their house wasn't very far from Baljaffray, was it?'

'If you'd not turned down that country road to the Academy, kept straight on, you would have come to the cottage. It's on a hillside below a farm. Really nice spot, lots of sheep in the fields.' She sighed again. 'Hard to know whether she'll stay there or not.'

'Won't she come back to school? After the holidays?' Abby did not look up to meet Maggie's eyes. Instead, she licked a finger and began picking up the crumbs of icing from her plate.

Maggie frowned. 'Wait and see, dear. She's been through such a lot.'

Abby nodded again, as though absorbed with the remains of her gingerbread.

She'd like to see her drama teacher again and it would be such a shame if she were to leave for good.

CHAPTER FIFTY-ONE

'I am so sorry for your loss,' Molly murmured as she shook hands with Fiona and Sandy Fairbairn. She turned to the third family member, Nigel's brother, Norman. He was more like his father in appearance, tall and fair-haired, whereas Nigel had favoured his mother, a short, slim woman whose well-cut black coat and scarf emphasised her pallor.

'Still can't believe it, even after . . . ' Sandy Fairbairn bit his lip as his eyes strayed back along the corridor where they had identified the body. 'He was so young, had so much going for him . . . '

Mrs Fairbairn was crying now, her husband's arm around her shoulders.

'When can we bring him home?' Sandy asked. 'Arrange a funeral?'

Molly stifled a sigh. 'The Fiscal will release your son's body once our investigation is concluded,' she advised him. 'I'm sorry that we cannot be more definite than that. But be assured we are doing all we can to find the perpetrator of Nigel's killing. And we will,' she added, taking the man's hand that he held out. It was a firm handshake, the sea-green eyes that looked at her full of sorrow.

She watched as they left the building, escorted by the family liaison officer, the parents bowed and broken, their son walking beside them. This was the worst part of the job, and overseeing Nigel Fairbairn's post-mortem next on her list of duties. Lorimer would be there, she reminded herself, suddenly glad that the man she respected so much would be by her side.

The post-mortem showed several lacerations on the victim's skull, the main artery to the brain severed by one of the blows. Had he lost consciousness right away? It was hard to tell, but the frenzied appearance of the attack would suggest that Nigel Fairbairn had been felled to the floor then battered to death.

'Posterior cerebral artery extensively damaged,' Rosie said aloud for the benefit of those watching from the viewing platform. 'He'd have been dead in seconds rather than minutes.' But several seconds of precious life might have given the young man moments of agony and anguish. That he'd known his attacker was something for the investigating team to decide. Rosie continued her examination, her observations noted by Lorimer, Molly and Alisha as well as a new face from the Fiscal's office, Hazel McKay. The woman had introduced herself earlier that morning, a nod to the police officers whom she had already met. There was no doubt of course that this was murder, and the Fiscal's office would be giving Lorimer's team every assistance that they could.

'A third death,' the woman murmured, eyebrows raised. But Rosie merely nodded.

Yes, the third victim from that theatre group was now on her stainless-steel examination table but to Rosie he was still an individual to be given as much special treatment as every other dead body that came her way. *A name and not a number,* she'd reminded her students. *Every cadaver is more than the flesh and bones that they leave behind. Each has a story to tell, and our job is to show as much of that as we can.*

'Any further on with house-to house?' Lorimer asked as they walked back to their cars.

'His neighbours at the flats heard hee-haw,' Molly told him. 'And nobody around the theatre appeared to have seen or heard anything. CCTV shows him driving back to his flat and entering the building at exactly eight-fifty p.m. so that tallies with what Standish told us.'

'And the back way out? Any joy?'

Molly made a face. 'CCTV's been out since last December. I talked to the maintenance people and gave them a rollicking. Anyone could have slipped out of the back court, crossed the road and disappeared into the night.'

'They'd have had to take the stairs or the lift,' Lorimer said.

'No cameras in the lift. Never have been,' Molly sighed.

'So, what are we looking for? A car parked nearby? A figure on foot? Where is the nearest CCTV to Fairbairn's flat?'

'There's one up the hill at the *Sunday Post* building and another at the Chinese wholesale warehouse,' she replied. 'But if our man had parked on the main road between, he could have got away scot-free.'

Lorimer took a deep breath and let it out again. Patience was needed for a case like this, every loophole examined.

'It looks to me as if our perp had it all carefully planned,' he said at last. 'Was this person waiting for Fairbairn to return home, darkness enabling a swift attack? How did they know that he'd be back later than normal? Only Standish knew that. And he claims to have left the theatre before Nigel.'

'We only have his word for that,' Molly said. 'If he'd left first and asked Nigel to lock up then he'd have had a head start on him. He's also got a more powerful car. His Audi against Fairbairn's old banger might have made the difference.'

'Motive?'

'Aye, I can't see one. At least not right now. But Standish is known for his temper.'

'Which suggests an impulsive attack not the premeditated one that I'm inclined to favour.'

It was Molly's turn to sigh as they stood beside their vehicles. 'It was frenzied,' she began. 'As if someone had a terrible spite against the man. Revenge for something?'

Lorimer shrugged. 'Could be. The manner of the attack doesn't rule out premeditation. Waiting for Fairbairn to return, our killer is perhaps all tensed up, ready to launch the first blow. And it wouldn't have taken too much strength to whack the man over the head with that stone.'

'Man or woman, then,' Molly concluded thoughtfully. There were several women playing parts in the production – a pretty student playing the part of Sweeney Todd's young wife and another taking on the role of the miserable beggar who is unmasked as that same woman years later. Then

326

there was Ada Galloway whose constant gossip had filled a few pages of the police reports. She'd actively helped them, so what motive could she possibly have? All the females in the production were easily capable of overcoming the slight figure of the new Sweeney Todd. He'd have known any one of them. But under cover of darkness, that fuse thrown … yes, Lorimer was right. This latest death had been carefully planned.

'Who would have wanted them dead?' she said aloud.

Lorimer gave her the faintest of smiles and raised his eyebrows in reply then entered the Lexus and drove off, leaving Molly no further forward.

CHAPTER FIFTY-TWO

Ada Galloway shut the ledger with a sigh. The students' rents helped a lot, but she had been depending on the new production to make her fortune at last. For all her youthful aspirations, Ada Galloway had remained no more than a jobbing actress who might be recognised by shoppers in the supermarket, a quick puzzled glance as they passed her in the vegetable aisle, but whose name was never remembered. Now that the curtain had finally come down on Standish's *Demon Barber* she needed to see her agent, find out what parts were up for grabs, see if there might be a TV series needing someone like her. Preferably for a decent run.

She lifted the telephone and dialled Desmond's number, already rehearsing her words.

'Desmond,' she purred, 'Ada here, Ada Galloway,' she added, in the unlikely case that the man had forgotten who she was.

'Ada, my dear. What terrible news,' Morgan replied, his

tone sincere and full of regret. 'That poor dear boy, what is the world coming to?'

Ada's eyes fell on the newspaper on her table. Nigel's death had not made the front page but had been of sufficient interest to be almost a full page in the *Gazette*. **THIRD MURDER IN BELEAGUERED THEATRE GROUP**, the headline stated, going on to suggest that there would be no forthcoming productions for the remainder of the season.

'I fear for the rest of us,' Ada said, putting as much emotion into her voice as she could muster.

'Oh, my dear. Who would want to kill a national treasure like yourself?' Morgan asked. This time his tone was less sincere, and Ada wondered, not for the first time, if Desmond Dylan Morgan was laughing at her. He had supported her for several big parts in the past but less so recently and so she had agreed to take the female lead in Standish's production, though the financial rewards were poorer unless it led to London's West End. There was no love lost between the agent and director, Morgan having taken several promising actors from Standish and landed them juicy parts down south. Theatreland was generally acknowledged to be in London, the provincial theatres paying far less to actors.

'I'm hardly that, Desmond,' Ada said wryly. 'But I can't depend on Jeffrey any longer and I want to get away from here. Is there anything in the offing, darling?' she asked, hearing the wheedling note in her voice and despising herself for it.

'Well, there are always parts for older ladies, not that I am suggesting you are old, dear, no, no, not at all. Just, you know, past that first flush of youthfulness.'

'What's on your books?' she asked, deciding that a direct approach was probably best after all. Desmond was far too wily an old fox to fall for an actor's airs.

'Pitlochry have an opening for someone to understudy Ranevskaya,' he began.

'*The Cherry Orchard*! I played that part myself,' Ada exclaimed. 'We did it in The Citz, three, maybe four years ago.'

'I remember,' Morgan said. 'It was actually about eight seasons ago, my dear. How time does fly! You shared the role with that lass who landed a big part in *Coronation Street*, didn't you?'

Ada made a face that thankfully Morgan could not see. The reviews for the other actress had been far more generous than for herself, but it had been a decent run and she'd been happy to have shared star billing. Eight years! Had she really wasted all that time with Jeffrey Standish?

'So, who's taking the lead? And what's the pay like?'

Ahmed looked up as the doorbell rang. He could hear other feet hastening down the stairs to reach the front door. Then there were voices, his heart sinking as he recognised them. Police. Again. More questions, probably about Nigel Fairbairn this time. What did it take for them to leave him alone? he thought angrily, fists curling into two tight balls.

'Ahmed!' he heard his mother's call, then slouched out of his room, leaving the light switched on and his laptop open.

Down below he saw the two police officers, the blonde-haired woman and the tall senior officer. What was Lorimer doing here? he thought, suddenly alarmed by the presence of the detective superintendent. Whatever it was, it must be serious to bring him here.

'Ahmed,' his mother repeated, shrilly, 'these police officers wish to talk to you. Go into the back lounge, please,' she ordered, wiping her hands together in a dismissive gesture.

Ahmed looked up at the pair then strode wordlessly along the corridor, leaving DI Newton and Lorimer to follow.

He slumped into a chair and glowered at them, then, remembering his manners, gave a wave as if to say *sit down*.

'Mr Patel,' Lorimer began. 'You will know by now that the St James's Theatre is closed due to this latest fatality.'

Ahmed nodded. He was jobless now, Standish having told him not to bother returning for the foreseeable future. Still, it might be a chance to do something different, if only people like these police officers would leave him alone.

'Yes,' he replied. 'Whole thing's finished. I'm out for good.' He gave a shrug. 'I've plenty of options, though. My uncles have good businesses and are always looking for someone reliable.'

'Lucky for you,' DI Newton said. 'Not all in the group will be so fortunate. Actors' jobs are harder to come by.'

He shrugged again. That wasn't his business. Frankly, he didn't care if the lot of them were out of work. None of them had ever shown much interest in him unless it was to ask for this or that property.

'We wanted to ask you about Nigel Fairbairn,' Lorimer began, his voice calm and polite. 'Can you tell us the last time you saw him?'

Ahmed frowned. He had been on duty during each of the

rehearsals, Standish insisting that he take notes about what stage props would be required at any given scene.

'He didn't turn up for that last rehearsal,' he began. 'The last one before ... I think it must have been three days ago ... wait a minute ...' he lifted a hand, examining his fingers. 'No, four days ago, sorry, it's been hard ever since we heard about it ...' He looked up at the officers and saw only sympathy in their faces.

'And how did he seem?' Lorimer asked.

'Fine,' Ahmed replied. 'He was enjoying playing the part of Sweeney, I could tell. Yes, I think he was in good spirits.' He nodded.

'And you didn't see him after that?'

He shook his head. 'No. I was downstairs after the rehearsal, checking that we had the correct props for the show and making a note of any more that might be needed. We hire rather than buy them,' he added. 'And that's— was ... my responsibility.' He looked from one to the other. 'That was definitely the last time I saw him. Standish was in a right state when he didn't turn up the next day. Thought he was going to have a stroke or something, he was that mad.'

'Did you ever visit Nigel's home?' DI Newton asked.

'His home?' Ahmed's eyes widened. 'I don't even know where he lived,' he said, gesturing with his hands turned upwards. 'Didn't know any of them that well at all,' he added.

'Did any of the others in the group show any animosity to you, Mr Patel?'

'Are you asking if they were racist?' Ahmed turned to the woman. 'No, nothing like that. They just weren't my type, that's all.'

'Have you seen anybody other than the usual members of the cast at the theatre recently?' Lorimer asked.

'No,' he replied. 'Caretaker, of course, but that's all. The kids who belong to junior theatre don't come in during Easter holidays. Oh, there was one other person I saw, but I was used to seeing her occasionally.'

He looked up to see them both staring intently, waiting for him to continue. Would he tell them everything? Or just what suited him?

'Ms St Claire visited after her fiancé died,' he said. 'To pick up stuff that Guy had left downstairs.' He shrugged again. 'That was a while ago.'

He saw the tall detective rise from the settee. Thank goodness, they were going at last. No more questions, he told himself, desperate to brush away that first trickle of sweat from his brow.

'Thanks again, Mr Patel. And good luck in whatever new job you are offered,' Lorimer said, grasping Ahmed's hand.

He watched them leave, his mother ready at the door to bid them a polite goodbye. Had they really thought that Nigel's death could have had anything to do with him? Or were they just visiting everyone who had known the actor? Ahmed Patel blinked as sunlight flashed from the side of their car, still curious to know if their questions had a deeper purpose behind them. Or if that really was the last time he'd have to face those officers.

'Anything?'

Lorimer shook his head. 'I can't see any connection between Patel, Milroy and Fairbairn. The only one he might have had a grudge against was Guy Richmond and it looks to me as if we are looking for a single killer.'

Molly nodded slowly, concentrating on the road ahead. 'So, we rule out Patel?'

'Probably, though he may know more than he's letting on. Maybe he has seen something that could be important, but just isn't telling us.'

At that moment his mobile rang.

'Lorimer.'

Molly snatched a quick glance at his face as he listened to the call. Something was up, these blue eyes suddenly widening. She waited till he had ended the call then looked across, expectantly.

'That was DS Giles. He's just heard from Northumberland Police. They think they've found the whereabouts of Pettifer and his wife.'

CHAPTER FIFTY-THREE

It was a simple mistake, pulling out her credit card and tapping the top of the machine at the checkout, no thought required. Despite Josh having told her repeatedly to just use cash, the moment was over before Mary Pettifer even realised what she had done. Afterwards, she'd been too afraid to tell her husband, worried about his reaction.

They'd been on the run for so long that this bungalow in the countryside now seemed like a safe haven, an obscure little place off a farm road, hidden by high hedges.

We'll be okay for a while, Josh had assured her. *Got a friend with a boat who can take us across the Channel. Then we can start afresh. Paris, maybe.*

Mary had believed him. She'd miss the big house in Killearn, though. A dream of a place for a wee lassie who'd been brought up in a council flat in Priesthill.

The woman gasped when she heard the noise of police sirens, Josh already on his feet, grabbing the holdall.

'Back way. Now!' he hissed.

Then he was gone, Mary scrambling to pick up her coat and bag, looking around distractedly to see what she needed to take on this latest flight from danger.

A cry and a man's voice made the woman stop dead.

It was too late. They'd been found.

Mary Pettifer sank back into her chair, pulling the sheepskin coat around her shoulders, her whole body beginning to tremble.

Then Josh appeared between two burly police officers, hands cuffed in front of him, his mouth shut fast, a warning glare telling her to keep her own mouth shut as he was escorted through the living room towards the front door.

'Mrs Mary Pettifer?' A woman in a dark raincoat was suddenly in front of her, blocking her view. Mary's last glimpse of her husband was his bowed back as the uniformed officers marched him out of the house.

'Mrs Pettifer?' the woman repeated, a little louder this time in a tone that demanded attention.

'Yes?' The word came out in a strangled note.

'I'm Detective Constable Irwin and I have a warrant for your arrest. You do not need to say anything . . . '

Mary's head began to swim, the remainder of the woman's words lost in a humming noise as a strange fog blurred her vision.

'They're on their way up now,' Lorimer told the team. 'We're treating Pettifer as a possible suspect for the murder of Guy Richmond, but, unless we find evidence that he returned to Glasgow, his disappearance will eliminate him from the murders of Sarra Milroy and Nigel Fairbairn.'

'Do we think he committed Richmond's murder?' DS Giles asked, with a frown.

Lorimer shook his head. 'He lied about his whereabouts that night, so I am certain we'll find he was up to no good. But whether he had anything to do with the man's death remains to be seen. However,' he gave a grim smile and looked around at the members of the assembled team, 'we can hold the pair of them on suspicion of that and perhaps Pettifer will be frightened enough to tell us something that is really pertinent to the case.'

Mary sat shivering in the cell. One of her pals had been inside and Mary remembered her story. It had been a drugs raid when a bloke had been stabbed. They'd taken all of her clothes and possessions, even the laces from her trainers, leaving her in a washed-out grey tracksuit, waiting to see what would happen next.

At least she had her own clothes, Mary thought, hugging her coat around her. But it was the waiting bit that was worst and when at last she heard the jangle of keys in the door, a wash of relief came over her. Surely Josh would have got a lawyer by now, done something to get them both out of here?

Molly Newton felt a wave of sympathy for the young woman who was sitting opposite, a female solicitor by her side. Mary Pettifer's eyes were wide with terror, dark smudges of mascara long rubbed off the false lashes. She sat huddled into a fake sheepskin coat, shoulders raised high with tension, hands clasped around the polystyrene cup of tea.

'Mrs Pettifer. Mary,' Molly began, smiling at the woman.

'We are going to record this meeting and so I'd advise you to answer all of my questions, not just nod or shake your head, do you understand?'

Mary nodded in reply until, nudged by the solicitor at her side, she managed a squeaky *yes*.

Once the date and time and those present had been established, Molly once more smiled at the trembling woman.

'We want to ask you questions about the night you told us your husband was at home with you when in fact you were with friends in Glasgow.' Molly paused, looking the woman straight in the eye. 'The night Guy Richmond was killed.'

The woman burst into tears, holding her head in both hands.

'I'm sorry, I'm sorry, it had nothing to do with me . . . Josh asked me to say he was at home with me!'

In another room Lorimer was looking across the table at a white-faced Josh Pettifer and his solicitor. Already he had challenged the man about his flight from Glasgow, suggesting that it gave the police a clue about running away from a murder charge. So far each question had been returned by a 'no comment' through gritted teeth.

'See, lying about your alibi makes us suspect that you saw Guy Richmond on the night that he died. And, you know, running away like you did, that doesn't look good for you, Josh. Not good at all. Murder . . . twenty-one years with no time off for good behaviour, how old would you be by then . . . ?' He turned to DS Giles at his side with a questioning look.

Pettifer exchanged an anxious glance with his solicitor who nodded at him briefly, then turned back to face Lorimer.

'I didn't kill him!' Pettifer sighed. 'How many more times do I have to tell you?'

'So, what happened that night?'

'Nothing. Nothing happened at all.' Pettifer licked his lips and darted anther frightened glance at his solicitor.

'I think my client would like to offer you some information,' the lawyer remarked. 'Go on, Mr Pettifer. Tell the superintendent what you told me.'

'If I tell you everything, can I go home?'

Lorimer raised his eyebrows and shrugged. 'All depends what you have to tell us.'

Pettifer sagged down in his seat, all his previous assurance gone.

'I was supposed see Richmond that night,' he began. 'Thought I had a deal with him.' He looked away from the detective superintendent then began chewing his lip. 'Not just the usual. He wanted a whole lot more.'

'Are you trying to tell me that Guy Richmond was a serious cocaine addict?'

'I don't know,' Pettifer said quietly. 'Texted me to meet him, didn't he. Then ... well when I got there he hadnae turned up. Not a soul there. Wasted my time driving all the way out to that fishing place. Called his number over and over but his phone was dead.'

'Slow down,' Lorimer said, raising a hand. 'When did Richmond text you?'

Pettifer gave a shrug. 'Earlier that Sunday. Mibbe ... afternoon?'

'And, what was your arrangement?'

Pettifer drew in a long breath before continuing.

'I was tae bring him a quantity of cocaine ... a large quantity like I says ... and he'd hand over the cash. Only, I got there and the place was deserted.'

'What time was that?'

'Text said I wasnae tae arrive till midnight,' Pettifer mumbled. 'S'pose he wis trying tae be dead secretive, like. All sort of cloak-an-dagger stuff. That's whit it read like anyway.'

'If this is true, why did you and your wife leave home in such a hurry and go into hiding?'

'Cos of whit's happening right now!' Pettifer insisted. 'I guessed you lot wid be after me as soon as you found I had no alibi for that night.'

'How did you first come to be supplying drugs to Guy Richmond?'

Pettifer licked his lips nervously. 'Met him when he was a student. Knew a few of them that hung around the drama school.'

'How often did Richmond buy drugs from you?'

Pettifer's leg was bouncing up and down rapidly and he turned his head away.

'Loads of times.'

'Once a week. More often?'

Pettifer ran his hands through his hair. 'No, no' really ... and not that often after he'd graduated. That wis why it was so strange, him suddenly asking for a load more ... '

The sweat was pouring off the man's brow now, his confession clearly affecting him badly.

'And can you show us these texts, Mr Pettifer?' Lorimer asked.

Pettifer looked towards his solicitor who once again nodded.

'Aye.'

'Your phone ...?'

The man heaved a sigh. 'It's at the warehouse, locked inside my desk.'

'We can easily obtain a warrant to search your premises and check that, then?'

'Aye. You'll see what I'm saying is true.'

Lorimer kept his face impassive. If what Pettifer had told them was true, then Richmond could have met up with someone else earlier on. Was the man spinning him a yarn, something concocted during the days he'd been away from Glasgow? The evidence on his phone might well put him in the clear. And yet, he could just as easily have pretended to call Richmond repeatedly after having dumped his body in the loch.

'Was he meant to be seeing you alone?'

Pettifer dropped his gaze.

'Aye,' he said quietly.

Lorimer's tone remained bland, though Pettifer's body language told him that the man was still hiding something.

Pettifer turned to his lawyer who whispered behind his hand. The drug dealer nodded then sat up straighter.

'See how I told you I'd arranged to meet Richmond? Ah didnae need tae tell youse anything, did I? But ah'm covering my back here.' He glanced again at the man at his side who nodded encouragement.

Lorimer sat back, thinking hard.

If this account by the drug dealer was in any way true,

then Richmond could have been murdered earlier that same evening, his body already in the fishing loch.

'What did you do with the drugs after you left the rendezvous?'

Lorimer saw a muscle move in the man's jaw as he looked back at him.

'No comment.'

It was back to stalemate again, from the look on Pettifer's face. He'd be able to hold him for a while yet, pending the search for the man's phone.

Pettifer's revelation had left them with plenty to think about. Had Meredith St Claire really been so unaware of the quantity of drugs Richmond had intended to obtain on the night of his death? There had been no trace of them at the cottage. And Pettifer was clamming up tight about what he'd done with them.

So, who had Richmond seen, possibly earlier that night? And why had that same person slit his throat? Was it one of the actors to whom he'd promised to sell a load of coke?

The idea, when it came, made Lorimer's heart beat a little faster.

Was it time to let Pettifer know that he was no longer a suspect in Richmond's murder? No, he was not yet finished with the drug dealer, sensing that some facts had been twisted during the interview.

'You will be charged with possession of a class A drug, Mr Pettifer, and with arranging to sell to another, as you have admitted today. Dealing drugs in such quantities will no doubt command a custodial sentence, but that will be for a judge to decide.'

CHAPTER FIFTY-FOUR

'It'll be nice, sure it will,' Netta assured her friend as they stepped out of Daniel's car. 'Molly's that busy at work the now, but she's obviously gone to all the trouble of having us over for a meal.'

Janette pulled her coat collar closer around her neck, the gusty wind threatening to blow her off her feet. Daniel was striding ahead, his whole demeanour showing how eager he was to be with his girlfriend again. She felt Netta's hand sliding into her arm to draw her closer.

'Awfie windy the night,' she murmured. 'But see me? My mammy always said I had a good grip o' Mother Earth.' She chuckled, pulling Janette up the slope of the car park as the wind roared through the leafless trees of Lilybank Gardens.

Daniel unlocked the door and stood aside, waving his mother and Netta inside. 'She'll not be long,' he said.

Molly Newton's flat came as a surprise to the Zimbabwean woman. It was bright, modern and as neat as her own little bungalow back home. She loitered in the hallway, admiring

343

the coloured photographs of Scottish scenery that lay behind glass clip frames arranged on the pale cream walls. Surely that was the mountain that Daniel had climbed with Mr Lorimer? Janette thought, staring at the photo of Buchaille Etive Mor, the one where that poor Dutchman had come to grief.

'Mother, come on in. Molly's left a surprise for us,' Daniel called.

Janette entered the sitting room, eyes widening at the comfortable furniture and a table set for four, a gauzy cloth covering plates of food. This was a cosy place to come home to, she realised with a pang. How often had Daniel relaxed into that squashy sofa after a long shift, Molly by his side? She did not notice her son bending to switch something on, but the strains of music that came from some hidden speakers was calming to the older woman. Mozart, she decided, recognising the famous composer's style. Hadn't she listened to her radio most evenings back home during the colder months, the British radio station one of her favourites? *Eine kleine Nachtmusik*, she thought, her lips turning up in a smile.

Then Netta was ushering her towards the white wooden table and matching chairs, their cushions a pretty pattern that matched the blinds by the window. Something delicious was wafting from the kitchen, Janette's nose told her.

'See she's gone tae a lot of trouble for us, bless her heart,' Netta declared after Daniel had swept off a nylon cover to reveal bowls of salad, platters of cold meat, smoked salmon and prawns.

'Her home-made potato salad is really good,' Daniel said, picking up the dish and offering it to his mother.

'Did she make thon Waldorf salad an' all?' Netta's eyebrows rose in admiration.

'She did.' As Daniel replied, his mother could hear a distinct note of pride in his voice.

'Good cook then, is she?' Netta continued, scooping up some salad onto her plate.

'Oh yes,' Daniel enthused. 'Doesn't have much time right now which is why she had to prepare a lot of this in advance, but I especially love her Italian dishes.'

'If she's a keen wee cook, mibbe ye could show her a few of yer ain recipes frae Zimbabwe,' Netta suggested to Janette who was beginning to revise her opinion of Detective Inspector Newton. Not just a hard-working cop with a pretty face, but a woman with skills that suggested she enjoyed being a homemaker.

The door to the sitting-cum-dining room opened, and Molly breezed in, taking off her jacket and slipping it onto the back of the vacant chair.

'So sorry to have kept you all waiting,' she said. 'Just let me take the pie out of the oven.'

'Were ye no feart it wid burn, lass?' Netta asked.

'Oh, I had it on a timer,' Molly laughed. 'It would never do to burn your dinner!'

Soon the dish was revealed, a chicken and mushroom pie that Molly dished up to them all, an especially generous portion for Daniel, Janette noted.

'We had a couple in custody that meant a longer time to interview them,' Molly said. 'But let's not talk about work, eh?' She looked sideways at Daniel.

The evening passed with Molly asking Janette about the

345

sorts of food she cooked back in Africa and the older woman was only too happy to tell her.

At last, it was time for them to drive back across the city to their Southside flat, Molly insisting that she wanted to clear up later. *You are my guests*, she had said firmly, giving both of the older women a hug.

Molly watched as they walked back to Daniel's car. She was tired now, the day's events and the strain she had felt before her visitors arrived making her yawn.

Molly put the thoughts of the murder cases from her mind and smiled as Daniel turned to wave, then she blew him a kiss before turning back into the room. For once she had sensed the Zimbabwean woman's approval. Perhaps now she and Daniel might embark on a new chapter in their relationship?

By the time she had filled the dishwasher and let the pie dish soak in the sink, Molly was ready for bed.

It was not long before sleep took her into dreams where she was stepping slowly down a long narrow aisle, a bouquet of flowers clutched in her hand, Daniel resplendent in a dark suit turning to beam at her, Mendelssohn's wedding music playing from a distant organ.

CHAPTER FIFTY-FIVE

'I think it is important that we talk to Sarra Milroy's parents again,' Molly told the assembled officers. 'See if there's any link between her and any of the St James's group that might give us an idea why she was killed.'

'It wasn't Pettifer, then?' Alisha asked.

Molly shook her head. 'We don't think so. Pettifer's confessed to having a deal to sell thousands of pounds' worth of cocaine to Richmond. We checked his mobile and it was exactly where he said it was. The transcript of the texts to and from Richmond are exactly as he told DS Giles and Superintendent Lorimer.'

'As to the money Pettifer was expecting to be paid, he mentions a rather large sum of cash in his text messages.' Giles raised his eyebrows as he addressed the assembled officers.

'Have we any follow up to that yet, Davie?'

DS Giles nodded. 'Yes, Richmond withdrew several large sums from his account in the weeks leading up to his death.

One theory is that he may have been amassing cash to pay Pettifer for drugs. When questioned about these withdrawals, Ms St Claire said they were probably to do with putting down deposits for their wedding. That's what he had told her, seemingly.' He caught Molly's eye and shook his head. 'But when we looked into that this morning, we found no trace of down payments for a venue or caterers.'

'Does she know this?' Molly asked.

'Not yet, ma'am.'

'Well, I think you and DC Mohammed need to pay her a visit. See how she reacts.

'So.' Molly turned to the whiteboard where the images of the three victims and those closest to them were pinned, along with the significant dates and times of each murder. 'Let's see who might have had reason to do away with Sarra Milroy.' She tapped the image of the young actress. 'Her death is the oddest of the three, given that she was pushed down a flight of stairs rather than assaulted with a weapon.'

Molly looked at each member of the team in turn. 'Now, what does that suggest?'

'A different killer?' one of the team offered.

'She had some knowledge of who had killed Richmond?' another suggested.

'Both possibilities but Detective Superintendent Lorimer wants us to follow up the latter,' Molly said. 'He is inclined to think that young Ms Milroy may have been meeting someone connected to the theatre. And now that we know about Pettifer's involvement with Richmond it may well have involved drugs.' She paused for a moment, eyeing the officers to see their reaction.

'And,' she added with a rueful grin, 'we know from experience never to discount any of the boss's inclinations.'

Meredith saw the car approaching as she stood at the window. Why had the police returned yet again? They'd already called to ask about Guy making withdrawals from their account. Was it possible that an arrest had now been made and they were about to inform her? She drew a long sigh. What a relief that would be. She swallowed hard. A funeral to arrange, people to see in a crowded crematorium (Guy had never liked churches, possibly a reaction against his Baptist-loving parents) and then ... oh, the very thought of it all being over made the woman draw her arms together in a hug.

'Ms St Claire? DS Giles and DC Mohammed.' The young man in the weatherproof jacket stood on her doorstep, warrant card in his hand. 'May we come in?'

'Of course.' Meredith stood aside and smiled at them both, remembering the young woman with the glossy black hair. 'Come on through to the kitchen. I was about to make some coffee ... ?' She ended with a question in her voice.

'No thanks, we don't want to keep you for too long,' Giles replied, settling himself on one of the kitchen chairs, the girl pulling out another and perching on its edge.

'We wanted to ask you about the wedding. I take it you cancelled all the arrangements after your fiancé's death?'

Meredith clutched the edge of the breakfast bar. 'Actually, no. I haven't gotten around to that yet,' she replied, twisting her diamond ring as though to remind herself of its existence.

'Why not?'

Meredith bristled. 'It just ...' she faltered, 'I have a funeral to arrange first and foremost,' she said. 'Untangling the wedding did not seem high on my list of priorities. Besides, it was Guy who'd arranged everything. I'm not sure I'd know where to begin.'

She saw a swift look between the pair and stiffened.

Something wasn't right.

'Where were you hoping to be married?' the Asian girl asked.

'Mar Hall. Out in Bishopton,' Meredith replied. 'Why?'

Again, a strange look passed between them.

'What's wrong?'

'I'm really sorry to inform you, Ms St Claire, but there is no booking for your wedding.'

Meredith stood up, staring wildly from one of the police officers to the other.

'What do you mean? Guy had everything arranged. He told me ... Mar Hall on July the fourth, American Independence Day. He joked that was his final time as an independent man ...'

She began to gasp, one hand clutching her throat, stumbling forward before the detective caught her in his arms and helped her onto a chair.

'Breathe, breathe,' she heard the girl say as she closed her eyes and felt hands pushing her head between her knees.

The sound of running water then the cold rim of a glass against her lips made Meredith sit up.

'I'm so sorry,' DS Giles murmured. 'You obviously had a shock. But I have to tell you that Mr Richmond did not book anything at all.'

350

Meredith clung onto his outstretched hand, her nails digging into his flesh.

'No ... you're wrong ... Guy booked everything; hotel, caterers, ceilidh band ... flowers ... he wanted it all to be a surprise for me ... I can't believe you,' she cried, looking at them wildly. 'There's been some sort of mistake!'

'You didn't think to ask the hotel for the return of his deposit?'

Meredith opened her mouth to reply then closed it again, shaking her head.

'Are you all right?' the young woman asked, her dark eyes full of sympathy.

Meredith nodded, grasping the glass of cold water that was being held out to her.

'Yes,' she whispered. Then, 'No, of course I'm not.' She looked up at them, a sudden fury in her expression. 'How can I be all right, when I find that the man I loved lied to me? Tell me that?'

Lorimer nodded as DS Giles related the bereaved woman's reaction. It made perfect sense to him that Meredith St Claire would react in that way. He watched as the door to his office closed, and turned to the window with a sigh.

It was all beginning to fit together now, and a wave of sadness came over him as he thought about the drama teacher.

It was up to the team to find sufficient evidence to make an arrest, of course. Perhaps their visit to the Milroys would bear fruit. Yet he was loath to tarnish their daughter's memory. If he was right, their burden in losing their girl was about to become even greater.

*

It was early evening when Lorimer and Molly stood at the door in Craigbank. The privet hedge round the small front garden looked in need of a trim and the long grass on the front lawn had not been cut for weeks. Tending to their garden would be the last thing on the minds of these parents, Lorimer realised. And now they would have to probe into wounds that were still raw. Dealing with a murder was never just about the one victim. As he had said to his officers many a time, it was like a stone being thrown into a deep pool, the ripples extending outwards to the many other victims damaged by the crime.

'Mr Milroy?'

Lorimer saw a man standing in the doorway.

'Yes?'

Lorimer and Molly held out their warrant cards.

'Detective Superintendent Lorimer and Detective Inspector Newton. May we come in?'

Gary Milroy nodded and opened the door to admit them. 'This is about Sarra, isn't it?'

He led them into a pleasant open-plan sitting room that led to a dining kitchen, motioning for them to sit down.

'I'll just get the wife,' he said, leaving them for a few moments. 'Angie. Come on down,' they heard him call. 'We've got visitors.'

There was the sound of footsteps on the stairs then Angela Milroy burst into the room, stopping as soon as she caught sight of the police officers.

'Oh,' she cried, one hand flying to cover her mouth.

'Come and sit down, love,' her husband said, stepping forward and taking her by the hand.

'We really are sorry to intrude again,' Lorimer began, 'but we have more questions about Sarra.'

'You haven't found who killed her, then?' Angela Milroy asked, her face crumpling in disappointment.

'Our investigation is ongoing,' Lorimer assured her. 'And we will be in touch the moment we have further news.'

'Oh,' she said again.

'I am sorry to have to ask you this, but had you any knowledge that Sarra might have been involved with drugs?' Molly asked.

The look between the parents was answer enough, Angela Milroy biting her lower lip, her husband clasping her hand, an expression of regret in his eyes.

'Aye, we did.' He sighed. 'That was the main reason that Sarra moved out,' he admitted. 'I told her we wouldn't tolerate her bringing any of that stuff under our roof.'

'Do you know what sort of drugs she might have been using?'

Angela Milroy shook her head at the same time as her husband nodded.

'Och, she was a silly lassie,' Gary groaned. 'If only I'd given her another chance ... '

'She wasn't using anything bad,' his wife protested. 'She just wanted something to make her feel a bit livelier. That's what she told me.'

'Cocaine is a class A drug, pet,' Gary said gently. 'She was getting mixed up with the wrong people.'

He looked across at Lorimer and Molly. 'I thought having rent to pay would keep her from spending her money on drugs,' he admitted. 'I wish now ... ' His eyes filled with tears. 'Sorry,' he mumbled.

'Do you know who was supplying cocaine to your daughter?'

Angela Milroy nodded. 'We thought it was Guy Richmond, the fellow who inherited all that money.'

'You are sure about that?'

The woman nodded. 'Sarra told me he had given her some to make her feel better after a show. One they did a few months back.' She exchanged a nervous look with her husband. 'I found some in her dressing table drawer and told her dad.'

'I said that was the end of it,' Gary sighed. 'She had to stop being so stupid or find another place to live.'

'Then he went and bought that place out in the country with Sarra's drama teacher. We thought they'd settle down and leave our Sarra alone once she moved to the flat in Darnley.'

'Did she keep on seeing him for drugs, then? Is that why she was . . . ?' Gary Milroy broke off, unable to finish his sentence.

'It's possible,' Lorimer replied. 'He was a very wealthy man and could afford to spend a great deal of money.'

'Buying drugs?'

Lorimer nodded. 'Yes.'

'Scum like that, giving drugs to wee lassies.' Sarra's father shook his head.

Then Gary Milroy's jaw tightened as he looked straight into Lorimer's blue eyes.

'I hate to speak ill of the dead,' he said. 'But I'm glad that bastard isn't around to inflict his poison on anyone else.'

CHAPTER FIFTY-SIX

Abigail Brightman looked up at the cloudless sky. It was a perfect day for a trip out to the countryside on her new bike. Dad and Ben had gone over to see Maggie Lorimer and Abby had told her parents that she was off on a picnic with her friend, Isabel. It was a fib that no one would ever find out, she hoped, but she did have a pang of guilt at not telling them the truth; that Izzy had gone away for a few days with her own family. That sense of abandonment by her best friend had left Abby feeling at a loose end. Mum was working (of course) and would be furious if she found out where her daughter was going. But ever since she had been given her new bicycle, the same idea had been circling around her brain. She'd be back home before dinner, Abby told herself, as she wheeled the bike along the pavement, mentally going over the route she had planned.

She smiled as she passed so many familiar landmarks, the Shish Mahal restaurant on Park Road, the bridge over the River Kelvin, then a little climb up and over to the junction beside the Botanic Gardens. It was a straight run all along Great Western Road, no problem. She'd looked at the maps in her dad's study as she'd plotted her route, curious to know why he had circled so many places in red. Something to do with mapping murder, perhaps, a subject he had tried to explain to her. Anyway, it didn't look that far on the pages, she decided.

The wind brought colour to Abby's cheeks as she cycled along, stopping now and then whenever the traffic lights changed to red. Once past Anniesland Cross and Knightswood, Abby fell into the rhythm of the cycle, careful to stay well away from cars whizzing past. Then she was signalling at several roundabouts, the signs ahead showing how close she was to Clydebank. The words of a poem she had learned at school came back to her as the girl smiled at the river of yellow all the way along the central reservation, *a host of golden daffodils*! It was truly springtime now and she hadn't a care in the world, Abby thought, freewheeling along the final stretch before the turn-off that would take her eventually to Milngavie.

After the stop-start cycle through some outlying suburbs, the countryside seemed to open up and soon Abby was heading towards the Stockiemuir road and her destination.

She glanced longingly up the hill towards Helmi's coffee shop as she approached the roundabout at Baljaffray, remembering the delicious cakes that she'd enjoyed there with Ben, a treat from the Brightman grandparents on their previous visit from London.

The road narrowed, twisting through trees that were still to show their leaves and past yet another roundabout, this one filled with more daffodils. Not far, now, she thought, avoiding a pothole on the road and keeping a sharp eye open for oncoming traffic. Then another climb, her breath beginning to labour a little, and past the turn-off to Douglas Academy.

Now Abby was in unfamiliar territory, her only hope of finding her teacher's cottage the few things that Maggie Lorimer had told her.

There was a farm high up on the left, sheep in the fields with a few tiny new lambs and then, a pretty cottage nestling on a plateau on the hillside. That must be it, Abby decided, spotting the red front door as she slowed down and turned towards the farm track. It was bumpy and a bit stony, so she dismounted, deciding to wheel the bike the rest of the way. She was surprised at how tired she felt after the journey which had taken much longer than she'd expected. Her legs were a bit like jelly, shoulders aching from the strain of gripping the handlebars, and so it was more difficult than she'd expected to push her bicycle slowly up towards the cottage. Maybe Miss St Claire would offer her a glass of cold water? Her throat was dry and her head beginning to throb, so she undid the strap of her cycle helmet, hooking it over the handlebars.

Abby paused as she reached the building, suddenly shy. She'd imagined this moment for ages, her drama teacher pleased to see her, of course, and glad of the company. What if she was out? Or, worse, what if she wasn't pleased to see her after all? The sky which had promised a fine day when she had set out was now full of clouds, a breeze chilling her bare neck.

The ideas struck her forcefully, the thought of a wasted journey suddenly overwhelming the girl. Nevertheless, she pushed on, making sure the bicycle tyres avoided muddy ruts where a tractor had been, till she came at last to the cottage itself. Abby looked at an upstairs window which was wide open, a pale curtain billowing inside, caught by the breeze. She *must* be in, surely?

A knock on the door did not elicit any response at first so Abby knocked again, harder this time.

The sound of feet thumping down a staircase was a relief. Then the door swung open.

'Yes?'

The pink-haired teacher stood there, her lime-green pleated skirt and purple shirt reminding the schoolgirl of how much she had always admired her teacher's flamboyant dress sense. But the face that looked down at her was pale, eyes devoid of her usual colourful make-up.

'Yes?' Meredith St Claire asked again.

'Miss, it's me. Abby Brightman. I've . . . I've come to visit you,' the girl stammered.

For a long moment nothing was said as the woman frowned at her.

'Abigail! Of course. I didn't recognise you out of your school uniform,' Meredith St Claire replied, a soft smile on her lips. 'Come in, won't you?'

Abby parked her bicycle against the cottage wall and entered the house. It was cool inside, and she jumped as somewhere within a door banged loudly. Perhaps the back door had been open, creating a draught? She shivered a little, following her teacher through the house, curious to see what the cottage was like, until she was led into a bright, modern kitchen.

'What a surprise,' Meredith St Claire said, looking at Abby strangely. 'Did you come on your own?'

Abby nodded. 'I cycled all the way,' she said, then bit her lip. 'It's a lot longer than I thought.'

'How on earth did you know where I live?'

Abby felt uncomfortable under her teacher's questioning gaze. Had she done the wrong thing to turn up unexpectedly like this?

'My godmother, Maggie Lorimer, told me,' Abby explained. 'Mr and Mrs Lorimer are my godparents. Do you remember Uncle Bill? He gave a talk at the careers seminar. You see, they gave me a new bike and I've been dying to ride out to see you. To see if . . . '

'Yes?'

'I wondered how you were,' Abby said in a small voice, her cheeks reddening. 'I mean, after . . . you know . . . '

Meredith's eyes softened. 'How kind,' she said. 'What a nice thought.' She paused for a moment and turned towards the back door, as if she was listening for something. 'And nobody came with you?'

Abby shook her head. 'I didn't tell anyone I was coming to see you. Thought it might not be allowed . . . I mean, it's a long way from Kelvingrove . . . '

'Poor child! You must be starving!' Meredith said, clapping Abby's shoulder. 'Let's see what I can make for you. A sandwich? Some cake? A cup of tea?'

Abby grinned and nodded. It was going to be all right after all.

'Yes please,' she said.

*

Lorimer looked at the papers in front of him and sighed deeply. He'd had his suspicions, of course. Every decent officer would have looked at this person with the utmost scrutiny and yet thus far they had managed to evade detection. Easy to do with such a background of knowledge, the theatrical training being put to a specific use. Now that he had seen these figures, he reckoned he had also found a motive behind the murder of Sarra Milroy.

His mind went back to that darkened stairway. Had the person who had pushed her followed swiftly, checked for a pulse? There had been no traces of DNA on the dead woman's body. Gloved hands, then, perhaps forensic quality that enabled the perpetrator to determine that life was extinct. If so, then they had been scrupulously careful not to contaminate the scenes of crime, no traces left to establish a contact. So clinical, so well planned . . .

And now he had some real evidence in the pages on his desk, it was time to talk to Joshua Pettifer once more.

'Oh, no, it's begun to rain.' Meredith looked up as a rattle of heavy raindrops swept onto the kitchen windows. 'How on earth are you going to get home in that!'

Abby's face fell. She had set off with such expectations but now the skies were much darker, rainclouds louring overhead. The thought of a return journey in such weather and arriving home soaking wet made her clench her teeth in anguish.

'My bike . . . it's still outside . . . '

'Come on,' Meredith said, opening the door. 'Put it in the garage, eh? That'll keep it dry meantime. Here's the key,' she added, taking a key from a hook by the back door. 'Run now, don't get too wet!'

And Abby did run, grabbing her precious bicycle and heading to the nearby wooden garage. There was a metal handle that twisted easily when she put in the small silver key that Meredith had given her, then she heaved the door open.

Inside there were several cartons stacked neatly to one side of her teacher's car and a tall freezer at the far end beside a wooden table. Overhead there were wooden beams where a folded sun umbrella had been laid, along with several long narrow boxes and what looked like a bundle of old clothes.

Abby squeezed past the side of the car, careful to keep her bike from any contact, then placed it carefully next to the freezer. As she made her way back, her sleeve caught on something sharp, and she pulled away in alarm, knocking over a long metal pole propped against the wall. It teetered sideways, catching something on the overhead beam.

Abby gave a cry and ducked as a dark shape descended, covering her face.

The girl battled with the cloth for a moment in sudden panic, then stepped back.

'Stupid!' she said aloud, her heart thumping. She bent to pick up the heap of black material from the floor, realising that it must have fallen from the beam above her.

Picking it up, Abby saw that it was a long garment, a costume of some kind, perhaps? Maybe Ms St Claire kept all her old theatrical costumes up there, she thought, gazing at the flat boxes. She looked down again, worried now that she might have dirtied the cloak, or whatever it was. She gave it a quick shake and swept her hand down the folds of heavy black fabric, then stopped, a frown on her face.

There were hard, dried patches along one side of the garment and, as she screwed up her eyes to see more clearly, flecks of dark reddish-brown. She ran her finger across them then stopped, her mind refusing to believe what her eyes were telling her.

'Abby?'

Abby whirled around, grasping the cloak with both hands, looking at her drama teacher as she slowly entered the garage.

'What have you got there?' Meredith asked, walking towards her.

Abby shook her head, suddenly too afraid to utter a single word.

'Give that to me, Abigail,' Meredith ordered.

Abby looked down, sure now of what it was that she could see on this black cloak, a queasy feeling in her stomach.

'Give it to me now, child!'

Abby froze then, hearing something quite different in the woman's tone.

And why did she look so angry?

Abby backed away, her hand finding the handlebar of her bike.

Snatches of conversation at home came back to her now, overhearing her mum and dad discussing the murders of these three actors. *Forensic evidence . . . blood spatter . . . Sarra Milroy, a former pupil at St Genesius.*

Then, as her teacher drew closer and closer, a horrible realisation began to dawn on Abigail Brightman.

CHAPTER FIFTY-SEVEN

'Abby?' Rosie Fergusson opened her daughter's bedroom door and frowned. That was strange. She had thought that Abby and her friend Isabel would have been back hours ago from their picnic, once the rain had started. Rosie pulled her mobile from her pocket and was soon listening to the recorded message. *Unavailable.* Where was she? Rosie wondered, with sudden irritation. Surely Abby would have called to ask if it was okay to change their plans and go off to the cinema or somewhere? Abby wasn't a rebellious child but perhaps this was the start of those teenage years she'd read about when one's kids began to assert themselves and do their own thing.

Rosie rang the Fleming house phone, Isabel's dad, Dr Fleming, having kept his landline for emergencies. But once again there were only the clipped tones of a pre-recorded voice, explaining that no one was at home right now.

'It's Rosie here, Abby's mum. Can you ask her to call us please?'

Rosie clicked off her phone. Where on earth had those girls got to? Abby's bike was not downstairs in the communal hall so she must still be out somewhere.

There was only one other person to call, and for a moment, Rosie felt a worm of unease as she lifted her phone again.

'Rosie? How are you? Sorry you couldn't join us today. Bill managed to come home to see Solly and Ben before they left. Think they'll be with you shortly,' Maggie Lorimer's cheerful voice told her.

'Thanks, Maggie. I'm just a bit anxious about Abby. I thought she and her pal, Izzy, were going off for a picnic but there's no sign of her and she's not answering her phone.'

'That's not like Abby,' Maggie replied. 'Don't worry, I'm sure they'll be sheltering somewhere. Maybe having a hot drink along at their favourite coffee shop on Gibson Street.'

'I'm sure you're right. Thanks, Maggie. Speak to you soon.'

Rosie leaned against the window and looked down towards the park where puddles were forming along the pathways. Nice weather for ducks, as Ben would say, but not for two teenage girls caught out in such a rainstorm.

Solly had never learned to drive and so it meant that he and Ben would have taken a bus and then the underground train to Kelvinbridge from the Lorimers' home in Giffnock. Would her husband have taken an umbrella? Probably not, Rosie thought with a smile. Solly's mind was often on less mundane matters than surviving a rain shower and she envisaged them both returning to the flat pretty well drookit.

Her face lit up as she saw them jogging along the pavement, her husband and little boy trying to see who would reach the front door first. Thank goodness they were back at least.

Rosie's smile faded as she thought again of Abby. She ought to have been home by now. Maybe she'd already called Solly and he would know their daughter's whereabouts.

'Abby? No, we haven't heard a peep, have we, Ben?' Solly grinned down at the youngster who was rubbing a towel across his head.

'Nope. But Auntie Maggie says can we go over for dinner on Sunday? All four of us?'

Rosie nodded. 'Sure. That's nice of her.'

'She says she's going to make her apple pie and get that ice cream from the wee Italian shop that we like. Ace!' Ben high-fived his father's hand.

'Off you go and change out of these wet things,' Rosie told her son. 'And don't leave them on the bathroom floor!' she called after his retreating figure.

'Hey, had a rough day?' Solly gathered his wife into his arms as Rosie breathed in the smell of wet hair and beard and the faint tang of peppermint.

'A bit. PM of a road accident. Poor kid on a motorbike. He'd had a heart condition. Must have lost consciousness before the bike veered off into the traffic.'

'Oh, I'm sorry. Always hard when it's someone so young.'

Rosie nodded then gave a huge sigh. 'And I've nothing in for dinner ... '

'Hey, how about we have pizza? Save either of us cooking,' Solly suggested.

Rosie smiled as she drew away from her husband, the front

of her jersey now damp from his hug. 'We should wait for Abby,' she said. 'Goodness knows where the pair of them have got to. She's not answering her phone and Izzy's folks all seem to be out.'

'Maybe they've taken the girls for a meal?'

Ben appeared, his dark hair sticking up in spikes.

'Who's taken who for a meal?' he demanded.

'Whom,' Rosie replied automatically.

'Izzy's parents might have taken Abby for dinner,' Solly explained. 'But we haven't heard from them yet.'

Ben looked from one of his parents to the other then shook his head.

'They're away on holiday, aren't they?' he said. 'Abby told me she was fed up cos Izzy was away for almost the whole school holiday.' He looked guiltily at his mother. 'I wasn't supposed to tell,' he said in a small voice.

Rosie took her son gently by the shoulders. 'Ben, where is your sister?'

A fat tear began to roll down the boy's cheek.

'I don't know,' he said huskily. 'She just told me she was going on an adventure on her new bike.'

Over their son's head Rosie and Solly were silent, recognising the expression of dread in each other's eyes.

CHAPTER FIFTY-EIGHT

She was so sleepy, her eyelids heavy, mouth tasting strange.

And she was cold, so cold.

Abby tried to open her eyes but there was something covering them tightly. And her sore arms ... why had she gone on such a long bike ride yesterday ... ?

The girl tried to sit up in the darkness but fell back, head striking a hard surface. What was wrong with her arms and legs ... ? So tight, so rigid ...

She took a deep breath that turned into a yawn. She must be dreaming, she decided, willing the darkness to take her once more.

Then she heard a familiar sound. It reverberated all around her and she could smell something that was both sweet and pungent.

Abby struggled against her bonds, the sudden realisation that her feet and hands were tied together, her eyes blindfolded.

367

As the car began to move, the teenager began to scream but her cries were lost under the sound of the car's engine.

Lorimer snatched up the phone. 'Any sign . . . ?'

There was a pause before Maggie spoke. 'Nothing. They have no idea where she's gone. All hospitals checked in case of an accident.' He heard the intake of breath before she went on. 'Is there anything you can do?'

Lorimer clenched his teeth. He was about to alert the team into a different sort of action from seeking a wayward teenager, one that would demand all of his resources.

'Rosie says she's got her phone with her?'

'It's ringing out but that's all. Either Abby's left it somewhere or she can't get to it . . . '

'I have her mobile number. I'll see what we can do from this end. But it is going to really hot up here tonight over the Richmond case and you're unlikely to see me again before the wee small hours. I was lucky to get home at all earlier.'

It would take just a few seconds of precious police time, but Lorimer knew it was important for his friends that Abby was found safe and well.

'Alisha, I've something I'd like you to do, please,' he asked the trainee detective before handing her Abby's mobile number. 'See where this is, okay? And, if she's on the move, let me know that too.'

All eyes were on the detective superintendent as he stood in front of the whiteboard with its handwritten notes and photographs.

'Now, I think we have cogent reasons for eliminating

368

several of those people from our enquiries,' he began, drawing a wearied hand across his brow.

'You know who it was that killed these three people,' Molly Newton said, nodding quietly in her place at the front of the team.

'I think so,' Lorimer said. 'But I still need proof.'

Molly shook her head and gave an exasperated sigh. It was evident that the boss wasn't going to share his thoughts just yet.

'Are you referring to one of these theatre folk? Standish? Ada Galloway? The Asian lad, Patel?'

Lorimer looked at her blankly, his blue gaze giving nothing away.

'I'd like a pair of you to go to Meredith St Claire's cottage,' he said at last. 'Take a forensic team and have another look around. Outhouses, garage, shed, anywhere they used for storage. If my theory's right, there must be traces of cocaine in that place. Meantime I'm off to question Joshua Pettifer. Molly?' He raised a hand her way and Molly Newton stood up and followed him.

The room had a stale smell of grease and sweat, from previous hours of interviews. It was lit by overhead fluorescent lighting, dusk having gathered and the sky outside a deep cobalt blue. Pettifer was already seated when they entered the room, and twisted round to see them. He looked nervous, Lorimer thought, the dealer's leg bouncing up and down beneath the table a dead giveaway.

'Mr Pettifer,' he began, seating himself opposite, his long

369

legs bumping against the man's feet. He nodded to the solicitor. He'd had a long day too, he realised. Probably wanted to
get home, have his dinner and watch TV but instead he was
sitting next to Josh Pettifer, glancing at him dispassionately
as he must do with all his clients.

After setting up the recording and giving dates, time and
those present, Lorimer stared at Pettifer, saying nothing for
several minutes. He had caused several hardened criminals
to crack under his blue gaze. Would Pettifer succumb now?
Or would it take the hint of further time spent in prison if
he withheld essential information?

Pettifer squirmed a little and hung his head.

'I have asked you here because I believe you have not told
the whole truth about the night that Guy Richmond died,'
Lorimer said at last.

'I didn't kill him! I told you before. You cannae pin that
on me!' Pettifer insisted, turning to the solicitor at his side.

'I'm inclined to believe you,' Lorimer sighed wearily. 'I
don't think you've got it in you to plan out the deaths of
those three people.'

'Three . . . ?' Pettifer began to look around wildly.

'Or even one,' Lorimer said quietly.

'But . . . ?' Pettifer's mouth fell open, the man clearly troubled by what the detective was saying.

'Three,' Lorimer mused. 'And yet . . . let's get back to
these text messages you spoke about.' His voice was matter-
of-fact, no accusation in his tone.

Pettifer looked at him for a moment. Did he see something
in the tall man's face that suggested he knew something else?

'We've examined your phone. Found it just where you

said it was. And we've established the facts about the texts between you and Richmond. However . . . '

Pettifer looked frightened now, his eyes flicking from the two detectives to his solicitor.

'There were also several calls made from Richmond's landline. What did you and Richmond talk about on these occasions?'

'I never spoke tae him. Havenae spoken tae him that much since he wis a student . . . ' Pettifer insisted.

'Then who was it that called you more recently on these different occasions, Josh?'

Then, as if caught in the beam of Lorimer's gaze, his shoulders slumped in defeat.

Lorimer tapped a pencil on the desk, a small sound but enough to keep the drug dealer focused on him.

'I need a name, Josh.'

'Her. Meredith. She was always the one placing the orders, asking for coke. Said it wis for him.'

And there it was, Lorimer thought, his heart heavy, though he had worked out this scenario already.

'Meredith St Claire?'

Pettifer nodded and sighed.

'Speak for the recording, please, Mr Pettifer.'

'It was Meredith St Claire who did the business. She told me never to come to their cottage. Had me running all over the country to do the deals. Said Guy had sent her . . . '

'And you believed her? You genuinely thought she was acting as a courier for her wealthy boyfriend?'

'I don't know,' he admitted. 'I jist assumed . . . '

*

371

Molly switched off the recording, her mind reeling with so many new possibilities. The night her fiancé was killed, Meredith St Claire had driven him to Glasgow, she'd told them, and dropped her fiancé in town. But what if that, too, was a lie?

'You don't think Meredith committed these murders, do you?' she whispered as she strode along the corridor, keeping up with Lorimer.

He stopped for a moment and gave her a sad look. Then nodded.

'I do,' he said. 'And before tonight is out, I think we will be having a very long conversation with our drama teacher.'

Molly shook her head. The poor woman had been in bits when they had broken the news about Richmond's death. Surely, just this once, Lorimer had got it all wrong?

They were met at the end of the corridor by DC Mohammed, her eyes fastening on the detective superintendent.

'Sir, we've located her,' Alisha began. 'Moving too fast for riding a bike, though. We think she's in a vehicle of some sort.'

Lorimer blew out a sigh of relief. 'Tell me she's on a bus going home,' he said.

Alisha looked at him and shook her head. 'Not unless she lives way out of the city. Her mobile shows a location on the far side of Paisley. Not far from the locus where that fisherman found the body.'

CHAPTER FIFTY-NINE

When the car stopped at last, Abby rolled to one side, her head aching.

There were voices and noises outside, loud music from a radio. She began to cry, but the reverberations from the heavy metal band drowned her screams.

Whoever was driving this car had deliberately turned up the music full blast.

Abby tried to remember what had happened after she had cycled past the road end to Douglas Academy, but everything was a blur, a nightmare where she had fallen into a black hole. Her head throbbed and she felt a wave of nausea. If only they would let her out . . .

The engine started again and she was shaken to one side of the car boot.

Abby began to sob, thinking of her mother. If only she'd not told that fib.

If only someone would come and get her out of here . . .

*

'A red bike?' Lorimer leapt up from his seat as the scene of crime officer related what she had discovered in the garage.

'We've also found traces of blood on a garment,' she added. 'And some yellow paint.'

'Get someone to bring that bicycle here. Now,' he commanded, his voice sharper than he'd intended.

He whirled around to meet the eyes of DI Newton and DS Giles.

'I think Abby went on a cycle ride to see Meredith St Claire. SOCO tells me there is no car in the garage but signs that it left recently. Fresh oil spillage on the garage floor.'

'You think Meredith has taken Abby somewhere?' Molly looked shocked.

Lorimer picked up his jacket and nodded. 'And I think we know exactly where she is going.'

Maggie Lorimer was humming to herself as she tipped Chancer's food into his bowl then watched as the old ginger cat padded forward. She smiled for a moment, wondering what age he might be now. They'd had him for . . . how long? Fifteen years, more? He'd been a stray, so it was impossible to know.

The mobile was just to hand on the breakfast bar and Maggie picked it up, still smiling. It would be Bill to say he was going to be late. Nothing unusual there, but he was always good enough to call when he could.

'Hi, darling . . .'

'Maggie, do you know if Abby had any idea how to get to her drama teacher's cottage?'

*

Lorimer stared straight ahead as the car began to twist through the countryside, trees darkening the road.

'I think my wife may inadvertently have told Abby how to get to the cottage,' he said quietly.

'Maggie?' Molly exclaimed.

Lorimer's mouth tightened. 'We gave her that bike recently. She's a good cyclist, careful. But I never expected that she'd go off ...' He swallowed hard. What had happened up at that remote house in the hills? He shivered, fearful of what lay awaiting them.

That the woman had murdered three people, he did not doubt now. She'd always had motive, of course. Money did strange things to people. And who was to say that Richmond had not changed his mind about spending the rest of his life with her? Hadn't Ada Galloway insisted that he ought to put his acting career first? There had been no wedding venue planned. No future Mrs Richmond, apart from that huge diamond on her finger. Somehow Sarra Milroy had been involved with the drugs, he thought. Had she suspected what Meredith had done? Blackmailed her, perhaps? One push down those basement stairs was all it had taken to silence the girl for good.

And Nigel Fairbairn? He'd known Meredith for many years. Had he guessed what she had done? And hoped to ingratiate himself with her once more? Had money and stardom been the twin temptations that brought about his death? Or, and here he felt an overwhelming sadness towards the young man from Kirkwall, had he really believed that Meredith would respond to his overtures, rekindle the flame he held for her?

And now, was she about to commit a fourth murder?

His eyes strained through the gloom to see the words **PRIVATE FISHING** written on the white sign.

'We're here, sir,' Molly whispered, cutting the lights and turning into the track she remembered from that cold day beside the loch.

Behind him, Davie Giles gripped the seat in front of him. 'I can see her car,' he said. 'Look. Beyond those trees.'

Molly reversed a little and turned the car around a bend until they were out of sight.

'Ready?' Lorimer's voice was steady. Backup had already been requested but for now the three plain clothes officers were on their own.

At last the car rolled to a stop and Abby heard a door slam. Then, silence. Where was she? And why ... the thought came to an abrupt halt as the boot was opened and a pair of strong hands pulled her out.

Then her blindfold was pulled away.

'Oh, miss! Miss St Claire!' Abby waited for the teacher to put her arms around her, take off the bindings from her arms and legs. She looked around, waiting to see her captor.

But there was nobody else in the windswept night.

Abby began to cry. 'Why are you doing this to me?' she asked, hearing her small voice caught by the wind. But the woman did not reply, nor did she look at Abby as she bent down to cut the ties on her legs.

'Walk,' Meredith demanded, giving Abby a hard shove that almost sent her flying onto the grass.

'I want to go home,' Abby sobbed. 'Please take me home,' she cried.

There was no reply to her plea, just the feeling of finger-nails digging into her skin as her captor gripped her arm.

Abby could hear noises now, water splashing nearby then a bird squawking as it took flight.

They moved together, the girl half-pushed along a muddy track towards the fishing loch.

Then, up above came a different sound, blades clacking and whirring as a helicopter roared overhead, its searchlight illuminating the water below.

Abby felt her hair lifted by the helicopter's downwash as it neared the ground, the noise growing louder every second.

Then she was shoved onto her front and dragged.

Abby twisted her face to one side, her head bouncing off the wet grass, the smell of earth filling her nostrils.

There were shouts, cries from not too far away and she felt the vibrations of feet running.

'Help!' she cried, but her voice was lost in the noise of the helicopter.

Then everything seemed to stop. Abby was no longer being dragged along the ground, but dumped by the loch side, her head already over the edge of the bank.

'Leave her, Meredith,' Abby heard a familiar voice call out. A gentle voice, one she'd known all her life.

'It's over, Meredith,' Lorimer said. 'What good can it do to hurt Abby?'

Abby squirmed around, digging in her heels and pulling herself into a sitting position.

There, on the bank, was her drama teacher, the bright pink hair illuminated like a mad halo beneath the helicopter's beam of light. For a moment she turned to look at Abby, her face a mask of fury, and the girl cringed.

'It would hurt you, though, wouldn't it, Superintendent?'

Abby watched in terror as the woman came at her, arms out, ready to push her into the water.

And then, out of the darkness, came two figures who leapt at Meredith and tumbled her to the ground.

'I've got you, darling, I've got you. You're safe now.'

Abby burst into fresh tears as her godfather held her against his chest, her sobs muffled as he caressed her hair.

'It's all right, lass. It's all right,' he told her. 'You're going home.'

Abigail Brightman would remember that night for many weeks to come, the flashing lights of squad cars, the uniformed police officers leading her teacher away, then the hours spent at Uncle Bill's place of work, her eyes everywhere, soaking up the details to tell Ben later. It would be dawn by the time her parents took her home again, no recriminations given, only heartfelt hugs.

CHAPTER SIXTY

Meredith St Claire sat opposite the two police officers in the small room off a corridor at the Helen Street police office, her eyes drawn to the tall man whom she had first met in the school car park. She was tired. Tired of playing her part, tired of being the focus of their enquiring eyes and questions, questions, questions. All she wanted now was to have it stop. To lie down on a soft bed and sleep. To wake up and find that it had never happened.

As Lorimer repeated the things she had carried out, her mouth turned up in a brief smile. She had been clever to deceive them for so long, he acknowledged. At least that was something.

'It was that book I borrowed from you that made me start to look harder at your acting skills,' he said at last. 'George Mackay Brown.'

Meredith opened her eyes wider. Had he really found out everything just from a book?

'You were the star of that play at school,' he went on.

'Marion Isbister, the so-called witch who is tortured in the most appalling manner.'

She nodded then, listening.

'That was when I knew how good you could be at screaming, fainting, acting out all these things. I guess you had rehearsed every scene of your plot in your imagination. Even when you came to me that day at Abby's school, you were acting out a part.'

She glared at him, furious that he had worked it out.

'And you did it all for money. A great deal of money. Guy Richmond had made you the major beneficiary in his will, hadn't he? Were you afraid he was going to change his mind?'

'Yes,' she agreed. 'And when he talked about seeing his solicitor to make some changes, that was when I knew I had to act.'

'And you set up Josh Pettifer as a scapegoat. That was clever of you.'

Meredith smiled at that and gave them a gracious little nod of acknowledgement as if she had been paid a compliment.

'I knew Josh couldn't resist the thought of a load of money. Guy had been giving me some from his account whenever I asked him. Made it look as if he was amassing cash for a drug deal.'

'And you very nearly got away with that, didn't you? It was you who texted the man, using Guy Richmond's phone, wasn't it?'

Again she gave them both a nod, a smile playing about her lips.

'Please answer for the recording,' Molly interjected.

'Yes, I set him up, texted Pettifer and made sure he would

be at the loch after I'd pushed Guy into the water. Got rid of the phone, too, if you must know. That's one thing you're never going to find,' she said, lifting her chin proudly.

'You said you had loved him very much,' the blonde woman, Newton, remarked.

Meredith gave a mirthless laugh. 'Love? Love a man who continually put me down? What was it he used to say? "Those who can, act; those who can't, teach." It was as if I was an inferior being to them all.'

'It was you who trashed the cottage, wasn't it?' Newton gasped, the truth evidently dawning on her now.

Meredith nodded.

'Speak for the tape, please.'

'Yes, that was me.' It had given her some satisfaction to rip all his precious photos to bits. In well-gloved hands, of course.

'Sarra was blackmailing you,' Lorimer stated. 'It was you who called her that night, asked her to come to the theatre, wasn't it?'

Meredith closed her eyes, remembering.

'Could have been an accident.' She shrugged.

'But it wasn't, was it?'

She blinked tired eyes against the fluorescent light flickering overhead.

'No, that was me. Silly girl wanted more money for drugs, and I couldn't give it to her till the solicitor declared probate, could I? She knew I was a user, threatened to tell everyone if I didn't give her a stupid amount of money. I couldn't risk that happening.'

'You could have sold that ring,' Newton said.

Then Meredith threw her head back and began to laugh and laugh till tears streamed down her cheeks.

'This thing?' she croaked, pulling it off then casting it onto the table where it rolled and sparkled under the light.

'That had you all fooled, didn't it? My expensive engagement ring! The one that Guy Richmond never even saw?' She lifted her head and looked at the two detectives. 'D'you know what that really is? A piece of cheap tat that I filched from the props drawer. Patel was none the wiser of its disappearance, stupid man!' she exclaimed.

She'd always been good at hysteria, but this time it was real, the dramatic irony ending in screams of rage.

'Poor Nigel Fairbairn,' Molly said later as she sat beside Daniel, holding his hand. 'The stone she killed him with was one they had found on the beach back home, a keepsake from better days. He knew Meredith better than anyone. Knew she was a talented actress, who'd had great ambitions and must have guessed she'd only hung around Richmond for his money. She was becoming paranoid, I think, terrified he'd sussed her out and would tell us far more about her than he already had. She couldn't take that risk. Yet he was probably the only one who'd really loved her.'

'What will happen now? To her?'

Molly snuggled into his arms. 'She's admitted her guilt so there will be no need for a trial by jury. We found the key to a safety deposit box in Stirling. Five packs of cocaine hidden in chocolate boxes. One more crime to add to the list,' she sighed. 'I expect she'll receive a very long sentence. Might not see the light of day again till her hair's gone grey.'

'And the theatre company? What will happen to their production of *Sweeney Todd*?'

'I doubt if that will happen this side of the border. I guess the actors' agents will be trying to secure them different roles elsewhere. Ada Galloway's left for a gig in Pitlochry. And I doubt if Ahmed will ever return to the theatre. As for Jeffrey Standish – who knows?'

'How did you know?' Maggie asked him as Lorimer clasped her hands.

'It began when I heard her singing,' he explained. 'Thought it was strange to be singing like that so soon after a devastating bereavement. In my experience most people undergoing a trauma tend to be quiet and withdrawn. Then there was that book.'

'George Mackay Brown. One of my favourite poets,' Maggie murmured. 'And Meredith had portrayed the poor innocent witch of the title.'

'The song she'd sung was about a shape-changing creature, a myth closely associated with islands. It made me wonder about appearance and reality. Had I been seeing what she wanted me to see, a grief-stricken woman, or was the reality something far darker?'

'And she knew Richmond was about to ditch her?'

Lorimer nodded. 'Wearing that ring was her way of showing other people that she was destined to be his wife, though of course he never saw it on her finger. Meredith found that Guy Richmond was going to see his lawyer and was afraid he was about to change his will, cut her out altogether, possibly. And she couldn't take that chance.'

'So, it was all about money,' Maggie replied sadly. '"The love of money is the root of all evil",' she quoted.

'And drugs. She's admitted it so far, so we know now that obtaining drugs from Pettifer was down to Meredith, rather than Guy. She was the one hiding them in that deposit box, not Guy, and I'm now convinced that Josh Pettifer has told us the real story. It was obvious he was hiding something when we first picked him up. It was greed that lured him to that loch, of course. As Meredith St Claire knew it would. She had it all worked out, hoped that we'd arrest Pettifer for the murder and she'd get off scot-free.'

'Did she really have to push that young girl to her death?'

'I think Sarra was also getting greedy. She was star-struck, snared with the thought of what a lot of money could do for her, wanting to get to Hollywood any way she could.'

'So, she was blackmailing Meredith?'

'Yes. Sarra had threatened to tell everyone about Meredith's drug use. There's a lot of other stuff that might never see the light of day, like how long she had planned to fleece Guy Richmond one way or another. Meredith St Claire is a consummate liar as well as a brilliant actress.'

If it had not been for the way that she had threatened Abby's life, then he might feel some pity for the woman. The casual cruelty of her boyfriend in putting her down must have rankled for years.

'Instead of following her own dream, she settled for teaching, possibly lured by a steady income. Then, when his parents died in that car crash, she saw her chance of becoming extremely rich, perhaps even pick up her acting career again.'

'So why didn't she stay with him, hope that they'd eventually marry?'

'My guess is that Richmond wanted to move on and not be tied to her. Perhaps everything that other people were telling him about not settling down finally made him think. He had a future as a big name and somehow being tied to a drama teacher with a drug habit wasn't a good look.'

'Meredith was a user?'

'Oh, we know now that it was Meredith buying drugs with Richmond's money. And I bet that day I saw Pettifer going to the cottage he was anxious to be paid for previous deals. Sarra Milroy's parents will be shocked when they learn the truth. They'd cast Richmond as the real villain.'

'Thank goodness Abby wasn't hurt. I'll never forgive myself for trying to describe whereabouts that cottage was.'

'Hush, she'll be fine. It's a hard way to grow up, finding someone you admired was not the person you thought they were. Solly and Rosie will help her through all of this.'

'And so will we,' Maggie replied firmly. 'Come on, I think it's well past our bedtime,' she added, taking her husband's hand.

As the morning light began to filter through the blinds, Daniel listened to her breathing until he was certain that Molly was fast asleep. Then he laid his dark head on the pillow next to hers. He had asked her a question that had been burning inside him for months. And she had said yes.

Today was a rest day and once they were properly awake, he had plans of his own for them both. Plans that included a visit to the city centre and Argyll Arcade, the best place,

Netta had told him, to buy a ring. A real diamond, not like the fake on a killer's finger that had fooled so many people.

There was a smile on his face as Daniel closed his eyes, hearing the sound of a blackbird singing to the dawn.

One case had ended.

And another day was just beginning.

ACKNOWLEDGEMENTS

Thanks first and foremost to my editor, Rosanna Forte, who has taken such meticulous care of my story in each stage of its journey to completion. The entire Sphere team is like a family who really care and work so hard to bring each of my books to my readers, and so may I also thank Liz, Brionee, Frances, Kayta plus Ella and everyone in the design department. This book is set in the world of the theatre and so it seemed a good time to say a special thank you to Joe Dunlop whose glorious voice has been enjoyed by so many listeners to my audio books over the years. Bless you, Joe.

Thanks to Christopher Pearson for permission to use his name in this book and of course to my dear friend, the lovely Molly Newton, who lived to a ripe ninety-five years. Also to the real Abigail, whose mum is pathologist (and regular helper for research) Dr Marjorie Turner.

My dear agent, Dr Jenny Brown, has been a massive support to me throughout the writing of this book so thank you, Jenny, for your friendship, advice and understanding. You are the best!

Last but not least, thanks to Donnie for his patience and for the endless cups of coffee that he brings upstairs to my study and for being the world's best roadie.